FLYING TOO CLOSE
TO THE SUN

George Jehn

RING OF FIRE PUBLISHING

ISBN-13: 978-0615735122
ISBN-10: 0615735126

Flying Too Close to the Sun

Published by
Ring of Fire Publishing
Seattle, Washington, U.S.A.

Cover image by kesipun. Cover design by Stephen Penner.

For Papa
You never knew how much you influenced my life.

CHAPTER ONE

Christine Shepard's heart was racing almost as quickly as her mind as she exited the neurologist's office located on Sixty-Third Street in Manhattan. She immediately took out her cell and phoned her boyfriend, David Bennedeto. He answered on the third ring. "You home?" she barked.

"Yeah."

"I've gotta speak with you. It's important. Could you meet me at the Starbucks near the subway stop? I'll be there in about fifteen minutes."

"Sure, but why—" The line went dead.

The ride on the air conditioned F local Eighth Avenue line to the Kew Gardens Queens station should have provided a respite from the heat, but hot air billowed in at each stop, fighting the car's a/c. Upon exiting a perspiring Christina saw David dressed in his usual summer garb, white muscleman tank top, tight cutoff jeans and sandals. They got two iced lattes and grabbed the only available seats, outside under a small striped umbrella. His tanned strapping body was wider than the ladder-backed, uneven metal chair that made the tacit statement to stay and enjoy your drink, just not for too long. That wouldn't be a problem today as the sun and unseasonable humidity were nearly unbearable.

"I visited a neurologist 'cause of the headaches and occasional speech problems I have when I wake up. The ones I told you about." She hesitated. "But it wasn't from migraine headaches, like I thought," she mumbled while scrunching her face, trying in vain to fight back tears from her mirrored eyes that stained the cotton summer weight dress. "This stuff's bitter," she muttered, but realized it wasn't the latte but the cramps born of stress and fear twisting in her stomach. She inhaled deeply and blurted out, "I have epilepsy," not wanting to believe that a Shuttle Air Boeing 727 captain and unofficial female pilot media spokesperson could fall victim to such a dreaded ailment.

"Holy shit! What are you, we, gonna do?" David asked loudly, immediately adding in a lower voice, "Can I catch it? We've been sleeping together now for…"

David, always number one. "It's a seizure disorder and not contagious. The doc, Friedman's his name, said the problem could be genetic or might be from a head injury I suffered as a kid while riding my bike. The headaches could be either the result of a nocturnal seizure I had while asleep or an aura, a sign of an impending one."

"That's probably why you've been moving around so much while you're sleeping." David hesitated. "Could he be wrong?"

"No. He was certain 'cause he administered an electroencephalogram to confirm the diagnosis. That's why my hair looks like a punk rocker's. It's from the glue used to attach the electrodes." As a light summer breeze blew she raised her right hand over her sparkling cobalt eyes to the unruly spikes of golden hair and tried to push them down with a sweeping motion, as if to say, *See. I still have complete control.* How long would that last? "He said the EEG *seemingly* indicates that I have the less severe form that produces partial, rather than Tonic-clonic seizures where you lose complete control. But he has to analyze the results further and wants me to get an MRI of the head to rule out a possible brain tumor. I'll have to save for that 'cause I won't, can't, use my medical insurance."

The stark reality of this new predicament awakened her instincts, the same instincts that guided her throughout her thirty-plus years. Although the ghastly diagnosis dictated accepting her fate, she would not relinquish control of her future. "I got his name from the phone book. He was kinda nerdy-looking, but nice. I used an alias and paid cash." Christina knew that neither the airline nor the Federal Aviation Administration could be allowed to find out about her condition because they would automatically ground her by revoking her Airline Transport Pilot license, which every pilot knows is mandatory when diagnosed with epilepsy. "I'll decide whether or not to stop flying." Shaking her head she whispered, "Hell, it's the only job I've ever known." Further thoughts of this horrid illness and how it would alter her life caused more brackish-tasting tears to involuntarily migrate into the corners of her mouth. David reached over to hand her a napkin, but instead she used the tip of her tongue to capture them, silently vowing to do whatever was necessary to insure she could live comfortably for the rest of her life. But the clock was ticking. It couldn't be seen or heard but she could almost feel each reverberation in her bones. She had to do *something*, quickly.

CHAPTER TWO

Pressing the button on her digital watch, the soft glow confirmed it was past departure time. Although she was in command, no one had informed Captain Christina Shepard why the jet's forward door and cargo holds weren't secured and the pushback from the gate commenced for the evening's final Boston to New York shuttle flight. They weren't waiting for fuel, as she had seen the fueler detach the long snake-like black hose that provided kerosene, the lifeline used by the three fuel-thirsty Pratt & Whitney fourteen thousand-pound thrust engines that powered her Boeing 727. Nonetheless, she glanced over her right shoulder to double-check the three fuel gauges located directly behind the copilot on the flight engineer's panel. The two wing and center fuel tanks each showed eight thousand pounds, twenty-four thousand pounds total, just under four thousand gallons. A 727 or tri-jet as it was better known in airline lingo could hold up to forty-six thousand pounds. With that amount you could practically fly coast to coast, meaning they had more than enough for their approximate forty-minute flight, even on a night like this with lousy weather. She recalled the wise words of an old-timer she had flown with as a new copilot, seemingly a lifetime ago. "The only time you have *too* much fuel is when you're on fire." The cursory smile faded as she glanced out the electrically heated cockpit window to the wet asphalt tarmac, so shiny it looked like smoked glass. Nothing was moving.

The weather had returned to normal for this time of the year, meaning the torrid heat was gone. This was a usual northern New England early summer night, with a gloomy sky hanging low over the entire airport like a shadowy tarp. This matched her mood due to her recent diagnosis. Everything from her hair to the plane's controls felt like a cold, damp mop. Cuddling up under a blanket with a good book in her tiny rental home in Queens would be a welcome respite. She was about to ask the flight engineer to radio the company when an out-of-breath boarding agent burst into the cockpit. "Sorry Captain, but your flight's gonna be a few more minutes late," he gasped in a thick Boston accent while handing Christina a large, sealed envelope. "We're waiting for a connecting passenger."

"You mean late, again?" Christina sighed. The fidgety agent exhaled and shrugged his shoulders, while offering what he probably hoped was a seductive smile as she swiveled around to face him. The four blue-and-silver-striped shoulder epaulets underscored her deep blue water-colored eyes that anchored the shiny, shortish blond hair framing her alluring Nordic features. "This is the third time this week," she added, ignoring the obvious come-on. "But thanks for letting me know."

Shepard knew so much was at stake with each flight that nothing could be accepted at face value. Her definition of the words flight safety meant stacking the odds in her passengers favor as much as humanly possible and confirming everything was in order. After opening the envelope she read the official contents, which again stated they were waiting for an armed United States sky marshal. The requirement to notify the plane's commander also specified no other crewmembers were to know the lawman was on board. Notification was a necessity since the airline attacks on American soil on 9/11. If a captain so desired and passed the required background security check and weapons training, a sidearm could be carried. No one wanted a shootout if a passenger was spotted with a gun. But the airlines' agreement with the federal government also stipulated the flight couldn't be delayed on account of the sky marshal program unless there was a known and immediate terrorist threat. There was nothing like that because yet another regulation also required notification. She was puzzled.

The balding agent, with flecks of dandruff decorating the shoulders of his dark blue uniform shirt remained standing in the cockpit entrance, so Christina asked, "You know who's responsible for these delays?"

"I don't have the slightest idea, Captain," he nervously blurted out. "I'm pretty low on the totem pole." He quickly exited from the doorway with a forced smile on his now slightly reddened face.

"Whatever the reason, this must be important," she muttered to her heavyset copilot, Howard Montgomery who went by the nickname, Woody. Montgomery had his feet propped up on the base of his instrument panel, nonchalantly scanning the late evening edition of the *Boston Globe*. She had always been curious about his nickname but never quite had the guts to glance down *there* to see if it was the case. The recorded ATIS or Automated Terminal Information Service for Boston's Logan airport that provided recorded information such as the weather and which runways were in use was blaring repeatedly over the cockpit speaker. Besides ignoring her comment Montgomery seemed oblivious to the repetitive message. There were a couple of reasons why she didn't care for Montgomery, the main one being he had a ridiculous air of macho immaturity about him. Plus, his body always had a very faint sweaty odor. The latter could signal that in reality he was apprehensive about flying and the mannerisms might be just a cover. So she kept a wary eye on him. "No one around here seems to know what's going on," she continued, attempting to use her glacier-like, I-am-the-captain cobalt stare. The older copilots like Woody always seemed to resent a woman's authority. But the coolness in her eyes that could have frozen his tabloid was wasted as Montgomery didn't even put the paper down. Shrugging his shoulders he finally replied in a gruff voice from behind his protective wall of newsprint, "If they won't tell a high-powered lady captain, why the hell would anyone say something to a low-life copilot?"

Christina wanted to rip the paper out of his hands, but didn't. Besides being against company policy to read in the cockpit, it was rude. "But why do you even care?" he added in his normal whiny tone. "We get paid by the hour and these nightly delays add up to a few more bucks each paycheck. I can use the extra dough."

This provided an opportunity to vent. "A bunch of our passengers complained to me about our last delay," she sarcastically added, "and I couldn't provide a reason other than the pilots earn a few more bucks."

Montgomery finally looked up, ran his fingers through thinning hair cut in a military style, let out a muted "Oh," and returned to reading.

Christina vowed to unearth the cause. Maybe the reason was locked somewhere in the airline's computer? The same one the pilots used for bidding their monthly schedule and vacation. She would check that out.

Just then the same agent stuck his head into the cockpit and in a poor Ed McMahon imitation announced, "Weeee're ready." After taking a final peek at the captain, he added with a broad smile, "Hope to see you again. Real soon."

With all doors now secured, Christina pleasantly asked, "Woody, please put the paper down and get us a pushback clearance from Ground Control. And, turn off the ATIS. Everyone in earshot has been listening to the same crap for the past twenty minutes. Let's read the *before starting engines checklist.*"

The copilot, also referred to as the first officer at Shuttle Air was required to read all of the checklists when the engines weren't running, with the flight engineer, or second officer taking over that duty when underway. As the mechanics smoothly pushed the plane away from the gate and onto the tarmac with a huge tug, Woody read the printed checklist aloud, with each pilot responding to their required items.

Erik Preis was the second officer, the systems operator and third member of the 727's cockpit crew. This was the starting position and he would next move to copilot and eventually captain. He hit the books hard for two months at Shuttle Air's flight school to secure his FAA Flight Engineer turbojet certification, which is different from a pilot license. The young man from Farmingdale, Long Island had just completed his first week on the job, finally realizing his airline pilot goal. To reach this point had taken over five years of grueling work. He had to first earn his FAA pilot and flight instructor certificates and then build additional flight hours by teaching others to fly. Each hour spent instructing also counted toward his total flight time, the means to gain the needed experience. The three metallic stripes on the sleeves of the uniform he now wore was recognition that passengers entrusted him with their most precious commodity. He was nearly able to leave his weighty personal problems behind whenever the shiny silver jet needle penetrated the deep indigo sky. Life was great—almost. Preis took his job of monitoring and running all of the 727's systems as seriously as a cop would a life or death situation. Even though his seat faced sideways for much of the flight he was a vital part of the crew. Hopefully, his opportunity to fly copilot would come soon. For now, hearing the moan of the hydraulics and smelling the big jet's aroma: a unique blend of brewing coffee and jet fuel was enough.

Preis had previously glimpsed Shepard on TV. Attractive on television, she was even more so in person. Although too young to be one of the first female airline pilots it was no doubt her beauty and confidence-exuding demeanor that caused the media outlets to seek her out for information pertaining to women in aviation. Her televised appearances translated into near-celebrity status within the airlines, but without her nose in the air. Although her flight bag bore the scars of many years of cockpit duty you couldn't say the same about her. She wore no makeup, seemingly immune to the ravages of time, exuding the same air of confidence as a female senior executive but without the hard shell. She was also an expert pilot who flew her plane with the finesse of a first-rate jockey in command of a thoroughbred.

With a short respite while the mechanic disconnected the tow bar from the jet's nose wheel Erik asked, "Will you both be flying these same three, five, seven and nine o'clock Shuttles for the entire month?"

Shepard half-jokingly replied. "Last month, this month and probably for at least the next six months," sincerely hoping that was true. "It's the only trip my lack of seniority in the captain ranks allows me to fly. Being on reserve – on call – goes to the senior captains who sit on their elderly butts at home and hardly ever work, while us junior pukes have to fly almost every day."

"I'm in the same boat with the copilots," Woody chimed in.

With blue eyes that felt as though they looked through Erik, she added, "With the hiring going on, you should be able to get more flight choices pretty soon."

After cranking up only the number one and three engines to conserve fuel, Shuttle Air 1540 was directed to taxi to Boston's runway 22 Right. Christina maneuvered the plane on the taxiways while Erik and Woody performed all their required functions. Once everything was running Erik got the weight and balance information over the Airborne Communications Apparatus or ACARS, filled in the required takeoff numbers with a black magic marker pen and handed Woody the completed takeoff data card. It fit neatly on the forward instrument panel and showed the pilots the number of passengers on board, amount of fuel, aircraft gross weight, along with the tail's stabilizer trim setting and the calculated takeoff speeds for their exact weight. The flip side would be used for the landing data. Erik recited the *before takeoff check list* with Christina and Woody first checking and then replying to each item. Approaching the active runway they fired up number two, finished up the checklist and were cleared for takeoff.

Rolling down the runway, when approaching the calculated critical V1 airspeed of 132 knots, Erik felt an abnormal vibration. Quickly checking his instruments all appeared normal. But swiveling his seat to the engine gauges on the pilots' forward instrument panel he noticed intermittent RPM fluctuations and an abnormally high Exhaust Gas Temperature on the number three engine. The EGT gauge was well into the red warning band. Simultaneously, Woody made the V1 callout, the speed at which the takeoff could no longer be aborted on the ground. A split-second later came his VR call, rotation speed. Just as Christina began rotating the nose wheel off the ground there was an earsplitting boom like a clap of thunder. Erik hollered, "*Something's wrong with number three!*"

CHAPTER THREE

"*Jesus!*" Christina shouted in a voice fueled by training and seat-of-the-pants instinct, "*Engine failure!*"

Like a doctor who is told a patient is coding, when a cockpit crew hears the words engine failure immediate actions are required to be performed from memory. Christina rammed the throttles full forward to get maximum power from the operating engines while Erik quickly reached to the top of his panel and rotated the essential power selector knob that carried the crucial electrical items from number three to the number one engine generator. He simultaneously turned off the jet's galley power to prevent an electrical overload and closed off the bleed air supply from the faulty engine so no smoke or fumes could enter the cabin, opening the same valve on the number two-engine.

Christina commanded Woody, "Gimme maximum power," seeing the throttles were already in the full forward position. Despite three thousand pounds of hydraulic assistance she had to press hard on the left rudder pedal to overcome the jet's powerful asymmetrical yaw and keep it centered on the runway. With only two engines the plane's acceleration was more sluggish, so she rotated the nose very slowly so as not to overcompensate and strike the tailskid, which could cause structural damage.

To Jim Ruppel, the Boston tower operator's trained eye Shuttle 1540's acceleration appeared to be sluggish and he was about to ask the pilots if everything was OK? Just then the jet finally broke ground and gained altitude, but the rate of climb appeared to be lagging.

Inside the cockpit it was like time stood still and they were glued to the runway. But the big jet finally broke gravity's grip and a hundred and fifty-two thousand pounds of gleaming metal staggered into the air. Once the vertical speed indicator confirmed they were climbing Christina directed Woody, "Gear up."

There was no reaction.

"Woody, raise the landing gear," she ordered. Seemingly spellbound, he just stared at the engine indications on the forward instrument panel. Erik quickly released his safety harness and seat belt, reached over Woody's shoulder and moved the large handle with the little wheel on it to the up position. With the gear retracted the plane would now climb more rapidly. Since the jet's three engines were at the rear of the fuselage and not visible from the cockpit, Christina wondered if the faulty one damaged any of the jet's other systems. If an engine broke up it could cause a catastrophic failure by cutting the fuel and hydraulic lines, along with the flight control cables. Was there a fire? Thoughts of 9/11 flashed through her mind faster than a jet flew through the air. Had terrorists targeted her flight? Despite these concerns, she performed her required flight duties with textbook precision. The passengers had placed their lives in her hands and she would not let them down. "Inform the tower we have an emergency and are taking it straight out until we get the flaps retracted," Christina directed Woody as the plane entered the low murkiness. "Then we'll need an immediate clearance to return for landing." Although not visible because they were in the clouds, she had to get the crippled bird over the looming metal masts of the mammoth cargo ships she knew were anchored in Boston harbor. She had frequently gazed in awe at these huge vessels sailing to mysterious, far-away destinations. But now their metal spars were like huge hands reaching straight up, trying to swat the big jet out of the sky. The first needed step was to achieve the correct thousand-foot level-off altitude where the flaps could be safely retracted.

No response from Woody. She wanted to reach over and shake him, see if he was alive. "Did you hear me? Call the tower and work with Erik to shut down number three and then run through the emergency checklists. I've got to concentrate on flying this bird."

"I've got it," Erik said picking up his microphone. "Logan tower, this is Shuttle Air 1540. Our number three engine's failed and we'll need to return for an immediate landing."

"Roger, 1540. Do you require the emergency equipment?" Ruppel replied.

"Affirmative. We'll be taking it straight out until we get the flaps retracted."

"The normal procedure is to turn left to a heading of 140 degrees—"

Erik cut him off. "We have an engine out. We'll be going straight out 'til we get the flaps up."

"Roger. All traffic will be cleared. Inform us if you require any other assistance. The emergency trucks will be standing by," the controller quickly added. "Runway 22 Left is the active landing runway. That runway's ten thousand feet long. The wind is two zero-zero at six knots. Will an ILS to 22 Left be good?"

Christina nodded her head in the affirmative. Erik figured that because of the poor weather they would have to make an instrument landing approach or ILS. "We'll expect an approach to

22 Left."

As taught, Erik grabbed the engine failure checklist. As the airspeed increased Christina performed Woody's job by retracting the flaps while Erik read the checklist aloud.

"Throttle, idle," he read.

"Idle," Christina's immediately replied, pointing to the number three engine throttle.

"Start lever: cutoff. Engine fire handle—pull," he said aloud. These combined emergency actions shut off the fuel and insured the closure of all the failed engine's bleed air valves so no fumes would enter the aircraft. Next, Erik had to disconnect the number three generator constant speed drive, rendering it useless. During his schooling the instructor had constantly stressed this was *the* most crucial emergency procedure step because if he made a mistake and disengaged the wrong one, the remaining generator would overload and plunge the cockpit into total darkness. The pilots' would have no instruments and without them they would crash. He was extra careful and disengaged the correct one.

While ensuring the completion of all his required items, Erik noted a mistake he'd made by not turning off the air conditioning unit on number three and opening the bleed air switch for the number-two engine. With a slight hand motion and a muted clicking sound, he corrected the error. They ran through the remaining items by the book, with Christina performing them and Erik verifying her actions. "The engine failure checklist is complete," a perspiring Erik announced.

"Tell the flight attendants we have an emergency and are returning to Boston," Christina instructed Woody in a loud voice, "and tell 'em to brief the passengers."

Suddenly, Woody snapped to, picked up the mike and rang the flight attendant call button. "We've got a serious problem and are returning to Boston. Prepare the cabin for an emergency landing."

"I heard a loud noise. What's going—?"

"Just do as I say."

Ruppel anxiously broke in. "How many souls and how much fuel are on board?"

Christina hated the use of the term souls. It was as if the passengers were already dead and on their way to heaven or hell. She swore it would be a cold day in the latter before that happened while she was in command. "Tell 'em there are a hundred and forty *passengers* on board and be certain to use that word," she told Woody, "and twenty-four thousand pounds of fuel." Woody did as instructed.

Ruppel picked up the bright red emergency hotline that went directly to the Massachusetts Port Authority police and informed the official-sounding voice that answered, "We've got a serious one in progress. A Shuttle Air 727 with a hundred and forty souls and twenty-four thousand pounds of fuel has an engine out and is returning for landing. Send your emergency and fire-fighting equipment along with all the security personnel you can muster to both ends of runway 22 Left. Now!"

The guy started to ask something, but Ruppel hung up.

While on the downwind leg of the traffic pattern Erik completed the landing data card, using the required thirty-degree flap setting for a two-engine landing. He asked, "Will we have to conduct an emergency evacuation after landing?"

"I hope not," Christina replied. "Inform the flight attendants there's a chance of that, but don't order it unless one of us tells 'em to." Christina knew there were usually many injuries if passengers used the escape slides that popped out of the plane's emergency exits like giant yellow tongues when opened.

"Assume the bracing position," Christina announced over the PA, briefly wondering what might be going through the minds of the terrified, hunched-over passengers who had no control over their destinies.

"This bird feels different on two engines," she muttered when turning from the base leg on to final approach. She cranked in the frequency of 109.9 for the Runway 22 Left ILS, a landing system that provided vertical and horizontal guidance to touchdown. This was a challenging maneuver in poor weather and even more so with only two engines. She silently prayed they weren't the victims of sabotage because there might be additional problems.

"Let's run through the *engine failure final checklist*. If you notice *anything* that was overlooked, speak up." As Erik and Woody began reading the checklist Christina ordered, "Landing gear down." Woody and Erik double-checked everything while Christina flew the precise profile called for in the flight manual. She constantly made minor corrections in heading and rate of descent, always keeping the V-shaped command bars on the flight director dead-centered, meaning they were right on course. "We're not taking it around for any reason," Christina stated after the gear extended normally. "I don't like the looks of number two engine. It's running hotter than normal." While glancing at the number two engine indications she could feel the hammering of her heart as it pounded up against her breastbone. Would number two continue to operate normally?

A supervisor and four other tower workers huddled around Ruppel, watching the tiny green blip on the radar screen that represented so much. Out of the corner of his eye Ruppel saw the huge door to the red-and-white firehouse open. Fire-fighting equipment, several ambulances and a number of other vehicles came wheeling out with sirens wailing and strobes flashing. As Ruppel monitored Shuttle Air's progress it evoked memories of Swissair flight 111, a MD-11 jumbo jet that had crashed some time prior. That pilot had reported smoke in the cockpit enroute from Kennedy Airport to Geneva, Switzerland. "Nothing too serious," he had calmly stated in his Germanic accent while over the North Atlantic asking to divert to Boston. It was clear things were more serious when he requested landing at the closer Halifax, Nova Scotia airport instead. A few moments later that tiny blip disappeared from the radar screen killing 229 people, including a number of children. The investigation uncovered a serious on-board fire had ignited the big jet's insulation, which in turn severed the flight controls causing it to nosedive into the frigid Atlantic. Ruppel had difficulty sleeping, contemplating how those people had died. Things got so bad that he considered quitting, but ultimately concluded he needed the money. But at this moment his GS-13 salary didn't seem worth it. "C'mon. You can make it," he beseechingly whispered.

CHAPTER FOUR

Shuttle Air 1540 broke out of the overcast at three hundred feet, aligned with runway 22 Left. With the high intensity sequenced strobe lights assisting Christina's depth perception the big tri-jet touched down at the fifteen hundred-foot marker and came to a smooth halt with approximately three thousand feet of runway remaining. Knowing how close they had come to disaster, the silence in the cockpit hung in the air like the thick fog outside. Emergency trucks with ear-shattering sirens blaring and blinding lights flashing broke the hush as they came to screeching halt planeside. As the crew and passengers anxiously peered out, security police with guns drawn, along with mechanics in fire-fighting garb and extinguishers in hand rushed out. With radios tuned to the ground control frequency of 121.9, a mechanic inquired, "Does everything appear normal in the cockpit?"

Christina responded, "Affirmative." The mechanic then stated he was going to visually inspect all of the engines and the landing gear. The security personnel remained at the ready, fingers on the triggers of their M-16's. A few long moments later he announced there were no visible signs of terrorism damage, fire, fluid leaks or other problems and that the jet could taxi to the terminal under its own power. "Woody, let the passengers know everything is under control and we'll be at the gate in a few moments."

After taxiing at a snail's pace, as the big jet came to a halt and the forward door was opened, Erik could feel his heart fluttering, like a bird banging against the side of a cage trying to escape.

To break the stress, a now-smiling Christina stated, "It's true that the life of an airline pilot is ninety-nine point nine-nine-nine percent total boredom and one thousandth percent sheer terror." They all managed a weak smile, even Woody who dabbed at his sweaty face with a handkerchief. As the cockpit door swung open a loud round of applause and cheers greeted them. Christina stood in the doorway, anticipating everyone would quickly deplane. But the same bumbling agent stood in the aisle making the other passengers wait until a frightened looking young man in 3-D got off; the seat the paperwork stated was occupied by the sky marshal. *What could this guy be up to?*

The entire episode had taken perhaps fifteen minutes and as he finger-combed his disheveled hair Erik asked, "Think anyone from the media's here?"

"It's pretty late. I doubt it," Christina replied. But upon entering the terminal it was bedlam. Apparently they had been notified and after learning the identity of the captain throngs of reporters sped to the airport and the crew stepped into the center ring of a circus.

"Christina! Captain Shepard! Over here," reporters shouted as they jostled for her attention, while others became entangled in the myriad of wires that cluttered the shiny marble floor like spaghetti on the bottom of a large bowl. Christina basked in the limelight. As flashbulbs popped her blue eyes challenged the cameras. Putting her arm around him and pulling Erik close she declared with a smile, "I want you to know that my entire crew and this handsome young man in particular helped save us from a possible disaster."

Erik smiled meekly into the lights and cameras, but felt great.

As things quieted down and the media folks left, another 727 was rolled out. They flew an uneventful return flight, but with fewer passengers. Christina said nothing to Woody about his performance. But, while riding in the rickety employee parking lot bus a subdued Montgomery informed Christina, "Maintenance believes a main engine rotor seized because of a faulty oil pump. By shutting it down as quickly as you did it prevented a disastrous engine failure keeping the thing from shattering into a million pieces."

"How do you know that?" she asked.

"I called Boston and spoke with the mechanics who gave the engine a quick once-over. As a former Air Force maintenance officer I'm friendly with a bunch of our maintenance people. Sometimes, I hang around after work just to see what they're up to or to BS a bit."

"Thanks for the info."

Woody seized the opportunity. "I'm really sorry for what happened," adding, "my father's very sick and only recently got out of the hospital. It's been very draining and because of that I've been drinking too much."

"Don't worry. It's over and everything turned out all right."

As a somber Woody exited the bus he walked with his head low and back rounded, as though his hands holding his flight bag went to the ground and some unseen weight bowed him over, making every step an effort. Although his apology was accepted, Christina considered giving an accounting of his performance to the LaGuardia chief pilot, Captain Michael O'Brien. She had received a message upon arrival, requesting her to call him first thing in the morning. A hard-ass member of management, he would probably want to know about Woody's reaction as the outcome would have been different if he'd been in command. Should she tell him?

Erik and Christina disembarked at the next stop and ambled slowly toward their cars. Erik asked, "You gonna tell anyone what happened with Woody?"

Christina stopped, turned and looked directly at Erik, her icy blue eyes seemingly burning a hole in his. "You'd better hope not, 'cause you also made some mistakes."

Erik felt his face redden. "I worked for a long time to get this job and I'd hate to think that because of one fuck-up I might—".

She held up her hand. "You're brand new and still on probation, which means you can be fired for virtually any reason, with no recourse. But your mistake could have caused the number-two engine to conk out. That's probably why it ran so hot. If that one also quit we would have really been up shit's creek."

Erik began to utter an apology, but she smiled. "No need. You also did Woody's job. But, I have to weigh everything, just in case he noticed. If I write him up…well, you never know what he might say about you. Just be certain to memorize and know *all* the emergency procedures," she added, patting him on the shoulder.

Erik thanked her, but wondered if she had already said anything.

While starting her car, without warning Christina's head began pounding. Next came a sensation of lightheadedness. She placed both hands under her thighs and sat on them as if to hold them in place. Her breathing became heavy. She considered crying out to Erik, but no matter how hard she tried, no intelligible words came forth. Then, as quickly as they had come on, the symptoms abated. She sat in her car confused and drained, unsure of what might happen next but certain her epilepsy was the cause. She finally very cautiously drove the fifteen minutes to her rental pad. She pulled into the driveway and switched on the car alarm, recalling that David wasn't there. He was having dinner with his parents and would be spending the night. She went right to bed feeling exhausted and awoke the following morning with a slight headache the only remnant. It was still raining lightly so she put up a pot of coffee and turned on the TV. After watching the news for a few minutes she felt a bit better and called O'Brien. His secretary Rose answered on the first ring.

"Hello Rose. It's Captain Shepard."

"Hi Captain Shepard. Captain O'Brien is awaiting your call. I'll put you through."

The Chief Pilot immediately came on the line barking, "How are you Captain Shepard?" Without waiting for a reply he added, "That was one hell of a job you did last night. On behalf of Shuttle Air I wanna thank you."

"It was nothing. I just did what they train us—"

"Nothing? You were great, taking a potentially disastrous situation and turning it into a routine job." A wary stirring in her gut said that more was coming. O'Brien wasn't the type to simply to bestow a pat on the back. He quickly added, "Were there any specific problems I need to look at?" his tone implying that he might know more.

Typical O'Brien she thought, probably referring to Woody. Perhaps he had already been informed about him, although she didn't think Erik would say anything. Exactly what did O'Brien know?

"Can you be more specific?"

"I'll be very specific," he bellowed. "We removed the cockpit voice recorder tape after your plane was towed to the hangar and heard everything that went on. So, I know what Montgomery did, or rather didn't do. However, your union contract prohibits us from using any information on the recorder for disciplinary purposes so there's nothing I can do unless you file a formal complaint." Before Christina could speak he cut her off. "But even if you did, I wouldn't take any action because like me Woody's a former military pilot and otherwise has an excellent safety record. I would simply have the instructor go over the emergency items more in-depth during his next annual proficiency check ride." He allowed a moment for his statements to sink in.

Christina figured Montgomery had already called or been to his office and given O'Brien his father/son mouth to ass resuscitation sob story, so she was probably wasting her time. "You wanna know why Montgomery fucked up? He was hung over from the night before. In my opinion he oughta be placed in rehab."

"You show me a pilot who says he doesn't drink and I'll show you a liar," O'Brien responded, obviously dismissing her statement. "What I really want to know is whether anything could have been done to *prevent* the damage. Was there something that your new second officer, Erik Preis might have missed during his preflight inspection that had he noticed would have averted the problem? Did he mention oil leaks or anything like that?"

"Wait a minute," she snapped. "Preis helped me while Montgomery just sat there with his head up his hung-over ass. He also accomplished quite a few of Woody's tasks in addition to doing his own job. I certainly don't think that—"

"Let me make this clear," O'Brien interrupted. "Management is *very* unhappy about what happened, and not from the standpoint of what was or was not done in the cockpit. What Woody failed to do didn't cost the airline a dime. But if there was some telltale warning sign that should have been picked up, a problem that could have been repaired beforehand, that responsibility would fall on Preis."

"I'm pretty sure if he had seen anything he would have said—"

"But, you're not one hundred percent certain that he would have told you? He's brand new and there was something about him I didn't like when he reported here after his schooling. He's not out of the military, looked very young and I sensed adolescence irresponsibility still running around inside him. Since he's on probation I can wash him out anytime during his first year. If his performance isn't up to snuff he could cost us a lot more somewhere down the road. Hell, the damage to that engine is going to cost Shuttle Air over two hundred thousand bucks and—"

"Like I said, he did an excellent job no matter how young he might look. For Christ's sake, I even said that with the cameras rolling," Christina replied, uncomfortable with where this discussion might be headed. "Let me ask you a question. Why are you looking for a scapegoat? Can't you accept that maybe it was an unavoidable accident that luckily didn't turn into a disaster?"

"I don't believe any shit like that just happens. There had to be a warning sign."

"In this case you're wrong."

An unyielding O'Brien just sighed into the phone. "Someone was responsible, perhaps Preis?"

Before ending the conversation Christina seized an opportunity. "Since you claim I did such a great job how about giving me today off, with pay?"

"This afternoon?"

"Yes."

"Let me put you on hold and see if we have another captain available." The line went silent and he came back on a moment later.

"We have coverage, so take the day off with full pay as a reward from the company."

"Oh, thank you," came the high-pitched, sarcastic reply.

After hanging up, Christina shook her head. Per the norm O'Brien was attempting to assess blame. He was on a military-like search and destroy mission looking for a scapegoat rather than correcting a problem like poor engine maintenance or Woody's shitty performance. For as long as she could recall this was his management technique, with fear and intimidation his *modus operandi*. She hoped he would drop his witch-hunt against Preis, but doubted it.

Her thoughts turned to the epilepsy and she went to the medicine chest in the small, grimy bathroom with the standup shower stall and plastic shower curtain that smelled of mildew, and removed a bottle of Epecol. Although the doctor said the medication *might* stop her seizures, he wasn't definite because each person's epilepsy could be different, depending upon the part of the brain causing the seizures. Last night proved it wouldn't. She took two tablets from the three-month supply the doctor had provided and would do so twice per day. Hopefully, it would work the next time?

She had asked the doctor if her epilepsy could be genetic. His explanation that it *might* be, caused her great consternation. From his studies he believed the disease is at least partially genetic, with female offspring being more predisposed to contracting it. He emphasized that the symptoms could also be brought on by stress and asked if she worked in a stressful environment. She informed him she was a housewife. Although he mentioned some promising new drugs, she held out little hope. Once again she felt as though she had suddenly crash-landed and couldn't extricate herself from the wreckage her life had become, overnight.

CHAPTER FIVE

When Erik arrived home his parents were asleep, but the blinking message light on the telephone got his attention. It contained a terse message from Captain Michael O'Brien summoning him to a meeting prior to his next day's flight. Did O'Brien want to thank him for his performance in Boston? But considering his fuck-up, he became concerned. Had Shepard or Montgomery said anything?

A tense Erik climbed the flight of steps from flight operations to O'Brien's office a full hour before his normal 2 PM check-in time and found O'Brien rigidly seated behind his large polished desk, waiting. Rumor had it the only time he stood was if the Shuttle Air President entered. The long desk looked like a dark mahogany aircraft carrier with more than a hint of power, underscored by the Bachelor of Science degree from the US Naval Academy hanging on the wall directly behind it. Without looking up, O'Brien waved him to enter. The heavyset man kept rubbing a rummy-looking nose while attempting to fasten the top button of his shirt, which looked like a size sixteen on an eighteen-inch neck. As the starched collar bit into his neck he finally admitted defeat and left his tie, which appeared to need a large dose of Viagra hanging at half-mast. He motioned Erik to a green faux leather chair across from him. Skipping any formalities, O'Brien asked in a raspy voice, "Prior to last night's engine problem did you see anything that didn't look right during your preflight inspection?"

"No sir," Erik immediately replied. "Everything appeared normal. There was no oil or other fluids on the engine cowling or the ground."

"Were you thorough enough?" O'Brien asked, raising one eyebrow above eyes as cold as the blue of ice. Without waiting for a reply he continued. "Management doesn't look lightly on what happened. In addition the high cost engine repair, the FAA will now scrutinize our maintenance procedures with a fine toothcomb. This translates into higher expenditures of scarce dollars." Erik opened his mouth to protest but O'Brien held up his hand. "Most pilots fly out lengthy careers without having a close call like that. If it weren't for Captain Shepard a whole planeload of people might've been killed." He immediately added, "I'll be following your actions closely and you'll be held accountable for any future incidents."

Following a long moment of uncomfortable silence and a stare-down, O'Brien asked about Montgomery's performance. Erik was troubled answering anything about Woody. Although just starting out, he knew the code of the airline pilot brotherhood demanded he keep his mouth shut. Any damaging statements would mark him forever as a lackey or a turncoat who would do or say anything to endear himself with management. Shuttle Air was a small airline and when the word filtered out, Erik suspected his would be a very long and lonely career. Plus, what happened was really between Woody and Christina. He stated in a calm voice that everything had gone as well as could be expected under the circumstances, with the proof in the final outcome. Erik was secretly pleased that O'Brien's face became beet red. The chief pilot growled something indecipherable under his breath, which Erik correctly took as his cue to leave. Hopefully this was the last time he would ever hear anything from *Captain* O'Brien.

CHAPTER SIX

Christina attempted to get her mind off her medical problem by immersing herself in paying bills, which only created more stress because of the small amount in her checkbook. She decided instead to drive to the airport to have coffee with David, a baggage handler at Shuttle Air and also a part-time student studying acting at NYU. Although they had been sharing a bed since her latest divorce, she had doubts about any long-term relationship.

With her photo ID prominently displayed, she proceeded to the security checkpoint and after being wanded by a Transportation Security Administration woman who looked more like a terrorist than a cop, she took the staircase down under the building into the central baggage loading area. It was ironic that following 9/11 the Feds instituted strict security measures for the airlines but the remainder of the aviation industry, in particular privately owned jets had none. One of Osama bin Laden's henchmen could be flying on one and the TSA wouldn't have a clue.

Christina passed a large room where a number of federal workers were busy x-raying, opening and going through passengers' checked luggage. They then re-secured and tagged them, placed them on a noisy conveyor belt for airline workers who threw them on one of the carts, all of which were then attached to a tug. A baggage worker like David would then load them into the belly of a flight. The entire area reeked of foul fumes and Christina's eyes burned as if she were in a room full of cigar smokers. Through squinty eyes she saw a number of video cameras. Were there were also hidden ones? David noticed her and flashed what resembled a toothpaste advertisement smile, removed his earplugs and facemask and shook hands. Christina made it clear there were to be no public displays of affection between them because she was a captain and he was a ramp worker. David said he told any fellow workers who inquired that he and Captain Shepard as he always referred to her, were simply good friends. She didn't know if that was true.

"You got time for a cup of coffee?" she hollered over the din of all the motors. When combined with the low-pitched racket of the loading belt, speaking in normal tones was impossible as there was nothing on the bare concrete floor to quiet the din.

"I'm due for a break. I'll meet you in the coffee shop," he shouted.

A stern-faced Christina went into the fluorescent-lit eatery and purchased two cups of cardboard-tasting coffee in Styrofoam cups from a clerk who sized her up with predatory eyes like a snake's. She drank hers with milk and sugar, but put only milk in David's because he didn't consume carbs. A moment later he slid into the seat alongside her. As they chatted Christina related the details of the engine problem and cockpit goings-on while sipping the bitter brew.

"That's pretty scary shit. Maybe they'll slip you a couple of days off with pay for the great job?"

"Today's the only day and I had to practically beg for it," she sighed. She steered the conversation back to the problem now constantly on her mind. "At this point I don't know what I'm going to do about the medical shit, other than *not* telling anyone. My next required FAA physical isn't for three more months." She hesitated a moment, altering her train of thought. "To make things even worse that prick O'Brien," pointing in the direction of the chief pilot's office, "asked me to call him this morning. I figured he would want to know the Boston details, and he did. He thanked me but then wanted to pin the blame on someone."

"But everything turned out fine."

"You've got to understand his military thought process. There always has to be fault assessed for *everything*. He believed the second officer should have seen oil leaking from the engine or some other bullshit so the whole thing would have been avoided."

"But it was the copilot—"

"He was the one who fucked up. But O'Brien's apparently got it in for the new second officer. I told him to leave the kid alone and if he wants to do something, then go after Montgomery. But he didn't want to hear that. So I might have to put something in writing?"

"All these management scumbags are nothing but selfish money-grubbers," David replied. "Speaking of money. Did you leave me a check for next term's tuition?"

"Like you requested I wrote a check for four grand and made it out to you, instead of the school. It's in an envelope on the kitchen table."

"Thanks. I also have my eye on a really nice Bose surround sound stereo system I saw on E-Bay. It would look out of this world on that empty shelf in the living room," a smiling David told her.

"Don't you care about my career? What's this latest crap cost?"

"I don't remember the exact amount, but it's not that much."

"Just like that Sony plasma giant screen TV you bought over the internet that went on *my* credit card? Either you don't understand or just refuse to accept it, but I need extra money to pay your bills and keep my head above water. I've got lots of other expenses and you pile on even more. And now with this epilepsy crap..." her voice grew faint.

"But you *are* an airline captain."

"Don't give me that. I've got child support and alimony payments. Plus, we Shuttle Air pilots haven't had a raise in almost three years. It's difficult to make ends meet and getting tougher each month. I need to come up with money, quickly. I don't know how much time I have left. I have a few months of sick time and then I'd go on disability, which is only half pay for a maximum of three years."

After a moment a pensive David replied, "I have an idea on how we just might do that."

"Do what?" Christina warily asked.

David paused, seemingly deep in thought, which Christina believed would be a first. He finally replied. "To get some dough. It might be possible for me to rifle through some passenger bags. Even though all the checked bags go through x-ray machines, there are still idiots who put money in their luggage. If I did come up with something the first suspects would be the TSA people that x-ray the bags. I read where some TSA workers at Kennedy were arrested for making off with eighty grand from some Pakistani asshole who stashed it in his bag."

"I don't know?" Christina replied, shaking her head. "There were some United Airlines baggage handlers like you in Los Angeles who were nailed for stealing items from luggage. It wasn't cash but other junk they fenced for pennies on the dollar. That's a lot of risk for some nickel and dime crap."

"I could do it quickly because the bags can't be locked," David added, ignoring her comment, "but I'd need a secure location."

"I don't like your idea one bit," Christina whispered, shaking her head.

"Not to worry. I could do it in that dark corner under the terminal near where you park on the last flight. It's in the deep shadows and as far as I can tell there are no video cameras. You could act as my lookout. Wait 'til the other pilots leave, stay in the cockpit and act like you're checking something. You can see me, but no one else can. If someone approaches sound the wheel well warning horn. Three toots then two, then one. I can just throw the bag back onto the cart and drive off. No one would be the wiser. I'll look for an expensive piece of Gucci luggage. Who knows..? I can do a test run tomorrow night."

Christina relented. "All right. But no petty-ante stuff, only twenty-five grand, cash, or more."

"Sure."

CHAPTER SEVEN

Erik entered the austere flight operations office where the emphasis was strictly on functionality and greeted Woody, saying nothing about his tense meeting with O'Brien. A few moments later, another captain named Jason Schmidt introduced himself, stating that he was filling in for Christina. All the flights came off without a hitch and nothing was mentioned about the previous evening's events.

Christina returned the following day, another dreary one with low ceilings and restricted visibility. As she was filling out the flight paperwork, with just the two of them present Erik asked, "Where were you yesterday? Did you speak with O'Brien?"

"I called him and he gave me the day off. Why do you ask?"

"There was a voice message on my home phone directing me to come to his office. When we met I got the distinct impression he was attempting to pin the Boston problem on me? Did you say anything?"

"No. But remember what I said. You need to study and be better prepared."

"You bring up anything with him about Woody?"

"Whatever I said stays between O'Brien and me."

"I don't know why he acted like that? I felt threatened."

"He is not a nice person. So take some advice and steer clear of him. I got the impression he doesn't care for you."

"Why?"

"I don't know for sure. It's just my gut feeling."

Woody arrived a short time later and the first three trips came off without a hitch. However, prior to the final leg the gate agent again announced there would be a delay awaiting a passenger. Christina was once again handed a paper stating they were awaiting a sky marshal who would be seated in 3D. While trying to make sense of this mystery, she noticed a set of approaching headlights on the ramp loading area. Any activity like this past departure time was unusual, and assumed it might somehow be connected to the delay. She stood and glanced out through the rain-distorted right rear cockpit window, allowing her to observe a section of the ramp neither Woody nor Erik could see. The window was cold to the touch because unlike the front ones it wasn't heated. Although unclear, she made out a dark panel truck pulling up planeside. A lanky young man in a raincoat with a shiny badge affixed hopped out, trying to shield his head from the light rain with a newspaper. She recognized him as the sky marshal. Was this some sort of government business? A couple of airline baggage loaders appeared out of nowhere but the fellow with the badge shooed them away with a simple hand motion. They ambled off, waited until the guy's back was turned and one returned a simple hand motion, the middle-finger salute. The handsome young policeman or whatever he was, finally uttered something into a small microphone affixed to his raincoat collar and several unformed guards immediately exited the van and began unloading large dark satchels onto a belt loader going directly into the forward cargo bin. They seemed to handle each with extra care, like something precious might be inside. Christina used her sleeve to wipe off the mist her breath was leaving on the window to get a better view of this puzzling scene. Through the swirling and drifting low cloud cover she caught quick glimpses of the brightly lit downtown Boston skyline off in the distance. A moment later the uniformed workers got back in the truck and drove off, while the fellow with the badge walked briskly toward the front of the plane. Her attention turned to the cabin, where he carefully folded his coat, placed it in the overhead compartment and took window seat, 3-D on the right side. There was no sign of his previously-visible badge. Just then the agent said they were ready to depart.

Christina returned to her seat. What was in those sacks? *If it's money I sure could use some.* But how could money or anything of value be tied into the sky marshal program?

US Treasury Agent Christopher Norton took his assigned seat and heard the familiar high-pitched whine of the jet engines starting, which meant approximately four million dollars of Uncle Sam's cash would again make it to its final New York City resting place.

As she carefully maneuvered the big jet tri-jet into the gate after landing at LaGuardia a now uptight Christina recalled David might be attempting his scam. There he was at the wheel of his tug and glancing in her direction. She saw what appeared to be an armored vehicle off in the distance, waiting. Should she sound the warning? Only seconds remained. She held her breath, knowing this was not worth the risk. Would he get caught? If apprehended would he implicate her? After reaching up to sound the horn she had second thoughts and stopped.

As the sky marshal hurriedly disembarked onto the jetway,

the umbilical cord that attached the 727 to the passenger terminal she saw David pull into a murky corner under the terminal building where his movements were concealed by the shadows cast by the concentrated lighting illuminating the outside ramp. He jumped off his tug with a piece of baggage in each hand, unzipped one and stuffed something into his pocket. While opening the second he glanced up, then quickly returned it to the cart and drove off. An instant later the sky marshal was standing next to the belt loader while the truck pulled up planeside and men in uniforms unloaded the bags into it. She immediately got out of there.

At home, Christina found David clad in checkered boxers and his usual muscleman tank, nursing a beer while lying on the dilapidated couch, watching a Mets game on TV. She plopped down alongside him and took a slug of his Bud.

"You see me tonight?" he asked.

"Yes. But I'm *very* uncomfortable with this whole thing."

He reached into his top pocket and pulled out a ring. "Oh yeah? Take a look at this baby. It ought to bring us an easy five hundred. Maybe more?"

She picked up a ring with what appeared to be an emerald setting and gave it a quick once-over. "I thought we agreed there would be no cheap shit like this?"

Ignoring her he said, "I was about to open another fancy-looking suitcase, but some guy came down the steps and walked right in front of your plane. Did you see him?"

"He was listed on my flight paperwork as a sky marshal. But he also—"

"A sky marshal! Holy shit! Those assholes carry guns. I could have been fucking shot! Why didn't you—?"

"He's been on board before."

"Why the hell didn't you warn me?" a fuming David

demanded.

Christina heatedly replied, "Warn you? I thought we agreed it would be twenty-five grand or better? If you didn't heist this cheap piece of garbage you wouldn't be worrying." Quickly cooling down, she changed the subject. "I think he also acts as some kind of guard?"

"The sky marshal? For what?" a now-composed David asked.

"I don't know. The guy's listed on the paperwork only as a marshal."

"If I didn't see him in time I might've been caught. And if I get nailed, you also—"

"I figured he would be busy supervising the unloading of some bags," she answered, taking note that David would implicate her if caught. Pointing to the ring she repeated through gritted teeth. "I told you that I do *not* want to run a risk for something like this."

As if ignoring her comment, David took another slug of beer and belched. "Any idea what's in those bags?"

Placing her anger on the back burner again Christina told him, "No. Have you heard anything?"

"Not a word. It must be some hush-hush deal. Let me see if I can find out anything."

She took another slug from his bottle. "I've got to get my hands on money. Fast. Not something like that," she again repeated pointing to the ring. "I do not like living with this epilepsy hanging over my head and never knowing if or when I might have a seizure. And you have got to *stop* buying all this pricey stuff that I get billed for. I saw where you bought a new Blackberry and put it on my credit card."

"But I needed it," he said trying to engage her with his dark eyes, like she was the most important person in the world. But the ploy didn't work.

"Just like this goddamned plasma TV? The expensive laptop computer, bedroom set and high-priced membership at the PUMP health club in New York City?" she said waving her arms. "Those also went on *my* credit card."

"C'mon. You like the TV. And I need the laptop for my college courses. And don't you want me to work out so I keep my sexy actor's physique?" a smiling David asked, standing up and flexing his biceps.

Christina didn't smile back, only removed her shoes and asked, "Did you get the check for four grand I left for your tuition?"

"Yeah. Thanks for making it out to me. The last time you wrote it out to the school and that created a whole shitload of problems. The names didn't match and the records were screwed up because they thought I never paid. This time everything will match up." A smiling David added, "I went to the gym and worked on these babies for an hour. Look at the size," he said, flexing his huge biceps. "But I didn't work out my love muscle, 'cause I'll let you pump up that one," David said scratching his crotch as he dragged her into the bedroom.

As usual David fell asleep immediately after their sex was done. Christina got out of bed feeling totally empty and went into the kitchen where she poured herself a glass of Evian water. In the bathroom she opened an unmarked small vial of pills and removed one 30-milligram capsule of Restoril, a powerful sleeping tablet. As if having epilepsy continually on her mind wasn't enough, she saw the ring lying on the table and it frightened her. A few hundred lousy bucks—maybe? But was there something worth taking a chance for in those mysterious sacks?

CHAPTER EIGHT

The weather was bright and sunny on Saturday, perfect for Erik's weekend flight instructing job at Republic Airport, located near his home on Long Island. He required extra money and the flight school needed an instructor, so by mutual agreement he was paid off the books. He and his heavyset student Joseph Jones, or JJ as he was called had just completed an hour of dual instruction in a single-engine Cessna 152. As JJ secured the plane Erik ambled back to the operations office that was adorned with black and white, framed photos of the numerous military aircraft that were produced by the airport's previous owner, Republic Aviation. Formerly called the Seversky Aircraft Company it was responsible for the design and production of many important US military planes of a bygone era, including the World War II P-47 and the F-105 Thunderchief fighter jet used in the Korean conflict. The company was long gone, along with thousands of jobs.

Erik went to the vending machine, put in four quarters, got a bottle of water and rechecked his appointments for the day. A first-timer named Sal Rodriguez was listed for the 4 PM session. It was just before two so he had time for the quick ten-minute drive to his parent's home where he was living until he finished his airline probationary period in just under a year. It was a hot day and the small planes weren't air conditioned so a cooling shower was in order.

"I'll be back for my four o'clock appointment," he informed Andrea, the school desk clerk with so much dyed jet-black hair piled on the top of her head that she looked as though she was in danger of tipping over. Erik looked at her ink covered arms and wondered how many tattoos she had on other body parts.

While driving, he passed neatly manicured lawns and row upon row of maple trees that bordered the streets in the middle-class Farmingdale, Long Island community. The homes here were quickly put in place in the sixties and all the houses on the street were pretty much cut from the same mold, but a generation of additions and landscaping changed that. This community was now mainly comprised of blue collar workers like cops and firemen. The neighborhood almost screamed out loud, *middle income only. No wealthy individuals allowed.* People like his parents who couldn't be classified as wealthy, but perhaps, comfortable. Only a short time ago this area, bordered roughly on the north by the Long Island Expressway, better known as the world's largest parking lot and the Southern State Parkway to the south was wall-to-wall potato farms. The roadways brought the people and as a result of the urban migration Farmingdale was now a suburb of the suburbs, waiting while one caught up with the other, creating the same urban environment most had moved here to escape.

Pulling into the driveway, Erik stepped back in time, his childhood all around him. But the memories that went with the starched tidiness weren't pleasant. He knew every floorboard, just as he knew the incendiary feelings of hurt and anger toward his parents that had been conveniently tucked away in a remote corner of his brain, only to ignite sporadically. Although he detested living

with them this would be the best he could do until next year when
he would make enough to begin paying off his debts and get his
own place. There might be a quicker way to make extra cash other
than flight instructing, but flying was his only livelihood. Recalling
how much money he owed, his stomach did flips and Erik felt like
he was in a plane and spinning out of control.

Entering the house he shouted in German, "*Guten Tag,
Mutter. Ich bin hier.*" Only stark silence returned his greeting. This
wasn't one of those massive ten-thousand square foot mansions that
dotted Long Island's Gold Coast on the money drenched North
Shore abutting Long Island Sound. The homes here were more in
the neighborhood of two-thousand square feet or slightly smaller
where you could hear someone drop a kitchen utensil from just
about anywhere. Formerly called starter homes, they used to be
occupied by newly married couples on their way up in the world or
retirees on their way out. But many like this had morphed into
lifelong residences.

Erik padded to the kitchen with the scrubbed white walls
and shiny green ceramic tile floor, removed the sweating orange
juice container from the refrigerator and took a long slug, careful
not to spill any. Although this place was outwardly pristine and full
of Old World antiques, he knew this amounted to shining fiction as
the unspoiled interior was permanently stained by the angst that
ran throughout, with distrust everywhere. His mother could buff
the floor continually but never wash away her acts or the venomous
words that came from his father's mouth. He could still smell the
cigarettes and booze on the old man's foul breath, feel the pain from
the wounding words. A place where senseless rage was Joe Preis'
answers for an unfaithful spouse; a time that turned what should
have been a period of love into a hardened heart. To this day it
remained cold and ugly, stripped of affection and joy. Along with

that went an abundant supply of alcohol to temporarily wash away the sins of the past and present.

Erik trekked upstairs to his room, his lair, and saw the source of his current anxiety lying on the desk; a certified letter from the bank that had financed his flying lessons stating they had run out of patience and were demanding repayment starting the following month. No matter where he went this followed him like a puppy yipping at his heels. With no clue where this money would come from, the letter went out of sight back into the drawer. But his dilemma remained in clear view.

After changing into a pair of cutoff jeans, Erik meandered bare-chested outside into the bright afternoon sun. He dragged a lounge chair from the garage onto the sun-drenched driveway of the two-story colonial and turned his sinewy, going on twenty-five body and face toward the sun. Comforting sunlight shimmered off the dark, wood-stained cedar shingles now slightly curled from years of heating and cooling. A faint, almost imperceptible summer breeze blew that ruffled the fine, almost invisible blond hairs on his forearms, while bright sunbeams dappled the colorful and symmetrical purple clematis, pink impatiens and roses that his mother had sown in the flowerbeds alongside the walkway that spelled a need for order. Like expensive perfume, the gentle puffs of air unfolded their exquisite fragrances so they mixed with and clung to every breath, while the dazzling sunlight lent a surreal radiance to the rich upholstery of contrasting colors. This was a day when you could almost *hear* the flowers growing. Erik closed his eyes and competed with them to soak up the soothing rays. Regardless of the great weather, uncontrollable cold storms raged deep within him. Even though everything *seemed* to be in perfect balance, no sunny memories were associated with this place, even on a day like this. His slender body only added to the illusion of perfection.

The next-door neighbor had just finished cutting the grass and the scent of the newly-mowed lawn mingled with the bouquet of the flora, adding to the eclectic surroundings woven together by the tapestry of diverse colors. The man saw Erik lying there and commented, "Your mother's roses are exquisite."

Erik thanked him for the pleasant words that should have cheered him up, but didn't. Instead, he felt his mother's flawless and fragrant roses piercing every inch of his psyche with their thorns. The neighbors apparently also got their thrills out of almost perfect, lush green lawns and rows upon rows of well-tended flowers, making him wonder what went on behind *their* leafy facades.

This pictured perfection was the public image his German immigrant parents had painstakingly constructed. To Josef and Ursula Preis, everything came down to an outward show of an undefined something Erik knew didn't exist. The *appearance* was all that mattered, making it impossible for Erik to forget a childhood that was as rancid as annuals left outside to rot over a long winter. Lying there he made a halfhearted effort to cheer up with some corporeal thoughts. He was in great shape, had a full head of dark blond, streaked hair that women paid hundreds of dollars to get washed in at a salon. To the best of his knowledge, at least for the time being, he still had a terrific flying job with great earnings potential just around the bend.

But his thoughts returned to his old man. The walls were thin and from overheard German language conversations, which neither parent knew he understood, Erik grasped that his father might once have been a meticulous European mechanic who after learning of his wife's affair added unsuccessful American alcoholic to his resume. It was Freud who stated that a person's mental health was gauged by their capacity to love and the ability to perform a day's work. Joe had no trouble with the latter, but lots with the former. Erik tried to retrieve a happy image of his father and although he could picture him laughing, it was always the drunken, cackling kind. Following Erik's birth Joe became poisoned after learning he was sexually betrayed by his stunning wife. For reasons unknown they remained married. His father's private American dream became determined by the amount of control he exercised over family members and number of possessions. The word *insane* didn't quite fit yet, but was getting close. Most parents might harm their children in some manner, perhaps by tilting the short-lived hourglass of youth a bit, spill out some sand through overindulgence or other forms of excess, while others like Joe smashed the glass entirely. Erik had done nothing to incur his wrath but was nonetheless forced to exist with this festering wound for as long as he could remember. Although he bore no physical scars, his father's first sin was one of total disregard followed by hostility. Even though they shared the same house, they never existed on the same planet. In an attempt to suppress his own anger, by his teenage years Erik began distancing himself and becoming the total opposite. The apple normally doesn't fall far from the tree, but in this case, like father *not* like son was more descriptive. He was aware one's personality is normally a blend of genes and nurture. He refused to go there because thinking of Joe, Erik *knew* what that meant for him. So, because Joe was narrow-minded, he became overly tolerant. The old man was unforgiving, so Erik was broadminded and rolled with life's punches, accomplishing everything by channeling all the negatives into motivation. He played ostrich for years burying his head in the sands of time, hoping tomorrow would be better. Except the tomorrows never arrived. He finally realized they never would, even though his father had it within his power to change everything through a simple paternity test. Erik didn't adopt quite the same attitude toward his mother, because while her conduct was at the root of the problems, he still looked to her for a meager amount of affection.

Once again, these carefully guarded emotions were relegated to the no trespassing, outermost recesses of his mind to keep the hurtful feelings away. He finished priming himself for skin cancer, followed by a shower. But he knew that no matter how hard he tried, sometimes these memories tugged at him like an unrelenting dog on a leash. He blew-dry his hair, donned a clean shirt and required tie and turned both ways to double-check his image in the mirror. Many times he wondered if perhaps his good looks might provide deliverance into a better world. This yearning came to fruition, but in a different way than expected when a friend's father invited him up for a flight in his newly purchased single-engine Cessna 150. While the man flew Erik carefully observed his every move and figured he could do as well. Or maybe even better? So, Erik asked if he could give it a whirl. When the man said that would be OK, his heart pounded, not from first-timer fright but rather from the mere thought of being able to soar when and where he wanted. There's a school of thought that says great pilots are born not made, and that fit Erik. He and the plane seemingly became one. The way he handled the plane that very first day was smooth as glass, no jerky movements, no over-controlling. His touch was so velvety that his buddy's Dad commented on how good he was. Those were the only words needed to head for the sky. A smile crossed his lips recalling the pent-up current of life that was released, making it easy for the huge transition from not knowing where he was headed to aviation highflyer. The feeling that rushed throughout his body made him wonder if there really was such a thing as destiny. Like a freedom flight, aviation became the personal morphine that dulled the home life pain. He wanted to become an airline pilot and every second thereafter was devoted to achieving that singular goal. It was a risky endeavor to live small yet dream so large. But without risk there could be no reward. So, he stepped outside into an entirely new world, living nothing but aviation. He had finally arrived at that destination, but now wondered if it would last.

Ursula Preis pulled into the driveway as Erik was closing the front door. He walked over to her squeaky clean Volkswagen, sparkling so much in the sunshine that he put his shades on. "Hi, Mom. Let me guess. You went to the beauty parlor and then got your car washed?" he offered with a toothy smile and eyes comfortably hidden behind the sunglasses. Like the landscaping, her golden mane was perfectly coiffed; not a blade of grass or single hair out of place. The hairstyle's soft waves accentuated her pleasant-looking, still wrinkle-free face and fair complexion, while the soft summer weight indigo cotton dress highlighted her deep sapphire-blue eyes, just like the dark red roses underscored the deep green color of the lawn.

"Why, yes," she replied without looking directly at him at the same time gently patting the right side of her head. "But why are you home so early?" she asked in a very soft voice with only a faint hint of an accent. "No students today?"

The car's air conditioner was running full blast and Erik could feel the undulating waves of cool air mixing with the breeze that carried a whiff of her roses with it. *Was that the a/c or his mother? Maybe that's why Joe never put air conditioning in the house?* "I do have students today, but I came home to shower and change." Pointing to his armpits, he added, "*sehr ubelriechend*, very smelly."

Ignoring his German comment out of innate fear that he could understand it, a frowning Ursula inquired in English, "Will you be home for dinner?"

No hesitation. "No. I have a new student at four. The first-timers normally take a while. I won't be finished 'til later." He purposely lied, as introductory lessons never lasted long because the beginner was usually jittery and also *ubelriechend*. "Don't wait for me."

"You are always rushing off lately. We hardly talk much, if at all. Even your father says—"

"What does *he* say?" Erik interrupted, raising his voice. "Since when does *he* want to speak with *me*?"

"Erik!" his mother shouted, with what he dubbed the pissed-off Kraut expression contorting her lovely face, "He really does care."

"Since when? Why do you always take his side?"

"If only *you* would try—" she began in a tortured voice suddenly as angst-ridden as if someone had stuck pins under her long, polished fingernails.

"We've driven down this road a hundred times. I gotta go or I'll be late." He turned away ending any further discussion. Yet in his car he slammed both hands hard on the steering wheel. It wasn't her fault his father was like Attila the Hun. Or was it? What kind of person was she, really? That was scary stuff that he still didn't even want to consider. Nonetheless he felt a pang of sorrow for her, which was easy to do if he blanked out everything prior to the last five minutes. Taking a shot at making amends, he honked the horn and waved goodbye while pulling away. But it went unnoticed. Ursula Preis walked up the driveway with her back to the rest of the world and into the unsullied silence of the perfect house.

CHAPTER NINE

Upon entering the seemingly deserted flight school office a short time later, Erik thought his first-timer had decided not to show. But Andrea whispered. "Your new student's here," adding with a nod that jiggled the huge knot of hair, "the skinny one."

"Wow," Erik exclaimed with a smile. "Who is *she*? Definitely not Sal Rodriguez." He immediately took special note of the slender and perhaps somewhat tomboyish appearing raven-haired girl sitting off in a corner near the water fountain dressed in a light blue pullover, contrasting dark tight-fitting cargo pants and tiny white sneakers. Even only thumbing through a magazine a certain aura surrounded her. The diffused light from the summer sun streaming through the window made her appear as though she was on stage instead of seated on a couch.

"She claims she's Carol Rodriguez."

"When I saw the name in the flight schedule I pictured some pain-in-the-ass, over-eager 18-year-old kid. I never expected—"

Turning away from Andrea when he felt his cheeks aflame, Erik quickly strode to the young student pilot and eagerly extended his hand. "Miss Rodriguez? I'm Erik, Erik Preis," he offered in a low, hopefully very masculine voice. "I'll be your flight instructor." Erik felt dumbstruck. She had small breasts above a flat stomach, skin as flawless and smooth as the ivories on a piano keyboard and delicate features to boot. She was so sexy that Erik didn't want to shake hands but take her in his arms.

Carol Rodriguez jumped up on slender legs like a girls' coach would instruct students to do with their nubile bodies, so quickly that as her hand extended to meet his it became entangled in the lanyard holding the huge gold rimmed Ray-Ban sunglasses that screamed out, *pilot*. After freeing herself she took his hand with warm fingers that were long, smooth and thin. Her touch jolted him, while the gaze from her dark almost black, brandy-colored eyes set in clear white riveted him in place. The shower smell still clung to her and his heart was melting quicker than an ice pop exposed to the summer sun. There was no wedding ring, in fact, no jewelry. It wasn't needed.

"Pleased to meet you, *Mister* Preis," she replied. Her slightly crooked smile was so effortless that it couldn't have burned any calories. There were endless lines of bright teeth resembling Chiclets and a sexy dimple cutting into her left cheek, along with just a smidge of lipstick or lip gloss. "Please, call me Carol."

"Then you call me Erik," he insisted, adding with a wave of his hand. None of the Mister stuff. And please, sit down."

"OK, Erik."

His new student exuded a certain aura of incredible sexuality, yet also with undefined choirgirl traits. The flawless skin and white teeth contrasted with gleaming dark eyes that seemed to light up from the inside drew him in like a pool of warm water in the dead of winter. When coupled with the glistening straight hair as black as the night, she attracted him like no one had before. Her feathered bangs were cut in such a way to perfectly frame the mesmerizing, makeup free face and bestow the embodiment of pure virtue. Yet her clothing did the opposite and accentuated every sexy curve. She was definitely his type. Pushing the lustful thoughts aside was about as easy as pouring an ice cold beer down the drain on a hot summer day. But Erik knew his first chore was to put the student at ease, relaxed enough so she even heard what was spoken. But this time he was the one who felt like a high schooler on a first date.

"Why do you want to learn to fly?" he asked.

"Well, my father—"

"Do you live nearby?" dying to know more about her.

"I live with my parents in Queens, a little less than an hour's drive away."

"You go to school?"

"Yes. I'm studying at Fordham University in the Bronx for my undergraduate teaching degree. My dad, Sal entered a contest in *FLYING* magazine and won an hour of free flight instruction here. He's a wannabe pilot and made the appointment, but then chickened out. They said he could do whatever he wanted with the hour so I told him I'd give it a whirl." She giggled and asked with eyes that lit up, "Is it scary?"

A few less than memorable flying experiences with students quickly came to mind as Erik replied with a smile, "Sometimes it can be, well, exciting. But if you listen it's easy and fun. For starters, let's go over the basics."

They sat down and Erik patiently explained the concepts of flight. He figured she might be a bit tense doing something new that she didn't yet fully understand, with someone she had just met. They were close enough that when she moved her head, the shiny hair would gently brush up against his face. Without going too deeply into detail he vividly explained the theories of speed, lift and drag, beginning by explaining how the speed of the air over and

correct spelling.

Feeling as though she was peering into a tender soul, she offered, "What about if you write down *your* phone number? In case I have some questions before the next…"

He immediately jotted down his cell and home numbers.

"Sure you don't mind if I call?"

"Any time."

While driving home Carol was thinking how she could really get into flying, especially with this cute guy. Arriving at her modest English Tudor brick home she found her parents, Sal and Anita Rodriguez seated at the kitchen table with faces betraying their anxiety.

"We were worried," her father, Sal told her. "It's late and I tried calling the school. There was only a recorded message saying it was closed."

"I'm sorry. I should have phoned. But my instructor kept me up a bit longer and then we went over stuff I need to know."

"Then you got to fly?" her mother, Anita interrupted, the don't-spoil-her-excitement look sent her husband's way.

"It was incredible, with the endless blue sky and tiny houses below. Just like in the movies. And my teacher is absolutely gorgeous!" She couldn't suppress a giggle. "His name's Erik Preis. I'd guess he's mid-twenties and tall, with flawless skin, no tattoos or pierced ears, blond hair and luminous emerald eyes, as green as an orchard of trees right after they bloom. Not regular eyes but the calm and assured type you'd expect on a pilot." She pleadingly asked, "I've scheduled some more lessons with him starting next Saturday. Alright?"

Her mother's animated look changed to concern so she quickly added, "Erik said I don't have to pay for the instructor, only the plane. Oh, please?"

"I guess under the circumstances a few more hours would be no big deal," Sal hesitantly answered. She thanked him, bounded up the stairs and disappeared into the bathroom before he could change his mind.

Erik stopped at a diner and grabbed a quick burger. His parents were having a drink when he arrived home, with the old man drinking Wild Turkey rye whiskey out of a beer glass. If Erik wanted to have a serious discussion with Joe it had to be when he was still clear-headed. Was he sober now? An uneasy Erik sat down with both parents in the living room with the fragrance of freshly cut flowers competing with the stench of the booze.

"I have a favor to ask."

"What is it?" his father replied, sloshing his fingers around in the glass and looking at him through brown eyes as frosty as the street outside after a snowstorm.

Erik got a whiff of the familiar halitosis cigarette and whiskey mixture, heard the heavier than normal accent. Was he already zoned-out? But there was no alternative. "I know that you recently raised my rent, but could I go for a while without paying you. I'll reimburse all the money I owe with interest once I resume the payments."

Joe ran his nicotine-stained hand over his face, washing it without water and after a silent communion with his drink inquired, "Are you in some kind of trouble?"

Always rapid fire, whiskey-based questions. "No. I'm just short on funds and will be until I get off probation." There was no way he could tell him about the loan.

"If you lived anywhere else you would have to pay more than you do here. Why should this be any different?"

"Because you're my father, I figured maybe—"

"I'm stupid? Well, I'm not."

"I never said that. I'm simply asking for help," Erik replied, looking to his mother for support. None was forthcoming.

"Let me make certain I understand. You don't want to pay rent, yet won't tell me why."

"I told you. My first year wages stink. I'll repay what I owe next year, with interest when I'll be making a lot more."

Joe Preis looked to Ursula, then at Erik. "You're a big shot airline pilot. If you didn't live here we would rent your room to someone else and charge even more. I count on that money."

Erik knew it was pointless to pursue this discussion. Even if Joe agreed it still wouldn't be nearly enough, perhaps allowing him to make only the first month's bank payment. But with the additional time he might be able to work out something else? Fueled by the years, simmering resentment surfaced like a scorching flame and Erik broke his silence. "Maybe you'd hear better if you ate some of the bullshit you're shoveling at me?"

Joe slammed his glass on the table and stood up, ready to unleash his blitzkrieg of cutting diatribe. Another dysfunctional family gathering came to an end as Erik took the stairs three at a time, slammed and locked the bedroom door. As he cooled down, an ice cold finger of fear touched him between the shoulder blades. What was he going to do?

Ursula stood, hand to her mouth. Speaking in their native tongue, she pleaded, "Why won't you help? He isn't asking much."

While glaring back through teeth clenched so tight that she feared his fillings would crack, Joe told her. "You should know the answer to that question. *You* were the one who had that affair. Now you ask *me* to help someone who's probably not even my son. You have no right."

"I've told you many times. If you want proof we could do a paternity test." A contrite Ursula pleaded, "I am certain Erik is *our* son. I openly confessed and begged for your forgiveness. I was young, foolish and confused, trying to adjust to a new life and culture in America. How many times must I beg you?" she uttered with raised hands, tears welling up in her azure blue eyes that caused the room lamps to reflect off them like headlights in a window.

"I did not want any tests back then and still don't. I was humiliated. You ruined my life. And maybe you can tell me why Erik doesn't even resemble me?"

"He takes after me. What more can I do or say?" a now weeping Ursula implored him.

He held her gaze. Even though she was ageless, he could no longer make love to her. He had tried many times, but the vision of the neighbor doing the same always returned and nothing worked. This rumination was revisited each time. That became his inescapable prison and he finally quit trying. He had originally hoped to find someone new, but that never happened. The years passed and the resentment built. "I don't want to discuss this when he's upstairs," Joe yelled, waving a shaky hand in the direction of Erik's room. "He might be listening. I know he understands some German. So shut the hell up!"

For what seemed like the thousandth time Erik understood what was being said through a door that barely filtered the words and it still disturbed him. Although no longer traumatized, recalling when he had first understood his father's rage, his mother's admission of infidelity confused a young Erik. He had double-checked what was said in a German/English dictionary and knew he was the bastard son Joe referred to, a tearful revelation he carried around bottled up inside ever since. These things were not supposed to happen with your asexual parents. How could he *not* be his father? What kind of person was his mother? Many times he considered telling Joe he knew. If they could bond in this knowledge *maybe* then he would get the paternity test and put this question to rest, forever? But that idea turned to fear, because what if it turned out he wasn't? Erik didn't want to think about that.

Joe Preis got up and stumbled to the master bedroom furnished with twin beds. The anger slowly abated like the heat from the dying embers of a fire due to the alcohol he consumed to extinguish them and enable sleep. His thoughts turned to the young man in the other room. Should he have done the paternity test years ago? Back then, as now, his embarrassment and Teutonic psyche wouldn't allow it. Instead, pent-up rage was vented on the only two people who were close enough to continually feel its fiery effects.

CHAPTER TEN

Christina skillfully guided the swept-wing stretched, denoting lengthened to accommodate more passengers, 727 toward a routine landing in Boston. It was the third segment of the two round-trip shuttle trips between New York's LaGuardia and Boston's Logan Field. The western sunset and beauty of the sparkling day's end reflecting off the blue waters that surrounded Logan should have cheered her up. But instead she was pensive. "This ain't as much fun as it used to be," she sighed, inexplicably recalling the many accolades her flight instructors had bestowed on her piloting abilities and how they didn't mean a damn thing now. "And boy, am I tired," she continued, yawning in Woody's direction. She learned from searching the Internet that fatigue could be a symptom of epilepsy and wondered if how she felt was due to her illness or state of mind? "But at least we earn decent wages." Pausing, she asked Woody, "Have you heard anything about new planes? You always claim to have the inside track."

"I heard from a confidential management source that Shuttle Air may be buying new jets to replace these aging 727's. Notwithstanding these days of planned obsolescence, these old 727's have held up well."

"At least we're better off than if we stayed with East Coast Airlines." Christina smiled faintly, pleased with having made the move when the entire shuttle operation was sold off. "I don't know what I'd be doing now that it has shut down."

But no matter what she pondered everything returned to the m-word; money. It was alimony for two ex-husbands and child support payments for her teenaged son Jimmy who lived in Florida with his father along with another sizeable expenditure that ate up a large chunk of every paycheck. Then there were also David's expenses.

Turning to Woody she asked, "You're married, aren't you?"

"Yeah. To the one and only for quite a few years."

"What about you?" he asked.

"I'm a two-time loser in the marital sweepstakes, divorced twice in the last seven years. I always figured flying was pretty much a single person's game due to the lifestyle. And my status as the female pilots' media representative exacerbated the situation 'cause that added extra time away for interviews and dinners. Both exes were the jealous type and sued me for divorce. The second one replaced me with a whiskey bottle," she mentioned in half-jest to determine Woody's reaction. But just then the Boston approach controller cleared them for landing, so she shifted gears. "Enough of the marital tour. Back to work. Flaps two degrees, put the landing gear down and let's perform the final checklist." Christina purposely omitted that the grounds of each divorce were allegations of her infidelity. There were also other secrets buried too deep for her to divulge.

Christina liked working with Erik Preis. He was young enough to eagerly accept working under a woman's command; not an old fart like Woody, a sexist who obviously resented a woman's authority. Thoughts of Erik reminded her to call her son, Jimmy after landing. Once at the gate she went off to an out-of-the-way corner of the chrome and steel, modernistic coldly-furnished terminal, took out her cell and punched in her ex's number in Miami. Jimmy answered.

"Hi honey. How are you?"

"I'm all right, Mom."

His voice sounded strangely distant, almost metallic even though there was an excellent connection. She changed her location slightly to see if that helped. "I was thinking perhaps you could fly up and spend a weekend. Maybe we could go to a Mets or Yankees game? It's been a while."

A pause. "Sorry. This weekend's no good. I've got a date Saturday night and my own ball game Sunday." Jimmy then added in a very clear tone, "And Mom, don't forget. My birthday's in a couple of weeks and you promised me that new iMac with the DVD burner, HP color laser printer and an iPhone."

"I didn't," she sighed. "We can look at some while you're here."

"I'll let you know. I gotta jet. Bye. Love ya."

"I love you too."

She heard rumblings in the pit of her stomach as though she hadn't eaten for a week. Why was Jimmy was so detached? When they finally got together she'd let him know about her epilepsy and what it might mean for him. A quick glance at her watch showed enough time remained, so she removed a small, black phone book from her uniform pocket. She hesitated, but then dialed a number in Minnesota. A woman answered after a couple of rings.

"Mimi. It's Christina Shepard."

"Oh. Hello, Mrs. Shepard."

It angered Christina when Mimi Johansen called her Mrs. Shepard because Mimi was actually five years her senior. There were also certain undertones in her voice that Christina was certain were used to make her feel unclean for what happened many years ago.

Forcing these emotions aside, Christina asked, "How's she doing?"

"She's fine. And Laurel is absolutely eye-popping," hesitating then adding, "kind of like you."

Christina could just picture her and smiled broadly.

"She got fantastic grades last semester and is about to enter her junior year," Mimi continued. "She's talking about perhaps going to law school after graduation." After a long moment of silence a condescending Mimi inquired, "Would law school cause any financial problems?"

"It might," Christina sighed, not expecting the question. She paused for a moment and added, "There's some doubt whether I'll even be able to continue paying her undergraduate tuition."

"But—"

"Something very serious has arisen and I have to speak with Laurel, as soon as possible."

"I can't let you do that," came the immediate, barbed retort. "You're fully aware of the agreement you and your mother signed when we adopted her. I don't think—"

"It's imperative," a fuming Christina interrupted with anger churning just below the surface. "It's a life and death matter."

"But then she would discover she's adopted." Mimi stuttered. "John and I kept that from her all of these years. I don't know how she'll react if she finds out. Why don't you tell me first what this is about and then I can relay it to Laurel if I decide it's important," Mimi reiterated in the voice Christina despised.

"Sorry. This is personal. Something I can share only with her."

"Can you at least give me some idea?"

Christina hesitated. "It's something that I must discuss in confidence with Laurel."

"Meaning she would have to know everything?"

"Yes."

"You've got to give me time to think this over. You call and out of the blue tell me after all of these years you want my daughter to know who her mother really is. With John gone, I have no one else to speak with—."

"I'm very sorry about his passing," Christina interrupted.

"It all happened so fast, seemingly he was fine one day and gone a week later. I'm afraid this knowledge, coming on the heels of her father's passing could devastate Laurel."

Christina said nothing more, figuring Mimi was worried Laurel might also leave and she would be all alone. The word alone triggered emotions of how much she had missed out on in giving Laurel up. The tiny, sweet body that smelled of baby powder, the runny noses, the beguiling smiles. Mimi's voice transported her back to the immediate task at hand.

"Could you call me back in a while?" Mimi finally asked.

"No. I can fly into Minneapolis and meet over the weekend, but I *must* speak with her. Perhaps we could meet at an airport restaurant?" Christina insisted. Notwithstanding a thousand signed agreements, with or without Mimi's permission she would contact Laurel.

"All right," Mimi moaned. "I'll call you back with a time and place. Give me your number. I have it someplace but I'm not certain where."

Christina supplied her cell and home numbers and hung up. After ingesting a tasteless burger she returned to the plane. Lately, everything she ate seemed to produce a case of heartburn. She was again handed official notification an armed sky marshal was on board, meaning another probable delay. She sat in her seat, fuming. She was angry about Mimi and frustrated over yet another late flight. When the same truck pulled up planeside she got out of her seat and informed a startled Woody, "You're in charge 'til I get back." Making certain her ID badge was prominently displayed Christina descended on to the ramp. As she walked around the nose of the jet, the young man with the badge put up his hand and commanded her at the top of his lungs, "Stop!" Then, he hollered, "She's all right. Put the weapons away." Wheeling around, Christina saw the guards had drawn their guns. No longer curious, she was terrified. "You're not allowed here," he shouted over the din of the plane's auxiliary power unit as he firmly grasped her arm and led her back toward the jetway steps.

She unsuccessfully tried to pull free from his rock solid grip. "Look," she said, pointing to her ID, "I'm the captain and trying to find out why we're being delayed every—"

"I don't give a shit who you are." Pointing to his badge, which she noted, read United States Treasury Department he brusquely informed her, "And this is official government business. Leave immediately or you *will* be arrested." He quickly led her up the narrow stairway back onto the jetway and returned outside without uttering another word. Regaining her composure and never having experienced treatment like this, she became convinced they had to be carrying something valuable. But this made no sense because the guy was listed as a sky marshal. Why would the government go through all the trouble to disguise a guard?

Once the loading of the bags was completed, Treasury Agent Christopher Norton scampered up the jetway and without uttering a word or even glancing into the cockpit took his assigned seat, 3D.

Once seated in her gray checkered fabric cockpit seat

Christina's concern became David and the luggage. She would warn him tonight. Once airborne thoughts of David were replaced by wondering what could be in those mysterious bags. Why the guns? She would find out, somehow.

Pulling into the gate Christina saw David with baggage cart in tow and sounded the alarm. She waited in the cockpit for a few minutes acting as though she was examining the ship's log. Once home, she found him in his usual spot on the old couch, watching television and nursing a Bud lite.

"Did you hear the warning?"

"Yeah. What was that all about? I wanted to try again and—"

"The sky marshal was on board again. I tried to speak with him on the Boston ramp but he started yelling and when I turned around the people with him took out guns. He said I'd better leave or he'd throw me in the slammer."

"Guns? Jail?" What the hell's going on?"

"You didn't find out anything?"

"No. But I did notice an armored car awaiting your arrival. A bunch of guys unloaded something from the forward cargo bin. What the hell could this be about?"

Christina simply shrugged her shoulders.

CHAPTER ELEVEN

Ostensibly as a gesture of thanks for the great job he did during the emergency, Christina invited Erik out for drinks after work a couple of nights later. "Let's unwind a bit. There's a place nearby called Parkers Pub. Be certain to remove your uniform 'cause if we got caught drinkin' the New York tabloids would be screaming out CROCKED-PIT or some such trash. I'll even buy," Christina added with a cute smile. Erik readily accepted and she gave him directions there. But she had another task to accomplish first. "I'll be there in a bit. I have to put in my next month's schedule," she told him. "I'll be bidding the same trips. How about you?"

"I already did," a smiling Erik replied, pleased that they would be flying together again.

Only Christina was in the deserted flight operations office with the quiet green glow of the computer screen and the softly humming vending machines that dispensed high-fat snacks. Hopefully, no one would enter while she was trying to dig up the needed info.

She was nervously logged into the "Pilots Only" section of the airline's super powerful mainframe. Would anyone discover her search? What about cookies or other telltale identification marks? Was she leaving any? She entered her employee number and confidential password and the usual screen appeared. Scrolling down, she double-clicked on a category marked OTHER. The monitor now displayed a multitude of additional choices, none of which were familiar. She finally clicked on an item marked Delay Codes and typed in flight number 1540 and the date she first encountered the mysterious sky marshal. A code appeared on the screen and she moved the cursor down to a corresponding number on the lower half of the screen and double-clicked on it. A warning immediately popped up stating only authorized personnel could view this information. Was someone monitoring the computer? The coded number for the delay was filed under the Abnormal Operations Section. She went ahead and typed it in and this time an entry made by a Boston supervisor popped up explaining the elaborate details of the flight delay, along with his suggestion that Shuttle Air not renew this contract when it expired in September. At that very moment she realized that the seemingly desperate plan she had formulated like a hopeful dream might work. But her window of opportunity was rapidly closing.

bonkers," she said, "and the first time on a 727."

The bartender interrupted, handing them two more drinks.

"The guy over there," he said, pointing to a heavy-set man Erik took to be in his sixties or seventies seated at one of the tables, "would like to buy you a drink. He said you did a helluva job. Whatever that means?"

Christina and Erik smiled and raised their drinks in a gesture of thanks and the man did likewise.

"Who's he?" Erik whispered. "He work for the airline?"

Christina took another slug of bourbon. "No. That's Doc Hartman. He gives FAA pilot physicals and I get mine twice yearly from him," she replied in breath now redolent with booze, referring to the requirement that a captain must maintain a current first-class medical certificate and wondering if he could pick up her epilepsy on the next. "You should get your FAA physicals from him. He's located at LaGuardia and is cheap compared to others. He also uses the old type of eye vision chart where *every* pilot knows the twenty/twenty line; DEFPOTEC. He probably saw us on TV the other night." Christina ordered another round, ignoring the neurologist's order that she have no more than two. "Perhaps you noticed, but whenever the cameras are rolling I put in a plug for women pilots. I had to put up with all the bullshit in the testosterone oozing cockpits that reeked with male hormones, crap like the not-too-quiet whispers of dyke and lesbo." She guzzled another long pull, stirring the half-melted cubes floating in the bottom of the glass with the straw and watching as they continued spinning and clinking against the sides of the glass. She was descending into that place where former secrets come to the surface and owing to the booze no longer cared. "Maybe I feel this way 'cause I came from a broken home, one affectionately dubbed today as a single parent household, which was a nightmare for my mother. After I saw her totally dependent on my father for financial support that never came I vowed that wouldn't happen to me."

"You mentioned you're divorced."

"Yeah. Twice. But I don't get a fucking dime from my two exes," she added with pride through clenched teeth. "I don't want my son and my —," she stopped herself, "anyone to do without. So I pay child support. Unfortunately, alimony went along with it."

To change the subject to a more pleasant one Erik asked, "How did you get into flying?"

"I started hanging around the local airport in my hometown of Lantana, Florida while attending Palm Beach State College. A friend worked there at the fixed base operation as a receptionist and I used to hang around. Aviation began as an escape, but flying also provided a sense of real accomplishment. The more I got into it the more I wanted to fly the big jets. Since most airline pilots were men it made landing the job more challenging. I had to be as good as or better than the boys. I got my licenses, flew seven days a week as an instructor and charter pilot and finally landed an airline job. But now, when I'm finished paying rent, taxes and child support and alimony there ain't much left."

For some individuals alcohol is like anesthesia on ice, but it had the opposite effect for Christina. A few bourbon blasts was as though the warden opened the jailhouse door. Erik didn't know what to say with this transformation. Taking another swig she continued, "Before I knew it, the media sought me out for information on women in aviation and the semi-celebrity status created a lethal marital mix. My first husband's lawyer argued because of my lifestyle and job, not only should he raise our son, but I should pay *him* alimony to become a househusband. My attorney tried to steer me away from agreeing, but pride and stupidity took over. After Michael's precedent it was pretty easy for number two, Charlie to get money even though we never had kids. No more of the marriage game for me 'cause it's anything but." She hesitated, and after another gulp continued. "I wish I had stepped out into the world earlier, like during the sixties, or there was a time machine to transport me back to when there was still lots of hope. From what I've read and seen on TV everything in aviation was new back then. But for pilots it was Jimmy Carter's airline deregulation, where pilots got fucked by big business and the government officials they bought, when their high expectations took an immediate nosedive. These assholes took a system that wasn't broke and supposedly fixed it. Despite the bullshit hype it only succeeded in destroying employees' stability. Hell, I haven't had a raise in over three years. Some of us tried to warn our colleagues that airline deregulation wasn't the route to fly but weren't successful in convincing the union hierarchy to go to the trenches with a nationwide stoppage of service. So the sixties' peace and love came to the current sorry state where the airline landscape is nastier and littered with lots of corpses. Used to be when you got a pilot job with a major airline, it was for life. But one stroke of the pen changed that. Job security is history so the management pricks and the investment bankers could fill their pockets and buy their big fucking mansions. Meanwhile we're always afraid, wondering if it's our airline, jobs, pensions and lives going down the shitter next. I liked the world better, pre-9/11. But then the security crap came along. Now we have to bend over each day in front of the passengers so some previously-unemployed TSA goon can look for a pair of killer sewing scissors."

Her comments made Erik picture where his life was heading and he didn't like the snapshot. He wanted to burn off his fear. "In every other business, hell, in life you get what you pay for," he chimed in, "but for some reason the passengers think airlines are different. For some unknown reason, they believe the FAA is looking out for them, when the FAA could give a shit less." He took another swig of beer. "I know what you're talking about when it comes to money," he involuntarily heard himself saying, his thoughts swimming with the Heineken in his gut. *Why was he was telling her this? Was she sister confessor or was it bottle courage? Or, maybe she had something to offer? A way out?*

"You couldn't. You're too young—"

"You might think so, but the post-9/11 pilot layoffs were followed by lots of airline bankruptcies. United, Delta, Northwest, US Airways, are just a few. Shuttle Air finally came through, but only after I sent out applications to every American and foreign airline, along with hefty rip-off application fees. Then there's another personal problem…"

"What's that?" a probing Christina asked.

"Like you, I worked my ass off building the flight hours needed to land this job. But the flight instructing pay was so low I barely earned enough money to get by, not to mention repay a debt—"

"What debt?" *Where might this be headed?*

To avert her intense stare he looked at her through the green bottle. "I simply kept pushing it aside, paying off a measly fifty or a hundred bucks a month. That was all I could afford. Hell, I still owe all of it and the interest just keeps pilin' on." After taking another hit of truth serum he looked directly into those sparkling eyes now glowing electric blue in anticipation. "I just kept putting it off. So when Shuttle Air hired me I was elated. They must've run a credit check, meaning they had to know about it. But for some reason it didn't matter," Erik recalled the guy who interviewed him seemed to be enamored by his good looks. "I figured a forty grand debt only made me a typical fiscally-challenged American male. I recently spoke with the bank manager where I borrowed the money for my flying lessons—"

"You borrowed the dough for your pilot licenses?"

"Yup. I told this banker asshole that I landed this job and would be making good money in just under a year. Our first year pay sucks, only about twenty-seven grand. Shit, by the time taxes and social security are taken out there's nothin'. I swore that next year I'd start repaying every last dime. I mentioned my extra weekend flight instructing job off the books. I'm even living at home to save money, which I hate because I have to pay my parents rent and put up with their bullshit."

"So what happened?"

"This prick was adamant that they weren't gonna give me another year, said they'd be calculating a full settlement timetable and if I didn't pay they'd go to my employer." His barstool squeaked loudly as he swiveled it to face Christina, the joy gone from his eyes. "To make things even worse the old man raised my rent and I've got three-hundred buck monthly payments plus life support for my bucket of bolts that's seen better days, along with credit card debt, cell phone, college loans, blah, blah…" He took another slug of beer. "The bank came up with an eighteen-month repayment schedule and said if I don't comply they're gonna call the loan with the full principal and interest immediately due. They wanted me to start last month but I convinced them to wait 'til July." He slammed his bottle onto the bar and pushed it away. "My fallback plan was to go to another bank or credit union, borrow money and pay off the first loan. But I discovered my name is in some fucking deadbeat data bank. No one will lend me a dime. So, July first it is. And that's only a short time—"

"What about your parents? Won't they—" Christina interrupted.

"No."

"Even with your job on the line?"

He looked directly at her with crimson cheeks. "They are *total* assholes, from another country and generation. I asked my old man to forego the rent for a while and his answer was to go fuck myself." He hesitated but realized it didn't matter. Nothing mattered. "I don't know why I'm telling you this, but you mentioned you were also in financial straits." Shrugging his shoulders he asked, "You know of any way that I can come up with quick forty grand?"

Christina hesitated for a moment. "Yours is *not* a good situation. I don't want to frighten you, but if the bank goes to management and garnishees your paycheck the airline could fire you. You also probably signed a contract agreeing to reimburse Shuttle Air for your flight engineer training if you either resign or get fired within the first two years…"

"Shit," Erik groaned, "I forgot about that."

"That's another sixty grand."

Erik felt like he was on a roller coaster, up and down but mostly down. "I can't let this shit fuck up my life when it's only starting."

"We've both got money problems. But yours are a lot more immediate."

Following several long moments of silence, Christina looked into Erik's sea-green eyes and whispered, "I don't want to raise false hopes, but I *might* have a way out," closely watching as he absorbed that.

Erik knew a person's life could turn around in a heartbeat; that each moment has the potential for tremendous change, good or bad. Sometimes it depends if a person is weighed down by conscience. She might be dangling a bait and he was pretty certain there was a hook hidden in it, somewhere. But he took it anyway. "How?"

"Gimme a couple of days."

Erik was torn between a yearning to know and an inexplicable fear of knowing.

"Remember I told you to steer clear of O'Brien? Well, if he knew you were about to default on a loan he'd fire you. There's strict company policy that requires pilots to be fiscally responsible."

"C'mon. Then you gotta tell me. What's your idea?"

She ordered another round. After the bartender brought them, she stood up and added, "Not just yet, 'cause I still have more details to work out. But I will tell you it's about money. Lots of it."

She might be just over five feet tall but Erik sensed that her last sentence might have a towering effect on *his* life.

They gulped down their remaining booze and left. Standing outside, greased by the smooth runners of alcohol Christina flaunted a seductive smile and told him, "I won't delay." She recalled David was off the next day and wouldn't be home. "I feel a bit woozy. Would you mind following me?"

"No problem. Where do you live?"

CHAPTER THIRTEEN

Fifteen minutes later Erik pulled up in front of a boxy brick Cape style cottage located on the wrong side of the tracks in Kew Gardens, Queens. The street was narrow with a huge amount of parked cars and her place was replete with security bars that partially hid unwashed windows that could have had *hopeless* written on them. The street was deserted, almost treeless and the pothole riddled pavement probably fried when the sun was shining. Erik found a spot, parked and walked Christina to the front door along a buckling sidewalk bordered by grassless dirt and an occasional weed. When finished unlocking two deadbolts, she offered a smile as appealing as a European bonbon that suggested come in. Stepping into the darkness of the silent hallway, after she flipped on a light Erik noticed that with the exception of a giant screen television and stereo, the décor of the living room with peeling vinyl floor was Spartan, furnished with what appeared to be Garage Sale bits and pieces. There was a threadbare fabric sofa, along with a table and a stick floor lamp that fit with the stale smell of poverty. The kitchen had scratched, light brown Formica countertops and a window facing the rear of the house that was wide open with no air conditioner protruding through the bars. She opened a grimy looking fridge and offered him a Bud, which he declined. The quick tour of her refuge from the world ended in the bedroom. Surprisingly, there was new furniture here including a double bed, with the edge of a clean white sheet protruding from its innards, a nice dresser and one end table with a reading light. There was a poster of Key West hanging on the wall along with a framed picture of a handsome, smiling teenaged boy on the bureau that Erik presumed was her son.

Without uttering a word he began unbuttoning his shirt. But she had an unspoken melancholy that created an inexplicable reflex to run. Could he summon up a life rope of passion to throw her? No words were spoken as she also began disrobing. He took note of how soft her skimpy lace bikini underwear appeared. Although his dick might eventually say yes, the larger head was saying definitely not. This mysterious brew of crosscurrents and conflicting emotions was a new-fangled feeling. Without explanation his thoughts shifted to Carol Rodriguez and he immediately buttoned up his shirt. A silent alarm screamed out that something here wasn't right. "I gotta go," he almost heard himself saying.

"What's the matter?" Christina asked while facing him, her eyes a beseeching blue with beckoning written all over them.

"I just gotta leave," he stammered. He felt guilty standing there fully clothed staring at her now half-naked body. An undefined awkwardness enveloped him like a mist, so thick he could hardly see her through it. Quickly retreating from the bedroom, he slammed the front door closed, hurried to his car and drove off, confused. But a short ride on that train of thought dictated that he had to make a quick U-turn, not out of longing but out of fear that maybe she wouldn't bring him into whatever might resolve his problem? After parking the car, as he jogged back toward the house. But his rest of the world-be-damned fake façade vanished and he stopped dead in his tracks. Another gut instinct screamed out that an intimate night with this lady might herald the end of a more important, budding relationship. He was drawn to Carol not Christina, for reasons he wouldn't be able to explain even to a shrink. This was something even *he* didn't understand. But he had a real dilemma because he couldn't write Christina off. He needed her potential salvation. Time was also needed to sort out this tangled mess of complex emotions. Suddenly, a potential temporary way out appeared. Breaking off a single wild climbing rose with huge, recently bloomed dark red petals growing alongside an abutting neighbor's fence, he inserted it into her front screen, rang the bell and quickly left.

A brooding Christina couldn't grasp why Erik had run off as like a frightened gazelle that had seen a lion stalking it. Maybe she intimidated him? Maybe he already had a girlfriend? Or was gay? She heard the doorbell ring and dressed. Did he decide to return? When she cautiously opened it only a solitary rose greeted her.

CHAPTER FOURTEEN

Christina spotted Erik before the next day's flight, looking like a person might appear before visiting the dentist. She folded her thin arms across her chest and glared at him with eyes ablaze like gas jets. Her glower made the stainless steel, glass and pale wood of the operations office with the white walls white linoleum floor and fluorescent lighting, seem warm. No batted lashes. No hand on the arm. "Don't think that leaving that rose would make up for what you did," she hissed though clenched teeth, a chill in the blue eyes and threat in her voice.

Erik attempted to walk the uneven terrain without tripping over his feet. "I'm really sorry."

Her eyes went dark. "You couldn't have hurt me more if you—"

"All right," he said holding up his hand. "Truth is I met this other girl who kept popping into my mind. Even I don't understand what happened."

Her plan outweighed *anything*, so she had to put the anger and embarrassment aside. But Erik wouldn't know that, just yet. Right now the front and center question was whether or not to include Woody. Besides a drinking problem, was he broke? Owe money? Gamble? Have someone on the side? The termination of the 7 PM Boston Shuttle was chowtime and hopefully would provide the opportunity to get answers.

After landing she asked Woody, "You gonna grab a bite?"

He hesitated only a moment. "Sure."

After stopping in the ladies' room she went to the employee greasy spoon, a self-service joint located in the basement of the terminal with a continual misty veil of smoke hanging in suspended animation in the grimy air, along with the smell of cooked bacon. Her order of a burger and fries more resembled a plate of lard that might cause a heart attack simply by looking at it. She took one of the creaky wooden seats right next to Woody and began the conversation on a light note by asking while pointing to his stew, "You working on clogging your arteries too?" His only reply was a weak grin.

Christina held many former military flyers like Woody in pretty low esteem as most were skeptical of a woman's piloting abilities. The irony of this wasn't lost on her after his hangover performance. All she knew of his personal life was that he lived in New Jersey, was married and had also transferred from East Coast Airlines when the operation was sold to Shuttle Air. Trying to lighten things up a bit, she asked, "You promised to tell me how you got your nickname. It wasn't like, a guy thing—was it?"

"Lots of friends thought that and razzed me all the time." He chewed slowly, as if deep in thought. "But the moniker came from my old man, a long story about getting hit on a head that was tough as wood."

A relieved Christina felt the time had arrived for *the* reason she was here. "You flew in the service. Right?"

"Yeah. I flew P-3's in the Navy, the military Lockheed Electra, a four-engine turboprop."

"You got all your flight time on the P-3?"

Woody's eyes blinked too many times. "Well, no." He hesitated. "Before my time was up, the Navy sent me to the Boeing plant in Seattle for a lengthy stint at aircraft repair school. I got all my FAA mechanic's licenses there."

This was strange. Like Shuttle Air the military had invested lots of money in their pilots' flight training. She knew other military pilots and none had done this. Why send a flyer to maintenance school? Maybe Woody also had problems there? If that was the case he would never admit to it, but his eye movement seemed to provide confirmation.

As if reading her mind, he continued. "The Navy loaned me to the Air Force where I oversaw repair work on KC-135's, the jet transports used to refuel fighters, the military equivalent of the Boeing 707. I learned the nuts and bolts of virtually every Boeing-built jet. The maintenance officer position was my assignment for the remainder of my tour."

Christina remained suspicious. There had to me more to this story. "How come you left the military?"

Another too-long pause. "I wanted to make more money. Plus my wife, Ingrid got tired of the military lifestyle. The only time we even came close to settling down was when I was in the maintenance program."

"What about our compensation?"

"Shuttle Air pays more than the military. But my wife still harps about money. She asks me how long until I get a raise? Make captain? Stuff like that." He paused to eat some more stew. "When word got out about my background, Shuttle Air's mechanics sought my advice on some complex maintenance problems. Sometimes I hang around and work with them. That's how I got the inside scoop on our engine problem."

"Where you living?"

"We own a home in Parsippany, New Jersey. I thought that would make Ingrid happier. But now she wants a new car. I feel like telling her to go get a job like lots of women today. The whole goddamn world's changing so fast, with mothers working and all. The bottom line is that I'm here for the bottom line."

His last comment afforded the needed opening. "You have enough?" she asked, hoping her question came across as spontaneous.

"Well. Well. Yeah. We're not starving."

By now Christina was pushing the food around on her plate like she was shoveling snow.

Woody changed the subject. "Like I mentioned, my father's been real sick. The doctor diagnosed him with a chronic heart condition due to high job-related stress. I visited him practically every day while he was in the hospital."

"What kind of job stressed him out so bad?"

"He owned a couple of businesses. One was a travel agency. That's how I got interested in flying. He used to bring home brochures showing all these exotic places. I figured if I could get paid for flying there, why not? But he wouldn't cough up the dough for private lessons so the military was my only option."

"How's he doing?"

"He's out of the hospital now, but is all shriveled and pathetic-looking. I don't think he's gonna make it? My mother passed a while back and it looks like this might be it for him."

"Sorry to hear that." Christina got up after hardly even touching her daily fat requirement. Woody was evasive and after this conversation she trusted him even less. Certainly not enough to bring him into her plan. When she returned to the cockpit, Erik was there and approximately ten minutes before departure the gate agent said there would be a short delay awaiting a connecting passenger. Neither Erik nor Woody took special note of the tall, dark-haired male passenger who boarded about ten minutes later. Christina simply grinned.

CHAPTER FIFTEEN

Christopher Norton plopped down in his reserved window seat, directly above the 727's forward cargo bin. Glancing at his wristwatch, he saw it was past nine. The handsome, dark-haired U.S. Treasury agent wanted to get tonight's Federal Reserve fortune flight, as he'd dubbed it over with. He was the sole armed guard overseeing one aspect of a lengthy process, the shipment of worn-out United States paper currency called fatigued bills in US Treasury jargon, to their final destination. Norton had signed on for this one-year tour of guard duty approximately seven months ago. Then, some unknown Homeland Security bureaucrat with the terrorism fight on his mind twenty-four, seven decided that Norton should be cross-trained as a sky marshal. In typical government fashion he was ordered to undergo eight weeks of intensive physical and psychological training at the William J. Hughes Technical Center in Atlantic City, NJ where all the instructors were fixated on the various Muslim terrorist factions, including Al Qaeda. For eight seemingly never-ending weeks all the gruesome details of what they believed was a holy war, a jihad, against western values was constantly driven home. But thank God, or Allah, or whoever, so far both jobs had been simply boring.

Notwithstanding the sky marshal training his chief task remained overseeing the transport of the old currency from downtown Boston to LaGuardia airport. The bills were carried in locked satchels closely resembling green army duffel bags in the forward cargo hold of Shuttle Air's final evening flight, right below his assigned seat. Four days per week he flew from New York City, where he lived in a trendy one-bedroom West Village apartment, to Boston. He flew on either the two or three o'clock shuttle flight, depending on the weather. Like most government functions there were overly complex and seemingly endless crosschecks used to ensure the money wasn't miscounted, lost or stolen. The mechanism was set in motion when a New England bank received mutilated or worn-out paper money in ten, twenty, fifty or larger denominations. The bill was flagged and sent to a commercial depository designated as a Federal Reserve collection agent. The agent bank would then verify the poor condition and amount and send replacement bills. The bills and receipts from banks throughout the New England area were next transported to the Boston central Federal Reserve location. Here, government workers under the ever-watchful eye of Big Brother's Japanese-made video camcorders, verified the amounts and packed the bills into satchels equipped with GPS devices attached to them for dispatch to their final New York City resting place.

His job officially began when the tattered money was ready for transport to the airport. Norton would ride from downtown Boston to Logan along with a supervisor and several guards. The satchels were loaded into the forward cargo bin. Just before the door was secured, Norton removed the heavy plastic fasteners holding the GPS devices in place and gave them to the supervisor, who would sign a paper attesting to the proper loading. Norton would then assume responsibility. The shipment was met at

LaGuardia by another contingent, where he would oversee the off-loading and reattachment of other GPS devices. His job finished, he'd drive home while the money was transported to the New York City Treasury building where it was recounted and the serial numbers scanned, officially removing the bills from circulation. The amounts were verified against the receipts in Boston and the currency was then fed directly into a giant shredder. Official Treasury estimates were that ten percent of United States' paper currency was destroyed annually in this manner. Norton often mused about how nice it would be if he could lay his hands on those fatigued bills. Spending them would be just as easy as the new. Maybe even easier?

CHAPTER SIXTEEN

Following five straight days of the shuttle, Erik arose early on Saturday to work at his flight instructing job. During breakfast his mother said, "You look tired."

He didn't want to tell her about what O'Brien had said. "I guess what happened in Boston was draining. Did Dad hear?"

"We both saw it on the news."

"He never mentioned anything."

"He probably forgot."

As Erik pulled out of the driveway a moment later Ursula stood at the window, bright sunlight streaming through windowpanes so clean the rays were unobstructed, recalling her family's emigration from *Deutschland* during the 1960's. Lots of hardship remained left over from the war and like many of their countrymen they were smitten with the young, handsome yet tough American president who had stood up in response to the Soviet threat and declared, *"Ich bin ein Berliner."* Although America welcomed them with open arms, her parents joined a German/American social club to recapture a portion of something left behind. That was where she and Joe had met. Their journey to the New World was always depicted as a fairy tale. But like many things the truth got lost somewhere in the mists of time. She was young, barely spoke the language and before long they were married, though it was a marriage of convenience and not love. After moving into their current home, she did fall in love, with a neighbor who seemingly provided the warmth Joe lacked. Considering divorce, she went as far as to rehearse in front of the bedroom mirror how she would tell him. But before anything could be put into action she awoke to find her lover had departed with his family for parts unknown. One night while drinking, another neighbor informed Joe what he already suspected. When confronted, she confessed. His cruel response made her contemplate leaving him anyway, but she had nowhere to go. Joe had made her and Erik's lives miserable ever since, thinking Erik might not be his child, a question still gnawing at him. She turned away and returned to cleaning the house.

Driving to the flight school Erik had the radio volume high, humming along with the songs. Although he didn't understand why, his mind was on one person, Carol Rodriguez. Whenever his thoughts turned to her everything else faded away. Strutting into the office he told Andrea, "You look marvelous."

"My, but you're in good spirits."

"Remember that pretty chick I flew with last week?"

"The skinny one who kept me here 'til almost 7:30?"

"Her second lesson is today."

Not pleased, Andrea had fantasized that one day Erik might invite her out. And, after getting to know her, well who knew? But apparently he had his sights set on this other girl.

"I just hope that she leaves a bit earlier," she muttered and turned back to her computer.

The day seemed never-ending, with Erik afraid that Carol might not show. But then he saw her enter the office dressed in second-skin jeans and equally tight-fitting pink tank top, her thick hair pulled back into a ponytail, carrying the books he had provided. The same huge shades hung around her neck.

Smiling, he asked, "Did you read them?" pointing to the books.

"Yes. But I couldn't understand it all."

"You should've called."

"I didn't want to bother you," she replied, not telling him that she had begun to dial his number several times but chickened out.

"You remember how to perform the preflight inspection?"

"I *think* I do."

"C'mon. I'll follow you," he said with a toothy grin.

All the inspection items were down pat, so Erik reviewed the cockpit instrumentation and procedures while keeping a close eye on *everything*. As they taxied out he handled the radio communications while Carol performed a flawless takeoff.

"Take her up to two thousand five hundred feet," he said pointing to the altimeter. "We'll review the fundamentals again." Carol was more self-assured and they returned to the field at twilight, just as the horizon was swallowing what was left of the sun. "This is the most magnificent time of the day to fly," he offered. "The air's smooth, no wind or sun-induced up or down drafts."

"It's the most gorgeous sight I've ever seen. I wish I'd brought my camera."

As the sky was beginning to deepen from watery blue to purple and the sun's late-day bolts barely penetrated the darkening clouds and touched the treetops, Erik floated in for a perfect touchdown. "Were you comfortable?" he asked.

"Yes. How did I do?"

"You should be able to fly solo pretty quickly."

"I'd better check with my father before thinking about that."

"Glancing at his watch Erik asked, "It's past six. Wanna grab a bite?"

Ten minutes later they were seated side-by-side in a small booth at the airport diner decorated with white walls, vivid red tables and edged with sparkling chrome called The Landing. She cupped her chin in her palms and stared at Erik with huge brown eyes. Two blinks. "How did you get into flying?" she asked, as though *every* word he uttered was important.

At that moment, feeling like God's gift to Carol Rodriguez, Erik surrendered to a shortened autobiography. "I was kind of drifting aimlessly, going to school, learning how to sleep 'til noon, working at different summer jobs, that kind of stuff. One thing I always knew was that I never wanted to get on the business world treadmill, the one you never get off. I finally spread my wings after going up with a buddy's father. Flying made me feel meaningful. I set my sights on becoming an airline pilot and never looked back."

"How could you afford the lessons? They're so expensive," her beauty shining like a magnet.

"I borrowed the money." He heard himself say, almost opening up too much. He steered the conversation in a different direction. "I'm a brand new 727 flight engineer for Shuttle Air, that new airline headquartered at LaGuardia, flying from New York to Boston and Washington. I'm teaching on the side just to earn some extra cash."

Another sexy blink. "You've got another job?"

"I've been there only a short time but was involved in an episode last week in Boston. One engine quit during takeoff. Maybe you read about it or saw something on the news? Lots of newspapers and TV stations carried it."

"I think I did." She hesitated a moment. "That was you? Was

it scary?" she asked, as though what he imparted was immeasurably important.

Erik recounted what happened moment by moment, omitting anything about Woody. "It happened so fast that I didn't have time to get scared 'til it was over."

She pictured him, calm and cool and a chill ran the length of her spine.

"The airline job was a godsend 'cause full-time instructing was taking its toll, with my patience the first thing to fly off into the sunset." He related an account about another student, omitting his name. "He's not a bad pilot. But, we began doing touch and go's, when you don't stop after landing but keep the plane rolling and take off again. Like I showed you, when you retard the engine throttle before landing you're also supposed to pull out the carburetor heat knob to direct the motor's warm air into the carburetor to keep ice from clogging it. But he was so edgy he mistakenly pulled the mixture control knob."

Carol put her hand to her mouth, gasping, "Doesn't that shut off the—?"

"Yup, the engine. Suddenly it got very quiet, very quickly. I was certain it would restart, but he was terrified and didn't want to fly any more that day."

Each time Carol giggled she tossed her hair and Erik noted a unique combination of virtue and seductiveness, an interesting but contradictory combo. A moment later he inquired, "You from a large family?"

"I'm an only brat," adding, "but with lots of relatives." She related some tales about her extended Hispanic family. "You've got to come to one of our gatherings. There must be over a hundred people."

"That's a part of life I've never experienced. It must be nice?

Plus, I really enjoy *fajitas* and *tacos*." He took a bite out of his cheeseburger. Surrendering a bit more autobiography he added, "I'm an only child too. My parents are German immigrants and the only family on this side of the Atlantic." He stopped speaking and glanced at the prints of fighter aircraft built by Fairchild Aviation, many during World War II when those family members were the enemy, so different from the way they were now viewed. Was there wisdom in *any* war? The company was long gone but the prints still adorned the walls. Like the cards you hold during a game of draw poker, as a rule Erik played his private life very close to the vest. But he felt inexplicably different with her and he opened up, a bit. "My parents aren't like the family picture you painted..." he hesitated, wondering if he had already said too much, "more like loners." He quickly added, "Josef and Ursula are their names." Mimicking a German accent he continued, "But zey are so American zat zey now go by Joe and Uli. Zey also changed our last name from Preismann to Preis; definitely more American-sounding."

"Why'd they come to the States?"

"I think it had to do with when JFK was President and stood up for the Germans in Berlin. The entire family worshipped him like a god." He took a long swig of soda and added, "I'm still living with them here in Farmingdale. That really sucks 'cause there's no privacy and I still have to put everything in its proper place. Plus, it's an hour-long drive to LaGuardia, more with traffic. But the rent is cheaper."

Carol sensed he might feel awkward, so she took his hand and the first thing she noticed was its warmth. Patting it, she added with mock pity, "Then you must come to a Rodriguez family get-together. Everyone would love to meet you if for no other reason than you'd be the only one with blond hair," she added in a tender voice.

"I'd love that. But for now let's concentrate on getting you flying solo."

"Oh my God! Me? Solo? How long does that take?"

"Sometimes only four or five hours for really sharp students like you. More for others."

Sitting there sipping sodas she asked out of the blue, "Are you married?" The question hung in the air for a few seconds begging for a response.

Do I look married? "No woman could ever live in the same house with my parents," adding, "I'm not even dating anyone right now."

Obviously embarrassed, her cheeks flushed. "That was pretty bold of me."

"Don't worry."

When finished she offered to pick up the tab. Though most airline pilots were so cheap they let less money slip through their fingers than air seep through the windows of their pressurized jets, she was different. "No way. I've got it." Erik quickly slid out of the booth, went to the cashier and paid the fourteen-dollar tab. While standing outside next to her black Subaru he reminded her. "Don't forget to hit the books before the next lesson; that is if your parents agree. You'll grasp a lot more since we've been up twice. We'll be practicing the same basics with the emphasis on you performing them without my help. Next come the touch and go's and after that you'll be ready to solo."

While extending her hand to thank him for the instruction and the burger their eyes made direct contact. "If you buy dinner for all your students, you'll go broke," she laughed with a twinkle.

No hesitation. "I save it only for the ones I like." But now he hesitated. "Would you like to get together in a more informal setting one night?"

"Are you asking me out?"

"I guess so."

"I would love that."

"How's tomorrow night?"

"That would be great," she immediately replied, noting he was a bit on the shy side, which she found to be *very* sexy. She also prayed that his reserved reaction wasn't from being burned in the past; afraid to touch the stove, again.

CHAPTER SEVENTEEN

Christina spent much of Saturday holed up in the bedroom, telling David she was studying for an upcoming check ride and didn't want to be disturbed. In reality, she was formulating an intricate plan. Once the basics were in place, she scrutinized it from every angle and could find no flaws, which brought an impending sense of freedom from her epilepsy. There was risk, but it could definitely work.

David knocked and stuck his head in the room as the afternoon shadows were forming outside. "Finished yet?" he asked.

Christina stretched on the bed, while closing the small pad she was using. "Just about. I was going over all the procedures. It's not like being tested in the aircraft where there were lots of maneuvers they were fearful of checking because if you screwed up everyone could get killed. Nowadays everything is done in the hi-tech flight simulator, meaning I've got to know and precisely perform each one. There's a lot more studying involved. Come and lie down next to me," she offered, patting his side of the king-sized bed.

Christina had been with David Bennedeto for roughly a year, after they met at a company-sponsored picnic. Initially a physical attraction, after getting to know him she knew he was not as advertised. He was narcissistic, but his negatives were offset by the crosswinds of emotions from a younger Christina who had experienced watching her mother try to cope after her father had run off. The corrosive effects of that total solitude destroyed her spirit. The dread of the same thing happening to her outweighed anything. But she still sporadically tried to convince herself that being alone might be better than with David and that it could deliver peaceful solitude. But the thought of such isolation subsequently returned to paralyze her, so David remained.

Lying there, he offhandedly remarked, "My grandmother was eighty this week and the family's celebrating tonight at her Brooklyn home. Wanna go?"

A surprised Christina immediately sat up. "Why…yes. I was wondering why you never introduced me to your relatives."

"Maybe now's the right time?" he mumbled.

They drove Christina's car in silence except for the radio, arriving at their destination on Sixty-Third Street in the very Italian Bay Ridge section of Brooklyn forty minutes later. Most of the last names on the mailboxes of the square-shaped brick homes lined up like Army barracks ended in vowels, although Christina also noticed Asian surnames. Like others in Brooklyn, this neighborhood was probably changing. After parking about a half a block away, instead of entering via the front door they went to the side and descended into a large living room, replete with an old black and white TV with no remote control, dog-eared rug and a plastic-covered couch with gaudy flowered patterns. The huge kitchen had a yellowed linoleum floor and an enormous table with too many place settings to count. Offsetting the decor were mouthwatering fragrances that seemed as dense as the Boston fog. At least seventy people were packed into two rooms with most screaming and communicating with hand gestures, while kids darted about. On the surface it appeared to be bedlam, but Christina quickly realized it wasn't. Coherent conversations were seemingly taking place. David walked around introducing her to everyone, eventually standing at the head of the long table beside an older woman with white, thinning hair and clouded eyes as if they were narrowed by a lifetime of disappointment. *Will I look like that if I make it to her age?* Christina wondered.

"How are you, Grandma?" David asked.

"I'm OK, darlin'." After hugging and kissing him, she asked while nodding toward Christina, "Who's your pretty friend?"

"This is my girlfriend, Captain Christina Shepard."

Christina was caught off guard by David's use of the word captain.

"Does she own a boat?"

David shook his head. "No. She's a jet captain at the airline."

Motioning with her hand the woman commanded, "Bring her here."

Extending her hand, Christina was caught off-guard when the woman pulled her into her full bosom and imparted a big, wet kiss smack on her lips. The lady actually felt like she had whiskers! Quickly stepping back, she sputtered, "Pleased to meet you, Mrs. Rosario."

"You call me Grandma. OK, Captain?" The eyes brightened, just a bit.

"Sure...Grandma."

"You Italian? You don't look Italian."

"No. I'm American."

Grandma said, "*Ciao,*" dismissing them with a wave of her hand and turned to others waiting to offer birthday greetings.

Christina grabbed a seat alongside David. Was it for protection? Before she knew it, table-cracking portions of pasta, followed by tasty homemade meatballs and sausage were passed out in chipped dishes with different patterns. One of David's aunts hollered, "C'mon, Captain, *mangia, mangia,*" as jugs of red wine were opened and tiny glasses were filled to overflowing.

Right after dinner everyone broke up into small groups. The women drank coffee, cleaned off the table, washed dishes and chatted, while the men played cards, smoked and conversed. Never one to join the dishwashing brigade, Christina sat with the men. Soon a short, stocky fellow with penetrating dark eyes, David's uncle Juni was seated beside her, as close as any married red-blooded Italian male could do without raising eyebrows. Between sips of espresso he said, "You must be the pilot David's dating."

"That's me."

"Did he tell you I used to work at a bank that did equity deals for the airlines?"

"He never mentioned that. You still work there?" she asked, crossing her legs.

After a not-too-furtive glance at the slender legs, he replied, "I left a few years back." Handing her a business card, he quickly added, "But if I can ever be of help, please call."

Christina thought it odd that the card gave the name of the Genoa Italian bakery and Juni Rosario, Owner, along with home and business phone numbers. Not quite in line with a bank job. She placed the card in her pocket and they went on to chat about various airlines' strong and weak points, pointing out the latter at Shuttle Air. Christina was concerned about many of the same things and also surprised at how well versed he was on the industry. "Maybe we should get together some time for dinner and discuss airlines in depth," Christina suggested, handing him her Shuttle Air business card containing her home and cell numbers.

A short time later David coolly let her know it was time to leave. They bid their goodbyes and while strolling to the car she told him, "That was a totally new experience for me. The food was fantastic." David didn't respond. They again drove in silence until Christina spoke. "Out of everyone I met, your Uncle Juni was the most interesting." David just kept glaring at the road with both hands seemingly glued to the wheel in the ten and two o'clock positions. She continued. "He knew a lot about airlines and mentioned he used to work for a bank. But his business card says bakery owner. What's up?"

"You did seem to really enjoy his company," David snapped.

"What..?"

"How come you gave him your phone number?"

"You are one jealous person. The man has lots of background on the airlines and it would be interesting to hear his thoughts on Shuttle Air's future."

"Over dinner?"

"I didn't know I was bound by the rules of Emily Post etiquette. Speaking of which, I thought you weren't supposed to tell anyone about my job? Every person there knew." There was no response. Christina also didn't mention that Juni might be an unanticipated key to a vital need.

After a brief period of silence a now-chastised David haltingly offered, "Juni's my mother's brother. His real name is Angelo Rosario, but goes by that nickname. He's married to Angela, the fat redheaded bimbo in the blue dress. They live in a split level in Lake Hopatcong, New Jersey probably mortgaged to the hilt. They have a couple of kids; a boy who's about seventeen, Antonio, and a younger girl, Andrea. I call them the A family, as in assholes. There's lots of stuff I don't know about him. There's a lot in his past, yet nothing at all. You know what I mean?"

"No."

"Well, he owes some family members more than a few bucks and hasn't repaid. I figured he'd seek you out because long ago I dubbed him the family's closet WASP."

"A what?"

"A person who's not happy being Italian. He was grandma's smartest kid and the only one to attend college, which he did the right way and went to Princeton on a scholarship. He told everyone he went there to break out of the Italian stereotype, whatever that's supposed to mean. Right after graduation he started working as a top-level officer at some Wall Street investment bank. Lots of relatives went out of their way to kiss his ass, probably figuring some of his money magic might rub off."

"He's very easy to speak with."

David's eyed her suspiciously. "Just be careful. I suspect there's more there. Maybe he's still just a *gavone* from Bay Ridge? Lots of folks used to pick on him because he was short and dumpy. But overnight, he was transformed and had the respect of the same people who used to laugh at him. He appeared to have a respectable, law-abiding lifestyle, supposedly on his way up the corporate ladder when somethin' strange happened."

"What?"

"The details were secret. But I do know that out of the blue he wasn't with the bank any longer and opened a bakery that's not doing well."

"Was he fired?"

"I overheard conversations about missing money and that he was one of the prime suspects."

"Did he go to jail? You think he took it?"

"He never went to jail and I don't really know, or care, if he did," David added with a shrug of his hefty shoulders. "But there's something else, an obnoxious attitude he has that I can't put my finger on. It's like he's angry at the whole world."

David's comments about his uncle made him the perfect candidate.

CHAPTER EIGHTEEN

Christina bought a ticket for one of the Northwest Airlines hourly flights from LaGuardia to Minneapolis to meet with Laurel. It was Sunday morning, so she dressed comfortably in a light-colored skirt and dark blouse and buzzed through security. There was plenty of room on the Boeing 757 jet and an apprehensive Christina had an entire row to herself. Most of the two and a half hour flight was spent contemplating what she would say and how she would say it. As the jet began its long descent for landing Christina observed what appeared to be thousands of black holes, which were actually lakes, stretching as far as the eye could see. Recalling the State of Minnesota's license plates identified it as the Land of 10,000 Lakes, she wanted to find the deepest one and jump in. How would Laurel react to her newfound knowledge? They pulled into the gate and Christina stood when the seat belt sign was extinguished, but allowed all the other passengers to disembark first, hesitating. Was she about to crash while meeting her daughter for the first time? Maybe she should return home, immediately? Everything in her life is always so complicated. Christina finally mustered the courage to disembark and spotted Mimi, a shorter woman with dark hair and crystal-blue eyes, exactly the same as she remembered her from a lifetime ago. Although attention-grabbing in her colorful dress with the floral pattern, she also wore her gloomy mood like a black necklace draped around her neck. The object of Christina's trip was standing alongside Mimi and she immediately recalled what it was like to carry her precious life. Laurel was stunning, a tall, blond-haired, blue-eyed beauty dressed in tight-fitting blue jeans and a white midriff blouse tied around her thin waist. Her resemblance to Christina was uncanny. It was as if she had turned back the clock and was staring at herself. Memories of that heated night flashed through her mind, when months of dating culminated in something she had never before experienced, but which she loved because she naively believed her boyfriend also loved her. Laurel's eyes were her eyes with a lifetime of stories behind them, accounts that would take weeks or months to share. But rather than joy Christina felt sadness at how much she had missed. Laurel appeared content, making her unsure if Mimi had told her why they were meeting? Christina nervously walked over to them and extended her hand.

"Hi, Mimi. It's good to see you," she said while shaking hands.

"Hi, Ms. Shepard" Mimi replied with a forced smile. "I'd like to introduce you to my daughter, Laurel." Mimi's use of the term my daughter didn't go unnoticed. So much for Laurel being informed of the reason for this gathering

"Hi, Laurel," Christina said while smiling and shaking hands, but really wanting to hug her. But that thought was only a mere whisper in her head, at least for now. "Please, call me Christina."

"I'm pleased to meet you, Christina," a smiling but obviously perplexed Laurel replied in a diffident tone. Did she notice their close resemblance?

Mimi continued. "There's a restaurant right here in the terminal called the Outer Marker. We can lunch there."

"That's fine," Christina replied with a smile, wondering if Mimi intended to join them. She didn't want Mimi to know. But if she did, the stipulation would be her condition must remain a secret between them. Once at the restaurant Mimi awkwardly stated she just remembered an important call she had to make and would return shortly, a not-too-graceful exit. "Order lunch and I'll join you later."

It was just the two of them and Christina felt like a teenager on her first date. The hostess led them to a table that overlooked the planes landing on runway Three Zero Right. After ordering two club sandwiches, Christina knew the time had finally arrived. "You know why we're meeting?" she asked, somehow summoning up the needed courage.

"Mom mentioned you wanted to meet, but didn't say why."

Christina took a deep breath. "I wanted to get together because I have something very important to impart, information that might—" to hell with the dancing. "You're my daughter," she blurted out.

A bewildered Laurel looked at her with disbelief written on her face, shaking her head from side to side.

Christina nodded her head up and down in response. "It was over nineteen years ago when I gave birth to you. My childhood and adolescence were fashioned by the perception that I was unloved, meaning I craved affection and searched for what I believed was love." The memory of the softness of that night when she was such easy prey crept back from her memory, but she forced it out. There wasn't any room right now. "When I learned I was pregnant, I confided in my mother. She was divorced and we discussed the consequences of keeping you at length and ultimately came to the gut-wrenching decision that I had to offer you for adoption. I've had to make some tough choices in my life, but nothing else came close to that one. I couldn't sleep for weeks. To make things worse, your father was killed in an auto accident a short time later."

"Why are you telling me this? Why now?" Laurel interrupted. "My mother is Mimi, Mrs. Johansen. And my father is, was, John."

"No, Laurel. I'm your biological mother. Just look at me and then yourself. We're mirror images. John and Mimi adopted you at the hospital in Palm Beach, Florida. Some parents decide to tell their children they're adopted, while others don't. They obviously decided on the latter. One reason I wanted to meet now is because I have something important to pass on that could affect your future health."

"My health?"

"Yes." Christina revealed everything she knew about epilepsy and then cautioned her. "The doctors aren't certain if the cause of is genetic or if an outside source triggers it, like being hit hard enough to cause brain damage. Mine believes it might be at least partially genetic. I'm an airline captain for Shuttle Air in New York and an epilepsy diagnosis means I would automatically be prohibited from using my pilot's license. But only if anyone knew."

After a moment of silence that felt like an hour, Laurel asked, "Why didn't you just let my Mom tell me this?"

The waitress thankfully interrupted, bringing their sandwiches.

She left and Christina continued. "Because I wanted to personally speak with you, see who and what you have become. I'm attempting to stretch out my career for as long as possible because I need the money. Besides paying your college tuition, I've got other large expenditures—"

"Pay my college tuition? Mom pays that."

Christina shook her head. "I'm the one who's been paying, which I did with pleasure. The only ones who knew that were your parents and me. But if the airline or the FAA even suspects I have epilepsy they would yank my medical certificate faster than you could say the word jet. Then, I'd be placed on disability pay meaning I would make only half for a few years. So, the fewer people who know make for better odds it won't be discovered."

"Does all this mean I won't have money to continue college?"

"I don't have an answer to that question—yet. I need a bit more time. However, I urge you to visit a neurologist as quickly as possible. But please keep what I said in your confidence."

"That might be difficult. I mean, you pop into my life after all of these years and then don't expect me to speak to Mom about this? I know she's going to ask what we spoke about and…"

"All right," Christina sighed. "Tell her. But only her. And she *must* keep what you say strictly confidential."

"I promise. But I have another question."

"Go ahead. I'll answer whatever I can."

"Who is – was – my father?"

That question ripped open an old wound. "I don't have a picture to show you. Your father's name was Brian Patterson and he was a very handsome and intelligent young man who I *thought* I loved deeply. At the time we were both high school seniors with all the graceless manners that went with that. Neither of us believed I would become pregnant. After that happened, we went our separate ways."

"Did he know you were pregnant? Did he ever see me after I was born?"

"The answer to those questions is, no," Christina lied. "He

died right after you were born." The truth was far different. Christina's mother had informed Brian's parents of the situation and they had attempted to talk her into forcing Christina to have an abortion. But her Catholic upbringing prohibited that. Until Brian's death approximately a year later, neither he nor his parents wanted anything to do with Christina, or Laurel. Christina slid her chair back squeakily on the hardwood floor. She stood up and requested the check, noting neither had touched their sandwich. Leaving the restaurant, Christina spotted Mimi seated on a metal bench on the concourse. "I told her," Christina informed a frowning Mimi. "There's another item that she has my permission to share with you and only you. I trust you will respect my wish."

Mimi nodded her head.

The three ladies stood there awkwardly looking from floor to ceiling. Christina felt things had gone as well as expected. No doubt Laurel had plenty running through her mind right now and needed time to digest it. Hopefully, they could eventually strike up a close relationship. Maybe even become best of friends? Christina had never allowed herself to become too attached to anyone since her last divorce. She had constructed a hidden wall with everyone except Jimmy, a structure she would tear down in a heartbeat for Laurel. Christina broke the awkward silence. "Here are my cell and home numbers. Think over what I've told you and call after the doctor's visit and let me know how it went." After again shaking hands she quickly headed to the departure gate for the next flight, two hours earlier than planned.

During the flight home Christina was pleased that she hadn't been totally rejected. She might even have detected a hint of childlike longing in Laurel's eyes? She'd give her a week or so to think everything over and visit the doctor. If she didn't call, then she would call her. Reclining her seat, Christina felt a slight headache and recalled the doctor's words about how stress and epilepsy went hand in hand. She certainly had enough of the former. She vowed to put her plan into operation as soon as possible.

CHAPTER NINETEEN

Upon arrival at the somewhat unkempt Rodriguez English Tudor home in Hollis, Queens, before reaching the front door it swung open and a smiling Carol greeted him with a peck on the cheek. Erik took note of her clingy dark blue dress with a slit up the side and mesh stockings, but before he could utter anything she informed him with a bright smile, "I'm so proud of you for helping save all those people that I got you something." She removed an unwrapped box from drawer in the small table by the door.

"For me?"

"Open it."

The box contained a white T-shirt with the words *MY HERO* emblazoned in bright red on the front and back.

"You shouldn't have," a blushing Erik lied. The truth was if his chest stuck out any farther someone would think he had just finished pumping iron. "Maybe I'll wear it to work?" he joked, recalling what O'Brien had said.

"I chose the words myself. You can try it on later 'cause I want to introduce you to my folks." She led him through a living room with French provincial furniture and quite a few books strewn about. One item in particular jumped out at him, a large, empty wooden picture frame hanging on the wall off to the left with the hand-stenciled word RESERVED in the center.

"What's that?" he asked as they passed it.

"That's where my degree will go. It's a reminder to study hard. Neither parent attended college, so it's special."

Erik could almost feel the difference between this home and his house, notwithstanding the lack of colorful flowers or weed-less lawn. It held a special karma he couldn't put his finger on, something that came from within and ran throughout. Entering a small den, a big man with a full head of wavy, gunmetal hair was seated behind a heavy oak desk, wearing dark linen trousers and striped, open collared shirt. The sloppy Persian-carpeted room also contained a long leather couch, accented by rustic, oak end tables along with two wrought iron bookshelves that contained what appeared to be over a hundred paperback and hardcover books. Erik's eyes were always attracted to books almost as much as a nice cleavage, because what a person reads revealed lots about their persona. These were mostly nonfiction, arranged on either side of a massive stone fireplace, which even in the heat of summer imparted warmth.

"Dad, I'd like you to meet my flight instructor, Erik Preis. Erik, this is my father, Sal Rodriguez."

"I'm pleased to meet you, Mr. Rodriguez." Sal Rodriguez was a man with a quarterback look, rolled up shirtsleeves that exposed Popeye-like forearms, a friendly smile and a square-shouldered heft more in keeping with the Timberland rather than Hugo Boss look. Rising to his feet and extending a huge, warm hand, Sal Rodriguez remarked in a soft spoken voice that made Erik feel warm inside, "The pleasure's all mine. And please call me Sal, otherwise I feel too damned old."

An attractive woman wearing a shortish black dress, white

enroute. Upon entering the crowded eatery, he was surprised when Monsieur DuBois personally greeted them and ushered them to a flawless center stage table surrounded by stylish art nouveau and urns of lush, exotic plants awash with exotic flowers like peace lilies. Pointing to Carol, DuBois inquired, "And who is this stunning young lady?"

"She's a very good friend of mine, Carol Rodriguez."

The owner kissed her hand, in the process mentioning Erik was fortunate to take such a divine woman on a dinner date. *God bless the French. They certainly know how to make you feel important.*

First came two glasses of smooth champagne. They clinked glasses and spoke in whispers in the soft light, mostly about flying. As she twirled the stem on her champagne glass and inspected the menu, both decided on the Steak Diane. Next came a bottle of fine *Chateau Latour* served in fluted glasses. Usually a beer man, Erik found the smoothness and fine taste of the red wine a bit bewildering. They enjoyed the leisurely dinner served in individual sterling hotplates, along with escargot. A delicious crepe dessert rounded everything out beautifully. The cultural differences between them were quickly vanishing in the flood of tasty food and wine. Finishing up their *café-au-lait*, Erik requested the check and was informed by the maître d' that the dinner was courtesy of Monsieur DuBois.

"You must be pretty important," Carol cooed. "We come to this fantastic place and don't even have to pay. Not too shabby."

"It's probably because Monsieur DuBois' son, Pete and I were friends throughout high school, actually closer to brothers."

"You're so unassuming. He probably saw your picture in the newspaper."

Erik left a nice tip for the waiter and as they were leaving, DuBois stopped them and offered in a heavily accented voice, "I hope you enjoyed your meal."

"Everything was fabulous," a beaming Erik replied, as Carol shook her head in agreement. "And thank you so much."

"It was the least I could do. I recognized your picture in the *Daily News*, and read about how you helped save that planeload of people."

"It was nothing."

"Ah, but it was," DuBois offered, shaking his finger.

"And, how is my friend Woodsy doing?"

"He is fine. He is working as a junior member of an accounting firm here in Manhattan. Sometimes he stops in for lunch, but other than that I do not see him often because he is so busy with work. He said that he eventually wants to become a CPA and a partner in the firm."

"That's great! Please, tell him I said hello."

"Where can he reach you?"

"I'm still living with my parents," a suddenly deflated Erik replied. "They have the same phone number."

"I will tell him to call."

Erik made a mental note to write a thank you note to DuBois for the dinner and red carpet treatment.

It was a clear and warm evening on the crowded Manhattan streets with couples strolling and a sky full of twinkling stars visible even from the sidewalks in the mostly residential East Side. While the city lights burned brightly on Fifth Avenue and the cabs' muted horns could be heard off in the distance, Erik said, "Where to now? Wanna mosey around here for a bit?"

"Nah. Let's go to my house instead. After what the owner said, I don't want to vie with any of the other eight-million for your attention. Don't forget, you're *my* personal hero."

"I'll never forget that," a smiling Erik told her. They

conversed about lots of things while driving and Erik detected a certain street shrewdness in Carol, an unanticipated trait that surprised him. They were so engrossed with each other that she had to remind Erik where to exit. Once inside the darkened Rodriguez home, Carol asked, "Go downstairs and turn on the television while I get us something to drink."

Erik descended into a comfortably furnished room, plopping down, remote control in hand on the end of a large white L-shaped couch, which when combined with the paintings and framed pictures lent a seashore atmosphere to the casual room. Carol came down a moment later.

"I brought you a beer and also made some tea. Which will it be?"

"Beer will be fine."

They watched TV for a few moments. "You want anything else?" she asked.

Erik didn't respond but began nervously scanning the channels, bypassing all of the dumb shows the fat and lazy entertainment industry produced for American viewers who fit the same description. He finally laid the remote on the end table with some rock music playing on a cable channel.

"I doubt if you'd give it to me," he said, sliding over to her. He placed his arm around her.

Carol could feel her heart hammering against her ribcage. This was a new sensation for her, as in the past she could always control herself. It was the guy who had trouble. For reasons unknown this time was different.

"You probably say the same thing to all your girlfriends."

"There are no others."

In response, she put her arm around Erik and kissed him on the lips. Carol's kiss felt as though it contained alternating current electricity and he quickly became aroused. He kissed her neck, which caused a pleasing shiver to run down her spine. As he moved one hand to her breast, she made no attempt to stop him. Her breathing became even more labored as he gently fondled her hardened nipple and moved his other hand to the light blue, flowered panties and began to rub her. With their tongues now rolling against each other he attempted to slip his hands inside, but when he touched her she immediately pulled away, blurting out, "We only met." But Erik felt as though he had known her for his entire life. The chemistry between them rendered those words meaningless. But just then came the telltale rattling of the electric garage door opening.

"My parents! Quick, the bathroom!" pushing him in that direction. He felt as though he'd just jumped from a sauna into a snowdrift. Did she have time to straighten her clothing?

"Hi Mom. Hi Dad. Gee, you're home early. I'm downstairs, c'mon down."

"Lots of people got tired," her father replied as Erik heard the thumping of shoes on the steps. I guess that's the price you pay when you're older? But it certainly beats the alternative." Pause. "Did Erik leave?"

"No. He wanted to wait 'til you returned. He's in the bathroom."

"Did you guys have a nice time?"

"It was fantastic. We went to this French restaurant in the city called *Chez Nous*. It was great."

Erik patted his hair down, smoothed out his crotch as best he could and checked for any other telltale signs. Finding none, he flushed the toilet and upon leaving the washroom feigned surprise.

"Hi. Carol said you'd be a while and I thought I'd keep her company 'til you returned."

"That was nice of you. All of the old folks started to leave, so we did the same," Sal said, adding with a wink, "actually I didn't want to spend any more time with my wife's family. They're a bunch of—"

"The true reason was you lost so much money playing poker," Anita chimed in.

"It wasn't *that* much."

"You're home, so I can leave now."

"No, please. Stay and finish your beer."

"It's getting late," he said, furtively gazing longingly at Carol. "Plus, I have to work tomorrow."

Good-byes were exchanged and Carol walked Erik to the front door. Wrapping her arms around his neck she imparted a long, sensual kiss. Feeling his hardness against her she sighed, "Call me when you have a few moments."

"Definitely."

He drove home swollen but strangely content, thinking about what could happen the next time they were together alone.

CHAPTER TWENTY

After hearing David leave for work, Christina donned her favorite tee and loose-fitting jeans and took out the same pad to put the finishing touches on her brainchild. Through whatever means, Preis had to be involved because her project couldn't get off the ground without him. On account of his monetary situation and difficulties with O'Brien, she counted him in. One other person was also needed and hopefully, Juni Rosario would be that someone. Soon, the sun was high in the blue sky and Christina went to the old stove-top and put up a pot of coffee. This job would be carried out in the same manner as she flew her jetliner, meaning everything would be planned so as to stack the odds as much as possible in her favor. The rich aroma of the imported South American Starbucks beans, combined with the delight knowing everything was quickly coming together kept her functioning at takeoff power.

While flying the shuttle later that day, the stimulation of anticipation flowed through her veins as quickly as sound travels through the air and enabled her to take precise mental notes of many topographical features while approaching Logan. On the return flight to LaGuardia Christina flipped up the paddle switches that placed the plane on autopilot, turned and casually asked Erik,

"Like today, we make our takeoffs in Boston on runway 22 Right. Know why?"

"Probably 'cause during the warm months the prevailing winds are from the south or southwest and we always take off into the wind." *Why's she asking me a basic aviation question?*

"That's true, but there's lots of history when it comes to the Logan field. Like you said, from day one every pilot is taught to take off and land into the wind. It's safer due to the slower ground speed, basic common sense. But for years common sense was one commodity lacking in the people who ran the airport. Ironically, the airport was named after General Edward Logan, a Spanish American war hero who never even saw a plane. Never having flown must have also been the case with the Massachusetts Port Authority bureaucrats, 'cause these idiots made noise-abatement procedures take precedence over flight safety by forcing us to make tail wind and horrendous crosswind takeoffs. Can you imagine, speeds over a hundred and fifty miles per hour and their procedures added on another ten or fifteen with needless tailwinds. This continued until a bunch of pilots, including yours truly, went public stating the situation was so dangerous that it was a disaster waiting to happen. But none of the pencil pushers cared. After lots of prodding, our union hierarchy finally sent up a red flag and the entire matter turned into a big political football. But the union held firm, publicly stating flight safety must take precedence over noise abatement. It was the ultimate threat of *total* noise abatement by airline pilots, no flights in or out of Logan that finally brought them to their senses."

"That little tool works every time," a smiling Woody interjected.

Christina still savored the victory. "Strict regulations were enacted, which is why we use 22 Right for takeoff during the warmer months when the prevailing south or southeast winds bring in heavy fog right around sunset. When we land on the seven o'clock shuttle, you can see the fog banks just lying in wait over the water, ready to cloak the airport. When the sun sets and the landside temperature drops, usually right around our final departure time, the fog rolls in so quickly that the visibility is reduced to near zero in a heartbeat. On 22 Right we only need an eighth of a mile for takeoff, six-hundred and sixty feet, which is damned little. This translates into always using that runway. The noise footprint on 22 Right is also fairly low, so everyone's happy. We get home safely and our takeoffs don't upset the locals who apparently vote with their ears."

Shortly after their arrival Woody jetted off to the employee cafeteria. Erik was about to leave when Christina's feathery fingers softly touched his left shoulder. "Let's chat—privately. Please close and bolt the cockpit door so no one can enter, even with a key." Christina swiveled around and faced him with her crystalline blue eyes seemingly taking in everything. But her expressionless demeanor gave back nothing. Why the secrecy? It was just the two of them surrounded by hundreds of dials and gauges, the myriad of blinking lights reflecting off their faces, giving both a luminescent, bizarre appearance. When Christina finally spoke, her voice was a mere whisper. "Shuttle Air is a small airline and I figure it's going to wind up in the garbage heap when the larger airlines and the government subsidized high speed trains take us on in the shuttle market. So besides your immediate problem, it would be nice to have a sizeable nest egg for future peace of mind."

"Amen," Erik replied. *What's coming next?*

To let her words sink in further she told him, "I double-checked in Volume One, the official Shuttle Air pilot handbook. Your bank problem means your job is at stake. Let me read you an excerpt." Reaching into her frayed black leather flight bag, she retrieved an approximate two-hundred-page, small, dark blue covered book with large white lettering entitled, *Shuttle Air Flight Operations Manual.* "This is the bible to management and addresses virtually every aspect of the airline from a pilot's perspective; how operations are to be conducted, dress code, on and off-duty conduct. Stuff like that." She turned to a folded-back page with a paragraph entitled *Fiscal Responsibility* and read it aloud: "'Assignment, attachment, garnishment of wages, complaints from creditors, and/or proven financial irresponsibility will subject the pilot to severe disciplinary action, including discharge.' It's crystal clear. If the bank goes to O'Brien and demands your debt be withheld from your paycheck, your employment will be history."

"Why are you..?"

She put up her hand. "But, if you take part in what I'm about to propose, all that goes by the wayside."

Erik added in an unusually shrill voice, "Enough!" sounding like he had a degree in advanced whimpery. "What is it?"

Pavlov was right she thought. "This is about money," she stated matter of factly, raising the brows above her previously cool blue eyes that were now afire. "And, a nice amount," attempting to come across as Miss Confidence. "You'll be able to repay your bank debt and we can both secure our futures no matter what happens to Shuttle Air. I can't do this by myself. It's illegal and we'll both do time if caught, although I'm certain that won't happen." She gave Erik a moment to absorb what was said and continued. "Before revealing more, I need your solemn pledge that what I tell you will go no further. We'll be in this together, all the way. No turning back." Short pause. "There's money onboard and we stand to make a lot..."

"How much?"

"Do I have your word you won't repeat this? To anyone?"

He nodded his head.

"Use an approximate figure of three quarters of a million each."

"Without robbing a bank?"

"Without even touching the money. Look, you have everything to gain and nothing to lose. You won't have to worry about O'Brien or your job. You'll be out of harm's way and have enough to tell O'Brien to fuck off, if that's what you want. And it should take only a short time to carry out."

"We use guns?"

"No violence and no one will get hurt. All we do is our normal routine with some minor variations."

"What you just dropped on me goes against everything I *thought* I stood for," Erik somberly replied.

"Then I guess I've already told you more than enough. Think it over and let me know. Let's join Woody, before he gets suspicious."

"Now *you* wait a fucking minute. You're can't leave me dangling like a yo-yo at the end of a string again, like at Parkers. You're asking me to make a life-altering decision."

"Sorry, but I have to know you're a hundred percent in before saying more," Christina replied in as blasé tone as she could muster. "Just let me know whatever and whenever you decide. But remember, *your* time is quickly running out," not letting on that without his participation her plan couldn't work.

Inside the dump that was called a cafeteria, Woody was nowhere in sight. Erik wanted to eat alone, his stomach already full—of Christina. After pecking at the overcooked steamed chicken and rice he left to perform his pre-flight inspection. As the day swiftly morphed into twilight, he could feel the penetrating New

England dampness. The sogginess of the rapidly cooling air made him shiver. Or was it out of fear of what Christina had said? With fog slithering into every nook and cranny of the field, in the short time it took to check the jet's exterior, the entire airport became blanketed in a white quilt. Once in the cockpit, Woody informed Erik, "I figured you guys were running late so I did the cockpit preflight inspection for you."

Erik thanked him, but his mind was elsewhere. During an uneventful flight to LaGuardia Erik brooded over Christina's offer. He was being corrupted, but didn't see much choice. Staring at the deep indigo sky that stretched like a twinkling canopy as far as the human eye could see, even with its open-ended vastness, Erik was trapped. If he didn't go along she would probably rat him out for fucking up. But, if he agreed..? Reality dictated there were no options. His thoughts turned to Carol and what she would think. For now, he was her hero and for the first time he felt close to capturing a unique commodity. What would happen to their relationship if he betrayed everything she believed he stood for? This was tempered by the thought of what would happen if he lost his job and owed a hundred grand.

The big jet commenced its descent toward the New York City lights, powerful beams that reached so high into the pitch-black night that even in a jet it seemed like you were looking up at them. Erik was normally mesmerized by these rays penetrating the polished, silver moon crescent that hung in a starlit sky replete with a few wispy clouds sailing across it like ships on a flat expanse of ocean. This sea of night appeared unsullied, the same as he was, until now. Until Christina Shepard had flown into his life. Although rationalizing, trying to justify or deny it, he was traveling into an unknown landscape more akin to the life and death culture below him in the city that devoured everything in its path. Yet, to reach his lifelong dreams and ambitions he had to hold onto this job. Reality grabbed him by the nuts. He would step into the darkness and release some heretofore concealed inner beast. When done, he would hopefully be able to recapture his personal Doctor Jekyll and seal it away back in the bottle, never to emerge again. He tried to justify this decision by believing that it wasn't the journey, but the destination that counted. Where would this train, in this case plane, take him? Erik felt a sea of change rolling through him as powerful and unstoppable as an incoming ocean tide. His life would never be the same.

CHAPTER TWENTY-ONE

Although Christina wanted nothing to do with David's baggage rip-off from the get go, while taxiing into the gate she saw him lurking in the shadows under the terminal. Woody and Erik said their goodbyes and she was alone in the cockpit. David *had* to know the guard was aboard because the armored vehicle was planeside. She lost sight of him as he drove around the left wing of the 727, careful not to pass under it. Management was adamant about this as any baggage piled too high would severely damage the wing, making it immediate grounds for dismissal. She saw him again as he drove off as if to place six or seven pieces of luggage on the carousel, but he stopped in the shadows, opened a bag and dumped its contents onto the cart, simultaneously throwing some items on the ground. Just then, Christina spotted another man dressed in a jacket and tie headed directly toward him. She immediately sounded the horn. But a jet was taking off on the adjacent runway, which must have drowned out the signal. Simultaneously, the cockpit door swung open and a mechanic entered.

David felt a light tap on his shoulder. His heart jumped into his mouth as he wheeled around.

"Can I help you?" a heavyset man with a prominently displayed gold-colored badge hollered to him over the deafening noise.

David was prepared in case something like this happened and was quick on his feet. "Why, uh, yes, if you don't mind. These items bounced off the cart when I hit that bump," he said, pointing to a protuberance built into the ramp to keep rainwater from flowing under the terminal building.

"Captain, you don't have to activate the wheel well warning," the mechanic declared, pointing to the overhead instrument panel where Christina had her finger poised. "We've already plugged in the external power."

"Oh, thanks," she sputtered, trying to see what was happening on the ramp. Someone was speaking with David, who kept glancing up toward the cockpit. Was he implicating her? She had already concocted a seemingly plausible explanation about why a pilot wouldn't be involved in a nickel and dime scheme. There was nothing further she could do, so Christina grabbed her flight bag and drove home. She paced back and forth, glass of wine in hand, totally stressed out, afraid of a seizure. Would the police knock on the door at any moment?

CHAPTER TWENTY-TWO

The heavyset guy assisted in gathering the contents and handed them to David, who stuffed them back inside the suitcases. "I try to be extra careful whenever I drive over that spot," he stammered, pointing to the bump, "but sometimes I forget."

"That doesn't seem to be a very smart place to put a speed bump."

"It's not a speed bump. It's there is to keep the water out." Changing the subject, David asked while pointing to the badge, "You work for the airline's security department?"

The man shook his head. "No. I'm with the Feds, here to check on an incoming shipment," pointing to the jet.

"Well, thanks for the help. I really appreciate it," David replied, not wanting to seem overly interested.

"At least now someone will be happy to get their belongings back," the man said with a smile as he strolled off.

After what seemed like an eternity, Christina finally heard David's car pull up. She yanked open the door. "What happened? I saw that big guy come over to you and—."

"Thanks very much. Why the fuck didn't you warn me?"

"I tried. But you couldn't hear it because a plane took off.

You all right?"

"Nothing I couldn't handle." Smug smile. "He believed me when I said it fell off my cart. He was wearing a federal government badge but I couldn't make out the department. He was checking on whatever was on your plane."

"I was afraid he collared you."

"Actually, he helped me pick the stuff up."

"You better back off, 'cause if that fellow worked for the airline..? It's not worth it over a lousy few bucks," Christina reiterated with a frown.

Ignoring her comment, David changed the subject. "What the hell's on your plane? First there's the guard. Then, that armored truck and now there's this guy checking. All of these people wouldn't be involved unless this was somethin' big."

"I haven't been able to come up with anything. It's probably top secret." After another pause a pensive Christina added, "But you have to stop with the bags." David said nothing. "Did you hear me?"

"No way." David hesitated a moment and added, "Well, maybe after a few scores?"

"You'll get caught," Christina insisted.

"Then don't do the lookout thing." If she wasn't involved he didn't have to share anything.

"Fine. I won't."

CHAPTER TWENTY-THREE

Erik's eighteen payments were calculated at $1965.33 per month, including interest. After receiving notification he again called in the hope the bank would push back the starting date or lower the monthly amount. However, the manager stated in what sounded like a recording, "We've been more than tolerant for well over two years. Per your request, we rearranged the financing so you could settle up over a longer period and also moved the starting date. Nothing more can be done."

Erik could picture this smug asshole sitting at a big desk on his fat ass, not caring what effect something like this would have on Erik's life. Since assistance from his parents was *kaput*, maybe Carol would help? He didn't want to ask, but pondering his dilemma, saw no other alternative. As the looming first month's deadline neared, he approached her, nerves on edge.

"I've got a serious problem. It's so bad it could cost me my job."

A startled Carol replied, "What? The airline or instructor job?"

"The airline." Erik hesitated. "I took out a loan to pay for my initial flight lessons. Back then everyone, the bank included believed pilot jobs were easy to come by. But then the recession hit and most pilot jobs flew off into the sunset faster than a supersonic fighter. I haven't started making enough yet to repay it and they're demanding I begin next month." He gulped. "I read the airline's ops manual and if I default and management learns, they'll probably fire me for fiscal irresponsibility." After providing the details he added, "I'm hoping to come up with some money in the near future, but could you help me? Now? Maybe with the first and second installments? I'll repay you. I promise."

Realizing his situation was not good, the following day she withdrew all the cash from her bank account, money she'd saved from various babysitting jobs. But it contained only a bit less than the first month's payment. Erik put up the rest. At least now he had some breathing room.

Christina approached Erik in the noisy, purely functional operations office and whispered, "I want to fill you in on the rest of the details. Let's chat in the cockpit again tonight. We'll manufacture some excuse for Woody."

After the second landing in Boston, Woody asked if Erik and Christina would be grabbing a bite.

"I have to stop in the ladies' room," Christina replied.

"And I have to call my girlfriend," Erik lied.

"Don't you folks like me anymore?"

"Not like you?" Christina smiled and added with a wink, "I'll be there shortly."

While walking across the ramp, Woody eyed Christina and Erik still in the cockpit, apparently immersed in conversation.

Erik inquired, "What've you cooked up?"

"I can't tell you if—"

"I'm in. It's final."

"A while back I discovered that we transport cash in our cargo compartment on the nine o'clock LaGuardia flight."

A nervous Erik began drumming his leg with his fingers like a tap dancer, now having an idea of where this conversation might be headed. "How did you find out? Whose money is it?" he interrupted, recalling his mother's favorite saying when it came to money. "The richest person isn't the one with the most, but one who needs the least."

"Ever wonder why we're always delayed on the final LaGuardia leg?"

"We're waiting for connecting pass—"

"That's just the standard bullshit. I thought it odd this happened every night, especially since I noticed the same guy boarding each time."

"The same person?"

"Not only that. He takes the identical seat, 3-D. I also receive official notification a sky marshal is on board."

"A sky marshal? That makes no…"

"The guy also wore a United States Treasury Department badge when I saw him on the ramp. But there was no sign of the badge when he boarded. To confuse things even more, according to the rules, a sky marshal isn't supposed to delay the flight or take the same seat every time. I was baffled. Everyone I asked claimed ignorance. One night, a bit past nine an unmarked van pulled up alongside and this guy hops out. After supervising the unloading of some heavy-looking satchels into our forward cargo bin he sprinted up the jetway again and took the same seat. As soon as he was onboard, the agent announced we were ready. This is the same scenario every night."

"How do you know we're carrying money?"

"Since I'm the captain, I wanted to know what the hell was

going on. So one time I went onto the ramp to find out. As I walked around the nose of the plane, the guards pulled guns on me."

"Guns? I thought you said no violence?"

"There won't be. I surprised them," an exasperated Christina said. "May I pulleeze finish? I rifled through the company's computer looking for the details and was able to dig them up. It's a highly classified Treasury Department operation." Christina hesitated and leaning closer to Erik and with her sweet breath on his face, whispered, "The guy has a dual role, working as a sky marshal and also guarding the sacks, which are full of old, worn-out paper currency—.

"So close, yet so far," Erik again interrupted.

"Near enough. After they're unloaded, the old bills are probably taken somewhere in New York City where the money goes through a shredder. I've seen pillows with cut-up bills stuffed inside. But catch this. The amounts listed on our flights were in excess of four million and these large shipments are what cause our delays."

A grimacing Erik felt as though his stomach was being run through a shredder knowing the feds were involved, meaning the FBI. "This happens every night?"

"I'm not certain about Friday, but the money's on board Monday through Thursday. From what I witnessed the ground portion is overseen by a number of people, but once it's aboard this guy assumes sole responsibility. And we have a unique opportunity before departing on 22 Right."

"How so?"

For about fifteen minutes, Christina outlined her step-by-step plan and when finished, Erik just whistled. "It *sounds* crazy, but just might work. Hell, if they're going to destroy it anyway, it's almost like we're not *really* stealing. But have you figured out every detail, because I'm wondering if there's anything you *don't* know about this or might have overlooked? And what about Woody?"

"I *think* I've got every base covered. But Woody remains a big question." Quickly glancing at her wristwatch, Christina saw only thirty minutes remained before departure. "We need to decide, but I'm against bringing Woody in. The forward cargo compartment is directly below and aft of his seat, so he can't see it. Plus if we include him it's less for us."

"I'm not sure we can trust him," Erik added.

"Me neither. But look, we certainly don't want him suspicious, so let's join him, now. I also want you to think matters through, because I still need a bit more time. I have someone lined up for our third person, but haven't spoken to him yet. I know your first payment is due in a couple of days, and..."

"I paid that."

"How?"

"I approached my girlfriend, Carol." Erik watched to see if there was any reaction from Christina after he mentioned her. There wasn't. "After I told her what was at stake, she cleaned out her bank account. All she had was enough for the first month's payment, but at least now I'm covered 'til August."

Christina frowned. "You *cannot* tell her—anyone—what we're up to."

"Don't worry. I won't," an annoyed Erik responded with a grimace.

While walking to grab two takeout burgers, a solemn Christina informed him, "After the job we'll be prime suspects. This means no calling each other from home or cell phones. And definitely no emails. This new world we live in is in reality a giant listening device for faceless bureaucrats. Maybe I'm only a gene away from the crackling winds of paranoia, but there aren't many secrets anymore. So let's touch base only in person or via a pay phone so there won't be any records. And keep the calls to vital ones."

"You're paranoid all right," Erik replied, feeling a bit that way himself, "if paranoia is defined as acute awareness."

They entered the eatery as Montgomery was putting his tray on the noisy conveyor belt. "Hey, where were you?" he innocently asked.

Christina immediately responded, "Erik was on the phone with his girlfriend. I made the mistake of standing close and all I could hear was yes dear, no dear. He's henpecked and not even married." Pointing to Woody's tray, she told him, "Glad you didn't wait for us. We'll grab a quick takeout."

"Fine. I'll return and get the clearance." Turning to Erik, he offered, "And I'll do your pre-flight inspection, again."

"Thanks." As Woody hurried back to the plane, Christina watched him, thinking they definitely did not want to use him.

Per what had become the norm, there was a delay waiting for connecting passengers. But this time Erik peered through the small peephole in the fortified cockpit door, taking note of the tall, dark-haired male passenger Christina had described taking seat 3-D. Outside, the moonlit, low wispy clouds with dim stars barely visible behind them were quickly replaced with fog and a ghostlike curtain dropped over the entire airport as they taxied for take-off on runway 22 Right. Erik found himself wishing the entire thing was over.

While taxiing Christina's mind was busy. What was the best method to rendezvous with Juni? After his grandmother's birthday party, David had mentioned something about a family picnic. This might provide the opportunity?

CHAPTER TWENTY-FOUR

When Christina arrived home David was in the process of wiring something.

"What's this?"

"The new Bose surround sound stereo that I picked up today. It can be used for music or the TV."

"Let me guess, you put it on my credit card?"

"Yes. You didn't say—"

"While I'm thinking of it," she interrupted with a more important item on her mind and a feigned smile on her face. "I've been meaning to tell you how much I enjoyed your grandmother's birthday party."

"From the feedback, everyone liked you too."

"Didn't you mention there was going to be another get-together soon, a picnic or something?"

"It's this Saturday at my Uncle Danny's beach house."

"That sounds like fun and I'm off. Wanna go?"

"Sure."

On Saturday they drove to the gathering held at a modest three-room bungalow located just a few short blocks from the

Atlantic Ocean on Rockaway Beach. It was a warm, bright day and Christina purposely wore a pair of cut-off, tight-fitting shorts. David told her, "Wow! Every member of my family is going to notice you."

"Hey, we *are* going to the beach." Christina was interested in getting only one person's attention. Forty-five minutes later they pulled up in front of the cottage in one of Long Island's few remaining Italian and Jewish ethnic seaside bastions. These two diverse, yet in many ways similar cultures had coexisted peacefully for years. Christina wondered if like the rest of American society, Rockaway would shed its colorful past. Aside from the hi-rise apartments built along the beach, the community consisted of old wooden row houses constructed in the 1930's or 40's. It appeared as though about half had been either meticulously maintained in their original condition or torn down and replaced by gaudy new millennium McMansions. David's uncle's place fit the former description. They went around the back of the small home where there was a tiny concrete yard and the only hint of soil was a small tomato garden in a sunny corner. The person she wanted to see, Juni Rosario gave her a peck on the cheek and asked, "How you been?"

"Good." David wasn't close by, so she whispered, "I'd like to speak with you, privately."

"OK...but let's wait a bit," Juni stammered, while eyeballing her skimpy outfit. "There would be lots of explaining if we just up and left. I'll signal you and then meet me on the boardwalk where it's crowded."

A smiling Christina nodded her head.

It was a perfect day for a beach outing, one of those comfortable yet warm New York summer days, with the moist and lazy sea breeze just strong enough to move the dry summer landside heat aside, eliciting mere whispers as the cooler air softly flowed through the entire area. The sky was clear and the air smelled sweet, like the water. It would only be a short time until the insufferable New York heat and humidity settled in for its annual stay, grasp the land by the throat and squeeze it until days like this would become a memory.

The luncheon menu consisted of tasty homemade Italian meatballs with fried eggplant. After that Christina shed the shorts revealing a skimpy bikini. As if to compete, David slipped into his Speedo, which didn't leave much to the imagination. They swam in water that felt like a cool blast of icy air wherever it touched the skin, helping to rejuvenate bodies that had grown lethargic from rich food. Next, a softball game was organized with another beach group. Since she wasn't interested, Christina put on her tank top and headed for the house, leaving David to flex his muscles and play ball. About halfway back she saw Juni walking in her direction. He almost imperceptibly nodded his head while passing. Christina casually changed course and once on the boardwalk looked, but didn't spot him. Had she misread the cue? An instant later the short man, wearing sunglasses so dark his eyes resembled two black holes, was standing right beside her.

"Where'd you come from?"

"Whaddaya mean?"

"Never mind."

Christina thought of how much their outfits clashed. Her chartreuse-colored bikini bottom and tank top might garner attention, but Juni's black pants and stark white shirt, his way of remaining unobtrusive, made him even more conspicuous. He would be more in place walking the streets in New York's Little Italy in February.

"Let's stroll a bit," he suggested. They walked on the

boardwalk beachside from the apartments that effectively walled off the beach. Young teenaged boys, rolling through summer on their bikes continually passed them. Others lounged on the benches looking at unconcealed female legs, low-cut tops and short-shorts that might afford a quick peek. At first she and Juni simply took in the sights: the people and fast-food eateries. Neither uttered a word and their visual spectacle was completed by the summertime mélange of cotton candy and popcorn intermingling with the ocean scent and uncollected trash.

Juni finally spoke. "What's so important we have to meet this way?" wondering what Christina's reply might be.

From the little David had told her she thought it would be best to act businesslike, get right to the point. She looked him in the eye and spoke directly. "Even though you and I have only met once before, on the drive home the night after your mother's party David told me you once worked for a bank and you either quit or were forced out over some missing money..."

Juni removed his sunglasses and looked deeply into Christina's blue eyes. His were so angry that she felt as though they might singe her hair. "He oughta know better."

"I normally wouldn't give it a second thought, until recently. I'm only interested in the future, *our* future, yours and mine. I need you for a deal where we stand to make a lot."

"Define a lot."

"For now, let's figure approximately three quarters of a million each."

"I'm all ears."

They immediately resumed walking, but much slower.

"You gotta promise that whatever I tell you stays between us."

"That goes without saying."

Christina spoke as they ambled, relating details from her divorces and alimony payments, to Erik's bank payments, to the perceived threats to Shuttle Air's future. She purposely omitted her epilepsy or Laurel. He concurred with her concerns about Shuttle Air. She provided a seemingly rapt Juni with the particulars, including the fact that the Boston supervisor who entered the delay code had also recommended the airline not renew the contract with the government after it expired in September. "This means we have to move quickly."

Juni asked, "At this point is anyone else other than you and this second officer involved?"

"No."

"Under no circumstances are you to tell David anything. If he happened to notice us speaking or says anything, threaten to cut him off."

"Don't worry. I'll handle him." She waited a moment. "Does that mean you're in?"

"Not yet," came the abrupt reply, "although I must admit what you outlined intrigues me. But, I can't commit now."

"Why not?"

"What kind of person you think I am? I run a legitimate business and have a wife and two kids to support."

"But I thought..."

"You thought what? That crap David told you about? You don't even know if this will work."

"It'll work; with or without you," she replied, now walking behind him.

After a few moments of awkward silence a frowning Juni spun around stopped, and allowed some humanity to show through. "The possibilities are enticing and I can use the dough..."

"It's the perfect crime," an uplifted Christina interjected.

"Perfect crime. Perfect marriage. No such things. When it comes to crimes there are only good ones, well planned out ahead of time so chances of getting caught are minimal. Arrogance only leads to mistakes. With today's technologies even clever isn't good enough 'cause there's always one small chance somethin' will be overlooked, no matter how trivial it *might* seem. I *may* become involved, but first have to fly to Boston and scope out the area. Gimme your phone number and if everything works out I'll get back with you to set up a meeting."

Christina provided her home and cell numbers and then removed two maps from her beach bag. "I brought these Boston airport charts in case you were interested."

Juni seemed to relax, just a bit and put an arm around her delicate shoulders. He laid the maps on the boardwalk railing and looked at them. "You know you'll be prime suspects?"

"If we play our cards right that's all we'll be, suspects."

He liked this woman for more than the obvious reasons. She didn't seem to have her nose in the air and her feet were firmly planted on the ground. "Sure you ain't Italian?"

Christina laughed. "I'm more akin to D.B. Cooper, that guy who hijacked a Northwest 727 back in '71, got two-hundred grand in ransom and parachuted out over the state of Washington, never to be seen or heard from. The cops never discovered his identity. There was lots of speculation, but they had nothing. In this case there should be lots of suspects *if* we play our cards right."

"Cooper was a solo operation. But remember, in this case if the cops really suspect your involvement they'll try everything, including playing you off against each other."

"What do you mean?"

"They'll tell you shit like the other pilot confessed. Or tell you he cut a deal and fed you to them. Maybe, the other way around? They can and will lie to you. Tricks are a part of the cops' and FBI's game, so don't fall for their ploys, no matter what they say. The government is allowed to bend all the rules. Consider *anything* they say to be a lie, 'cause if they do something like that it will only be a gimmick. Be certain you relay this to the second officer."

"That's pretty scary. But we will need a credible way to account for the money."

"Don't get too far ahead of yourself." After a moment Juni added, "Remember, you can't go throwing money around because unlike Cooper you'll get nailed. And if you get caught the chances are good I will—*if* I'm involved." A fierce darkness came into his eyes again. "You have to launder your shares correctly. I might be able to help 'cause I still have some contacts in the banking business. I'll get back to you on that one."

She handed him a small piece of paper with some telephone numbers.

"What's this?"

"The second officer, Erik Preis' home and cell phone numbers. He only recently hired on. I also included our work numbers, the operations offices at both LaGuardia and Boston. If you phone either of us use a pay phone."

"I make most of my calls that way. Since you brought it up, never call the cells." He crossed off the cell numbers. They are easy to trace. The cops will probably wire your home phones. They'll get a court order, go back months and check all your calls. Also, absolutely no emails, because those are the easiest to trace. You'll be my primary contact. What's the best time to reach you at work? That would probably be the best place to contact you."

"We fly the afternoon and evening Shuttles and the first departs at three. We check in at two, so call between two and two-thirty." She rattled off the operations number and he jotted it down. "If you reach me on the job, tell whoever answers that you're the flight dispatcher and want to speak with Captain Shepard. Dispatchers are FAA-licensed and do the flight planning. They frequently call so no one will be the wiser. In an emergency you can normally reach me at home either before eleven in the morning or after eleven at night."

"I'd rather not do that. Not only because of the cops, but David."

She nodded her head in agreement. "Another important thing we haven't decided is whether or not to bring in the copilot. Mull that over."

"What's this guy like? Is he smart or the type who thinks he has to study for a urine test? Do we need him? Can we trust 'em?"

"I don't trust him one bit," she said, while handing him a small spiral pad.

"What's this?"

"I jotted down my ideas in it. When you're done, destroy it. I feel uncomfortable having it around David."

"No problem," Juni said, placing the small pad in his trouser pocket. "I'll get back to you as quickly as possible."

"When?"

"It won't be long."

They shook hands and Christina immediately returned to the house, while Juni lingered so they wouldn't show up together. Leaning against the wooden boardwalk railing he fired up another Marlboro while staring out at the cobalt expanse of water that looked like an unfurled tapestry. Juni was uncertain of his involvement with this attractive lady as her waspy appearance rekindled old memories of his fellow students during his college days. A number had initially sought him out, fascinated with his

chipping in."

David looked into Christina's eyes and she stared back with an intensity that felt like it went clear through him. Nothing more was said. Maybe she was tiring of him or had found someone else?

Christina and Erik flew together after the picnic, but she said nothing until the seven o'clock shuttle was at the gate. Woody left and Christina told him to lock the door. "I discussed the plan with the guy I want to bring in. He's originally from Brooklyn, now living in Jersey. His name is Juni Rosario and I believe he's got the needed savvy you and me lack. He's gonna scout the area and then we'll get together to finalize everything. He wouldn't give me a specific timeframe but knows this is time sensitive. He asked questions, one of which was whether to include Woody. We'll discuss that when we get together."

"Did he commit?"

"No. But I got the impression he would."

Glancing at his watch, Erik added, "If our decision is not to include Woody, I don't want him recalling anything out of the ordinary. It's best not to have any more cockpit discussions. If we need to speak let's do it in another out of the way place either before or after work.

"Agreed."

When they arrived a smiling Woody was preparing to leave. "I didn't know how long you'd be so I went ahead and ate. You have plenty of time, 'cause I'll do the pre-flight inspection. But I'll send Erik a bill at the end of the month."

After he left Erik said, "You might think Woody's an asshole, but he's OK in my book."

"That's 'cause he's doin' your work."

Just before departure time, Christina was again handed a

sealed envelope and informed they would be delayed for connecting passengers. Barely noticeable smiles crossed Erik's and Christina's faces.

CHAPTER TWENTY-FIVE

When Christina was called to the phone in flight ops a couple of days later, she was pleasantly surprised to hear Juni's voice. "I'm at Newark airport. I just returned from Boston where I surveyed the area. Let's meet Friday night at an Italian eatery I know. It's called Pepi's located on Sixty-eighth Street and Fourteenth Avenue in Brooklyn. Can you both be there between nine-thirty and ten to do some brainstorming?"

"The time's good, but is the place secure?"

"I'm goin' there tomorrow night to make certain. If not, we'll switch locations. If you don't hear from me the meeting's on for Friday night." He provided directions.

"This mean you're in?" an anxious Christina asked, but the line went dead.

Pulling into the driveway at home Juni's old Chevy practically disappeared into a huge pothole. *When did that happen? I gotta fix that along with painting the entire house.* His wife Angela was sitting in the kitchen and he gently kissed her. As he removed a piece of bakery cheesecake from the refrigerator and prepared a cup of coffee, she told him, "The washing machine broke today, so I used the public laundry."

"I'll try to get my hands on a new one." He was sorry for her and felt like he was caught in a washing machine tumbler. Glancing around, he brooded over how a Princeton graduate, instead of making a good living was running a bakery on a shoestring, all because of a crime he was falsely accused of. He threw the cheesecake into the garbage and went to his wife. "I'm sorry about all this," waving his hand at the house. "You're entitled to better."

She tenderly took his face between her hands and looked knowingly into his dark eyes. "Maybe someday you'll catch that break? You can't help the hand you were dealt."

"I love you."

"I love you too."

CHAPTER TWENTY-SIX

The grimy Chevy ground to a halt in the parking lot of Pepi's. The worn-out springs groaned and the engine ticked and pinged, ridding itself of heat created by the hour-long drive. Juni dragged himself from the air conditioned-by-nature interior that reeked of stale smoke. After mopping his face with a handkerchief, as the summer heat continued its late day assault he straightened his striped silver and black tie and grudgingly donned his jacket, knowing that appearances were important in Brooklyn.

Entering the eatery was like unlocking a portal back in time. No trendy pâté and brie, henpecked men pushing kids in strollers with overbearing wives staring over their shoulders or other such crap. Unlike other cities like L.A. where everyone was from somewhere else, no doubt these people all either resided or grew up in Brooklyn. The front doorway still led directly into the dimly lit bar, with an equally shadowy, spotless dining room off to the right. Each wooden table was covered with the same red and white checkered cloth tablecloth under a single white chrysanthemum floating in a water-filled fine Lenox vase. Neatly arranged gold-framed vistas of Italy adorned the dark red velvet-papered walls, while the spicy fragrances of northern Italian cooking hung heavy in the air and made his mouth water even though he had already eaten. Juni stepped into the bar that smelled of nicotine and hard work, the conditioned air a welcomed relief. Frank Sinatra's *Summer Wind* began playing as he hovered in the shadows with his cigarette, ignoring the black and formerly white but now yellowed official New York City sign that boldly stated, **Smoking Prohibited**. His exhaled smoke added to the thick man-made haze layer hanging like a ghost under each tiny bar lamp.

"The summer wind comes blowin' in from across the sea," the mellow tune began. *"It lingers there, to touch your hair, and walk with me..."* As the muted trumpets kicked in Juni instinctively began swaying ever so slightly, as memories flooded back. He took another long drag, but shook his head. He hadn't come here to listen to Old Blue Eyes. Not spotting the person he was seeking Juni drifted into the softly lit dining room. Maybe the guy had sold the place? Juni's tailored suit and expensive leather shoes created an impressive persona. Only one person tracked his moves and when their eyes met the older guy, with bushy eyebrows that came together and a two-day blue-black and gray stubble on his face grinned, the smile emphasizing three missing teeth. Juni's was probably the only full set of ivories in the entire joint. Why did old-time Italians rarely have good teeth, taking better care of their cars than choppers? The owner, who might qualify as being athletic if barroom brawling could be passed off as a sport, was clad in the expected baggy pleated black trousers and a stark white, open collared shirt that exposed a large gold chain and cross hung around his neck, partially buried in a tangle of gray chest hairs. Was a nickel-plated pistol also hidden there? He appeared surprised and perhaps a bit tense at encountering this person from a bygone era. Curiosity apparently overcame anxiety as he slapped Juni on the shoulder with a smile. "Holy shit! Juni the Lid! What's happenin'? I

ain't seen ya in ages. Must be way more than a dozen years." Eyeing the charcoal-colored *Armani* suit, he raised one thick eyebrow, "But ya certainly look like you're doin' OK."

Feels like a thousand years, Juni thought as the two men hugged, an Italian custom he never understood. A smiling Juni stepped back, unbuttoned his jacket and scrutinized his host, "Carmine DiLiberto you old *sonamabitch*. It's at least that long and you and the place haven't changed. Damn, you look even younger. Hey, never mind me, how you been? Everything still good with you and Maria?"

"I've been married to the same broad for so long it's like I'm reading the married man's *Penthouse*; a couple of different stories but the same goddamned centerfold every month." Making the sign of the cross, DiLiberto continued, "The only words that'll be inscribed on my tombstone will be restaurant owner—forty fuckin' years." Cutting to the chase, he asked, "What brings ya back?"

After the expected glance over his shoulder, a solemn Juni whispered in a suddenly reacquired thick Brooklyn accent, "Ya got somewhere we can chat? Privately?"

"Sure. I still got my conference room over there." DiLiberto nodded in the direction of the tiny table he'd come from with two chairs off in a remote corner. Juni could still picture him discussing matters with the big boys at that table, with most probably dead by now. They sat down and Juni fired up another Marlboro as DiLiberto leaned over and asked, "Can I get ya a bite to *mangia*? Maybe a little macaroni or lasagna?"

"No, thanks. I ate at home earlier this evening with the wife and kids."

Shaking his head DiLiberto muttered, "Wife and kids? Where the hell *does* the time go?"

Time had flown since Juni gained respect from DiLiberto

and other lowlifes like him. Only Juni knew it was undeserved, because none knew the true circumstances surrounding the incident that took place during the '86 World Series. Never a great baseball player because of his build, like almost everyone else in the Big Apple Juni got caught up in the Mets run at their second World Series title against the Red Sox. So much so that he purchased a Mets hat that declared them the winners before the series ended and proudly wore it everywhere he went. In Little Italy one night an inebriated, connected thug named Antonio "Big Boy" Gallo came out of Mama Sorrento's restaurant, saw the hat and demanded Juni turn it over to him. But Juni ran away as quickly as possible, which wasn't very fast, around the corner and down a dead-end alleyway. To his chagrin Gallo pursued him. With nowhere to go, Juni meekly took off the hat and handed it to his pursuer who had actually drawn a gun. Gallo was so drunk that walking out of the alleyway with Juni's Mets hat in hand, he tripped over a garbage pail and the pistol discharged. The bullet went into his stomach and severed an artery, killing him. After retrieving his hat, Juni ran off. But Gallo's *goombahs* believed a struggle had ensued, with Juni disarming and shooting him. Perception became reality. Gary Carter might have been the most popular Met, but God was Juni's best fan that night because loads of unearned respect was piled on him. He immediately became known as Juni the Lid and adopted phony mannerisms to go along with his newfound status. No one but Juni and the cops knew the whole thing was a sham.

Juni returned to the present when DiLiberto snapped his fingers, commanding the heavyset waitress with the constant smile, "Maria, bring us a bottle of good wine, the '88 *Venizie Pinot Noir*." Turning to Juni he added, "Only the best for you." After the waitress poured the wine Juni grasped the small goblet in his thick mitt and both men raised their goblets, simultaneously reciting, "*saluti*."

DiLiberto looked directly into Juni's dark eyes and as a faint smile crossed his lips knowingly asked, "To what do I *really* owe the honor of your return?"

Another peek over his shoulder. "I need a spot for an important meeting with some, er, business associates," he whispered. "We gotta have good food *and* privacy, not worried about anybody listenin'," Juni added, "or even rememberin' we were here, if you know what I mean?"

Knowing exactly what he meant, DiLiberto replied, "You got nothin' to worry about 'cause if anyone like that hung out here, someone would burn my joint down."

Juni abruptly pushed his chair back from the table and stood, ready to depart Memory Lane.

"You'll be comin' in?"

"Yeah. Make a mental reservation at a secluded table for this Friday. There will be three of us for a late dinner between nine-thirty and ten-thirty. I'll let you know if anythin' changes."

"Consider it done." They again hugged and DiLiberto put his arm around him. "C'mon, have a bite. A small plate of pasta or some fried *calamari*?"

"No, thanks." Juni took a twenty from his wallet. "But give this to Maria. And put me down for one of your pasta plates on Friday."

"Your order is placed." A serious DiLiberto leaned over and whispered, "As far as anyone's concerned I never spoke with or even seen ya tonight. I'll instruct Maria on the same thing."

Juni smiled. Returning to his car the smile disappeared as he felt dejected for reverting to his previously self-despised creature. His internal civil war picked up where it left off years ago, black versus white; evil as opposed to good. But the conflict didn't last long, as a singular thought, do or die, overshadowed everything.

While driving to his Jersey home, a somber Juni pondered how fate or whatever else you might dub it, had taken three total strangers whose lives had collided a short time ago and dropped an opportunity in their laps, no doubt changing their destinies.

CHAPTER TWENTY-SEVEN

After concluding his Shuttle Air flights, Erik checked the pilots' computer and discovered another notice from O'Brien demanding to see him prior to his next trip. *What could he want this time?*

Erik showed up as ordered the following day and without so much as a handshake the large man ushered him into his office. A frowning O'Brien sat down with such a crash that it jostled his full mane of stark white hair. There was an open personnel file lying on the huge desk. O'Brien spoke while pointing to it. "During your first year management reviews your employment record at least twice. I've been going over yours and even though there's nothing negative, I remain concerned about your role in the Boston incident."

"Like I told you, it had nothing to do with me." Was O'Brien on a fishing expedition or had Woody or Christina said something?

Ignoring Erik's comment, a red-faced O'Brien continued. "In retrospect, do you want to fill me in on any other details?"

"There's nothing more to say," Erik replied with a shrug of his shoulders.

Erik could see the lines in his face and crow's feet around

O'Brien's eyes deepening. He asked Erik, "Are you're nervous with your job?"

"No. I'm very comfortable."

A stern-faced O'Brien began. "Captain Shepard wrote about..." but stopped. He quickly closed the folder and told him. "You can leave now."

While checking in for his flight Erik pondered what, if any connection there might be between Christina's plan and O'Brien's grilling? He would ask her when the opportunity arose.

Christina heard nothing further from Juni so after work that Friday she provided Erik with directions. He desperately wanted to get her take on O'Brien's most recent fishing expedition, but decided to see if she said anything first. Erik changed into jeans and tee shirt in his car, while Christina left her uniform blouse and slacks on, removing any items that could identify her. Christina pulled up next to his car, telling him. "Let's take two cars."

The dented Chevy the size of a cabin cruiser that seemed to instinctively dodge the Brooklyn potholes came to an abrupt halt in the parking lot and Juni exited. Running beefy hands over the suit lapels, he fired up a Marlboro. All the medical hoopla notwithstanding, he wouldn't quit smoking for fear of gaining more weight. He glanced into the outside rearview mirror and patted down his well-greased, gray/black hair combed in the pompadour style. A full head of hair was important to his image. Recalling the words of an old *paisan*, "For us *guineas*, when you get old, you lose hair where you want it and find it growing where you don't," he paid extra attention to a small thinning spot he'd noticed recently on the crown, making sure it was covered. Since it was unknown who might be watching, with the butt dangling from his lips he unbuttoned his jacket and paraded across the street in his best Brooklyn swagger, leather heels thundering on the concrete.

He entered the crowded restaurant and after a warm greeting the owner ushered him to an out of the way table. It was easy to pick out the few made men who had proven themselves in some manner and taken a solemn oath of allegiance to the Mafia organization, La Cosa Nostra that police insisted no longer existed, post-Giuliani. These well dressed and bejeweled guys were surrounded by their hangers-on. The remainder were mostly old-time Italians sporting five o'clock shadows; the hard-working guys, masons, carpenters and the like, marked by their permanently dirty fingernails. Most had emigrated from different sections of the old country, now fortunate to be able to afford to eat dinner out once or twice a month with the old lady. The latter usually the result of an arranged marriage and the immediate acquisition of a coveted green card. Their wives were mostly first-generation Brooklyn/Italian; short, pudgy, with fat thighs who stuffed three or four cream-filled cannolis into their mouth for dessert, but made certain to put Sweet and Low into their cappuccino. Juni recently heard rumors that the neighborhood was changing, with many Italians moving to the suburbs, replaced by first-generation Asians and newly-arrived Russian/Jewish immigrants. But obvious from the numbers, the *paisans* that might no longer live here still drove to get the food.

Erik parked behind Christina and entering together, many patrons gave them the once-over. Pepi's was roughly thirty miles and a universe away from Farmingdale. Would someone be needed to do cultural interpretations? Between the barroom jukebox and loud conversations, there was a constant buzz. Was this done purposely to make electronic eavesdropping impossible? Christina mentioned Juni's name to a grungy-looking maître d' with thick eyebrows and some missing teeth and was ushered to an isolated table where a short, more horizontal than vertical forty-something guy with black hair fading to gray, looking worn down by hardship, work or both, sat. Maybe a bit Neanderthal? Although his body exuded an undefined intensity, he resembled any other Italian guy. Pointing to Erik Juni asked, "Who's the kid? I thought you were bringing another pilot with you?"

"He's the one." Christina introduced them.

They shook hands and Juni said, "Jesus Christ, you still in high school?" as he blew pungent smoke into Erik's face.

Erik glared back and Juni immediately apologized. "Hey, I'm sorry. That was out of line. But I thought airline pilots were, well, older."

"You have to start sometime."

"Why do you want to get involved in this shit when you still have your entire life in front of you?"

Erik relaxed and opened up, which he inexplicably found easy to do, quickly synopsizing the story about his loan that Christina had only partially related. Juni muttered while shaking his head, "A woman captain and a kid pilot? I guess times have changed."

"It's a new world out there," Christina added.

"Forgive me. Right now I feel like an asshole in a room full of proctologists. I'm not certain I like this new world a hell of a lot."

"It's no Dick and Jane fairyland any more, but there's nothing we can do about it." To lighten things up Christina added with a wide grin, "The next thing we'll work on in this new world is changing the name of the COCKpit." They all laughed.

The toothless guy came and took drink orders. Juni requested a bottle of white wine and recommended the *fruitti di mare* seafood pasta, which sounded good to all of them. Erik asked, "Will anyone recall seeing us? Lots of people stared when we entered."

Juni scratched the scalp under what looked like greasy hair, while shaking his head. "Memories are good here, but also short. Let's get to why we're here. I flew to Boston and spent a few hours reconnoitering the airfield and the town you described across the bay from Logan. It's called East Boston, a rundown New England burg seemingly straight out of a time warp that unlike me wasn't able to adjust to this changing world." Small smile. "A bunch of Hispanics live there, but also still quite a few *paisans*. I pretended to be just another *guinea*—and only I can use that term here, like a black person using the n-word in Harlem—thinking of moving there. If I were, I would be welcomed with open arms. Here's a tide chart I picked up at a local tackle store." Juni placed it on the table. The chart disappeared and the conversation changed to food when the smiling waitress brought plates overflowing with delicious linguini loaded with clams, mussels, calamari and pieces of tender sea bass, all covered with a delicate *livornese* sauce. Once she left Juni stated he felt that barring a merger with a larger airline Shuttle Air's long-term survival appeared uncertain. Both pilots simply looked at each other. "Let's get back to the job at hand. What do the money sacks and locks look like?"

"They're large dark green satchels with padlocks on top," Christina replied, "like the duffel bags I've seen in Army/Navy stores."

"Meaning I can get identical fakes?"

"Probably."

"That's important, 'cause if the bags aren't the same, they'll immediately know something's wrong when the cargo hold is opened. Replacing them with look-alikes will increase the odds in our favor. If they're transported before anyone knows somethin's up it will give us more time and the suspect list will be longer. We have to think like the cops and try to stay one step ahead."

Cops? Robbery? All Erik wanted was to be an airline pilot. Juni's voice jolted him back to the present.

"What about the locks?" he asked, while jotting things on a napkin.

"They looked like every day brass locks to me."

"Long or short? Key or combination?"

"The short ones. And I didn't see any numbers."

"I'll buy four. I might even have two key locks at home from college, so old that chances are they're untraceable."

The waitress again interrupted, this time bringing three cappuccinos courtesy of the house. After thanking her Juni asked, "What else?"

"What about transportation?" Christina said. "How are you getting to Boston?" adding with a toothy smile, "and how will you bring *our* money back?"

"My wife's Buick. I had it tuned up and the oil changed. I'll get my hands on some Massachusetts plates." Juni continued as they sipped their cappuccino. "The East Boston Holiday Inn is where I'll stay under an assumed name. Here's the number," he said, handing Erik and Christina tiny slips of torn paper with the telephone number in pencil. "Once we're done, get rid of those. Once I get fake ID, I'll let you know the name I'm using. My story will be the same. I'm checking out the area in anticipation of moving there. Any questions?"

Christina said, "I guess you're in?"

"You guessed right."

After a sigh of relief Christina took some pages copied from her 727 flight manual from her handbag that described the forward cargo compartment door and its operation. She handed them to Juni, pointing out one unique feature: because the aircraft was pressurized, to prevent it from blowing off, the counterbalanced, smooth ball-bearing-hinged door opened inward. "Don't make any noise 'cause the guard is seated directly above it," she cautioned him.

"That might present a problem. I'll probably have to slam it closed."

"You won't. Just twist the handle. They keep it well lubed."

Erik said in half-jest, "Maybe you can leave Sunday and we can be done with this by Monday?"

Juni held up his hand like a stop sign. "Sunday? Monday? I doubt it. I can't rush 'cause I gotta be thinking four or five steps ahead. Plus, more groundwork is needed. I gotta get materials, drive to Boston and find out where the cops are stationed, if they patrol and how busy the marina is after dark. That'll take time. I *might* be able to accomplish everything in a few days, but don't count on it 'cause if I make a mistake it's not like erasing chalk off a blackboard."

Christina changed the subject to something nagging at her like an overwrought spouse. "What about Woody? Do we bring him in?" Turning to Juni, she added, "He's the copilot."

"Woody! Is this guy named after a dick?"

Christina giggled. "I wondered about that too. But he said it was from getting hit on the head a lot."

"What are *your* thoughts?" a suddenly serious Juni said.

"After speaking with him and mulling it over, I believe we'd be better off without him. I can keep his attention diverted by telling him to handle the radio or something similar."

"Will he do as he's told?"

"Definitely" she said, looking at Erik. Christina sipped her cappuccino and nodding toward Erik, added, "After our engine problem I'm certain he'll go out of his way to please."

"You sure?" Juni asked.

"Yeah. We had an engine quit working a while back and Woody didn't do shit when we needed him. And I don't trust him. There's something else that I can't put my finger on. Call it woman's intuition or whatever. I did some subtle probing at dinner one night and didn't like his answers. Hell, he might even go to the cops to endear himself with management and we'd have no way of knowing. Plus, including him means less for us."

"I agree," Juni added, gently slapping his palm on the tablecloth. "Is it unanimous, Erik? Just the three of us?"

Erik concurred.

As he was finishing his cappuccino Juni asked, "What other info you got on this sky marshal? I think the jets the rag heads crashed into the World Trade Center came out of Boston and I don't wanna get shot."

"They did. But the sky marshal part mainly concerns anything inside the plane. It'll be dark and he won't be able to see or hear anything outside, provided you don't screw up." She hesitated. "Remember, we can't wait too long to act. Like I said, this contract won't be renewed in September. I also heard the Feds might attempt to fence in all the areas of large airports that are bordered by water. I sure wouldn't want to see you having to climb over barbed wire—"

"I heard that too," a somber Erik interrupted.

"I agree that we have to move as quickly as possible. But that raises another concern. Are there motion sensors around the airport border?"

"Why, I, I don't know," Christina stammered, "but I have noticed small, evenly spaced poles along the perimeter that *might* be sensors."

"If they are, those could be our undoing. Is there any way to find out without tipping our hand?"

"I don't think so."

"I need to know before I go traipsing around."

Christina said, "If I ask that question it'll just arouse more suspicion later. Why would I be asking?" She hesitated. "I pride myself on logic, so let's take the worst possible scenario by assuming there are sensors." Juni and Erik listened attentively. Looking directly at Juni she said, "You'll be operating when the weather is so poor that no one can see you. When the weather's good and the devices are triggered, the controllers would probably first try to locate the cause by peering through binoculars or a telescope from the tower. It stands to reason that only if they couldn't tell what set them off would they send out a vehicle to investigate. Odds are high that a seagull set it off. But, when the visibility is so lousy that nothing can be seen, I'd be willing to bet they're deactivated 'cause it would be senseless to send a car as the driver wouldn't be able to see anything either. They'd also have to stop or delay every jet from taxiing and taking off while the car was out there for fear a jet might run into it, or vice versa. The airlines would never stand for monumental delays caused by someone chasing invisible gremlins."

A thoughtful Juni lit another butt. Erik believed more smoke came out of this guy's mouth than his old man's diesel Mercedes.

Christina insisted, "It *must* be FAA policy to disable them when the visibility drops below a certain value. I've flown in and out of Boston a lot in bad weather and never experienced a delay like that."

But Juni remained concerned. "Suppose what you've said is wrong and when I come ashore the cops arrest me?"

"Believe me, I know that *won't* happen."

"All right," he finally sighed, waving his hand in the air. "I'm willing to roll the dice."

"Look," Christina added, "I also want the odds in our favor as much as possible, but do *not* see a problem."

Juni continued. "Another thing. Suppose the satchels have tracing devices, like a GPS attached? They'll know exactly where and when they're removed."

"They can't."

"Why not?"

"It would interfere with the plane's navigation system."

"You sure?"

"Positive. Another non-issue."

They continued discussing a few more unresolved details until they were satisfied. At that point Juni added, "Do not mention anything to another soul. All calls to each other are to be made from a pay phone and only if absolutely necessary. No cell calls or email messages. Shortly after I get the money, I'll give your homes one ring. This will be followed by another single ring twenty seconds later. Do *not* pick up the phone. After that, nothing unless there's a dire emergency 'cause at some point the cops will tap your phones. And remember, you can't throw money around or we'll get nailed. It has to be laundered overseas because the bills' serial numbers must be recorded, somewhere, sometime. I'm not certain where and when, but if there was a data entry made before we get them and a large chunk is spent at once, it'll be easy to track. The laundering must be done in a former Iron Curtain or Far Eastern country. Once the money goes into an overseas institution it will be impossible to track because it will be handled by lots of people before working its way back into the States. I'm familiar with how to handle this. It will cost a small percentage of the take and is somewhat complicated, but is money well spent. I'll provide the details when I'm back. You guys will still have to sit on your shares and can't go tossing it around 'cause the cops will have you under a microscope for a long time."

"We keep it in our mattress like Italians?" Christina asked.

"Whaddaya think? Italians are the only ones? You don't have to go *quite* that far, but you can't spend it immediately. In the modern world this storm will blow itself out because any crime, irrespective of its size is followed by another even larger. I still know a few people in the investment banking business that can bury it for you for a few years while it earns interest. For now let's just concentrate on getting it."

Erik said, "What about paying off my loan?"

"That'll be easier because the amount is relatively small. I'll immediately provide you with a certified check from a former business associate to reimburse the bank. My contact is willing to acknowledge through certain channels he loaned you the money irrespective of your crummy credit rating, at a rate bordering on usury. Christina mentioned repayment wouldn't be a problem for you next year. Is that right?"

"Yeah. I get off probation and—"

"He's agreed to wait until then for you to start repaying a bit at a time. When questioned, all of your answers will have sound explanations. Of course you have to hand over three thousand in extra interest. That OK?"

"Fine."

Juni paid the bill and on the way out put an arm around both pilots. Turning to Christina he said, "There was something I liked about you beyond the obvious the first time we met. Remember, after the job you and I can't be seen together. One of us will have to make some excuse why we can't come to family gatherings whenever the other is present."

"That won't be a problem." Christina assured him. *David would be out of her life once this was a done deal.* Juni shook hands and to Erik it was as though he'd stuck his hand into a warm loaf of Italian bread.

Outside, Erik and Christina discussed some work items while Juni was lost in thoughts of yesteryear. While silently surveying the familiar surroundings, memories of a younger world and simpler times painted a smile on his face. It was a period before progress and savagery grew at the same rate, when nothing changed, year after year. He could still smell the bouquet of fragrances caused by the newly bloomed lilacs mingling with the Italian cooking scents oozing from the row houses; hear the muffled sounds of people speaking in cramped, hot rooms with open windows and no air conditioners; see the backyard clotheslines; all mementos of a poorer, yet more carefree era. Ah, Brooklyn. A place where life was still tough and even talking was a hassle due to the incessant traffic and jangling horns. Where exhaust fumes coat the air. A further stroll down memory lane was unavoidable because big events had occurred within walking distance of this very spot. It was right up the street, in the schoolyard of Public School 132 on a warm summer evening like this where he'd first proven his manhood, gone all the way with a young dark-haired beauty named Nancy Colucci. He was fifteen and she a mere fourteen years old. An era when the sex was safe, but the streets could be dangerous. Worried that he'd gotten her pregnant after that embarrassingly brief encounter, when it turned out he hadn't his Catholic upbringing mandated confession. The following Saturday, fearful of recognition he'd nervously sought Almighty forgiveness by declaring his carnal sin in a disguised voice to Father Anthony Monasco, or Padre Tony as he was known to the young parishioners at St. Theresa's. The priest asked intimate and probing questions, "What did it feel like?" and "How long did it last?" Only years later did Juni realize that the Padre was probably getting his jollies over every sordid detail. Four long city blocks away was Alley Park, where he got drunk for the first time with his best buddy, Billy Peluso. After throwing down a pint of cheap Italian Swiss Colony Muscatel both teenagers laughed so hard at absolutely nothing that they tumbled to the ground, hysterical. No matter how hard they tried, the next day neither could recall what was so funny. It wasn't funny ten years later, when Billy was gunned down. His murder remained unsolved, an open case. When translated from Brooklynese this meant he had crossed some powerful individuals and paid the ultimate price. The floodgates opened and more memories poured forth, recalling standing on the top stoop of these same homes, watching brown water cascade down the street after a sudden summer thunderstorm. This brought on thoughts of pastimes like stoopball and stickball, which made him long to return. But he forced himself to stop. Like Billy, the fucking past was dead. All Juni was concerned about now was the future, his and his family's.

Erik and Christina were still speaking when Juni returned to the present, gave her a peck on the cheek and again shook Erik's hand. Cranking up his car for the hour-long drive home, the Chevy with more rust than metal wouldn't start on the first two attempts. He whacked the cracked, dried-out dashboard, but didn't get angry. *With this deal, I'll be drivin' a brand-new Caddy.*

As he drove off Christina asked, "What do you think of him?"

"I guess we're fortunate to have him." The truth be known, Erik was close to not wanting anything more to do with this harebrained scheme. But those words just wouldn't cross his lips. "Right now *you're* the captain in command of my future," was all he could manage.

Standing there, the lights from the passing cars cast an

attractive sheen over Erik, highlighting his European features, clear complexion and bright eyes imbued with the deep green hue of shallow Caribbean water. To Christina he was always attractive, but tonight, even more so, due to the silky cloak of the warm summer night air. But recalling what happened last time made her cast these thoughts aside.

As if reading her mind, Erik spoke. "After our pictures were in the newspapers, my girlfriend wondered if there was anything between us."

"I already have a boyfriend."

"I didn't know."

"No one at the airline does. But now you do. His name is David Bennedeto, a Shuttle Air baggage slammer and studying at NYU. That's how I met Juni. He's his uncle. But if you should ever meet or speak with David, don't mention his uncle's name."

"You and David living together?"

"Yeah. But also keep this tidbit to yourself. I don't want anyone at work to know. I learned a long time ago not to advertise my private life and recommend the same to you. Most pilots are like washwomen because flying is mostly tedium and *everything* gets discussed."

"Will you be all right driving home alone?" he asked, intentionally changing the subject.

"Perhaps you could follow me. It is late and I've heard that some sections of Brooklyn aren't the safest."

Approximately thirty-five minutes later they pulled to a halt in front of her place and she walked over to Erik's window.

"Thanks. I appreciate it."

Erik summoned the courage to get out and stammered, "I'll walk you to the door."

"Only as far as the front door." She unlocked the double

security locks and stepped inside the darkened house while Erik waited on the stoop. She went to the bedroom and stuck her head inside. Returning, she said, "Everything's fine."

Erik stepped inside without an invite, but she immediately grabbed his arm, which felt much thinner than David's and quickly led him outside. "Thanks. I'll see you at work." She sarcastically added with a forced smile, "And, no more roses."

Embarrassed, he said nothing. Just then a car wheeled into the driveway and a big guy dressed in a tight-fitting, muscleman top and equally tight jeans with wavy hair exited. Ignoring Erik, he went to Christina and gave her a smooch. She said, "I want to introduce you to the second officer I'm flying with. David, this is Erik Preis. Erik, this is David Bennedeto."

The two men shook hands and David's mitt felt huge.

"How long you been with Shuttle Air?" David asked.

"Only a few months." To play dumb Erik asked, "You a pilot?"

"Nah. I just date the pretty ones." He pulled Christina closer. "I work at the airline and study acting."

"You've got excellent taste in women," Erik awkwardly replied, not knowing what else to say. "I gotta be going." He quickly drove off.

As they stood outside and watched him, David said, "A little young for you, isn't he? His mommy might be worried that he's not home yet."

She pushed him away. "What the hell is that supposed to mean?"

"You weren't working this late, if you know what *I* mean?"

"I don't. Why don't you be more specific? A lot more specific."

"What the hell was he doing here?"

"We work together and went out to grab a bite. He's the kid I told you the Chief Pilot is gunning for. Man, you are one jealous son-of-a-bitch. What are you trying to do trigger another seizure with all of your bullshit stress?"

David felt the anger radiating from her like heat from an oven. He put up both hands as if to stave it off. "I'm sorry. It's just that I come home and you're here with a good-looking guy and well…"

"Well, what? Like he said, he's brand new and I wanted to give him a few pointers."

David again took her in his arms. "I just couldn't stand the thought of another man touching you."

Christina just glared at him.

Erik now had another reason for not accepting Christina's invitation the last time. They probably would have been caught, tonight. And that gorilla boyfriend had that steroid look in his eyes.

Alone in his darkened den, Juni dialed his brother-in-law, Gene DiAndressi. He needed expense money for this operation and would put the squeeze on him. Gene owned a successful plumbing supply company. The phone was picked up on the second ring.

"Gene, it's me."

The heavyset DiAndressi groaned, "For Christ's sake Juni, it's late."

"Did I wake you?"

DiAndressi was dressed in his pajamas about ready to call it a night and this conversation was the last thing he wanted. "Look, Juni…"

"I won't keep you long."

"What do you want? Like I don't already know."

"I'm working on a deal and need to borrow some dough."

"You mean some *more* dough, don't you? You still haven't paid back the three thou I lent you last year, plus the other from..."

"This isn't for the business. It's for somethin' else."

"What's it this time?"

"I'm not at liberty to say."

"Oh no? Then maybe I'm not at liberty to give you another fuckin' dime! How do you like that shit?" DiAndressi screamed into the phone.

"Calm down. There's zero risk for either of us and we stand to make a lot."

"What the hell's this *we* shit? How can I be part of somethin' you won't tell me about? What do you take me for, a fuckin' moron?"

"I gotta have it," Juni begged, "or the deal will have to be scrapped."

Cooling down, Gene demanded, "How much?"

"Only twenty-five hundred."

"Twenty-five hundred bucks!"

"And you're better off not knowin' what it's for," Juni quickly added. "When this is complete, and it'll be a done deal soon, I'll repay you seven thou."

"Let me get this straight. You're gonna reimburse me seven grand?"

"Plus the original money I borrowed, with interest."

"This I gotta see."

"Does that mean you'll loan it to me?"

"If for no other reason then to keep you from calling again at this hour. Come by the office tomorrow afternoon and I'll have it in fifties and hundreds."

"Thanks, Gene."

"Don't give me this thanks Gene crap. If you weren't my

brother-in-law you'd never see a nickel of mine."

"I'll be at your office tomorrow about three. 'Night, Gene, and give my best to Diana." Juni hung up and muttered, "I'd like to tell him to stuff the twenty-five hundred up his big fat ass. There's nothin' worse than an uppity Eye-talian. Let him join one of those waspy country clubs and he'd find out pretty damn quick what those types think of a *WOP* who's got some loose change." Done grumbling, Juni felt better, as just about everything was in place and ready to launch.

CHAPTER TWENTY-EIGHT

Saturday was Carol's third flying lesson and Erik's final one of the day. He phoned the evening before.

"I was waiting for your call," she cooed. "Don't forget. We have some flying to do tomorrow."

"I didn't forget. We're scheduled for—"

"Four o'clock and I wouldn't miss it."

The day dragged on until she entered the office dressed in tight jeans, white sneakers and a light fabric, flowered blouse. From their conversations Erik again detected a different spirit, a sense of street smarts that didn't quite go along with the way she normally carried herself. Someone not afraid to get down in the dirt and fight. After flying together for an hour Erik told her with a knowing grin, "Let's conduct our post-flight de-briefing at another location."

She drove behind him on the narrow, tree-lined streets replete with speed bumps Erik had mentioned were put in place to keep the local mechanics in business until he finally pulled into a bluestone driveway of a Colonial-style house. Although he knew every inch of it, stepping inside he still felt like an unwanted intruder in the house draped in sadness. She figured this was his parent's place and noted the lovely roses and other flora growing alongside the split rail wooden fence. Erik unlocked the door and shouted greetings to the parents he knew weren't there.

Carol exclaimed, "I love it. It's so old-world." She walked around, gently stroking a few of the framed delicate needlepoint works. "These are exquisite," she said, pointing to the needlepoint. "Who stitched them?"

"My mother. She's good at it."

"When will I meet her?"

"Maybe tonight?"

"I'd also like to meet your father 'cause—."

"I don't want to discuss him," a now-serious Erik growled.

"Why not?"

"That's a *very* long story," he replied with a scowl. These feelings began to fade as he led her upstairs by the hand. "Sorry for the heat," he meekly whispered in his bedroom, "but my folks don't believe in air conditioning." He went to the window and flipped on the fan. The fan-made wind made its way into the room and the rhythmic puffs of breeze washed over their bodies.

"I thought all the heat was from us? I love your room! Let me guess. You're a pilot?" she joked, pointing to all the aviation paraphernalia that adorned the shelves and walls. "And since there's no a/c, how about letting me cool you off?"

"Cool me off? Not!" Smiling, he raised his hands over his head and she tenderly peeled off his undershirt. Taking her in his arms, the hard edges caused by thoughts of his father disappeared, replaced by others so powerful they couldn't coexist with anything else. It felt like a love genie popped out of Erik's personal bottle after being locked up for over twenty years. He'd been alone for so long, but now it all changed in a heartbeat.

She tasted great as they kissed and her clothing quickly evaporated. As he inserted his middle finger into her warm wetness, with difficulty she tugged down his boxers. He felt her legs around him and her cheeks were flush with expectation, their reddish tint making her appear even more innocent and appealing. Since there was no chance of their lovemaking being interrupted, they took their time, caressing and probing, hair, breast and thighs. Minutes that felt like seconds. Her knees felt weak as he gently entered her. She gave of herself in a way that made it clear she was his. For the first time Erik felt loved and appreciated, sheltered from everything bad, a strange and exotic place he had never before visited. When he could no longer hold back, bathing in the sweet scents of sex and sweat, they both reached climax together. Totally immersed in each other, he remained inside her while he ran his fingers though her thick, disheveled hair. They drifted off into a dreamlike state. Not a single word was uttered, yet so much passed between them. As they lay there together, each knew their world had changed. There was no going back as a powerful current held them tightly in its grip.

Gazing at Erik's sinewy body, Carol wondered how every other woman could *not* see him in the same light as she. These thoughts were interrupted when they rolled out of bed onto the floor, giggling. They stood up and barefoot she barely came to his shoulders. He platonically kissed the top of her head and headed to take a shower. She quickly dressed and meandered throughout the house. There were no family photos, which she thought strange. She finally spotted one of Erik and a beautiful woman she took to be his mother. Both were smiling, but the smiles were those of people who have been told to do so, with lots of flashy teeth showing but without true happiness in the eyes. Rather, it was as if despair found a place in his mother's eyes.

After hearing the water stop, Carol returned upstairs and slid her fingernails sensually over his dripping body, an action that made not only the hair on the nape of his neck stand up. "I'm ready for round two," he said, pointing. After seriously considering that he added, "But my parents might return." Trying to drag his corporeal thoughts away from her he mentioned, "I know this little Italian restaurant not too far from here. You think pasta and wine might force lustful feelings aside?"

"Or, have exactly the opposite effect. But let me call my folks first." She took out her cell.

He whispered over her shoulder with a broad smile. "Hi, Mom. Erik and I just finished flying, er, making love and it was great!"

She threw him a playful look and hit memory button number one. A second later her mother answered. "Hi, Mom. I finished my lesson and Erik and I are going to grab a bite."

They took separate cars to the *La Pizzetta* restaurant where Erik suggested the linguini with red clam sauce. "Although this place isn't fancy like *Chez Nous*, they make their own macaroni and use fresh calms." They both ordered that dish. The dinner conversation was conducted in high spirits as Erik related stories about some of his student pilots without mentioning them by name. They finished off the meal with homemade cheesecake that was more like home comfort. While sipping coffee, Carol asked, "What's up you and your old man? When I mentioned him, you were like a different person."

Erik didn't want to plumb those deep waters. Could he even begin to convey about his mother cheating and his father's reaction? That answer was no. "It's gotta be the cultural differences," he finally stammered. "My parents are from another country. My father doesn't like the way I do things and makes my life miserable." He'd probably divulge everything eventually, but needed more time.

Very reluctant goodbye kisses were exchanged in the parking lot and Erik returned to a darkened house. He went directly to his bedroom and locked the door. The windows were still wide open, but the oppressive air still wasn't ready to surrender the day's heat to the night's coolness, even with the chugging fan. He removed his clothing and lay down, knowing there would never be air conditioning in this house. His father loved to quote the German philosopher Friedrich Nietzsche. "That which doesn't kill you makes you stronger." The old man repeated that over and over. Erik wanted to tell him that Nietzsche eventually suffered a mental collapse, was institutionalized and died from syphilis, but never did. Instead he let him live in his bullshit world. While lying there he glanced at the blue and white aviation navigation charts he'd pinned to the walls seemingly eons ago so his imagination could fly off anywhere, anytime. Retracing the route he and Carol had flown, he found himself wishing she was still there with him.

He also longed for his problems to be put behind him. But the inability to wish them away caused the dreaded anxiety to return. His mind and stomach churned as a fitful slumber finally came. But in his nightmare he wasn't flying with Carol, but was on a bus with bars on the windows and headed to prison.

CHAPTER TWENTY-NINE

The game was about to begin and although Juni was the only player and still wasn't certain of the rules, hopefully victory would be his. Right now the scoreboard read zero. Dispensing with the phony confidence he had displayed with his partners, after many thoughtful hours he had come up with his plan. He'd leave for Boston tomorrow and would lie low during the day, maybe take in a baseball game at Fenway Park, major league baseball's oldest stadium. Nighttime would be different. He'd always felt more comfortable moving about under a shroud of darkness, a black slipstream where he could look out, but no one could see in. Although doubtful they'd be able to quickly pull off the job even though the tide would be favorable, and notwithstanding that the weather might cooperate there were still other items to accomplish, like finding the right boat.

Juni descended to a locked home basement closet and rechecked his gear: a hand-held compass, wet suit, diver's gloves and booties, snorkel, small LCD flashlight, wire cutters, set of copper wires, latex gloves and a portable VOR radio. Christina said pilots used the latter to navigate, and it was essential. He loaded everything into the car, except for the borrowed money, a bag of smoked sausage and four loaves of Italian bread. He would depart the next afternoon for the approximate four-hour drive. He told Angela that he was going on an unspecified business trip and needed her car. The cable TV Weather Channel forecast for the following two days in New York and Boston was for partly cloudy skies with a chance of thunderstorms toward evening, with the four-day extended forecast calling for deteriorating conditions due to a stalled stationary warm weather front to the south. He drove to a pay phone and placed a call to area code 718—Brooklyn. It was picked up after a few rings. "Joey Martino. It's Juni Rosario. How you been?"

"Juni the Lid, you old fart. I ain't seen ya in ages. I thought you croaked or somethin'. What's happenin'?"

Skipping the formalities, Juni told him, "I need somethin' fast for an important deal," silently praying that Martino could deliver.

"What you need?"

"A Massachusetts driver's license and some matching credit cards—by tomorrow afternoon."

"Tomorrow fuckin' afternoon! Holy shit, that's a pretty tall order. My contact will have to get 'em today and FedEx or drive 'em down."

"Hey, ain't that what old pals are for?"

After a moment's silence Joey offered, "In this hi-tech age I can probably work somethin' out. But I gotta make a few calls. Give me the number you're at. If you don't hear from me within fifteen minutes, pick the stuff up tomorrow afternoon at Lenny's Lounge over on Twenty-First. But it'll cost a little extra to get 'em so quick."

"How much for everything?"

"About a grand."

"No problem."

Juni was sure that Joey added a couple hundred for himself. He stood by the phone for a half-hour, but no call came through.

On Sunday, after attending the eleven o'clock mass with his family and not hearing a single word, Juni departed. Dressed in a comfortable short-sleeved shirt and pair of light fabric slacks, he first drove to Lenny's Lounge in Bay Ridge, a shady joint that used to be called Lombardo's Bar and Restaurant. The hangout had been bought by one of the connected boys who converted it to a gin mill that was now used for conducting this type of business. Juni sat on one of the creaky bar stools in the smoke filled, noisy saloon with the jukebox turned up full blast to prevent any wires from picking up conversations, and forked over a thousand bucks in hundreds to a heavy breathing Martino. His jacket and pants must have been a size fifty or larger and he not only resembled an overstuffed Italian sausage but also smelled like one. For his grand, Juni got what to his eyes looked like a Massachusetts driver's license and matching set of stolen credit cards.

Martino was curious and hollered at Juni over the blaring rock music, "If you don't mind me askin', why you need a Massachusetts license?" Before Juni could respond he added, "And why so fast? My guy had to pull in a bunch of IOU's to get this shit on such short notice."

"I ain't got time for small talk, but I need it for a big deal I've got cookin' in that area." Juni hesitated, finally adding, "There's absolutely nothin' that feels as good as takin' back money from a good uncle, in this case uncle fucking Sam. I mean, he's been stealin' from us for our entire lives."

Martino let a soft whistle out of his chipmunk shaped cheeks. "Don't get fuckin' caught. The Feds ain't too kind when it comes to people filchin' from 'em."

"Who said anything about that? All I said was that I was

gonna take back what's mine."

"Just be *very* fuckin' careful," Joey reiterated raising his thick gray, almost white eyebrows.

Juni bought Joey a drink and left, but did he make a mistake. Should he have mentioned anything? But on second thought, Joey was good people and knew enough to keep his mouth shut. Juni quickly glanced at his new ID and saw he was now Frank Sciotta. If anyone asked, Sciotta would be a self-described businessman from Pittsfield, Massachusetts, the address on the license. His story line would be that due to a pending divorce, a move to the Boston area was needed. He didn't intend to use the credit cards, with the only exception being in the unlikely event the hotel refused to accept cash. Putting Brooklyn out of his mind on the drive, he first pulled over at a newspaper-recycling bin in the Bronx, removed three bound piles of New York tabloids and threw them into the trunk. He next stopped at an Army/Navy store in the same area and another in Hartford, where he purchased a couple of Army duffel bags. After checking for video recorders and seeing none, he bought brass locks in two separate auto-supply stores in Dedham and Brookline, Massachusetts all the while listening to different rock 'n roll stations on the radio as he clicked off the approximate two-hundred and fifty mile drive. The Boston skyline appeared just before dark and after a quick dinner of hamburgers and fries at a roadside diner just off the Mass Pike, he drove to Logan Airport and entered the long-term parking lot where people left their cars while on extended trips. It was a multi-tiered cement structure with loads of graffiti that smelled of gasoline, rubber and old exhaust. The graffiti meant there were no video cameras to catch the assholes that drew what they tried to pass off as artwork. A quick check confirmed that. On the second tier he stopped alongside a same year blue Buick parked head in. He got out and removed only the front Massachusetts license plate and did the same on the fifth level. When both owners returned chances were good they wouldn't discover the missing front plate. But if they did, they'd no doubt assume it simply fell off and neither would be reported as stolen. Juni stopped in a deserted section of the garage and replaced his New York tags. The entire process took approximately half an hour. As he exited the lot a hitch occurred when the black gate attendant became suspicious, not raising the bar allowing him to exit. Juni felt perspiration soaking his underarms. Could he drive through the bar without damaging the car?

"This is the long-term lot. What were you up to in there for such a short time?"

Juni responded, "Scuza, but I no speaka too gooda English." All the time praying the guy wouldn't make a move for the phone. There was definitely a surveillance camera here because cash changed hands. If forced to make a quick escape, it meant ending everything. "I looka for my little brother Alfonso. He fly toa Italy tonighta on Alitalia. Is thisa where I parka to meet him?"

"No," the guy sighed. Pointing, he said, "You gotta go out here and make a right. Then, another right at the first light and park in the short-term lot."

"I go outa here and thenna two times righta?"

"Yeah, but first you gotta pay."

"How mucha?"

"You know you're in the wrong lot?"

Juni just sat with a quizzical look on his face. The bar remained down.

"It costs twenty dollars." After making certain there were no other cars in line the attendant hollered even louder, "Twenty dollars."

"Twenty dollars to parka the car?"

"Yeah."

Juni handed the guy his ticket and a twenty-dollar bill for forty minutes. According to the posted sign it should have cost three bucks. As the gate was finally raised, a relieved Juni added, "Thanka you very mucha." Ten minutes later a relaxed Juni pulled into the Holiday Inn parking lot, a couple of spots from an overflowing dumpster and tight up against the hotel wall so only the rear plate was visible. This was good because even in the daylight the car would be pretty much incognito from all but one side. Inside, he found the standard American hotel. Plastic everywhere, including the clerks who had plastic smiles to go with plastic ID tags with their name and hometown written on them. There were fat-dispensing vending machines everywhere with crackers, candy, potato chips and the like, along with a typical American restaurant off to the right, most likely with frozen food tasting like shit. After registering as Frank Sciotta he wrote in the car's rear license plate number. While filling out the documents he struck up a conversation with the room clerk, an attractive, slight girl with light blue eyes and long, fake eyelashes that he estimated was in her late teens or early twenties. Her name was Irene and according to her nametag her hometown was Boston.

"Between us," he whispered while winking, "I'm getting divorced. I'll be staying for about six days. Instead of using a credit card, can I pay for everything in cash? In advance?" He took out a fistful of greenbacks.

"That'll be OK provided you give me enough for your entire stay. You'll also have to pay cash for any hotel services."

"No problem."

She carefully counted the money, which was probably more than she earned in a month and handed him a receipt.

"Once my divorce is finalized I'm considering moving to

East Boston," he added, folding the voucher. "The town seems nice, but I'd like to explore the neighborhood a bit. Maybe I'll buy a place here and—"

"I've got a pretty good idea what you're going through, Mr. Sciotta," she interrupted sympathetically. "My parents divorced a few years back and it got messy. You should do well house hunting because lots of homes are for sale. You can probably find some good bargains. Which part of town are you interested in?"

"I'm not familiar with East Boston, but maybe close to the water?"

"In that case, try Smith's Real Estate on Bennington Street. They handle the nicest waterfront and water-view homes."

The chambermaid would no doubt see the wetsuit and other paraphernalia, so he wanted to cover himself. "Do you know if there's a beach where snorkeling is allowed? It's my favorite hobby."

"There's Orient Heights public beach and as long as you don't use a spear gun you can snorkel. I dated a guy who liked to dive and he told me the water there is pretty murky and cold, meaning you probably won't be able to see much and will definitely need a wetsuit."

"I brought mine along. Thanks for the info."

"That's what we're here for."

Taking the briefcase containing the cash and some gear from the trunk, Juni went to the room with plastic veneer furniture camouflaged to resemble wood. It was clean and contained an air conditioner large enough to freeze over the entire Boston Bay, along with a chained-down color television with remote control. He had paid a twenty-dollar deposit for the latter. There was also a well-stocked bar that charged five bucks for a lousy ounce-and-a-half bottle of booze. He figured there was a water saver on the showerhead and a quick glance confirmed that.

CHAPTER THIRTY

A perspiring Woody Montgomery ambled down the quiet, dimly-lit corridor of the Intensive Care Unit at St. Francis, the famed Long Island cardiac hospital. He hated all hospitals. The antiseptic odors, blood pressure cuffs and the like were synonymous with death. From the phone call early that morning, he knew his old man's case was classified as a life-and-death situation, and closer to the latter. After identifying himself to the rotund nurse in charge who had more rolls on her stomach than a French bakery had behind the counter, he was ushered into his father's room. The eerie silence was only punctuated by the hissing sounds of the ventilator used to keep the old man alive. The room smelled of disinfectant, with an underlying scent of something else Woody classified as disease. Glancing at the chart affixed to the end of his bed, Woody saw that lots of things were wrong with him. Once the nurse softly closed the door, it was just father and son. Although listless, Errol Montgomery was conscious but couldn't speak due to the life-support system. Woody's first task was to devise a means of communicating. While holding his father's ashen hand he whispered that one squeeze meant yes, two no, three good and four meant bad. Asked if he understood, his father responded with a single squeeze.

"How are you?"

Four feeble squeezes."They're doing all they can for you."

One.

Father and son had never been close, especially after Woody's mother, Evelyn passed away several years earlier. Woody subsequently learned the old man had kept a young mistress in a lavish Manhattan apartment for years, while forcing his wife and son to endure with the barest of necessities. Woody had confided in his wife, Ingrid that his father was a selfish codger who had only one use for women. As a result, she despised him. But they put up with him for a single reason—money. During the little time they'd spent together, he usually drank too much and mentioned cash he had stashed away, somewhere. When sober he was more wary and wouldn't utter a word about his finances. As a result, neither Woody nor Ingrid was certain about his true financial status. Over the years he and Ingrid had been careful not to let on how they really felt, but as soon as word arrived of his grave heart attack she'd dispatched Woody in case the alcohol-induced accounts were true. Maybe now he'd come clean?"Dad, I know it isn't the best time to raise this 'cause you're going to be fine. But since I'm the only family left, I want to make sure everything's in order...just in case," he whispered. Hesitation.

One squeeze.

"Do you have a trust agreement or anything like that?"

Two squeezes.

"Even though you'll be fine, I think it best you sign a trust in order to avoid probate. That can be time consuming and costly."

One squeeze.

He released his father's hand.

"I had a lawyer draw up this document." Woody exhaled a long breath and removed two neatly folded pieces of paper from his breast pocket. "It makes certain you get the best care possible and in case anything bad happens, leaves everything to me in a way to make the tax implications minimal." Taking his father's hand again, he whispered, "Do you understand?"

One squeeze.

"Do you mind?"

Two squeezes.Woody summoned the same nurse to witness his father's signature. The plump woman watched as Errol Montgomery scribbled his barely legible name at the bottom of a document he couldn't read and probably wouldn't understand even if able to. She then signed in the space provided for a witness, thinking that Woody was one crass bastard. But she'd seen shit like this so many times she was getting used to it.

Once finished, Woody stayed for another fifteen minutes watching television. "You're gonna be OK," he assured his father before leaving, but knowing he'd never see him alive again and not really caring. In his detached opinion, life amounted to a bunch of different relationships and this was one he really didn't give a damn about. Outside the hospital he experienced a momentary coating of misery and pang of guilt, similar to the feeling he got when passing a homeless guy on a street corner. But this emotion quickly abated. He was simply returning the treatment the old man had given his mother and him.

He stopped at a local bar near home for some drinks and made a single call from the pay phone. "The paper's signed. The old man's not gonna make it," he said and hung up. Pleased with himself, Woody proceeded to get thoroughly smashed for the first time since the night before the Boston emergency. Then, he had been out at this same bar drinking his favorite gin and tonic until closing. He had sworn off after that, figuring his drinking might cost him his job. But it didn't, so what the hell?

CHAPTER THIRTY-ONE

Juni spent much of the following day wearing latex gloves to prevent DNA, tearing up New York newspapers and stuffing the shreds into the four duffels. When finished he locked each. Looking outside, it appeared as though the air had grown soggier as the sunlight waned and quickly turned to darkness, time for a first-hand survey of East Boston. After donning a light parka, he exited the hotel through the back, locked the duffels in the trunk and walked in an easterly direction along Saratoga Street, the main drag running through town. He made mental notes of the location of the police booth and single cruiser, along with several Italian restaurants. Closer to the bay the entire make-up changed from commercial to residential with quite a few "Room for Rent" signs hanging outside the old wooden New England-style frame homes. It was easy to imagine how charming the area was before the constant din of the jet engines shattered the serenity. Closer to the water, the delicious New England saltwater scent you could almost lick from the air changed into a stench when it mixed with the jets' kerosene exhaust, with no way to escape the vile taste. His estimated mile-long trek brought him to the pothole-riddled, pebble parking lot of the East Boston Yacht Club. The driving time from the hotel would be only four to five minutes. From appearances the name of the marina was a misnomer as none of the boats vaguely fit the description of a yacht. Although there were a few sailboats, their masts like tall oaks peering above a forest of small pines, most were smaller powerboats between twenty and twenty-five feet, no doubt used for fishing. The nice weather meant the marina was alive, with fishermen entering and leaving with their gear. Juni walked inside while the one entranceway gate was ajar. There were a number of unpainted wooden storage lockers off to the right, the numbers on them seemingly corresponding to the ones on the slips. Grubby-looking, unshaven anglers were in the process of removing fishing poles, smelly bait and other gear from the lockers and transporting it to some of the seventy-odd berthed boats. He walked onto the wooden dock that floated on the water with worn planks that resembled exposed human ribs, his footsteps hollow-sounding. Small waves gently lapped at the pilings holding the dock in place. The airport was clearly visible about three-quarters of a mile to the south-southeast across the bay. He could hear the high-pitched whining sound as the jets awaited their turn in line for departure, which changed into a thunderous roar that shook everything as takeoff power was applied.

Sizing up the place, the locked cyclone fence gate leading to the plain wooden clubhouse and slips wouldn't present a problem. He could enter easily by jamming the rudimentary fastening mechanism open with a small piece of wood or cardboard. It was also possible to gain access by swinging his body around the right side of the gate, bypassing it completely. But this would entail a messy descent down a slippery mud bank, followed by a vault from shore to the dock, so he would use it as a last resort. There were no security guards or video cameras and there weren't even any of the huge spotlights common in other marinas, probably due to the smaller size of the boats. While meandering along he used a pen to jot down the slip numbers where the berthed boat hulls were smeared with a large amount of slimy growth, indicating they weren't used often. Anglers were sitting around drinking beer. To pry some information he told one. "I'm supposed to go fishing with a buddy of mine who keeps his boat here. What happens if the weather's foggy? Think we'll still go?"

The guy was outfitted in bright yellow foul weather gear and rubber boots, looking like he stepped out of one of those fishing catalogs. He was holding a can of Bud and replied in a voice heavy with a Boston accent, "Practically no one fishes when the weather's bad 'cause the striped bass move around so much it's almost impossible to locate them, even with one of those satellite global navigation systems and a fish-finder. You're better off staying home, having a few beers and wait for better weather."

Juni thanked the guy and slipped back into the crowd. He didn't want anyone to remember him. Since he had the needed info, quickly exited through the same gate, discovering no key was needed as it could be opened from the inside simply by rotating the latch. Strolling farther in a northeasterly direction along Saratoga Street, he passed the Orient Heights beach where the hotel clerk said snorkeling was allowed. There were also four well-attended softball games in progress on the diamonds, with most of the players jabbering away in Spanish. Like much of Boston, baseball was *the* sport and watching a few games would be another way to kill some time. A smiling Juni now knew for certain their plan would work. All he needed was the cover. Hopefully cliffs of needed fog would move in for a weeklong stay. He turned back toward the hotel, sensing that if the weather did cooperate, maybe he could move quickly?

CHAPTER THIRTY-TWO

Woody returned the following day and Christina asked, "How's your father?"

"He was on a respirator and the prognosis isn't good," a somber Woody replied. "They're putting him in hospice care today."

"I'm sorry to hear that."

In Boston Christina telephoned the Holiday Inn, but there was no response from Juni's room. After the next landing, she asked Erik to call. "If he's there, tell him to forget it 'cause the weather's too good."

A few moments later he returned and informed her, "No answer."

Both pilots were edgy. Could Woody sense it? The angst was particularly draining on Erik. After work he joined Carol for a late dinner but only picked at the leftover pot roast, food being the last thing on his mind. He didn't even become aroused when she kissed him and began unbuttoning his shirt.

"What's wrong? Did I say or do something?"

"No. It's not you. I've just got a lot on my mind."

She figured he was concerned with the looming second payment deadline, but said nothing, hoping he'd eventually open up. Erik stayed only a short time and before leaving, apologized for his conduct.

Lying in bed at home while fear cheated him of any sleep, he detected the very faint, almost imperceptible pitter-patter of rain a bit before two in the morning. It wasn't the heavy pellet-like precipitation that occurs when a front moves through, nor could he detect the distinctive ozone odor that precedes a thunderstorm. The ashen-like white rain seemed to just hang in the air like a heavy mist. The calm wind meant the coming weather wouldn't be rushed. Had the time arrived? He was finally able to pull himself out of bed, trudged to the window barefoot and opened it: no traffic, not a single leaf stirred on the steaming street below. The heavy mist whispering through the dense foliage imparted a wet, almost black sheen, with the stillness broken only by the summer sounds of crickets, while damp air flooded into the room through the rattling window fan. While taking deep breaths, he stalked the room with restless energy, knowing the clouds would soon roll up the coast like a camouflaged army battalion, with accompanying fog rolling in from the sea shrouding the shape of everything. As terror built deep inside, the unrelenting anxiety finally gave way to thoughts of Carol and what would happen to her, to them, if he was caught. Did he ever *really* intend to go through with this insanity?

He silently padded to the living room and grabbed the phone. With churning stomach and pounding head, he cursed Juni for the command not to call him. He had the power in his hand that very moment to call off this idiotic scheme. But canceling meant all his life expectancies would come to an abrupt end. The phone went back on its cradle. Erik hobbled back upstairs and again peered through the window, offering a voiceless prayer that by morning brilliant sunshine from ninety-three million miles away would chase the dreaded fog away. But he knew differently in his gut, where the truest feelings lived. He returned to bed and pressed weak fingertips over his eyes, seeing nothing but sparks. He finally dozed off while trying to convince himself that he was *not* afraid.

Christina was also finding no sanctuary. She was as awake as an owl even after ingesting two powerful Restoril sleeping pills. Even though this was twice the normal dosage, sleeplessness remained her only true companion. While listening to the soft rain, she turned toward David who was beside her, snoring loudly and smelling of his favorite aftershave. She found everything about him increasingly repulsive. Still wide awake, her thoughts turned to her childhood. Since her father had deserted the family, the only religion she practiced now was the dreaded fear of being alone, a medical condition known as autophobia. She recalled that her very first reaction after hearing her shrink's clinical diagnosis was to tell him that she wasn't afraid of cars. With a slight smile, he explained it had nothing to do with automobiles. A number of subsequent sessions had given her valuable insight. Although she tried not to wear this phobia like a crucifix, it remained *the* driving force in her personal life choices. Although she sometimes needed solitude, a door one voluntarily closed, it was the second kind that terrified her; when the world rejects *you*, leaving you alone. David *had* filled a void in her life in keeping out the emotional isolation, but she would soon be ready to move on. Her eyelids finally involuntarily closed under the combined weight of these thoughts and medication into a sporadic slumber, with ruminations still running through her mind as fast as a racehorse at Belmont.

Both pilots looked exhausted when they showed up for work. "I can't continue like this," Christina hoarsely whispered to Erik after passing through security. "I have a knot in my stomach that feels like a boulder." She was also concerned that all the stress would trigger a seizure.

Erik couldn't help but notice the redness around and bags under her eyes that looked more like valises. "I was up all night too. My eyes feel like someone poured a pail of sand into them." A moment later he asked, "Did you see the forecast for Boston? That stationary weather front is slowly working its way up the coast just a bit offshore," he said, with fear having its teeth firmly embedded in him.

A featherlike rain carried on a light breeze had begun prior to their first Boston landing. The visibility was reported as three-quarters of a mile restricted by showers and fog, not as poor as they needed. Maybe this wouldn't be the night after all?

After their first Boston landing on runway 15, Christina checked the forecast for nine P.M. and it called for lower ceilings of one hundred feet, with the visibility dropping to an eighth of a mile in fog, light rain and mist, along with a south wind at three to five knots. Shuttle Air's weather people were housed in an air-conditioned, windowless building, so maybe their forecast would be wrong? But if so, this might be it. Would Juni agree? Was he set to go? Christina went to the pay phone and after making certain no one was within earshot, dialed Sciotta. When Juni answered she said, "Tonight might be a go," in a voice an octave higher than normal. "Runway 22 Right's in use for takeoff and the visibility is forecast to be near zero. Our tail number is N838SA. Erik or I will call after our next arrival. It's your decision. Everything ready on your end?"

"I haven't tested the boat yet."

"Is that a yes or no?"

There was only silence on the other end.

"For Christ's sake Juni, c'mon."

"All right, it's a go. But only if the weather's as shitty as you say."

"The visibility was three-quarters of a mile when we landed, so it ain't gonna be clear skies and a bright moon by nine."

"I'll be here."

Although the weather was damp and cool, Christina was anything but. Damp yes, but definitely not cool. And that distinct tingling was once again present in her fingers. She prayed all of this wouldn't trigger a seizure, not tonight. After she returned to the plane Woody popped his head into the cockpit saying he was going to phone for an updated report on his father's condition. Once he departed, Christina related her conversation with Juni to Erik, who simply rolled his eyes.

CHAPTER THIRTY-THREE

On this dreary, penetrating day, per the usual routine Chris Norton grabbed a taxi from Logan to the Federal Reserve building located on Atlantic Avenue in downtown Boston. After passing no fewer than three security checkpoints he asked the young black woman in charge of the counting process that was located in the basement, "How much tonight?"

"I don't know for certain yet, but probably close to four million."

Norton groaned, knowing that any amount over three million would take approximately three hours to verify, count and prepare for shipment. This meant once again delaying the outbound flight. Under the terms of the government's contract with Shuttle Air he was empowered to do so to ensure he and the money made it on board. "Please hurry. I'd rather not hold up another flight. Some passengers bitched about last week's half-hour delay. The airline called my boss and gave him hell when they discovered that amount was under three million."

The young clerk started to explain that particular glitch was due to several workers calling in sick, but said nothing. Norton wasn't her boss. Instead she smiled and shrugged her shoulders.

Norton sauntered down the hallway to the men's room and stood unusually close to the urinal while relieving himself wondering if this room also had hidden cameras? He then went to the agents' waiting room, picked up a copy of the *Boston Globe* and began reading it front to back as he probably had several hours to kill. When thumbing through the business section his eyelids grew heavy and he dozed. After what felt like several minutes but was just over an hour he awoke, stretched and glanced at his watch. Enough time remained to grab a bite. At the in-house deli he ordered turkey on rye and as he was finishing a supervisor entered and signaled they were ready. Norton stood up, Styrofoam cup of coffee in hand and felt for the heavy .40-caliber Smith & Wesson automatic in a shoulder harness under his jacket. The nine o'clock flight would have to be delayed, hopefully only for a few minutes this time. He gulped down the coffee while dialing the Shuttle Air manager and gave him the news.

"I've recommended the airline not renew this contract when it comes up in September," the guy replied.

Norton had met him only once and didn't like him for a number of reasons, mainly his indifferent attitude. "That's your choice. I'm sure Delta would love it."

"You're a typical government worker who doesn't know shit about running an on-time business."

Norton had heard this before and quickly replied with a feigned yawn, "We'll be there about nine-oh-five."

To his surprise the guy continued. "Tonight you're in luck. Our flights have been running late anyway due to the lousy weather. So, I'm not going to bitch—too much."

Juni finished the conversation with Christina and hurried to his car, noting more of the blind fingers of vapor embracing the area with each passing moment. He ran a final check. He had everything. Driving to a nearby supermarket dumpster he grabbed a cardboard carton, then drove to the yacht club. He waited the few precious moments he allotted for this purpose, while nervously tapping the steering column with cigarette-yellowed fingers, hoping someone with a key would roll up. Just then a car entered the lot and Juni removed the large empty carton from the trunk, pretending to struggle with it. The other fellow noticed him and held open the gate. Juni thanked and followed him inside. Once alone, he tore off a small piece of the box and jammed open the small dead bolt, tossed the carton into the trash. He hurried to slip #42 where a small wooden boat christened *Pride of the Navy* was berthed. He jumped aboard and as the boat listed to starboard he peered into the tank to ensure there was enough fuel and then hurried back to the hotel.

Per the usual routine, Christina piloted the first flight to Boston, while Woody flew the middle two segments. She would fly the final leg. Although delayed en route earlier, they had arrived in New York close to schedule and while filling out the paperwork for the Boston leg, the operations agent notified Christina that the Boston weather had deteriorated.

"Is it still above landing minimums?"

"Barely. The visibility is down to a half, variable three-eighths of a mile."

"I'd rather be safe than sorry, so we'll take an extra three thousand pounds of fuel in case of holding. I'd hate to return because we didn't have enough."

"Roger. I'll take care of that, Captain" the man crisply replied.

With a nod of the head, she motioned Erik into the hallway.

"This could be it."

"I'm scared shitless."

"Me too," she said wringing her hands. As the embers of anxiety burned, she remained concerned about a crippling seizure. "You remember all the details?"

"I think so."

"Let's go over it once more while we walk."

After passing security, Erik whispered, "What about the flight data recorder?"

"What about it?"

"We missed this, but there are different types. I'm not certain which is installed on this plane? I don't know what flight parameters other than speed, flap settings and the like it registers. Would a cargo door opening show up?"

Christina stopped dead in her tracks, turned and looked at him with alarm that darkened the blue of her eyes. She finally stammered, "I, I don't know." A moment later she added, "I think we can get around that problem if you pull the recorder's circuit breaker before any of the others and then reset them in reverse order, with the exception of the generator control circuit breaker. Reset that one last. This way if anyone examines the flight recorder, the difficulty with the generator will be the only problem that shows."

"I don't think that'll work 'cause if it's a new one it would show a time gap when the recorder wasn't functioning."

"Shit. You're right. How the hell did we miss that?" she said, shaking her head. "We'll just leave the recorder alone and roll the dice, hoping it has one of the older models that won't show a door opening on the ground. Had I thought of this I could have found out ahead of time which type is installed."

"We weren't supposed to take any more chances. You wanna call this off?"

"If we told him, Juni would probably shit-can the whole thing. If it has the new type, we're fucked," a solemn Christina added. "But these are old planes and I pray it doesn't. Let's go with that."

"I hope you're right."

"So do I."

The combination of dusk and fog had smothered the daylight when they arrived in the Boston area, with the visibility still hovering right around half a mile. Other than having to execute an instrument approach almost to touchdown, the landing on runway 15 Right was routine. While taxiing, the tower reported the visibility had dropped even lower to one-half, variable one-quarter of a mile in fog, still adequate for takeoff.

Bill Francis, the diminutive and balding Boston tower operator checked with his supervisor, Tony Heinz a career Air Traffic controller with over thirty years on the job under his sizeable belt, and then turned off the motion sensors that surrounded the airport perimeter, as called for in the Mass Port Authority and TSA security procedures. This system had been installed for some time, but thus far there had been nothing but false alarms and plenty of those, usually caused by seagulls. It was not a well-kept secret that some tower personnel furtively turned them off as one of their first orders of business so as not to be disturbed by bogus warnings. The timid Francis was different. He didn't want to risk his job over this or any other item as he had been in serious trouble a short time ago while routing planes on ground control. He had granted a clearance for one jet to cross runway 4 Left while another was landing on the same runway. It was only the pilot's last minute evasive action by aborting the landing that averted a potential disaster. Francis said that coordination between two controllers was the problem, but he was the only one placed on probation for a year. This meant if he screwed up, made even a minor error during that time he'd be fired. So, he did everything exactly by the book because he had a wife and two children to support. The regulations stated that if the visibility increased beyond a half-mile he had to again check with Heinz and turn the sensors back on if ordered to do so.

Once at the gate Woody quickly deplaned to check his father's condition. Christina immediately went to a deserted section of the terminal and called Juni. "The conditions are right. But because of the weather we may be off the gate late and there might also be departure delays."

"I'll be there," Juni said and hung up, hoping he would indeed make it. His watch showed 8:15. There wasn't much time. *Never enough fucking time!* His Buick accelerated with a cloud of blue smoke as it exited the hotel lot and cut a swath through the swirling fog. Closer to the water the headlights had difficulty penetrating the billowing veils of mist that obscured everything and painted horizontal ribbons of rainbow-like shades tinted in every color of the spectrum across the windshield. In the yacht club's parking lot his tires kicked up pieces of gravel and came to an abrupt halt. The conditions were so bad the only thing barely visible was another car, a dark brown SUV. The top of the marina's gangway lights were bare smudges, with their dull yellowish glow attempting to cut through the fog. They resembled angelic halos no brighter than gaslights peering down from atop the poles. The syrupy air was turning into more of a soupy blackness. Looking toward town Juni saw the jellylike fog rolling down the street like a silent serpent, slithering through and filling the empty spaces between the square wooden frame houses, creating what appeared to be rows of mausoleums. The vapor wrapped around everything and was so dense that Juni felt as though he could cut it with his knife. A very light rain began falling and as the water-mirrored depressions in the parking lot gravel filled, his excitement built. With senses wide open, his anxiety level was rising as quickly as the incoming tide. He exhaled in short bursts like a machine gun with several misfires, the moisture from his breath clinging to his body. With footsteps falling as silently as in snow he opened the trunk and donned the tight-fitting diving gloves. After grabbing some gear and two duffel bags, he prayed the entrance lock was still jammed. Gently pushing on the gate, his damp fingers almost slipped off, but it swung open ever so slowly, inviting him to enter. As he passed by the wooden clubhouse, a bag in each hand, he squinted. There was a broad-shouldered, bearded fellow with kinky hair the color of a rusty pipe, dressed in a stark white baseball jersey with EAST BOSTON MARAUDERS inscribed in black, sitting there. The man was on a porch rocker nursing a beer. His face looked like it was cast from cement, with haunting gray eyes on the top. Did the fog distort his appearance? Pleased this wasn't a social type fishing club, Juni simply nodded as he passed the stranger. The fellow responded with a barely detectable wave, beer in hand. Juni turned his attention to the task at hand.

At the boat, he placed everything on the deck and returned to the car, again waving to the man as he passed by. After removing the rest of the gear and two remaining bags, Juni made his way back down the slippery walkway. He gingerly stepped aboard the uncovered *Pride of the Navy*. It listed to starboard and quickly righted itself. All was quiet except for the hardware clinking against the aluminum masts of sailboats berthed nearby. After stowing everything, he raised the lid of the sixty-horsepower Evinrude outboard, grateful for overhearing friends' conversations on how to hot-wire cars on the Brooklyn streets. Holding the small penlight between his teeth, its beam cut through the darkness smoother than a hot knife through butter. After fumbling with the pliers, he snipped one end off the starter ignition wires and stripped away the damp plastic coating. He then connected the ignition to the battery lead wires and touched them to the starter line. The outboard coughed and came to life, ready to do its work. The motor would run so long as the ignition remained attached to the battery lead.

Due to the gloves, with difficulty he changed into the constricted wet suit and diving boots and compared the reading on his hand-held compass to the one on the boat's Airglide marine compass, noting they differed by only a couple of degrees. He turned on the portable Very High Omni Range navigation unit, the VOR radio, which would be his means of accurately navigating to the airport in the near-zero visibility conditions. After tuning the digital dial to frequency 112.7, the Boston VOR, as instructed by Christina he selected the 168-degree radial. While doing this he recalled their meeting at Pepi's when he had pointed out that the most important ingredient, piss poor visibility, could also hinder success. "Picture this," he told Christina and Erik. "The visibility is so shitty I can't be seen navigating to your plane, meaning I also won't be able to see anything. There's a powerful current running in the three-quarter mile wide channel between the marina and airport, ruling out using only a compass. This means I gotta have a way to navigate with pinpoint precision." He went on to explain that the tide also had to be at least halfway in during the flood stage, because this way he would come ashore within easy walking distance of the taxiway where they would be waiting. The incoming tide also meant Mother Nature would reclaim its rightful territory and quickly erase all signs that anyone had ever set foot there. Neither Christina nor Erik had considered the navigation element. "Presuming I make it to the airport, my position could be anywhere and the wrong location would cost the crucial element we don't have; time. I'll have only two to three minutes. And each trip to the boat and back means two duffel bags, but four is the number I'll be shooting for. Plus, I'll not only be removing the money bags but replacing them with dummies. I can't be running all over the airport 'cause with this terrorist shit, someone might spot me and report it. If that happens, the cops will put two and two together and implicate you. Bottom line is I *gotta* have a way to get to your exact location."

Erik floated the idea of using a personal GPS unit that is accurate to within feet. But Christina quashed that. "Those satellites are sent up by a government agency, the Department of Defense. I believe there's a record of the coordinates that are selected. So, it would probably be easy to download that information, allowing the cops to trace it and quickly crack exactly what happened." They fell into silence, but a moment later Christina's face lit up. "I've got it," she exclaimed and told Juni about the hand-held portable VOR radio. "It might seem a bit difficult for a non-pilot to understand, but we navigate our planes on avenues in the sky formed by flying from one VOR to another. A VOR is a line-of-sight homing device that sends out signals shaped like a wagon wheel with the VOR located at the center. Each spoke or radial, as they're called, represents one compass degree. All you do to navigate precisely is select a particular radial and keep the needle on your radio centered. Your only other requirement is to be tuned to the Boston VOR frequency of 112.7. You'll be steering to the VOR facility located on the airport and you can reach the *exact* spot where we'll be waiting. And, there's no way anyone can track you down. In order to return to the dock you use the same procedure but with the reciprocal radial, a hundred and eighty degrees different." She later provided the specific radial to pinpoint their location.

Juni was ready and with gurgling stomach stood motionless, staring out at the pitch black expanse, straining to see beyond the murkiness that engulfed everything. He inhaled deeply and untied the boat, leaving the ropes so they could be reached effortlessly upon return. He motored ever so slowly away from the dock, staying close enough to maintain visual contact until he reached the end. At that point he slipped into what felt like another dimension, a sinister world of eerie blackness, with the surface of the water resembling a slab of gray slate occasionally moved up and down by some unseen force beneath. He feared the darkness, but would never confess that to anyone. Besides the chugging of the engine, the only other sound was his own nervous gasps coming in short staccato bursts that caused his heart to beat so hard he felt as though it was bouncing off his ribcage. But the die was cast and there was no turning back.

As instructed, he took up a heading of 150 degrees and held this course until intercepting the 168-degree radial. The only other noise was the gentle slapping of waves against the wooden hull, the material purposely chosen to avoid possible radar detection. The boat amounted to an acoustic sponge that smelled of salt and oil. Suddenly, the din of an idling jet engine was followed by a deafening roar, a spine-chilling sound that interrupted the tranquility with throbbing felt to the bone. As a feeling of dread came over him, Juni shook so hard that it was as though his sweat had frozen and turned to ice. But the noise did provide some solace, proving that he wasn't on an uninhabited, lifeless planet. But the sounds were only out there somewhere, an oppressive force with the power to disorient. Once the jet departed the silence was once again so oppressive it seemed to have substance. The can of Coke he drank earlier worked its way through his system and he fought off the urge to vomit, instead whispering aloud, trying to convince himself there was a splendid canvas of moon and stars somewhere above the enveloping gloom. But the blackness seemed solid and eternal. Christina had hammered home the point that just like a pilot he must place *complete* faith in his instruments. Indeed, the success of the job and perhaps his life hinged on his compass and radio.

After what seemed like an eternity, the VOR needle finally centered on the 168-degree radial, meaning he was on course. But this was a short-lived respite. He and Christina had previously practiced near a VOR facility located at Riverhead, Long Island. But that was from a stationary car. Now, whenever he glanced at the radio, the boat's heading would shift by thirty or forty degrees. But if he paid attention to the compass, the VOR indicator would deflect full scale showing off-course. He felt like the Lone Ranger, but without Tonto. He occasionally looked toward the sky searching for the lunar face that had to be there, somewhere. Juni assumed the navigation would be a piece of cake, but he should have known better because nothing in his life came easy. In spite of sweating, his teeth were chattering, slamming together like torrents from a rifle firing round after round inside his brain. "I'd like to get my hands on that broad and that kid right now. Those fucking Germans always got some tricky shit up their conniving *sauerkraut* sleeves. If I overshoot the goddamn airport..?" He even contemplated turning back since Christina said all he needed to do was reverse the procedure one hundred and eighty degrees. At least the marina was still behind him. Or was it? One real fear remained. He didn't want to die. *Please God, not now.*

Christina and Erik were in the cockpit, when at approximately 8:40 a ground supervisor asked, "Any weather-related departure delays?"

Woody hadn't returned, so Christina radioed Boston's clearance delivery. "Any delays into LaGuardia?"

"They're minimal, running ten to fifteen minutes at most."

She passed on this information to the guy, who replied, "That'll work out fine. We have a short wait for a connecting passenger and now I can pin the delay on air traffic control."

After hearing the magic words connecting passenger, Christina glanced at Erik, but neither uttered a word. Just then, Woody returned, looking alarmed. "My old man's taken a turn for the worse. Are there any delays getting out? This is probably his last night."

"I just checked," Christina said softly, welcoming the momentary respite. "Boston's right at landing minimums, but there should be no difficulty departing. There are only minimal delays outbound, ten to fifteen minutes, which we would have had anyway because we're waiting for a passenger. The LaGuardia weather's above landing minimums, so we should arrive close to schedule."

"Thanks. I'll let the doctor know that I'll be there later tonight." Woody left the cockpit.

At exactly 8:50 the heavy metal doors of the armored truck were slammed shut and padlocked for the approximate ten-minute ride to Logan airport's cargo section via the Fitzgerald Expressway and Callahan Tunnel. Although a GPS device monitored their every move, Norton disliked the tunnel part because he felt if anyone were going to attack them it would be the perfect location, as all it would take were two cars to block any escape route. His senses were always on full alert and sidearm at the ready during this portion of the journey. However, there was nothing out of the ordinary other than the trip taking a few minutes longer due to the drizzle and fog. As they approached the airport, Norton hoped their flight wouldn't be delayed long because he had a date that evening. A few moments later, after meticulously checking Norton's eye retina and ID on a hi-tech scanner, the airport guards raised the steel reinforced barrier gate allowing the armored car onto the airport perimeter road. Planeside, in dampness that was so penetrating he shivered regardless of wearing a raincoat, Norton oversaw the loading of eight bags containing a little over four million dollars. When finished, he peered inside the forward cargo hold to make certain nothing other than the money was there. Once the cargo door was slammed shut he signed a document attesting to the number of bags and their proper loading, sprinted up the jetway and took his reserved seat directly above the cargo compartment. The armored vehicle would wait next to the jet with its occupants observing it until it began taxiing.

While Woody was busy reciting the Before Starting checklist, Erik silently removed the two tiny light bulbs from behind the *forward cargo door open* indicator light and placed them in his shirt pocket. His metabolism was in such high gear with a heartbeat so deafening that he feared he wouldn't hear anything spoken. Next, he tripped the circuit breaker for the cargo compartment's interior lights. To buy the needed time, he then pulled the large, number two engine generator control circuit breaker. All cockpit indicators would now show that generator as inoperative.

Juni cursed everything and everyone, including the wooden boat that wouldn't steer straight. He was still shivering inside the wetsuit, his chilly sweat akin to cold rainwater dripping down a windowpane. But in this case it was his back. How could you be sweating, freezing and frightened to death simultaneously? Even worse, the fog and sweat combination began to sting his eyes, causing more misery. He'd been in the tiny boat for what seemed like an eternity and had to be getting close to *something*, although he had no way of knowing what. As he held the VOR radio on top of the compass so he could observe both at once, the needle remained centered, indicating he was on course. Then suddenly and without warning there was a loud crunching sound and the boat lurched, coming to such an abrupt halt that Juni was knocked from his seat onto the deck. Back on his feet, he shifted into neutral, went to the engine and quickly detached the ignition wire, shutting down the engine. Squinting, he was barely able to make out the fog-shrouded outline of a shoreline. All was quiet except for the lapping of the waves. Was this the airport? From the charts he knew the runway jutted out into the bay, forming a U-shaped peninsula. But it seemed way too quiet. Maybe he'd landed someplace else? He stepped gingerly off the bow onto a blob of soft green marsh grass, his boots making a squishing sound from the suction. The sodden earth shuddered and gave way slightly under his weight, like Jell-O in a bowl when you place a spoon on it. Constantly glancing at his handheld compass, he cautiously walked on the required heading for approximately seventy-five feet. As he peered through the thick air he spotted a large yellow sign with bold, black letters stating, 'AIRPORT – NO TRESPASSING.' A chill of wonder still coupled with a goodly amount of fright ran down his spine as he murmured, "Goddamn, I made it!"

CHAPTER THIRTY-FOUR

Although in awe, Juni still didn't know his exact airport location. He continued walking in the direction of 168 degrees and a few moments later came upon a paved area that was bordered by blue lights with a row of green, recessed lighting running down the center. Christina had described these as taxiway lights. Once on the taxiway he moved in a northeasterly direction, which brought him to another bright yellow reflective sign with black letters reading N-2, the agreed-upon intersection. To validate this, he turned right and walked another hundred feet or so on southeasterly track until the white edge lights of runway 22 Right appeared. He hurried back to the boat, passing one of the small poles on the way. Was it a motion sensor? Were the cops on the way now? His wristwatch showed 9:05, meaning there were probably ten to fifteen minutes until rendezvous time. Back at the boat he lifted two of the duffels with the intention of placing them in the grass alongside the taxiway, but stopped. In case the cops were dispatched, he'd remain with the boat to make a quick getaway. Plus, forensic tests would no doubt link the bags to the mud. So, he left them on the boat and sat on the bow waiting for the now familiar high-pitched jet engine whine and hopefully not a police siren.

Bill Francis glanced at the Runway Visual Range monitor in the tower and was surprised to see the airport visibility had increased to slightly more than a half-mile, with the RVR at three-thousand feet. He immediately went to the portly Heinz and asked, "The RVR on runway 22 indicates three-thousand feet. You want me to turn the motion sensors back on?"

Heinz looked incredulous. "What're you, fucking nuts? We'll be lucky if it stays at three-thousand feet for even another five seconds, never mind five minutes, the time it takes to get them up and running. Leave 'em off."

"Whatever you say, but the regulations call for—"

"Goddamn it, Bill. I know what the regs state. Just do what I say."

"OK, it's your call."

Approximately a minute later the visibility dipped back to a quarter-mile. Pointing to the meter, Heinz said, "See. What'd I tell you?"

The huge tractor pushed the tri-jet back onto the ramp as easily as a child would roll a toy plane. Christina ordered the number one and three engines started and instructed Erik to leave the Auxiliary Power Unit, the APU, running to provide needed compressed air to start the remaining one. Woody called for taxi clearance and they were cleared to runway 22 Right via Alpha and November taxiways. The poor visibility required a reduced taxi speed.

"You guys were lucky to have arrived earlier," Francis commented, "when the visibility was better. Right now we're running delays up to thirty minutes inbound and we've already had a couple of missed approaches."

"Are there any departure delays?" Woody anxiously inquired.

"No. All I need is a release from the En Route Center, which should take only a few minutes."

They crossed over runway 15 Right and Francis instructed them to change to the tower frequency of 119.1. The big jet entered November taxiway, which ran parallel to 22 Right. The partially fog-obscured bright yellow sign indicating taxiway N2 soon came into view. They stopped at N2 and Christina positioned the 727 to block it so no other departing aircraft would be able to observe their forward cargo compartment door. As she set the parking brake the lever almost slipped from her sweaty fingertips.

"How long until our clearance comes through?" Woody asked the tower.

"I called the High Altitude Center and it should only be a few more minutes."

"Let's crank up number two," Christina commanded.

Erik reached up with trembling hands and shut off the air conditioning units to get the compressed air needed for start and turned on the four center tank fuel boost pump switches. Extending his arm, he could feel the damp perspiration under his armpit and the fine hairs on the nape of his neck quivering.

"We've got enough air pressure," he announced.

Juni heard the sounds of an approaching jet and a moment later brilliant smudges emerged from the cloaked mist, as though a shroud had been lifted. Once it passed by, he ran to the edge of the taxiway and confirmed it was a Shuttle Air 727. But he still couldn't make out the registration number on the tail. The noise was deafening and as he observed the plane came to a smooth halt. Juni ran toward the tail section until he could make out the number, N838SA. He dashed back to the boat and grabbed two duffel bags.

Hugging the fuselage as he ran to the area near the forward cargo bin, he dropped them to the pavement, returned and got the other two. The roar of the engines increased and he figured they must be starting the final engine.

"Shuttle Air 1540 your clearance came in. You ready to copy?"

"Affirmative. Go ahead," Woody replied as he copied and then read back the ATC clearance.

"You're cleared into position and hold on Runway 22 Right."

"Roger. It'll be a moment 'til we're ready," Woody replied, as the N2 gauge on the now-running number two engine reached thirty-five percent and Christina released the start switch.

"Let's perform the remaining items on the After Start checklist," she directed.

Erik interrupted. "Number two engine generator won't come on line. I can't get the breaker to close."

She swiveled in her seat to get a better look at the engineer's panel. "Try again," she ordered. But the second attempt also failed. "What do the generator frequency and voltage show?"

"Both indicate zero."

Woody turned around, attempting to get a look at the indications, but Christina stopped him. "Erik and I'll handle this. Please notify the tower we're holding on the taxiway with a mechanical problem and keep an eye out for conflicting traffic."

Woody did as instructed. The tower operator wanted to know if the trouble required any type of assistance and asked for their exact location.

"Negative on the help. Hopefully, we can rectify it. We're stopped on November taxiway at the intersection of N2."

"Have you blocked access to the runway?"

"Affirmative. If anyone needs to get to 22 Right they can

enter the runway at the taxiway behind us and back-taxi on the runway to the end."

"Roger. Keep us informed of your status."

"Take out your manual and check the possible causes," Christina told Erik. "I don't want to depart in this crummy weather with only two generators."

"A circuit breaker might have popped." Woody chimed in.

"Woody, please keep your eyes and ears outside. If you feel like you've got to do something else, pick up the PA and tell the passengers there will be a short delay while we try to resolve this."

"Good evening, ladies and gentlemen and welcome aboard. This is First Officer Montgomery speaking. We were delayed a few minutes leaving the gate due to the inclement weather, but the weather conditions at LaGuardia are much better, so we don't anticipate any inbound delays and should arrive on schedule. We're currently experiencing a minor mechanical problem, which should be resolved in a few moments. Our flying time to New York will be approximately thirty-five minutes. Thank you for flying with Shuttle Air."

The noise level was now much higher and Juni figured all three engines had to be running, meaning he had two minutes at most. *Never enough fucking time!* He spun the latch for the forward cargo door and it swung inward as smoothly and silently as night turns into day, just like Christina said. It was pitch black inside, so a breathless Juni turned on the small penlight held between his teeth and peered in. Suddenly, the clouds parted and slid away, exposing the moon. Was the fog lifting? But just as quickly dense murkiness again descended and placed a tight lid over everything. He could see the shape of two duffels right near the front, so he grabbed and dropped them to the hard taxiway. The remaining bags were inside. He reminded himself to think like a cop, meaning he had to keep

the compass resolved the problem. His ass was still dragging but his mind was already in Jersey counting the money. Approximately fifteen minutes later the dull lights of the yacht club began sporadically peeking through the thick fog like the cheerful blinking lights on a Christmas tree. He dropped the VOR radio overboard, where it immediately sank out of sight. Not another soul was around as he slowly chugged by the long wharf and turned into slip 42. He removed the copper jumpers and the engine quit. The wires went overboard and he made certain the boat was berthed in precisely the same manner. Although difficult, Juni refrained from breaking off a lock and peering inside one of the bags. He should have enough to pay off his debts and get on with his life. Although he wanted to let out a loud Brooklyn cheer, there would be plenty of time to celebrate later. After stripping off the diving suit and changing back into jeans and flannel shirt, he wrapped the other gear up in the wetsuit, tied the arms to secure it and placed the entire bundle on the dock. His watch read 9:44, meaning he would be home by two-thirty or three. After double-checking the boat and systematically wiping it down with the sleeve of his shirt, a quick glance confirmed the dock was deserted. This pleased him because it would take two trips to haul everything back to the car. He carefully placed two of the bags sideways on the narrow floating walkway between the boats so they couldn't roll off into the water, picked up the gear and two other bags and walked to his car with some difficulty. He had a nagging feeling that he wasn't alone. Sure enough, passing the clubhouse he saw the same guy still sitting outside nursing a beer. He simply gazed at the boats, while stroking a sizable birthmark on his left cheek. Juni again nodded as he passed close by. Even in the thick fog the fellow's voice carried from the porch with radio-like clarity. "Nasty evening for boating," he offered in a copious Boston accent.

"I cut my diving trip short because of this piss-poor weather. I couldn't see a damn thing. Maybe tomorrow night?" Juni replied. At the car, he felt uneasy, but couldn't put his finger on why. He dumped the gear and two bags into the trunk and locked it. Returning to the boat, the guy was no longer sitting on the porch, but was ambling toward him. Juni noticed that he was carrying a wooden softball bat in his large hands, confirming he'd come from a local game. As he passed Juni paused, an innate animal-like alarm stiffened his muscles and an internal siren screamed inside his head that this was a dangerous man. Something wasn't right. The peril suddenly came together in the viscous air. *Why would he have a wooden bat? Everyone uses metal today. With this lousy weather there couldn't have been any games. Fight or flight? No time. No choice.* With clenched fists and flexed muscles, Juni wheeled around to confront the stranger. But there was only a thunderous crack followed by searing pain that spread from his head down into his neck, followed by a descent into a bottomless pit of a slowly revolving abyss.

CHAPTER THIRTY-FIVE

"Shuttle Air 1540 is cleared for an ILS approach to LaGuardia Runway 22. The ceiling measured three hundred feet overcast, three-quarters of a mile visibility in light rain and fog. Wind, one nine zero degrees at seven knots. Cleared to land."

As the 727 touched down, Christina put a handful of levers controlling almost fifty thousand pounds of Pratt and Whitney jet engine thrust into reverse and came to a smooth halt at the Charlie turnoff. She slowly taxied to the terminal via the Inner taxiway. After securing the aircraft the crew quickly gathered their belongings. Woody had left his car in the short-term lot right across from the terminal in order to quickly get to his father's side. Erik and Christina didn't speak during the seemingly endless ride to the employee lot, where they simply shook hands before driving off.

There was endless darkness just outside Erik's line of sight on both sides of the road on the drive home, the air heavy with expectancy. McDonald's provided a quick respite to stave off the hunger. Once home, he went to the fridge and cracked one of the old man's Warsteiner beers and tried to settle back with bottle and remote in hand. He heard nothing while alternately glancing from the TV to the seemingly stationary hands of the old Bauhaus Moller clock, anxiously awaiting the agreed-upon signal.

CHAPTER THIRTY-SIX

"Mister. You all right? Wake up. Please!"

Juni looked up and could barely make out the blurry outline of two dark-haired teenaged boys, twins, leaning over him.

"You don't look good. You slip on the dock or something?" one asked, his brown eyes wide with fear.

"Where am I? Who are you? What happened?" As Juni lay there motionless, the caustic stench of creosote and coal tar arose from the dock, which when mixed with the metallic odor of his dried blood made him wonder if he was dead and embalmed. But then it came back that he was at a marina. The excruciating pain made it difficult to bring anything into focus. While attempting to get to his feet, Juni discovered that wouldn't happen, as his body seemed to be at involuntary rest. His brain felt as though it was too big for his head, which throbbed in rhythm with every heartbeat.

"Whoa, easy. You must have taken some spill. Want me to call an ambulance?"

"No!" Juni exclaimed, but then murmured, "I'll be OK. Just give me a few minutes." He took some slow, deep breaths, trying to clear his head and the hurt finally subsided to an endurable level. When his equilibrium returned, with the youth's help he slowly sat up. He finally stood with his world spinning and swaying on his feet with legs that felt like rubber bands. This vertigo sensation, when combined with the slight pitching of the dock made him almost tumble over.

"I came down to check on my dad's boat 'cause I wanted to make sure the bilge pump was working. Then I saw you lying here..." The boy gulped, obviously holding back tears.

"Don't worry. I'm all right." Juni softly patted the lad's shoulder, wondering where his brother had gone. But he realized there was only one boy. He'd been seeing double. "I must've slipped on the dock and hit my head," he said while looking down at his blood, now thinned by the rain, oozing between the boards and dripping into the murky brine. Juni took a handkerchief from his pocket, noting his keys were missing and gently touched the back of his head and grimaced, feeling sizeable swelling along with a good amount of fresh and partially dried blood in his matted hair. How long had he been out? "You know the time?"

"I don't have a watch, but it must be a little after ten."

Remembering his own, he looked down at its luminescent dial that showed a fuzzy 10:25.

"What's your name, son?"

"Anthony. Anthony Conte, sir."

Juni looked off in the direction of his car, thanked and dismissed him. As he staggered toward the ramp, he saw the lad still watching, so he gave a hopefully reassuring wave. The last thing he wanted was for an ambulance or the police to be summoned. They'd ask questions he couldn't answer. Slowly making his way up the gangway, the minute he saw them though the soggy mist the pain was forgotten as his keys protruding from the car's trunk lock told the story. Juni hoped, but knew better as he peered inside and saw the wetsuit, praying the money was still there. Seeing no bags or cash, the throbbing in his head returned with a vengeance; not only the duffels, but also the remaining borrowed money that had been in his briefcase were gone. He looked around, but the lot was deserted. He put the keys in his pocket and had a sinking feeling in the pit of his stomach as he stumbled his way back down to the *Pride of the Navy*. There was no sign of the other duffels. With his body feeling somewhere above sheer agony he returned to the car, somehow remembering to remove the cardboard from the marina lock. What would he tell Erik and Christina? How would he break the news to his brother-in-law? What the hell was he going to do?

CHAPTER THIRTY-SEVEN

It was late and United States Treasury employee Sara Jones, a young, single parent, hurried to finish up her nighttime job. She disdained the cold, fluorescent-lit government building where she worked and was anxious to return to the snug environ of her two-bedroom apartment in Washington Heights where her young children were waiting with a baby-sitter who was hopefully watching them closely. The attractive dark-haired, emerald-eyed young lady detested the walk from the US Treasury building, located on New York's Sixth Avenue to the Eighth Avenue subway line for the fifteen-minute journey to her place. Being required to follow the Federal government's strict dress guidelines meant wearing a skirt or dress. Most nights it was like running a gauntlet while walking past the derelict buildings dotting the area, as the lowlifes who called them home hooted foul things. But there was no choice because she couldn't afford many cab rides on her GS-11 salary.

She placed a key in one bag's padlock to empty its contents, scan and record the bill's serial numbers and to confirm the amounts, as she had done thousands of times before. But this time the lock wouldn't budge. She immediately summoned her supervisor Jim Hennesy, a career civil servant who she believed never had an original thought in his life. "Something's wrong with this lock. My key won't open it."

Hennesy, whose glasses were so thick she didn't understand how he could see *anything*, stood over her, looking down with disdain. He confidently inserted his master key in what turned out to be a futile, almost comical attempt to unlock it. He tried the same thing on the seven remaining bags and only four opened. A now ashen-faced Hennesy hiked up his pants waistband normally near his shoulders even further, and hollered at Sara, although she was sitting right next to him, "Call inspector Hank Selac at extension 552 and get him down here—now!"

Fitful sleep finally came, but a startled Erik was awakened on the couch by the doorbell's ring. The only other noise was the TV, with some nonsensical infomercial stating why the viewer should buy a product to promote hair growth. His first brain wave questioned why would Juni come to the house? Squinting, he turned on the dim hallway light and clad in his boxers apprehensively opened the door with veils of sleep still clinging to his eyes, keeping them partially closed. Confronted by two burly men dressed in ties and jackets, a quick glance back at the clock showed it was 1:30. The street was deep in shadows and sopping August heat, with the breathless darkness combining to make it all seem surreal.

"Are you Erik Preis?" the obviously better fed of the two asked, holding up a gold-colored badge in the faint light. These were the vultures who would be circling, looking for the guilty carcass. Although Erik knew they would be coming and soon, he still felt unprepared. As the skin on the back of his neck tingled with gooseflesh he suddenly felt more exhausted than ever before and only wanted to get this over with. Turning around, he saw both parents peering down from the upstairs hallway.

"Yes, sir," he replied with a gulp, feeling the blood rush to his head and the roses in his cheeks involuntarily blossoming.

"I'm FBI Chief Inspector John Daly," adding, "and this is Sergeant Frank Morganthaler of the Port Authority Police. May we come in?"

"Of course. I'm sorry," he said nodding his head and gesturing with his hand. The two men seemed to bring more of the heat and humidity inside with them. Erik estimated the gray-haired, pot-bellied FBI man whose jowls had lost the battle against gravity to be about fifty-five. The younger, fortyish sergeant was built like an inverted pyramid that went along with a pair of distrusting ice cold cop's eyes that seemingly knew your darkest secrets at a single glance. They shook hands, with Erik surprised that the older Daly had a vise for a grip, while the other guy's felt more like a wet mop.

What hit Daly as they stepped into the tastefully decorated house was the unique scent: more accurately, the essence. This caused him to recall a girlfriend from the distant past. Johanna Schumacher's parents had emigrated from Austria and this place had the same aroma. It was a unique fragrance far different from an American household, an alluring combination of European soap with a tiny, almost insignificant hint of a human. Not body odor per se, just a human body. This caused erotic flashbacks of Johanna, his bewitching, blond *schoen Fraulein* of a lifetime ago. Thinking back, he could actually feel body and soul stir. She had done great things to and for him. Too bad his wife, Nancy no longer had the hots for him, now generating a different type of body heat, the elevated temps of menopause. No doubt the same condition had caused her to complain loudly when his cell phone had chirped earlier while asleep, summoning him to this case. That was all they ever did in bed now, sleep, leaving only yesterday's memories to evoke how things had once been. Now, he was married only to the FBI. *Where was Johanna? What did she look like today?*

Erik's words snapped him back to the present. "Excuse me. It's late and I was out like a light." Leaving the sleep behind he added, "Let me put on some decent clothes." Running up the steps like a benched basketball player sent into a close game, Erik hurried past his parents as he sprinted into his bedroom. He managed to calm himself enough to slip on a loose-fitting pair of blue jeans and plain white tee. He descended the steps two at a time like someone anxious to help, hoping this wasn't lost on the cops. "Sorry to keep you waiting. What can I do for you?" Erik cheerfully offered between breaths, even though there was a chill in the pit of his stomach. Was there a telling flaw or did the cops picture him as a calm, cool pilot? Truth be known, he was sick with anxiety and his heart was pounding like a jackhammer. Recalling Juni's words, he tried to think like a cop. But that went by the wayside as he couldn't help but wonder if the cuffs would go on if they even simply *thought* he was involved? "Please," he offered, gesturing toward the couch, while he took a seat on another chair. Both policemen pulled out small notebooks, their eyes honed in so intently that Erik felt glued in place by their laser-like stares.

It was previously agreed that Daly would conduct this interrogation. Morganthaler removed a small, portable digital tape recorder from his shirt pocket and placed it on the table, explaining, "This device will record what's said so we can review it later. Is that acceptable?" They were using the opportunity to lock in his story and would go back, listening for any inconsistencies, knowing that many cases turned on a minute detail, perhaps a seemingly inconsequential item during the initial interview. Listening later might provide the key.

"Sure."

"Would you please state your full name and address for the record?" Erik did as requested and Daly continued. "Shuttle Air informed us you were a member of the cockpit crew on flight 1540 tonight from Boston to New York," he somberly began, ladders of wrinkles over his deeply furrowed eyebrows. Seemingly looking at a sheet of paper he was holding at arm's length, he was actually looking over it and directly into Erik's eyes trying to pick up any subtleties. Years of experience said the eyes always told the truth.

"Yes. Is something the matter?" Erik quickly added, while looking directly into Daly's blue eyes and blinking. Green-eyed innocence? "Did I do something wrong?"

Ignoring his question, Daly asked, "Did you observe anything you might classify as strange or out of the ordinary?"

Just then, Joe scurried downstairs clad in his pajamas and bathrobe. Erik was happy for the diversion when he demanded, "What is going on?"

"I don't know, Dad. These men are police officers."

"Police?"

There were no introductions and the elder Preis' face was as red as a Coke can. He mumbled incoherently and sat on the far end of the couch, glaring. Nursing a hangover, the repulsive stench of stale whiskey enveloped him and floated throughout the room like a swarm of buzzing flies alighting on everyone present. "I will stay here," he announced.

Daly wanted to question Erik alone but continued, ignoring the old man. But if he interrupted he would be told to leave. "For example, did you see anyone snooping around the plane or notice anything you might classify as uncommon? Out of the ordinary?"

Ignoring his father and still looking directly at Daly, Erik hesitated for a moment and then his face brightened. "There was something."

The FBI man glanced at Morganthaler who shifted slightly in his seat as if anticipating vital information.

"We had a mechanical problem, difficulty with a generator. The captain and I resolved it." Without waiting for a response he continued, "I haven't worked for Shuttle Air very long, but I have flown that trip before and except for the generator and some poor weather, everything else was pretty routine."

"Tell me about the generator."

Erik repeated the story he'd gone over in his mind seemingly a thousand times hoping it would appear spontaneous, not wanting to come across like an actor trapped in a bad play. "To conserve fuel, Shuttle Air's standard procedure is to wait 'til just before receiving takeoff clearance to start the final engine. On the 727 that's the center, or number two. When we got to the departure end of 22 Right, the runway we were using for takeoff, there was difficulty with that generator. Its speed is constant and is governed by a constant speed drive or CSD, and it wouldn't go on line…"

"Whoa. Slow down. I'm no pilot. To me the cockpit is just a bunch of dials and gauges."

"Sorry. Each engine has its own generator that provides electrical power to different items like air conditioning units, hydraulic pumps and the like. There is a maximum allowable electrical load for the entire plane, so when one isn't working, it puts added stress on the ones that are."

"OK. I *think* I understand better now." Daly hesitated. "If one was broken, why didn't you return to get it fixed?"

"We might have because I don't think the captain would have wanted to take off in crummy weather without it. But resetting a circuit breaker got it working and we departed."

"How long did that take?"

"I dunno. Maybe a couple of minutes..?"

"You sure about the time?"

"Yeah. A few minutes, at the most."

Daly wrote something in his notebook and asked, "Is there a portable phone in the house? Do you use a cell phone? A computer?"

"There's a portable and I also have a cell and an old laptop upstairs."

"May I see the portable?"

Erik took the white Panasonic phone from its cradle on the end table and handed it to Daly, who passed it to Morganthaler. He took out a pen and copied down the numbers and times of the received and dialed calls that were shown as he scrolled though the last twenty-five numbers.

"May I also have your cell number and the name of your cell service and internet provider?"

"My cell company is AT&T," and he provided the number, "but I don't have access to the internet." Looking meekly at his father he added, "My Dad doesn't want me tying up the phone line."

"May we take your cell and laptop? Both will be returned to you in a few days."

"Sure." Erik went back upstairs and handed them to Morganthaler.

"We'd also like to look inside your car?"

"OK. It's the blue Toyota parked at the curb. It's, well, kind of dirty. I didn't have a chance to wash it." He went into the kitchen and returned with the keys.

"Thank you, Mr. Preis," Daly stood and again extended his hand. Based on his experience and internal lie detector he liked the kid. But he also knew a good actor might beat him. "Here's my card. We'll probably have some additional questions for you later...oh, and one more thing. On the 727 is it possible to access the forward cargo compartment from the cockpit?"

A truly surprised Erik replied. "Why, no. That's impossible. But why would anyone—?"

"Sorry to have awakened you."

Erik hesitated, thinking he should appear curious. "What's this about? Did something happen? Did I do something wrong?"

"All I'm at liberty to say is that a substantial amount of money being transported on your flight is missing."

"How much?"

"I can't divulge that."

"I hope you get it back."

"We will."

Once the door closed Joe began his grilling. "What are you mixed up in?" he loudly demanded, sweating profusely, a hangover sweat.

"Nothing," Erik replied, holding up his hand trying to keep the putrid breath away.

"You are lying."

"So you say..."

At that moment the doorbell rang. Daly returned Erik's keys, thanked him and left.

When the door closed Ursula Preis rushed downstairs clad in a light fabric pink nightgown, with hair pulled back and pinned in a bun. "Come to bed, Josef," she said gesturing toward the bedroom. "Erik didn't know why they came here."

"He knows."

"For God's sake, he was sound asleep on the—"

"I don't care what he thinks. If I had money, I'd get the hell away from you," Erik yelled over his shoulder at Joe while heading to his room.

Once ensconced in their bedroom and speaking in German, Ursula pleaded, "Why are you so hard on Erik? You should treat him with respect."

"Don't give me that respect crap. You know he's been very different since he was born, doesn't resemble me and is too Americanized. His values stink. And because of you I don't even know if he's my son. Now, he's involved in something that brought the police. What will the neighbors think?"

"It's late. The neighbors won't even know," adding a wave of her hand. "He has a good job. Why would he be mixed up with anything dishonest? And as I've told you many times he is *our* son."

"And, I do *not* want to discuss this any more," Joe shouted.

Lying in bed, after overhearing his parents' conversation, thoughts from jubilant to terrifying raced through Erik's brain. The joy and fear caused a sweat with a distinctive odor. He would indulge himself with a long shower in the morning. His thoughts turned to Juni, who probably got the money, but didn't want to take a chance on calling. Good thing the phone didn't ring while the cops were there. He pictured what his share looked like, mentally stacking the money on the spotless floor. Perhaps now he could seriously consider asking Carol to marry him? She was the only person he'd ever shared that indefinable bond with.

Walking through the mist to their unmarked vehicle, the cops concluded Preis *seemed* to give honest answers. "It was a good idea to question the pilots first, especially the kid. The young ones are usually a lot easier to trip up," Morganthaler offered.

"My gut says he's not the kind to get caught up in this stuff," Daly responded in a soft voice normally reserved for kids. "He's got a good job and was sound asleep, not the signs of someone involved in a serious crime. But there was lots of friction between him and the old man."

"Like millions of others," Morganthaler interjected.

"I guess..?"

The two cops meandered in silence back to the FBI blue Ford Victoria, deep in thought, knowing the hours immediately following the crime were crucial. As a Port Authority cop, Morganthaler was somewhat accustomed to working in the middle of the night, usually on drug busts at one of the New York or Jersey airports that the PA police oversaw. Actually, he would do most anything to get out of the dingy Port Authority police station at LaGuardia, a faceless, grimy building where you froze in winter and cooked in summer. No doubt he'd bring the street smarts to this investigation, while in his opinion Daly existed in the la-la land of the Feds, a desk jockey, paper pusher who never got into the down and dirty of an assignment. But this case was intriguing, even working under Daly, the lead investigator with proprietary jurisdiction. Referred to by other cops as the big G's or suits, the FBI people were rarely awakened and required to dress in the compulsory jacket and tie and work all night. But justice never slept, meaning they still had to drive to Queens, then Jersey. It was ironic that they would be up all night yet the first person they interrogated was sound asleep and was probably back in slumber land.

"Airline pilots make good money. Why does the kid still live with his parents?" Daly muttered as they got into the car. "If I was young and good-looking like him, with a job like his, the last thing I'd want would be to live with Mommy and Daddy, especially after what we just witnessed. I'd be too busy shacking up with every stewardess I could get my body parts on."

"You're showin' your age, John. There are no more stewardesses. Nowadays they're called flight attendants." A serious Morganthaler removed a paper from his jacket pocket. "The quick stats from the airline and our cursory computer background check show he's twenty-five and brand-new, which he mentioned. Maybe that's the reason? But I'll run credit and further checks and see what I come up with. You wanna get a court order to tap the pilots' phones?" Morganthaler knew that it would be difficult for the local cops to get enough evidence to present to a judge, but the Feds carried sufficient weight to get it done without a hassle, even without clear-cut evidence.

Daly was deep in thought. "No, not yet. We have nothing. Maybe later," he sighed. "Let's start by visiting the flight attendants, as you like to call 'em and the other two pilots. After we check their backgrounds, computers, home and cell phones, maybe we'll come up with something definitive? If so, then I'll go for the wires. If any of the crew was involved, they wouldn't be pros and would make mistakes."

"The kid doesn't use the internet," Morganthaler reminded him.

"That's what he said, but maybe he's bullshitting us? His laptop will tell."

"Except his old man was sitting right there. That prick would have said something if the kid was lying."

"What really pisses me off is the switch wasn't discovered sooner, before the bags arrived in Manhattan." Daly heaved a sigh as he started the Ford, turning the air conditioning up full blast. "These fucking Fords suck. Why the hell can't they give us something decent like a Honda?" he wondered aloud as the blast of cold air hit him right in the face.

"Maybe it didn't happen 'til the bags got to Manhattan," Morganthaler ruminated aloud.

Daly didn't want to hear any of Morganthaler's Sherlock, off-the-cuff Holmes hypotheses. He was accustomed to first logically breaking down all the possibilities and doing the timeline, alone. Here, that amounted to a huge block of info that had to be whittled down, eliminating the pieces that didn't fit. Although currency was stolen, making it a federal offense, because the crime might have taken place on NY airport property the Port Authority cops were brought in, meaning Daly was stuck with Morganthaler, at least for the foreseeable future. That was OK, at least at the outset because Morganthaler better knew the inner workings of the New York airports. "In this goddamn weather either you cook or freeze," Daly interjected, feeling the dampness penetrating his flesh. "Our list of possible scenarios and perps is way too long."

"Maybe some federal government workers did it right there, in Boston or New York, or at the airport—anywhere."

"Spoken like a true cop. That narrows it down to about a hundred fucking people," Daly replied with more than a bit of sarcasm in his voice. But, if this turned out to be the case it would turn out to be the FBI's sole jurisdiction. "The one thing we do know now is that anything could have happened. Anywhere. It's a totally different world today where the bad guy doesn't always lose or get what he deserves 'cause there are lots of loose ends that never come together." Daly often made major breakthroughs by grinding everything down, which was like lifting a veil. But a repetitive routine like the transport and destruction of the money creates huge cracks in any security blanket. This was especially true for someone with insider knowledge who could outwit the system. He would have to first work out a precise time and location, T and L theory, try to see when and where the best opportunity was afforded the thief or thieves and look for a crucial piece of the puzzle. Jealousy and distrust between the feds and locals would make this process thornier. Trying to move past that he stated, "Look, Frank. We've got to immediately pool all our information. Don't shut me out.

And, no inter-agency bullshit squabbling or clash of cultures. We have to share every shred of info without going through the customary channels, even if egos get bruised and toes stepped on. That way we both win."

"You have my word there won't be anything like that between you and I. But the agency stuff could be different. Our people don't like being treated like gofers and then left on the street like dog shit. Remember what went on with the Big G, post-9/11. That was a fucking disgrace. Even though the Towers were PA property, you Feds put up a firewall as thick as a bank vault. It's a two-way information highway. I know you're never impressed with the locals, but…"

"I'll speak with my people, but old habits die hard. Make sure your guys understand that, so I won't have to pull out the gold," referring to his FBI badge, as if PA cops would genuflect in awe. Reality dictated this would have as much impact as whipping out his dick. Daly put the car in gear and turned to his new partner and using carefully chosen words said, "This ain't gonna be an easy one. It's like sinking your teeth into one end of a calzone, when the hot cheese comes out the other end and burns you. Solving this is a mission for me, like the robbery was an art form for the perp or perps." Daly hesitated and added, "I do *not* like to lose," intense beads of sweat slowly forming under the collar of his starched shirt.

"Just so *you* know. Neither do I."

Along with a throbbing skull Juni also had burning anger, but wouldn't phone Christina or Erik. No doubt the cops had already interrogated them. He found an old Mets cap in the trunk, moved the clips to the largest position and gingerly covered his head. For now, his singular priority was to get out of town, to put as much distance between himself and the rotten city of Boston, as quickly as possible. But he vowed to return, patronizing some local saloons and softball games in the hope of running into the scumbag who clobbered him. Gobbling up the asphalt on I-90 as quickly as his condition and the weather allowed, he constantly rubbed his neck and forehead in a vain attempt to rid himself of the pain emanating from inside his skull. There was still a decent river of traffic and the first roadside rest provided a dark enough location to discard the stolen license plates and purchase gauze and aspirin in the 24-hour convenience store. As the adrenaline rush from the run-in with Mr. Concrete Face dissipated, driving down the glistening, night-draped interstates, the fog and light drizzle occasionally changed into an intermittent lashing rain that clattered down, snapping against the windshield like pebbles. He studied the rain as if it held an answer. As the dark highway whipped past, the hour got later and the traffic lightened. Although exhausted and hurting, especially when he had to move his head horizontally, the weather required slower speed, which provided a bizarre form of relief, allowing him to perhaps come up with a vital but missing piece. He liked short and finite moves to solve a mystery, so during the arduous journey he repeatedly went over and over what happened. But despair replaced hope with each passing mile. Closer to home he lit up a butt. But even that tasted lousy and he threw it out the window, vowing to quit. After passing through towns that were just waking, he pulled into the driveway a bit past four, in a constant drizzle. Everything appeared ugly as the summer sun was ineffectually attempting to spread its first gray tint on top of the cloudy eastern sky and the sopping wet air was beginning to warm ever so slightly. With mist still hiding the dawn he went to bed after fitting large gauze pads on his wound so no blood would stain the pillow case. After penning a note for his wife asking not to be awakened, he was wide awake anyway because lying on his back to shield the wound from view meant placing more pressure on it. Although his head felt pulverized, anger took the top spot because he had failed. If his instincts were running in high gear knowing what that ugly bastard was up to would have surfaced in time. It also scared the hell out of him to contemplate his future. He finally dozed off, pondering how different this could have ended, with no one but himself to blame.

The investigators spent the remainder of the night conducting interrogations and took possession of the cell phones and laptops of Christina, the four flight attendants and Woody. The interviews were fairly brief because they didn't have any leads to pursue, yet. At Christina's place, considering her earnings they were surprised at how shoddy it was and that immediately raised a red flag. They took note of a new giant screen TV and expensive Bose stereo. When asked, she produced her previously-dated credit card receipts for them. They were also able to get a pretty good idea of her finances, in the process suspecting that her credit card was maxed out. Daly asked, "Does anyone else live here?"

"I have a boyfriend who occasionally spends some time here."

"Is he also a pilot?"

"No. He's a baggage handler for the same airline at LaGuardia."

"Meaning he has access to the aircraft?"

"Yes. His name is David Bennedeto. But, what is this all about?"

Both cops jotted down his name. "All we can tell you is that a substantial amount of money that was aboard your aircraft is missing."

She laughed nervously. "How much? I sure could use some."

"We can't divulge that."

"If David's got it tell him to give me some," she joked, hoping this would demonstrate her non-involvement.

Walking to the car, Daly told Morganthaler to run a credit check on her first thing in the morning. "I'm willing to bet she's hurting financially, which could provide a motive."

"I was also surprised a captain would live in a dump like that."

"Let's not jump to conclusions. Wait and see what turns up."

They interviewed the flight attendants, all of whom also lived in Queens. Nothing new was unearthed, with all four seemingly in decent shape financially.

The final stop was Woody's. Knowing that you never *really* knew people fully, that everyone had a small private room where they hid the truth about something, Morganthaler asked him, "Do you three fraternize after work, visit each other's homes, go out for drinks, stuff like that?"

Woody hesitated and finally answered, his face growing crimson. "I wouldn't hang around with that fucking bitch if she was the only other person on the face of...," he snapped. But then he stopped and glanced meekly at the cops as though this statement might somehow incriminate him.

"Oh? Why not?" Daly immediately asked, liking what he heard because it might break open a tiny crack to squeeze information through.

Woody again hesitated and then answered with a question. "You guys have any lady cops who are your boss?"

Both men shook their heads. "But that doesn't answer our question."

"Yes it does. If you did, then maybe you'd understand. That broad and I have absolutely nothing in common other than the job."

Although late, Woody's interrogation continued a while longer. Both cops came to the same conclusion. There was no way he would be involved in anything with Shepard.

While driving to work the following afternoon Erik tuned in 1010 WINS, a New York all-news radio station, but heard nothing about the heist. He also stopped at several newspaper boxes, fumbled with some coins and grabbed copies of *Newsday*, the *Daily News* and the *NY Post*. He quickly thumbed through them, but again, nothing. Hopefully, robberies were like fast food, quick and forgettable.

When the crew assembled in the brightly lit flight operations office, the previous evening's clouds were whipped away on stiff northwest winds that carried a taste of promise along with blue skies as polished as a new car. The white décor of the operations office normally made the surroundings seem cold, as this area was set up only with total efficiency in mind. But for Christina this felt like the first uplifting day in a long time. While signing the flight plan Christina saw Woody and Erik enter. "Did the two Dick Tracys, with the emphasis on the first name, visit you last night?" A jovial Christina said she told them that other than the generator problem, nothing out of the ordinary occurred. Both agreed. Christina's voice was so buoyant Erik believed Juni must have contacted her.

After Woody disappeared to grab a coffee, the operations agent motioned Christina to the phone. Hearing Juni's voice she felt another shot of adrenaline. Moving the phone behind the counter out of earshot, she pointed to the mouthpiece and silently mouthed the word J-u-n-i to Erik.

"I didn't want to call your place 'cause your phones are probably wired."

"How much?" she hoarsely whispered, barely able to contain herself. "Just tell me how much."

After a sigh on the other end of the line. "Nothing. I had it, but someone hit me and took it."

Juni's words could have been a solid punch to her jaw. She paused as she felt a cold finger of dread slice down her spine. "Whaddaya mean someone stole our money? You take me for a fucking moron."

Erik motioned with his palms for her to pipe down. Her face was now cherry red and he didn't want to draw attention to her.

"I swear on my mother. It's the truth. A guy hit me over the head with a bat and took it all."

She could envision a double-dealing Juni pushing a huge boulder to the edge of a cliff that was about to tumble off and squeeze the life out of her. "Go to hell. Where are you? I'll come there and whack you again." Breathing heavily, she stopped and rubbed her head to collect her thoughts. "Who was this guy? What did he look like? Have you ever seen him before? When and where did all this happen?"

Erik was standing far enough away so that he couldn't overhear, but Christina's expression betrayed her angst. The office was bright, but her appearance spoke darkness.

"It happened right on the dock. I don't know who he was. Did you or Erik mention anything to anyone? Someone had to know because there wasn't another person in the entire marina other than this blotchy-faced asshole. He had to be stalking me."

"I can't answer for Erik, but I never said a word, to anyone." But her mind raced back to David because she had briefly discussed the possibility they were carrying something valuable with him. And he later grilled her about what she'd uncovered. Did he somehow unearth what they were up to? Did she know any friends of David's with a mottled complexion? "The only people I ever discussed this with were you and Erik."

"I had four bags, probably over two mill—"

"I don't wanna hear that! It doesn't matter if it was fifty fucking cents. Erik's gonna be mad as hell when I tell him; unless he already knows 'cause you're in this rip-off together." Christina inhaled deeply, attempting to calm herself. Her head felt like she'd been hit. She implored Juni, "Tell me this is some kind of sick joke."

"I wish it were."

"The cops already questioned the crew."

"Look. It's no good talking over the phone. I never suspected anything like this could happen. It's a big risk but we have to meet again. Let's shoot for tonight after work at the same place as last time. Drive in separate cars and make certain there's no tail."

"How the hell am I supposed to know if someone's following me?"

"Drive a while. Then get off the parkway and double back to somewhere, like the lot where you originally parked. Or get out of your car for soda or gum, always watching for the same car with two guys who just look like cops. Keep checking in your rearview mirror for a Ford Crown Victoria 'cause that's the unmarked the cops drive. Change lanes or exit quickly and see if another car does the same. If you even *think* someone's following, go home. *Capisce?*"

"Yeah, I *capisce* all right. Now you understand or *capisce*, as you like to say," Christina growled. "We'll be there. And I'll break the news to Erik, unless like I said, he already knows." She slammed down the receiver but without enough force to attract attention.

"What bullshit are you feeding me? You take me for a fucking idiot!" an incredulous Erik shouted when they were alone. "I didn't like this from the get-go. But after putting up with so much crap, I'm entitled."

"That's all I know. Juni said he'll fill us in tonight. He emphasized to make certain we're not being tailed," repeating his precautions.

"This is one sick joke you're trying to pull." *Exactly who were the good and bad guys?* "You two in this together?"

"Don't give me that," Christina immediately shot back.

"Go to hell."

"The three of us are probably going to wind up there anyway."

Christina suddenly felt a throbbing headache that could be an aura. She immediately called crew scheduling, said she felt ill and they replaced her. Erik was livid. She hauled him into this mess, was probably trying to cheat him out of his share and now left him to stew, alone.

After spending the rest of the day in bed her headache abated enough to drive. She wore loose-fitting jeans with a matching light blue top. Nothing sexy because she felt anything but, and drove to the restaurant using Juni's precautions. Erik wasn't certain if she would show but decided to go anyway, if for no other reason than to confront Juni.

Christina arrived at Pepi's and Erik followed a few moments later. Juni was already there, wearing hurt on his sleeve like a neon sign. Sitting at the same secluded table, Erik looked at a different, pale, perhaps even smaller man. They ordered pizza and beer accompanied by an awkward silence that was easy to recognize but difficult to accurately define.

Fuck the pizza. Erik was hungry for information. The tension between them was thick, like prize fighters in the ring just before the opening bell. Erik had tough questions and would demand hard answers. He threw the first jab. Trying to ignore Juni's physical condition, he said, "You two trying to cut me out?"

Juni's features hardened and his raspy reply came. "Cut *you* out? I was the one who got beat. I wanna discover who got *our* money." He paused. "We can waste time if you want, but the guy who hit me was ugly and bearded, about forty-five, maybe five-ten, stocky, built like a weightlifter, but with a fatter midsection. He had thinning blond hair and a blotchy complexion with a birthmark, a brownish colored mole on the left cheek." Juni pointed to the area on his own cheek. "He probably shaved off the beard by now. Does this match anyone you know?"

Christina didn't utter a word, but the word weightlifter got her attention. Did this mystery person work out? With David?

No reply. "If you guys still don't believe me there was a local kid named Tony Conte who found me. His family's boat's docked there. If you want, I'll track 'em down and get his phone number so you can speak to him. You have to accept what I'm saying as the truth 'cause it's the first important step in getting *our* money back."

Erik figured the truth *might* be here, somewhere. Who could he trust? "I don't wanna go on a walk down some bullshit memory lane with you. If you were whacked so goddamned hard, how come you're here? Why aren't you in the hospital? I've got two sickies on my hands. This one called in sick today and left me with rage as my only companion," he said pointing to Christina.

"I was, was under the weather, you ungrateful little—" Christina started to say, but Juni interrupted.

"I probably have a concussion. But I'm not a doctor and I'm not goin' to one."

"Oh? Why not?" Christina chimed in.

"Whaddaya crazy? The first thing a doc would ask is what happened and if I try to bullshit the guy, he might call the cops. I'll take my chances."

"Why don't you show me where this mystery man

supposedly whacked you?"

Juni wheeled around, took Erik's hand and gingerly placed it on the back of his head. "You believe me now?"

Erik immediately pulled his hand away from the swelling in Juni's skull that was bandaged but still damp. Juni's eyebrows came together, creating creases across his forehead. Erik wondered if that created pain from pulling on the wound. Juni pleaded. "Now it's my turn. You have to be a hundred percent honest with me. None of this makes sense, 'cause the guy left the keys in the fuckin' trunk lock. For some reason he *wanted* me to get outta there. Why?" Juni whispered. "Something is *very* wrong. Did either of you slip, disclose our plan to someone? *Anyone?* Mistakes can be undone. Wrongs righted."

"I didn't say shit," Erik insisted, but then recalled the night he had begun to relate the story to Carol, but stopped. Was that enough for her to relay what was said to someone else? Could that person have passed it on? Carol wouldn't harm him but someone else might. His mind raced. What would he do now? He was right back in the same predicament. He started to speak, "If your story's true—"

"It's the truth! How much goddamn proof you need? C'mon, put it all on the table. You still don't trust me, do you?" Looking from Erik to Christina and back, Juni curled his hands into tight fists and held them in front of him as if trying to pull apart a rope. "Suspicion can eat away at people like acid, so for your information I did not take *our* money." Something, maybe resentment thumped in his temples and tears involuntarily ran down his cheeks, which he quickly wiped away. Not relishing bringing up the ghosts of the past he informed them with redness of embarrassment on his cheeks, "You wanna know the truth? This was unchartered waters for me. But it wasn't the first time somethin' like this happened. I had a good, legit job at a bank and was set for life until the day money was missing. Guess who was the *guinea* that got blamed? I always used an ethical knife with a very sharp blade at the bank, but when some private dicks they hired discovered I had been suspected of straying while in high school that was enough. A chill suddenly came over my fellow workers. Then corporate amnesia set in and all my skilled work was conveniently forgotten. People I knew for years, the same ones I worked with and called friends avoided me like I had the fuckin' plague. Overnight I was like shit on their shoes and all they wanted was to wipe me away, write me off like a bad check. I got physically sick from the pressure and finally resigned. The whole thing was hushed up and no charges were ever filed. I didn't take that dough, but knew who did. But I couldn't rat the guy out. The WASP asshole who stole it is still workin' there and probably still stealin'. The old expression that justice is blind is accurate. Overnight, I stepped from one universe into another. I was forced to deal with what appeared to be failure or worse to everyone except me and my wife, the only ones who knew what *really* happened. But silence cost me my job and long-term security," he shouted. "How do you think I felt reverting into the fuckin' fake I hated so much? I thought that person had been left behind, forever. I didn't want to do this job but stepped back into the darkness only for what it would mean for my family. So I wouldn't have to borrow from some new Peter to pay Paul. And just like the pricks at the bank you think *I* stole it." A number of diners turned and looked at them as Juni again wiped his eyes with his fingertips.

"Lower your voice," Erik demanded.

"My word is my bond," Juni growled, making blood vessels surface in his temples. "Maybe you two can't grasp the meaning of that, but we shook hands, ate and drank together. If that makes me old-fashioned in your young minds then I'm guilty as charged. Friendship is about trust and I'm no rat. The only reason I took a chance on meeting like this was to try to figure out who did it. I've always been well served by using hard logic and believe if we put our heads together and use these tools, we *might* be able to at least begin to get to the bottom of who it was. I jeopardized a lot just by comin' here. Think about that. Why would I risk meeting with two prime suspects? Instead, I'd be putting mucho distance between you and me. The cops don't even know I exist. I'm even gonna drive back to Boston hoping to spot the prick."

"All right," Christina sighed, as she peered into mahogany eyes that seemed to mirror a warm heart. Her mind was still on David. "You asked us, but maybe you mentioned something to someone?"

Juni recalled the mere fragment he revealed to Martino. There was *probably* no way Joey could have figured out what he was up to. But if he did, prying anything out of him would be hard. "You take me for an idiot?"

"It's just that we came so close," she whispered, constantly wringing her hands to force feeling back into them, at the same time trying to force feeling for Juni into her heart. They spoke in hushed tones while lucidly going over the smallest details until closing time, but couldn't come up with anything. Juni sensed they were missing an important piece of the puzzle, but didn't know what. He finally offered, "Whoever it was either had to know every detail or was the luckiest son of a bitch in the world."

"Maybe this guy was after your wallet and only discovered the money afterwards," Erik offered.

"C'mon. No one would wait like that with a baseball bat on a deserted dock just to roll someone, not knowing if the guy had a dime."

"For now it's the only plausible explanation."

"I'm returning to Boston for a couple of days. Maybe Mister Asshole will do something really dumb, like driving to the ball field in a flashy new Jag or bedecked with jewelry? It's a long shot, but might pay off."

"Does anyone know how much we had?" a dejected Christina asked. She wanted to forgive, but found that difficult.

"The cops will keep that hushed up," Juni added. "But it had to be at least a couple of million."

"I asked them that question. Their only reply was that it was a substantial amount," Erik added. He was out of fuel and running on fumes. "Can either of you help me?" he pleaded. "My deadline's almost here."

Christina wondered about *her* future and how she could pay the next term's tuition for Laurel and buy Jimmy's I-Mac and printer. What effect would all of this have on her relationship with both? On top of everything else, she just discovered David's tuition money never made it to the school. The bursar had called and said he still owed it. No grades would be issued until it was paid. He probably pocketed the cash. For the foreseeable future he was the only constant in her life and she didn't want him out—yet. Although he didn't make her heart melt like the water in a frozen stream at spring's first thaw, she was more terrified of being all alone, like her mother. "I'd like to," she replied, "but I'm broke."

Erik looked to Juni. "Sorry, but the guy even grabbed money I borrowed. I got plenty to worry about."

Erik's brain raced. What the hell was he going to do? He chewed on that during the seemingly endless drive home and again in bed, until he finally fell asleep.

CHAPTER THIRTY-EIGHT

Daly, Morganthaler and a sizeable cadre of FBI and Port Authority police pored over all the possible angles during their systematic investigation. After securing a list of crew and passenger names they painstakingly checked out each, looking for criminal records, mob-related activity or other connections. Daly ran a background check on all possible suspects in similar crimes nationwide, while Morganthaler, with the help of some contacts in the NYPD reached out to confidential informants, small-time hoodlums on the cops' payroll. Per chance, someone might have attempted to dispose of old bills through the criminal world. But all these came up empty-handed.

The FBI's forensic experts that worked at headquarters on Pennsylvania Avenue in Washington weren't much help either. The 727 was pulled out of service the following day over Shuttle Air's objection, and they went over the forward cargo bin with a fine tooth comb. But no fingerprints, blood, fibers or other material that couldn't be accounted for was found. Although human hairs were discovered, no matches were in the FBI's criminal DNA data base. The same was true for the duffels. The latter turned out to be unnumbered, imitation army surplus sold in thousands of outlets throughout the US, Europe and Asia. The same held true for the locks, two of which were so old as to be untraceable. The newer ones were eventually tracked to auto-supply stores in Dedham and Newton, Massachusetts. There were no surveillance cameras in either store and interrogations of the cashiers were no help. None recalled the purchases nor could they could identify any suspects from snapshots provided by police, including the crewmembers' photos. A list of potential suspects, including government workers, passengers and other airline workers was drawn up. Some were grilled at length, but this also came up empty handed.

A routine credit check uncovered Erik's financial dilemma and showed Christina's credit card was borrowed to the max. So the possibility of flight crew involvement raised some eyebrows. The two men met at Daly's office, where the first split between the locals and FBI surfaced when Morganthaler said, "Let's bring 'em in and lean on 'em."

"Who?"

"The kid and the broad. Let's tell the young one, the kid, that she implicated him. He would probably lose his nerve after ten minutes alone and the Stockholm syndrome would kick in. He'd work with us."

"That's fucking asinine," an unyielding Daly replied. "You're overreaching out of frustration. You think if he planned out some complex plot that he'd just cave? So, he owes some money and Shepard's credit card is maxed out. We've got to come up with better evidence, so let's wait for Preis' bank deadline and see what happens."

No doubt the suits would fuck things up, again. "If it was up to me I'd lock the kid in a room for as long as it took to get some answers."

"Well, it's not your call." To appease him somewhat, after re-reading the tower's transcribed conversation tapes, Daly suggested they again interrogate each pilot separately to discuss the particulars of the aircraft's generator problem in greater detail. "Just don't let on that we know about the money Preis owes or Shepard's debts."

Morganthaler reluctantly agreed, but nothing new came from these interrogations. They then reconfirmed with Boeing that there was no possible way to access the cargo compartment from the cockpit, in the process verifying that the generator problem was almost an everyday occurrence for a jet of that age. But a subsequent check of that particular aircraft's maintenance log revealed that jet had no previous history of this particular malfunction, which raised a tiny red flag. The delay had been slightly less than four minutes. Was that long enough to pull off a well-executed robbery? It also came to light that Shepard had reported to her chief pilot about Montgomery's questionable performance during a previous flight emergency, strongly recommending he be sent to alcohol rehab or if he refused, his employment be terminated. This was certainly not the action of a partner in crime. Montgomery remained the odd man out, so he was also re-interviewed.

Daly and Morganthaler arrived at his chic suburban New Jersey home early in the evening. His wife, Ingrid answered the door and ushered them into the den where Woody was watching TV. He clicked it off and invited them to be seated.

"We won't take much of your time," Daly told him, "but want to ask you some additional questions about the ground delay in question." Woody nodded his head. "In your opinion, could someone have opened and removed anything from the forward cargo bin while the crew was busy resolving the electrical malfunction? If so, could the cockpit crew have missed it?"

Montgomery put on a pensive expression. "I don't believe that would have been possible. Shepard had given me specific instructions to keep my attention focused on cockpit communications and the surrounding area because she didn't want anything to happen..."

"Like what?"

"Conflicting traffic or crucial missed communications with the tower would be the two best examples. There have been a number of near misses in Boston involving aircraft taxiing while others were landing or taking off."

"Can you be more specific?"

"I worked the radios, informed the passengers about our short delay and kept an eye peeled outside. If the forward cargo door had been opened, I almost certainly would have seen or heard *something*."

"Are you saying it would have been impossible?"

"Probably. Plus, there's a door light that would illuminate on Preis' panel if that door were opened." Woody then added, "Our delay was only a few minutes. There just wouldn't have been enough time to do anything."

The lawmen thanked Woody and left. Other policemen interviewed every passenger once again, attempting to establish any potential link between one and any crewmember, airline or government personnel, a time-consuming task that again came up empty. Next, Daly and Morganthaler went over all of the written interview summaries, along with a computerized spreadsheet on which all the possible witnesses and suspects were placed at different, case-important times and places. These T and L sheets are used to identify and possibly come up with a list of suspects with the highest probability of involvement. They were able to track with a large degree of certainty the movement of the bags from beginning to end of the journey with the exception being from the time the plane began taxiing until it landed and parked at the gate. Although there was no hard evidence implicating them, Shepard and Preis remained high up on the suspect list because of the T and L sheets.

After speaking with Transportation Security Administration officials, Daly and Morganthaler learned that infrared motion detectors that sensed heat and/or motion had been installed along the area bordering the bay adjacent to Runway 22 Right. The TSA officials said these were tied into warning devices located in the air traffic control ground controller's work area. If anyone had ventured onto the airport boundary near the plane, their movements should have set them off. However, the standard operating procedure was to deactivate them when the airport visibility dropped below a half a mile. This was done to prevent any possible conflict between a car sent to investigate and aircraft taxiing for takeoff. They had been deactivated prior to the time Shuttle Air 1540 pushed back from the gate. But the weather bureau records showed the visibility had improved to above a half-mile for a brief period, yet the detectors weren't reactivated. The cops interviewed Bill Francis and wanted to know why. He responded that he had brought this to the attention of the tower supervisor, Tony Heinz who had ordered they be left off because he felt the weather would quickly drop back below the minimum, which it did within moments. The cops interviewed Heinz and he confirmed that. A quick check of Heinz's finances showed nothing awry. He was married with a couple of older, married children and had a few bucks in the bank. During Heinz's interrogation he mentioned Francis' previous error and how he was faced with the loss of his job if he screwed up again. He felt that was why he had asked Heinz to reactivate the sensors. Could Francis somehow be involved? His name was added to the suspect list.

After consulting with the FBI's aviation experts, the cops went to Shuttle Air with a request to pull the plane's flight data and voice recorders to have them analyzed. The voice recorder had a constant erase feature that went back only forty-five minutes, rendering it useless. But if the forward cargo door was opened would it show on the flight data recorder? This analysis was an expensive and time-consuming process. After assuring the airline that they would pick up the tab, Shuttle Air sent the flight data recorder to Data Link, a high tech laboratory located just outside of New Orleans, where its contents were decoded and carefully analyzed. However, this jet still had the older type of recorder installed, and any door opening wouldn't show up provided the aircraft was on the ground. Only if the door opened once airborne would that show. There were no irregularities evident other than the generator problem.

Daly raised the possibility that perhaps someone could have come over in a boat and somehow managed to access the cargo bin without anyone the wiser. He called Boston FAA officials, identified himself and got the latitude/longitude coordinates for the departure end of runway 22 Right. He contacted Department of Defense officials to ascertain if a global positioning device, a GPS was used to navigate to or from any location with those approximate coordinates the night in question. It would have been only a short distance, so something like that should be easily recognizable. The DOD officials checked the date and time for six hours before and after the flight departed, but came up empty-handed. No coordinates were selected other than for flights that relied upon GPS and all of these matched the exact numbers for their departure gates.

The increasingly-frustrated investigators concluded if any pilots were involved it must have been Shepard because the captain should be aware of everything. Her alimony, high credit card balances and child-support payments might provide the motive. Maybe she stayed in the background while another person carried it out? They called and spoke with her exes, both of whom supplied credible alibis for the night in question. The cops checked them out and were satisfied with both. Each ex spoke about her with more than a hint of disdain in their voice.

They had Shuttle Air pull up Shepard's computer records and a red flag was immediately raised when it was discovered she had rummaged around in a restricted area of the airline's mainframe. This potential breakthrough got their adrenalin flowing and the cops wanted to question her further. Although unable to squeeze her more without other still-missing details, they drove to LaGuardia and caught her off guard as she sat in a remote corner of the airport coffee shop prior to her first flight. Daly grabbed a cup of coffee and sat down right next to her, blocking any exit, while Morganthaler sat across the table. They might finally have come up with a solid lead.

"Did you recently snoop in an area of your Company's computer where you weren't authorized?" a somber Daly asked, grimacing after burning his mouth on the steaming, foul-tasting brew, hoping she would deny it.

Although the question was not unexpected, Christina felt the cold finger of fear poke at her psyche. Outwardly composed, but inwardly nervous, she calmly replied, "Yes. Once," wondering if they could see through her façade?

"Why?"

"'Cause the final flight was being delayed almost every night and as captain, I wanted to know why." She hesitated, a solemn look on her face. Her plan all along was to put them on the defensive if this arose. "Please confirm that your positions allow you to be privy to what I am about to say because it concerns airline security. Are you?"

"We'll ask the questions," Daly replied, "but the answer is yes."

"If I find out later you're not, you'll have hell to pay," she countered, attempting to display confidence she wasn't certain she had. "As required by TSA and FAA regulations, each night I received notification that an armed sky marshal would be riding in the cabin and that we were being delayed until he boarded. But we weren't supposed to incur a delay for that reason unless there was a known terrorist threat. If that was the case, I was also supposed to be informed. Yet no one said a word about that. So, I checked in the computer after work and discovered the reason," she responded a nonchalantly as possible, while looking both men directly in the eye.

Morganthaler asked with gray eyes as cold as steel, "So you knew about the armed guard and the money?"

"Only after I discovered a Treasury agent was doubling as the sky marshal. That explained the delays and was all I cared about. The rest didn't concern me."

"Let me repeat myself. You did know there was money on board your flight. Correct?"

"Of course. But I didn't know how much."

"Why didn't you tell us about this?"

"Because it's strictly a security issue and didn't have anything to do with your supposedly missing money."

The cops just stared blankly at each other. Yet another stone wall.

"Who else lives with you?" Morganthaler continued,

grasping for something, anything.

She sighed. "Like I told you, I have a friend who's a baggage handler and stays over occasionally." When asked, she voluntarily provided additional information about David, including the gym where he worked out in Manhattan. After the cops left Christina immediately called his cell, but there was no answer. The phone was probably in his locker and she didn't want to leave a voice message.

The two policemen drove to the upscale PUMP health club in midtown Manhattan and parked their unmarked in front of a fire hydrant. Daly placed his official FBI business tag on the dashboard, hoping they wouldn't be ticketed. After showing their credentials, the clerk pointed out David, who was bench pressing a lot of weight.

"Mr. Bennedeto?" Daly asked the powerfully built man.

"Who are you?" David answered, continuing to lift.

Both men took out their shields. "I'm chief FBI inspector John Daly and this is Port Authority Police Sergeant Frank Morganthaler. Stop what you're doing and take a seat over here," Daly said, pointing to a small table in an area where shakes and protein drinks were dispensed. After David re-racked the weights he became visibly antsy. Maybe the cops wanted to question him about the missing baggage items? Both policemen immediately took note of his edginess. Daly's innards involuntarily tightened and his cop's sixth sense, which was really a sharply-polished talent of close observation and interpretation, honed in. The cops stood while David was seated and kept his eyes on the table, not looking directly at either policeman. Daly read him like a polygraph machine. "Where were you on Wednesday night the 10th at approximately 9 P.M.?"

His mind raced. When had he pilfered the ring? "I, uh, think

I was working."

"What do you mean you *think* you were working? Were you or not? Just to refresh your memory, it was raining lightly that night and we wanna know exactly what you were doing."

"Yes. I worked that night at LaGuardia airport where I'm employed as a baggage handler for Shuttle Air. My shift runs 'til around 10 P.M. when the final flights arrive."

"Can you prove that?"

"I'm paid by the hour. The airline has a record of all of my time down to the minute."

"We're not referring to an official record. Are there any fellow workers who can vouch for you?" a frowning Daly asked, knowing it was likely that the heist didn't occur at LaGuardia as the jet never stopped until at the gate. After that, no unauthorized persons were near the forward cargo hold. But something was definitely amiss here. This guy's behavior said he was lying or withholding something.

As his mind started to clear, David recalled the last time he lifted any jewelry was before the 10th. This must concern something else. Finally looking up, he said, "There were a number of people I worked with for the entire time."

"Write down their names," Morganthaler demanded, handing him a pad and pen. David jotted down the first and last names of three people, one a supervisor and two other co-workers who could verify his presence.

"You know Captain Christina Shepard?"

David glanced from one cop to the other, still avoiding prolonged eye contact. "Why do you ask?"

"Let's get something straight, right now. We'll ask the fucking questions; that is unless you would rather do this at the stationhouse?" Daly said.

"Go ahead and ask," David replied. Both cops noticed beads of sweat on his forehead that weren't there before.

"Are you living with her?"

"What goes on between us is our business. I didn't know it was a crime to live with another consenting adult," a more confident, almost sneering David replied. "I don't think it's proper for you to be asking me this question."

Morganthaler was pissed. "Not proper? Oh really? A serious crime was committed, and—"

"I don't know nothin' about any of that shit," David interrupted. "All I do is slam bags at the airline, go to school and work out at here—"

"Shut the fuck up," a now red-faced Morganthaler told him. "I'm tired of listening to you. You have another address other than Shepard's where we can reach you? Or like I said, we can get the information in a more formal setting? You'll also have the right to an attorney there."

The word attorney immediately got David's attention. "Yes. I have a small place I rent in Brooklyn," he gulped, not wanting to go anywhere near a police station or lawyer. "I sleep there sometimes, usually when I work out late. But listen, Shepard doesn't know about that and—"

"Give us the address and phone number," Daly ordered. He was losing patience with this asshole. "Do you use email and/or the internet? Have a cell phone?"

"Yes."

"Jot down the cell number, your internet provider and your email address."

David scribbled all the requested information, stating that he used a jointly owned laptop with Shepard for the internet.

"You don't have your own?"

"No. I use hers for school."

"We'll find out if you're lying."

"I swear. I'm not." He whined.

"You'd better not be." The two policemen looked suspiciously at him and handed him their cards. "Rest assured that we'll be speaking with you again, shortly. Can we assume you'll either be here, at work, Shepard's or at this other dump?" Morganthaler added, knowing the lousy section where it was located.

"Yes," a now contrite David replied.

After leaving the gym Daly commented, "I do not like that sleaze. He's mixed up in something that he's trying to hide. I doubt if it had to do with the money, but we'll keep a close eye on him. Why would Shepard hang out with a scumbag like that?"

"I don't know, but I agree with your opinion."

David hurriedly changed into street clothing and sped to Christina's. A haggard-looking Christina was lying on the couch, watching television. "How was your workout?" she softly asked.

"Don't give me your bullshit," he immediately replied in a high-pitched tone. "What the hell have you been up to?"

"What do you mean?" a stunned Christina asked, standing up.

"Two fucking cops paid *me* a visit at the gym over something."

"Maybe it had to do with your stupid luggage scam?"

"I doubt it, since one was FBI," he replied, poking her hard on the shoulder. "I think you stole something off your plane."

"That hurt," she said rubbing her shoulder. "Keep your goddamned hands off me. What're the steroids you're taking making you crazy? For your information, you're messing with interstate commerce, so the FBI *would* be involved with your baggage shit. I tried to warn you, but—"

"This probably has something to do with that guy you told me about," he screamed. "You got something. Was it money?"

She turned away and when he spun her around, she was crying. "My epilepsy symptoms have returned even though I'm taking medication. Probably 'cause of all the stress you pile on me. Don't add to it."

"Let me see if I've got this right. You expect me to feel sorry for you over some bullshit disease. What do you take me for, a fuckin' moron?" Without saying another word he stormed out, slamming the door with a loud crash.

Christina went to the phone and dialed Mimi's number. The time had arrived. She *had to* forge a closer relationship with Laurel. She also had to relay the bad news about next semester's tuition. How would she react? The phone was picked up on the second ring. "Hi, Mimi. It's Christina," she said, trying to sound chipper but not doing a very good job.

"Oh. Hello, Mrs. Shep, er, Christina."

"I'd like to speak with Laurel."

Mimi hesitated, finally sighing, "Hold on. I'll get her."

She could picture Laurel and at the sound of her voice, Christina's spirits would be lifted as though sunshine had just broken through the clouds at thirty-five thousand feet.

"Hello."

"How are you, honey? It's your mother."

"I'm OK."

"Did you follow my advice and see a neurologist?"

"Yes. He mentioned that studies show epilepsy *could* be genetic. Doctors have recently isolated the genes that might be responsible. He did a blood test and I don't have any of the genetic markers. So, everything should be fine."

Christina sensed a common bond rapidly slipping away.

"He also said that I shouldn't lose any sleep worrying."

Christina found herself at a loss for words. "That's great," she managed. "I also have a bit of bad news. I'm frequently getting partial complex seizures. That means I can't take a chance and fly, so I won't be able to come up with next term's tuition."

"After you told me about your epilepsy I expected that might happen, so I went to see the dean. I explained the details of the situation without mentioning your disease and asked if the school could help."

"What did he say?"

"Because my grades were so good, they offered me a full scholarship for the remainder of my undergraduate work and will assist me in securing one for law school."

"Oh, I'm so happy for you." Fortunately, Laurel couldn't see the frown on her face.

"I have to be honest," Laurel continued, "my feelings toward you are ambivalent. I don't dislike you, but really don't know you either. I do appreciate your telling me about what happened with my father. Although we don't know where we're headed when we depart this life it's nice to hear the details about the arrival." Slight hesitation. "But *you* walked out of my life. And now barge back in expecting me to embrace you. I can't do that, at least not yet. Mimi is the only mother I've ever known and loved. It will take me time to see if I can adjust and feel the same way about you."

Christina mustered all the strength she could and told her, "I want you to know that while you're deciding, I'll always be here for you." Deafening silence came from the other end, followed by a frosty goodbye that perhaps mistakenly sounded final. This meant she was at the one place she dreaded most, *completely* alone.

She went to bed but even after taking two strong sleeping

pills couldn't sleep. Everything in her life seemed to be crashing down around her. Why could she never catch a break?

CHAPTER THIRTY-NINE

As Erik's August first deadline approached and no check arrived, the bank manger phoned the airline executive offices and was eventually routed to O'Brien. After a lengthy discussion the bank granted an additional fifteen-day grace period. He would have to come up with the entire amount by that time.

Daly secured a secret court order allowing him to keep tabs on Erik's, Christina's and David's finances. At Morganthaler's insistence he also went to a friendly Federal Judge in the Manhattan Eastern District Court and got permission to wire Christina's and Erik's home phones. Everything they laid their hands on showed Erik was flat broke. The pilot involvement theory began running into strong headwinds. This became more evident after the FBI's examination of the pilots' cells, home phones and computers showed they had never contacted each other. They anxiously awaited Erik's new deadline, as the potential loss of his job might force a move.

Daly took all the known facts and shook them down, alone in his office, surrounded only by the FBI's reference books and Manual of Rules and Regulations, better known as the Big Manual.

As he sat behind his hopefully intimidating desk, he was perplexed. Although the T and L sheets pointed to the flight, his hypothesis changed once he looked at the evidence garnered thus far. The fact that Shepard and Preis were virtually penniless and that Montgomery saw or heard nothing meant things pointed elsewhere, in another direction. But where? Maybe during the transport or counting process, with an insider knowing how to fool the system? The torn-up newspapers indicated New York, although the lock purchases were closer to Boston. Daly knew he had to keep an open mind on *everything*. He reviewed the videos of the counting process a number of times, but they showed nothing out of the ordinary.

This meant that despite his high security clearance, Chris Norton might be involved. Since he was a Federal employee, Daly got a court ordered wiretap, and his cell phone, computer, personal life and financial statements were intensely scrutinized. They discovered his bank accounts contained large balances, more than expected based on his government income. From the wiretaps they learned he had another business. It was decided to bring him to Morganthaler's office for questioning. Morganthaler was running late, so Daly watched Norton through a one-way mirror as he sat in the interrogation room alone, cooling his heels. It was obvious that he was not accustomed to being on this side of the mirror in a place that reeked of coercion. He reminded Daly of a new age cop, young and handsome with a dapper appearance, lots of hype and bullshit. Morganthaler finally arrived and both cops entered the room. "You know why you're here." They purposely hesitated, sipping coffee. "Where do you get your money? Your accounts contain way more than someone with your job should have."

"I own a business."

"We know that. What type? And don't bullshit us."

"Since you know so much about me, then you should also

know I'm a personal trainer and nutritionist. Those were my majors in college. I provide diet and workout guidance, mainly for Baby Boomers like you," he said nodding toward Daly. "Older, fat people who want to lose weight and/or tone up." Daly glanced at his protruding gut, hopefully covertly. Speaking directly to Daly, he said, "After my clients answer questions pertaining to their lifestyle, daily routine, eating and drinking habits, I recommend a combination of exercise, diet and supplements. Since I have mornings off, I also train and counsel them. I get paid hourly and recently expanded my business by instituting a specific regimen in conjunction with a doctor who specializes in geriatric medicine for people with age-related problems like high blood pressure, high cholesterol or diabetes." Daly thought of his own blood pressure, which was elevated the last time he had it checked. "Because of the aging US population this has plenty of potential. The results so far prove this correct."

"What's this doctor's name?"

"Gus Miller . His office is in Manhattan." He sighed. "Look, you're wasting your time. Every movement of the armored car was tracked by GPS units." Without waiting for a reply he continued, "So you know my vehicle was always moving. I couldn't, wouldn't be involved," he pleaded. "You think I like this happening on my watch? We're on the same side."

Ignoring his comment, Morganthaler asked, "Shut up. You see or hear anyone open the cargo compartment?"

"No. If someone opened it I would probably have heard, and definitely would have gone to the cockpit and told the crew to return to the gate. I have that power. It's in the contract with the airline. One time we even simulated someone opening and closing the door while I was blindfolded and I definitely heard it."

"You're saying that would have been impossible?"

"I don't like to use the word impossible. Highly unlikely would be better."

Daly continued. "There are GPS units locked onto each bag when they leave the downtown Boston location, correct?"

"Yes."

"But they're removed just before they're loaded onto the plane. Correct?"

"Yes."

"Why?"

"I made the suggestion they be left on, but the airline wouldn't allow it, said it might interfere with the plane's navigation system. So, the seat position was the next best thing. The GPS units are reattached immediately at LaGuardia."

The cops later confirmed everything Norton had said. With nothing more to go on all they could do was continue monitoring him. But nothing surfaced. "I just can't dismiss this guy," Morganthaler declared a week later. "Maybe there's a dark secret somewhere in his personal closet and he's being blackmailed? Or caught up in some kind of conspiracy? His explanations are a bit too pat. I'd like to continue his surveillance."

"Even if all of that is true it still doesn't even begin to explain how he pulled this off," Daly sighed. Since it was the cops watching him, once again he reluctantly went along. No subsequent findings even remotely pointed to Norton, so Daly downgraded him to a lower priority in his book. The entire investigation was going nowhere. It was like playing poker without a full deck. Frustration set in. The latest dead-end meant they needed to start over again, maybe look elsewhere.

The time between when the plane began taxiing until takeoff and between taxiing and arrival at the gate continually surfaced on the T and L sheet as a high possibility, so the new definition of elsewhere was FAA ground controller Bill Francis. They knew Francis was in trouble for the near miss. Heinz had downplayed the blunder as the controllers for each runway operated on different radio frequencies, meaning that besides speaking with the pilots they also needed to coordinate with each other. A harried Francis stated he had done so, but the other controller denied it. The investigation came down to who they believed. Francis became the fall guy.

Another court order was secured and Francis' financial records were scrutinized. Nothing of substance turned up, so Daly and Morganthaler flew to Boston, rented a car and visited him at his New Hampshire home. It was a modest, old clapboard farmhouse with an adjacent small plot where he, his wife and two young daughters grew organic vegetables. Very bucolic.

"Mister Francis?"

"Yes."

"I'm FBI Chief Inspector John Daly and this is Sergeant Frank Morganthaler."

Francis face went pale. The two cops immediately noted that.

"May we come in?"

Francis didn't utter a word, just motioned them inside. His wife and children were in the garden, so it was just the three of them. Awkward pleasantries were exchanged and Daly got right into the business at hand.

"What is your financial situation?"

"I'm not a millionaire, but I do OK."

"We know you're an air traffic controller." Francis began to speak, but Daly cut him off. "We also know about your near miss problem at work, and—"

"That wasn't my fault. The other controller—"

"That's not why we're here. This concerns another matter."

"What?"

"We're not at liberty to say, but it involves stolen money."

"Stolen money?" An incredulous Francis told them, "I don't know anything about that."

"Then for starters we presume you wouldn't mind giving us your cell phone, computer and internet provider so we can check out some items. They'll be returned to you shortly."

He started rapidly tapping his feet and small beads of perspiration formed on his upper lip. "You can have my cell, but the laptop contains confidential financial information I don't want anyone to view."

"Look," an angry Morganthaler stated, "we can either do this the easy way or the hard way. We can and *will* get a Court order for the computer, within a few minutes."

Francis was visibly upset, but went into another room, returning a few moments later with a HP laptop. "All I ask is that you don't tell my wife," as he handed it to Daly.

"Tell her what?" he asked in his best Father Confessor voice. "This relate to the theft? Is there anything else you want to tell me?" almost adding, "my son."

"No. You'll see."

"Is this your only computer?"

"Yes."

"We'll find out if you're lying. And, if you try to clear out, you'll be tracked down."

"I'm not."

A subsequent check of the computer's hard drive at the FBI's lab showed Francis fear was caused by his gawking at young, naked boys and girls in various sexual acts. He paid the substantial charges that went along with his leering. But since all the participants were purportedly eighteen years old, no action was taken. His computer was eventually FedExed back to him, with nothing further said. Another dead end.

CHAPTER FORTY

Erik flew a morning shuttle the following week with O'Brien in command. Under FAA regulations the minimum requirement is every pilot, including the chief pilot must have three takeoffs and three landings every ninety days. Maybe O'Brien was simply meeting that obligation? This appeared to be so when he informed the disappointed copilot that he would be handling every takeoff and landing. The bright, blue hue of the sky made the high thin cirrus clouds resemble white sheets billowing softly on a clothesline in a light breeze. The weather conditions might have been nice, but the atmosphere O'Brien emitted was more akin to an approaching cloudburst. The vibes were so ominous that Erik felt like a frightening tsunami was gathering, about to break. Not Mother Nature, but the crushing power of corporate America.

Although the two roundtrips came off without a hitch, Erik sensed his every move was being watched. This was confirmed when O'Brien told him to report to his office. Could he make it there with all the weight he was carrying on his shoulders? The acrid stench of fear and tension screamed out that his entire life might be at stake. He was brusquely told to be seated by the heavyset secretary whose flowery dress couldn't disguise her disdain. What did she know that he didn't? The room was eerily silent except for a wall clock loudly ticking in the background. After what seemed like an eternity of covert glances between Erik and her, a stern-faced O'Brien emerged and motioned him inside. Erik took the seat on one side of the huge desk adorned with a model Shuttle Air 727. As O'Brien sat down his immense belly pressed against the other side. "All right. Let's get right down to business. The top bosses have been notified by the police that you're under investigation concerning the theft of money missing off one of our flights."

Erik felt his heart fluttering like the leaves on a tree just before a storm, his hands gripping the arms of the chair so hard his knuckles hurt. Did the cops uncover something? Were they going to take him into custody?

"I flew today to check on your performance and also questioned Captain Shepard about your work. She reported you do an excellent job and are a loyal employee."

Erik breathed a slight sigh of relief, making a mental note to thank her.

"Shuttle Air has invested beaucoup bucks in your training. Your flight engineer's license cost us approximately sixty thousand. If you leave the employ of Shuttle Air for *any* reason during your first two years, you signed an agreement to reimburse us that amount."

Erik felt his stomach churning like the sea before a powerful storm.

"The police investigation also uncovered that you are about to default on a sizeable bank loan, approximately forty thousand dollars."

"I—"

"I'm not finished. As to the missing money, all the police will say is that the flight crew is suspect. I doubt Captain Shepard or

First Officer Montgomery would have any involvement in that sort of thing and told them so. You, I don't know about. However, I am *very* troubled about your bank debt. Let me read what's contained in our Flight Operations Manual as it relates to this." O'Brien picked up the thick book and began to thumb through it.

"I'm already familiar with that passage. I've missed only one payment and plan on speaking with the bank to see if an arrangement can be worked out 'til next year, when—."

"Don't bother. Their collections manager called me and you have only until the fifteenth of this month. There aren't going to be any more extensions. You'll have to come up with *all* the money by then or I'll fire you—period. That means you'll not only owe the money to the bank, you'll also be on the hook for our sixty grand." O'Brien looked at a paper lying in front of him on the desk and shook his head. "I cannot understand why you were hired with knowledge of this liability. All the head of Human Resources would say was that they knew, but still offered you the job. You're probably aware that if you're fired it will be impossible to get another flying job. *Anywhere.*"

Erik felt the blood rushing to his head and knew that his cheeks were aflame. O'Brien's eyes seemingly indicated he was enjoying this.

"The *only* way to hold on to your job is to pay off your entire debt by the deadline. You know the consequences if you don't."

"That's not possible," Erik stammered, a large lump forming in his throat.

"That's not my problem."

"It's not like I used the money for drugs or gambling. I borrowed it for flying lessons."

"I don't give a shit. And don't think what Shepard said will protect you. You're running on empty, mister and better come up with something, fast."

The furrows in O'Brien's face seemed even more pronounced, highlighting his importance in Erik's life at the moment. His career might still be salvaged if he could somehow get the needed cash, somewhere. "What if I repay the loan in full by the deadline?"

"That's your *only* option." O'Brien waited a long moment and added, "Or, I'll allow you to resign. Now. At least that way you *might* be able to find another flying job." He slid an official, typed document across the desk. "Of course, you'll still have to reimburse us for the training costs."

Erik couldn't believe O'Brien had a typed resignation letter ready for his signature. No wonder his secretary looked troubled. "No! I, I worked too long, too hard for this job. Plus, I'd owe even more."

"You have two weeks."

An icy dread immediately formed in Erik's brain. Everything seemed so remote, so surreal it was as though he was seeing O'Brien through a telescope with an out of focus lens. His brain pounded and his mind flew faster than a jet. Searing hot tears involuntarily sprang from his eyes, ran down his cheeks and onto his neck, staining his collar, while his throat burned from refluxed stomach acid. "But, but this job is everything to me."

"Oh, please! You think I'm running a day care center here? You should've considered that beforehand. Your failure to repay definitely fits the definition of being fiscally irresponsible." O'Brien got up from his chair and turned away. "You know your choices. Pull the door closed as you leave." O'Brien disliked Preis even more. No doubt he had everything handed to him on a silver platter because of his good looks. The faggot personnel pencil pushers probably gave him the job because he fit their handsome airline pilot image. Hell, they probably fawned over him. O'Brien couldn't wait 'til two weeks passed to fire him. After Erik departed he picked up the phone and reported to upper management what had transpired. This way when it came time for his pink slip there would be no overriding him.

Erik just sat in his parked car for several moments with blurred vision, silently watching the fuzzy-looking jets taking off and landing through the sun drenched windshield. A sense of isolation came over him. Would it be fight or flight? He recalled the words of a friend who had stated that life was really hell. It wasn't fire and brimstone but the here and now. Erik had thought that asinine, but now he agreed. He finally drove off with the punishing knowledge he had less than two weeks to come up with forty grand. Unlike the Rolling Stones, time wasn't on his side. He'd fight, but would need help.

CHAPTER FORTY-ONE

He had no other choice. Only with great reluctance Erik decided to ask his father for a loan, hoping he would help. But his heart knew better. If there was the slightest chance of success, this had to be accomplished before the old man embarked upon his nightly booze ritual and subsequent descent into the womb of an alcoholic haze.

"Dad, there's an important matter I need to speak about with you."

"What is it?" looking like he was poured into his chair, his voice thick. The bottle was almost empty. Was he already hammered? His mother also sat down as Erik explained what happened, the deadline he was up against and what the consequences would be. A loan meant he could avoid all these problems and would repay the full amount, with interest, starting the following year. When Erik finished an ugly silence engulfed the room as an unshaven Joe lit a cigarette, inhaled deeply and in a raspy smoker's voice asked, "What type of a person are you, *really*?"

"I borrowed the money to pursue a career, to be a success. And I'm *almost* to the finish line." Erik continued. "When 9/11 came along everything changed. People became scared of flying and the tailwind was taken out of the pilot job market."

A seemingly-reflective Joe replied in alcohol-soured breath Erik could smell from across the room. "I don't have that amount."

"Could you borrow it? A home equity loan might—"

Joe lifted the glass in his heavy fingers and interrupted. "I'm not going to do that. Like the bank, you'll probably stiff me." More silence. "What would happen to *my* credit rating?" he shot back with a sweeping arm gesture, his arms almost knocking the bottle off the antique end table. He collared it before it fell. "I could lose this house."

"But my entire *life* is on the line," Erik begged, his fear turning to panic.

"I don't owe you a thing. You should have thought about that before. It's the bottom of the ninth inning with two outs for you and you just struck out. I want you to leave. Right now and for good," Joe sputtered with hatred coming through loud and clear.

"I ask for help and instead you're throwing me out?" Erik said in disbelief, breathing in and out through his mouth, trying to keep the twenty-plus year reservoir of rage from breaking his personal dam.

A livid Joe lifted his right palm up to his face. "This says, out." Then he lifted the left. "Oh, too bad. This one says the same thing." Next, the glass of booze went to his mouth as he pointed toward the door with a smirk on his face. "Looks like you lose either way." Ursula put a hand to her mouth and gasped, but he cast a shut up look her way.

Erik ground his molars so hard he thought they might crack. As despair engulfed him he looked pleadingly to his mother. She sat with frigid immobility, unable or unwilling to utter anything. She finally turned up her palms, got up and left the room. In the immaculate kitchen her body shook and she cupped her chin in her hands. Should she tell Erik the reason Joe harbored such bitterness? She said nothing.

You can't argue with an irrational person. Yet so much repressed hurt surfaced that Erik's immediate urge was to vent everything, by stating he had long known of his mother's infidelity and just to rub it in, adding that he applauded what she'd done. That would hurt. But Joe's response would probably be explosive. So he went to the closet and pulled out the suitcase he used while away during flight engineer school. A breath of stale air was released as it opened and he threw in his belongings.

He knew what had to be done. He went to his parent's bathroom as the cigarette and booze perfume followed him, and he grabbed Joe's toothbrush and secured it in a Ziploc baggie. Although no longer trapped behind invisible bars of unremitting fear, he didn't feel liberated. His shoulders drooped as he slammed the door and drove away from the immaculately kept house on Violet Lane, with grim expectations and smoldering hatred as companions. The night exploded and anxiety engulfed him while driving. A time that should have been one of celebration over his new job and first love, was instead an impending disaster. He *had to* get back on course. Carol was all he had left. Would she be there?

After Erik left Ursula implored Joe, "Please. Help him."

"Why?" he responded with a wave of his hand. "He screwed a bank and would do the same to me. You want to lose this house and live in poverty? We'll rent out his room to someone else and charge more." After a moment of awkward silence he snarled, "He certainly doesn't take after his father. But you already know that, don't you? Cheating seems to be a common trait in both of you." He stormed upstairs and slammed the bedroom door.

While driving aimlessly Erik contemplated his father's actions. Even during times when nothing seems to go right, children are *supposed* to be a source of joy. He would get proof, one way or the other whether or not he fit that definition. As his thoughts began to focus, the idea of spending the night alone in a hotel room didn't sit well. He recalled a flyer posted in the operations office stating there was a room available in a small commuter apartment near the pilot ghetto. There would probably be at least a half-dozen other pilots and the rent most likely wouldn't be cheap, but he wouldn't be alone. He drove to the airport, took out his cell and called the number. The place was still available. The landlord offered the first two weeks for free as an incentive. He dropped off his belongings and sat down in the kitchen. If a person swims far enough into the ocean you can lose direction, not knowing the way back to shore. He knew what had to be done and phoned Carol.

"Can I come over? Now?" he hoarsely whispered.

"Sure," she replied, concerned by his tone.

Erik arrived approximately fifteen minutes later. "Let's go downstairs. I have something to tell you." Carol could tell his mind was running at warp speed. They plopped down facing each other on the couch and he fired off his story. "The bank contacted Shuttle Air and my job is at risk. I only have two weeks to make full restitution." He paused. "And it's not only that. If I get canned I have to repay Shuttle Air an additional sixty thou for my training. That's almost a hundred grand. I asked my father to loan me the money. I thought that maybe when he heard what was at stake, he'd help. But the dysfunctional bastard became irate and kicked me out of the house."

"Hold on. Slow down! Your father threw you out?"

"Yeah, and told me not to come back. I moved all my shit into a commuter apartment near the airport." Erik wanted to tell Carol every lurid detail of the heist, but couldn't bring himself to do that. Maybe she would kick him out too. She was all he had and had to hold onto her at all costs.

"He knew you'd lose your job if he didn't lend a hand?"

"Yeah."

"Why would he help carry the rope to your lynching?"

"He said he'd have to take a loan on the house and didn't want to take a chance on losing it. Bottom line, he doesn't trust me."

After a moment she added, "We'll work this out, together. He abandoned you, but I won't."

Following another moment's silence he said, "There's more."

"More?"

"There was some money on one of my flights and it's missing."

"Are you a suspect? Did you take it?"

Erik couldn't bring himself to lie directly to her, so he skated. "It was a lot and if I had, I wouldn't be in this mess." He quickly related the information the police had given him about the money. To get off this subject he asked, "I need to look up a business address for another important matter. Can I use your computer?"

"You know where it is," she said, pointing to the next room. *Maybe he's looking for a way to come up with the money?*

Erik returned a few moments later after having written down the address of a DNA testing lab.

"Did you find what you were looking for?"

"Yeah."

As she took Erik in her arms and hugged him tightly Carol got a reality jolt. This was the only man she'd ever loved and that they *must* find a way to resolve this.

CHAPTER FORTY-TWO

Throughout the seemingly-endless night Christina Shepard felt like her leaden body was sewn to the mattress. With the loneliness and desperation now working twenty-four, seven she felt more akin to languishing in prison. Finally dragging herself out of bed, she peered through sandy eyes at the fuzzy numbers on the clock for the umpteenth time, desperate for light. She squinted through the filthy windowpanes, while gloomy shadows still engulfed the streets. Looking in the mirror, her normally dazzling blue eyes more resembled dim roads traveled only by sorrow. David's spot in the bed was empty, like the now-bare spaces in the living room for the TV and stereo. She'd heard him enter one night but didn't have the energy to confront him as he carted them off.

The official start of autumn might still be a few weeks away, but Mother Nature was in charge and had no regard for the Roman calendar. It was as though she had her fill of summer and wanted autumn to begin. The gray dawn finally bloomed, a dreary day that presaged the early arrival of damp weather. Gazing into the mirror again, only exhaustion stared back. Scraggly hair that would be more befitting a witch on a broom than a jet captain. Aside from not preventing her seizures, the Epecol had other side effects. The dull morning light finally bled through the soiled curtains, but the streets remained a ghost town. She watched as a man scurried about, attempting to keep out the unrelenting dampness, his breath leaving a long vapor trail like a 727. Out of habit she began to brew a pot of coffee, but stopped. Angry at the world, she flung the empty cup emblazoned with the blue and silver Shuttle Air insignia against the wall where it shattered into a thousand pieces, exactly what she was trying to prevent happening to her life. She had heard crew scheduling leaving numerous voice mail messages inquiring if she was well enough yet to fly. She didn't answer because unless the promising new medication called Keppra worked as advertised, her career was over. The years of schooling, flight training, tributes from her instructors, television interviews, sixty-hour workweeks, all meant nothing unless something stopped the seizures. She held out hope because her neurologist mentioned that his other patients whose EEG's indicated irregular left temporal lobe activity like hers had experienced no seizures or other side effects while taking Keppra. He was also happy to hear that his unknown to him, fictitious patient, Megan Bauer was staying with a close friend in Kew Gardens, Queens, when she had asked him to mail the Keppra to a Miss Christina Sheppard, with two P's. But for now, garbled, unintelligible speech remained a real threat. Her partial complex seizures were very frustrating because although she knew what she wanted to say, the words wouldn't flow. Hopefully, she wouldn't experience any more until the new medicine arrived later that day or the next. Even if the Keppra worked as promised, she couldn't tell the airline or the FAA because she would still be automatically grounded. David was the only one who knew and he'd better keep his mouth shut or she would threaten to expose his rip-off scheme. Going to jail would make him think twice.

It had been only a short time since the robbery, her

salvation, had gone awry. But it felt like eons ago. Gazing into the mirror made her appreciate how fragile youth was and how fleeting it now seemed to be. She decided to call David at the number he had given as his parents' home to deliver her warning. But a youthful female voice answered instead.

"Please, put David on the line."

"Hello."

"Hi. It's me. Who answered?"

"That's none of your fucking business." A moment of awkward silence. "How much did you get?"

"I told you, I never got anything. Not a penny."

"Yeah. Sure. Bye, Christina." There was a dull click on the line and it went dead.

"Don't you hang up on me, you fucking—"

Although her logic wasn't fully functional, she still wondered if an accomplice of David's had made off with their money. If so, he would take up with someone younger because he didn't need her any more. At least he was out of her life.

She next dialed her former husband, Michael in Florida. Was it sunny and warm there? She still had Jimmy and desperately wanted to speak with him, try to explain why there would be no birthday presents. He answered on the second ring. "Mike, please let me speak with Jimmy."

"You know the cops called here," a nasty intonation in his voice.

"Look. I wanna speak with Jimmy."

There was a long moment of silence until a groggy-sounding teenage voice came on the line.

"Hi, Mom. Why you callin' so early?"

"I had trouble sleeping and figured the sound of your voice would cheer me up." She forced a grin, as if he could see her from a thousand miles away.

Jimmy moaned, "When're you going to get me that new computer and printer you've been promising? It's been a while, and—"

She hesitated. "I'll eventually get to it."

"C'mon, Mom. I really need that stuff for school. You've been promising me—"

"I know. But things haven't been going too smoothly here."

"I gotta go. I have school today and need to get some more shuteye. Can you call back another time?"

"Sure." Standing on the edge of this warm sea of memories, but unable to plunge in, she quietly uttered the words, "I love you." She lightly ran her feminine fingers like rosary beads over a framed photo of Jimmy, a handsome teenage boy hanging on the wall right next to the phone. She longed for a picture of Laurel to place alongside it. With the receiver dangling from her fingertips, she sighed as she wiped away the tears. No longer shining lights, instead her eyes were desolate pools awash with painful emotions. But she was still able to see the dreadful shape of the future for Shuttle Air. Between the high-speed train and the larger airlines that were poised to jump into the lucrative shuttle market, the outlook was grim. The end wouldn't come suddenly but slowly and painfully, presaged by pay cuts and labor strife that would also portend the end of her small disability pay and retirement. History was replete with airlines doing exactly that.

Meandering aimlessly, she touched many keepsakes while trying to relive what went with them: the framed articles written about her, including numerous pictures as the female airline pilot spokesperson: her first set of pilot wings, with all the pride and expectancy oozing from them: photos of a smiling younger woman, surrounded by friends and family. She ran her fingers over the collage of images knowing that she could never reclaim their essence, return her to those happier days, a time when a much younger and simpler life was filled with family, love, joy and anticipation.

Flicking on the kitchen light brought to mind that flying was always about lights. There were the seemingly motionless northern lights shining brightly in a black sky; breaking out of the clouds and seeing the welcoming runway approach lights; caution lights and the delicate lights of Saint Elmo's fire dancing across the jet's windscreen like threads during a nighttime storm. Then, there was the most important light—the one left burning in the window by the person you loved.

Maybe when she signed on to this life she had boarded a train, or a plane, that was headed for a predetermined, shitty ending. Whichever that might be, she couldn't, no wouldn't, jump off now. She was committed and would ride this journey to the very end, whatever that might be.

Suddenly, she pictured those warm lights shining brightly and not through the prism of her memory. Those were extinguished. But even though the yesterdays no longer existed and she was no longer the excited young girl in those snapshots, the expectations lived on. If, no *when*, the new medication worked as expected, if need be she could get another flying job when Shuttle Air folded. Perhaps something in the corporate jet field? She would *never* accept defeat. She would always be the captain.

CHAPTER FORTY-THREE

When Erik finished flying two New York to Washington roundtrip morning shuttles, per the norm he noted any items requiring maintenance in the aircraft log. The copilot had mentioned that the voice recorder had been intermittently operating. "You want me to write that up?" he asked the captain, Charlie Davis, who went by the nickname of Skip.

"Sure," the handsome, gray-haired captain replied with a warm smile. "The plane will be on the ground for two hours, enough time to repair it."

While the crew was reciting the Securing checklist, a mechanic decked out in the normal dark blue garb entered the cockpit and grabbed the logbook. Erik was about to leave when the guy mentioned, "You sure have hard luck with voice recorders."

"What do you mean?"

"You brought in flight 1540 a while back and I performed the overnight check. It was a different plane, but I discovered the voice recorder wasn't working. When I checked further, the entire mechanism was missing, nowhere to be found. Nothing was written in the log, so I figured another mechanic removed it because the voice recorder circuit breaker in the aft airstair area was pulled. But no one here or in Boston knew anything. It turned out that although the cockpit indication showed it was working properly, it was nowhere to be found. I've never seen anything like that."

Erik's face lit up like a hundred watt light bulb as he asked as calmly as possible, "When did this take place?"

"Maybe a couple of weeks ago. If you want, I can get the exact date."

"No need," was all Erik could manage, while quickly gathering his belongings. He almost ran over a dozen people sprinting to a pay phone, fumbling for change. The juices were flowing and he needed to speak with Christina, now. But recalling Juni's words that the cops would likely place taps on their phones, just as quickly he decided not to call. All his other thoughts were replaced with searing anger wrapped in rage. Hours spent trying to put the pieces together had resulted in nothing. But a chance encounter with a mechanic and *voila*, everything added up on a cerebral level. Erik took a deep breath and vowed to do what was needed—alone—then bring Christina and Juni in.

But before anything else could be accomplished the bank deadline was approaching quicker than water runs through a sieve and had to take top priority. A burden settled in his heart, as only one way remained to resolve it. He nervously phoned Carol. "My deadline's almost here."

"What are we going to do?"

"Can I come over? Is your father home?"

"Yes. But—?" The line went dead.

When Erik arrived Carol got a whiff of fear wrapped in desperation as they descended to the basement. They sat down and Erik's hands clawed the fabric on the couch, as if trying to gouge away the past. What was done was done, so he finally blurted out, "Would you speak with your father and ask if he'll loan me the money? He's my only salvation." He never wanted to hear those words come out of his mouth, but the fear of losing everything meant there was no other choice.

"Why'd you wait so long?"

"I thought I could come up with enough without involving him, but couldn't. Not knowing how he'll react, I don't want to lose you. But he's it."

Without hesitation she said, "I'll speak with him, now." She went upstairs.

Erik paced back and forth. Was he the "piece of shit" his father claimed? Would he discover new strengths? Would Sal help? Would he hold on to Carol? His career? His life?

After explaining the entire story and the amount owed, with tears in her eyes she pleaded, "Dad, Erik desperately needs your help."

"I can't access that amount immediately," he muttered. As he looked at the young lady standing before him, he recalled when he had first fallen in love with Anita, a lifetime ago. Like her mother, Carol had the same warm heart, worth more than all the glamour in Hollywood. "You have to answer one question before I'll even consider this." He hesitated. "Do you love Erik?" adding with a knowing sigh, "and I don't mean only a physical attraction. I can probably get a home equity loan, quickly. But the cost will be burdensome. Will he repay me?"

Carol wouldn't beg and replied with so much conviction that it surprised even her, "I do love him, very much. I can't define what that means right now. But, I'm absolutely certain he'll repay you as soon as possible. Without you he'll lose his, our, future."

"What about his parents?"

"They're a whole different story, from a different country and culture and drink a lot."

"Where are they from?"

"Germany. I believe that because of them Erik has lots of private wounds that are hopefully, in the process of healing. The bottom line's that his father wouldn't loan him a dime and threw him out of the house. It's you or nothing."

"All right," Sal finally whispered, wondering how *anyone* couldn't help their child in a time of dire need. Glancing at his watch, he said, "I'll go to the bank first thing in the morning. My credit rating's good, so it won't take long."

"There's more."

"What?"

She told him the missing money story and how it might appear when money suddenly surfaced.

Sal dismissed her concern with a mere wave of the hand. "Don't worry. Just have him tell whoever asks I advanced it. I have nothing to hide."

"Thanks, Dad. I love you." Carol kissed him and immediately relayed the good news to Erik. As a wave of gratitude ran through him, he went to Sal and also thanked him profusely.

Erik's stomach was churning when he arrived at the Rodriguez household late the following morning. Maybe Sal changed his mind? He and Carol cautiously stepped into the den, together. As they sat down Sal sensed the anxiety, so he immediately handed over a cashier's check for full restitution.

"I can never thank you enough for what you've done." Erik took a step forward and seeing the older man through tear distorted vision hugged him. "I'll repay every last cent. You have my word."

Sal let out a large breath and embraced Erik, the son he never had, while brushing his own tears aside. "Life's a bitch. Get the hell out of here and to the bank. Now!"

Erik drove there at twice the posted limit and handed over

the check. He then called O'Brien.

With disappointment seemingly in his voice, O'Brien told him, "I'll be closely monitoring you," and hung up.

Erik next phoned Morganthaler and told him the details of how he repaid the loan. Morganthaler demanded information about Sal that Erik couldn't supply. "You can rest assured I'll check him out." Maybe he could find inconsistencies in this all-too-convenient way out?

He called Daly and relayed the information Preis had supplied. "What's this guy Rodriguez's relationship with Preis?"

"His daughter's dating him."

"Sounds a bit too easy."

"I agree. I'll check him out."

But his investigation turned up nothing other than some previous traffic violations. They drove to his home and grilled Sal in depth. But the income tax returns, pay stubs and bank statements he supplied showed his finances were in order, so unremarkable that the cops felt like they already knew him. They were right back where they had begun: nowhere.

With the weighty repayment off his back, Erik became all business; money business. At his apartment he penned a note to Juni and in it he outlined what he believed happened, sealed and placed a stamp on it. After marking it *personal*, he dropped it in the mail box on the corner for pick up the following day.

He returned, took a cotton ball, thoroughly swabbed the inside of his mouth and placed it another baggie alongside the one containing his father's toothbrush. The FedEx office was a few blocks away, so he drove there and sent both items at the airline employee reduced rate via overnight delivery to Genetrack Bio Laboratory, including a return FedEx package. He next called Shuttle Air's crew scheduling department. "I think I'm coming down with a cold. Can you cover my trips for a few days?"

"We have plenty of reserves. Feel better soon."

As his thoughts returned to what happened, hatred won out over every emotion and he turned his total attention to the impending task.

CHAPTER FORTY-FOUR

After awakening from a short nap Christina checked for the mail, discovering the new medication hadn't yet arrived. She went into the grimy bathroom, showered and washed her hair. After applying a liberal amount of conditioner, she blew it dry, noticing that the shine was returning. According to her doctor's strict regimen she also took two Epecol caplets. Hopefully, the Keppra would arrive later that day or tomorrow via UPS. Thoughts of putting her seizures behind her, forever, actually made her feel like a Catholic school girl on her first date. As a kind of celebration of a seizure free life, she dressed in a light pink top accentuated by tight-fitting jeans and drove to a nearby Burger King. While waiting in line she dug money out of her purse and patiently waited her turn in the slowly moving procession of people that wound its way between two heavy chrome railings. She planned to order two double cheeseburgers, fries and a root beer. This was her first time out in days and it was great just to hear the sound of other peoples' voices.

The counterman finally asked, "What can I get for you?"

She began to speak, but her reply came out garbled and made no sense.

The young man looked at her strangely and asked, "Miss? You alright?"

She wanted to tell him what was wrong, but couldn't. Suddenly, she grasped for her chest, as she was having difficulty breathing. From somewhere, a voice asked, "You feeling OK? You don't look good. Miss! Miss!" Why did he sound so far away? Why was she having trouble breathing? *Heart attack? Not in my family.* Suddenly, everything faded and she could no longer stand. Her knees buckled as everything in the room whirled about. With the full weight of her body behind it, she crashed headfirst into the chrome waiting line railing. She was on the floor and felt as though a hundred people were standing over her and looking down. She could hear them screaming something but couldn't understand what. All she could feel was immense pain along with something warm spurting from her head. Then, the pain disappeared and she was spiraling toward the brightest and warmest light she had ever come in contact with.

CHAPTER FORTY-FIVE

Woody and Ingrid Montgomery were seated in their newly-renovated New Jersey ranch style home. They were in the living room done in contrasting hues of soft white, with both reading. The heavyset Ingrid shifted in her seat, put down her copy of the *New York Times* and spoke as she patted her swept back, dyed blond hair that attempted to convey a wind-blown look, but was so overdone it looked like she was inside a wind tunnel. "What are you going to do now?" she asked.

"I dunno," Woody exhaled noisily, shaking his head. He laid his copy of the *NY Post* on the coffee table. "I do know that I'm done with flying, finished. With all the new security crap and alcohol testing it's no fun anymore. Plus, I don't see any long-term future at Shuttle Air. Your brother, Billy told me how well our investment in his new company will do, so maybe I'll work with him?" Woody paused, "Why don't you invite him for dinner? Do you think he'd object if I ask about coming aboard?"

A knowing smile appeared on her face. "He'd probably be thrilled. You guys have always gotten along so well. If you think it's secure, I'll invite him."

"That would be fine. Just make it an innocuous conversation in case of, you know, the phone thing that we discussed after the police were here the last time."

CHAPTER FORTY-SIX

Dressed in blue jeans, black tee and old tennis shoes, after making certain of no tail, Erik drove into New Jersey via the Holland Tunnel. He checked into one of the grubby motels ringing Newark Airport or Sew-ark, as pilots regularly called it due to the nauseating stenches emanating from the countless refineries and other heavy industries that ringed it. The single-story fleabag with peeling paint he chose was situated near the always busy New Jersey turnpike interchange used by eighteen wheelers. Its presence was announced by a huge red neon sign, with the last letter of the name *The Newark Country Motel* either broken or burned out, making it *The Newark Country Mote*. After ensuring it wasn't surrounded by water, even with the misspelled word, he parked in the rear and walked into the closet-sized lobby. Judging by the scarcity of cars in the lot, it was mostly empty. Probably a cheaters joint. A skinny white guy in his twenties, with a pimply face and long, unwashed hair sat behind a bulletproof partition. Even through the divider he smelled like he hadn't gone near a shower for days. It was a dismal place with fluorescent lights and a noisy Coke dispenser. "Can I pay cash?"

"Cash is *always* good here," the dirtbag replied and handed

Erik a registration card.

After sizing Erik up, the creep mentioned at least four times there were free X-rated movies in each room, with a new one every night. This meant the movies were probably changed more often than the sheets. After discovering no ID was requested or desired, he registered under the name John Smith and paid a hundred bucks cash for two nights. At one time this might have been a decent place, but the merciless march of time had left it far behind with no attempt to catch up.

His room had bars on the windows and smelled of chlorine disinfectant. Although he wasn't expecting a robe on the bed and mints on the pillow, gloom hung over every corner just like outside, with the entire place glowing an off-shade of sulfurous yellow. Besides a twin-sized bed, the tiny room was adorned with a cigarette-scarred, scratched Formica nightstand with initials and phone numbers inviting a call etched everywhere. This décor matched the badly discolored dresser and streaked mirror. Stale cigarette stench was permanently suspended throughout and the plywood-walled closet was bare, except for rows upon rows of empty wire hangers hanging on an unpainted wooden pole. Erik didn't unpack his clothing or toiletries, fearful of what might find its way into his underwear or worse yet, toothpaste. Trying to focus on the task at hand, he finally got up the courage to sit on the creaky bed that almost dipped to the floor and pore over a map providing directions to the Parsippany, New Jersey street address he'd found in the phone book for Mr. Howard Montgomery. The smoldering embers of hatred spread throughout his body screaming out only one word, revenge. He anxiously awaited the needed darkness, which seemed to never come. It was as though the light was working well past its normal quitting time. But when the blackness finally arrived, with it came an accompanying taste of promise.

CHAPTER FORTY-SEVEN

The Montgomery front doorbell rang at five-thirty sharp. Ingrid's strapping brother, Billy was a walking timepiece. After hugging and kissing him, she took his hand and led him into the living room. He and Woody shook hands and embraced. "It's great to see you," Woody clucked as he took a step back and looked at Billy Rhodes who was dressed in designer jeans and open collar, short-sleeved shirt that exposed his hairy chest and meaty forearms. "But I just can't picture you with a beard."

"My whole fucking face was itchy. I couldn't wait to shave it off."

"I'm glad it's gone." Woody said, "We sent Stephanie to a friend's for a sleepover, so it's just the three of us for a leisurely dinner.

The word dinner sent Rhodes scurrying into the kitchen with the gleaming checked ceramic black and white tiled floor and glistening granite countertops. Opening the stainless steel Viking oven, he exclaimed, "Rib roast. My favorite!"

"I remembered," a beaming Ingrid cooed as she gave it a final basting.

"But I feel bad that I won't see Stef."

"You can see her next time."

As they sat down for dinner, Billy admired the fine red wine, holding it up. He gingerly scrutinized the bottle in the muted light of the gaudy crystal chandelier hanging over the table. "*1976 Chateau Lefils*! It must have cost a fortune. You shouldn't have."

"When the going gets tough, the tough go shopping," Ingrid clucked.

They made small talk and as dinner was ending Woody finally asked, "How is our investment doing?"

"I printed these out. Just for you," Billy smiled with a wink and removed some spreadsheets from his pants pocket.

"One thing I always admire about you," a jovial Woody added pointing to the papers. "Everything is planned well ahead of time, down to the smallest detail."

Billy arranged the crumpled papers on the black glass coffee table, pressing them down with his hands. "These show your half of our, er, investment was worth a bit over a million, one million, one hundred and sixteen thousand bucks, to be exact." He chuckled, adding, "The cash is safe and sound, still in those gorgeous green sacks, minus the locks. From what I've lined up, it looks like our small enterprise should have initial annual sales of a bit below three million and just over two-hundred grand in earnings. I'm estimating the really big bucks and profits will begin rolling in next year when sales should reach almost twenty million, even in a sluggish economy. The profits should be just under a million after tax breaks and start-up costs. Since everyone wants to feel green today, recycled paper is an up and coming enterprise. The big boys, including the mob people, are no doubt watching closely. Once things get up and running I'm pretty sure they'll make an offer to buy us out, if for no other reason than to eliminate the competition. Then, we just sit back and count our money. Bottom line is that right now I'm projecting your original investment to be worth just under three million by next year. If someone buys us, well that would be off the chart."

Woody interjected, "I'm glad to hear that. Since 9/11 there's no more fun in airline flying. Plus, all I ever hear from management is negative bullshit, with constant intimidation along with it. So, I resigned and probably can't return, which is fine by me. Unfortunately, I can't collect my retirement money 'til age 60, if there's any left by then."

Rhodes didn't hesitate. "That's OK, 'cause I can offer you an executive position, Director of Marketing at a starting base salary of two hundred and fifty grand a year, plus expenses and profit sharing." Billy paused to savor the bouquet of the fine wine.

"That's fantastic!"

"Wait. There's more. You'll also have a direct partnership. I'll issue you privately held stock with a face value equal to the amount of your original investment, fifty percent of the startup capital."

"I've said many times that your business savvy borders on brilliance."

Billy waved away the compliment and took another sip of the velvety vino. "Speaking of brilliance, weren't you the one who first discovered what those two shit-for-brains pilots and that pudgy *guinea* were up to?"

"Yeah. But give Shepard some of the credit. I couldn't believe she thought up the whole thing down to the tiniest details; a brilliant fucking scheme. But she was also dumb. Can you imagine discussing everything in the cockpit? She must have actually believed that their entire conversation would be wiped out in forty-five short minutes..."

"But didn't you say that would have happened if—"

Woody held up his hand. "The voice recorder does have a

constant erase feature. Except, when I suspected they were up to no good, during the preflight inspection I did as a favor for Preis, I secretly removed its power source by pulling a circuit breaker in the jet's aft airstair area. That preserved its contents, even if they believed they deleted it by pressing the erase button in the cockpit." A smiling Woody nodded his head. "I got to hear their entire conversation, intact."

"How'd you do it?"

"That part was easy. Back at LaGuardia I simply hung around the maintenance shack for a while like I often did. The first time it took me almost twenty minutes to open the recorder's metal cover and remove the eight track tape cassette. You probably remember those babies from the good old rock 'n roll days."

Rhodes smiled and shook his head. "In this modern age they still use ancient shit like that?"

"They do on the older 727's. The newer jets have more advanced digital systems. Fortunately, the same was true for the flight data recorder. If it had been the new digital type, then the door opening on the ground would have shown. But Shepard probably checked that out ahead of time and knew it didn't? I don't know, but *we* were still covered either way. Once I got my hands on that tape, I listened right here on my stereo. They were speaking on the ground and their conversation was crystal clear. I realized there was lots of money to be made, but still needed more details."

"What'd you do with the tape?"

"The first time I took it home and burned it in the fireplace. But it would only be a matter of time until some maintenance guy became suspicious if another tape mysteriously disappeared. If that happened Shepard or Preis might hear about it and put two and two together, meaning no more cockpit discussions. Or worse yet, a changed or cancelled plan. Next time I brought along a portable tape player, listened in my car and then reinstalled it. Since I had done it before, that entire process only took about twenty-five minutes. I brought you in when I had all the needed info," Woody added with a shrug of his shoulders. "I have to admit, the entire set-up was foolproof. They took all the risks and became prime suspects, and we got the dough."

"Not a bad deal!" Rhodes exclaimed.

A smiling Woody continued, "I even made Shepard and Preis hurry up during the robbery when I thought they were taking too much time. I didn't want to make them appear *too* suspicious."

Ingrid got up and poured more wine. "It was flawless," she added with a wry smile. "Woody even slipped with the cops and made his disdain for Shepard known. Can you imagine, that little bimbo complained to Woody's boss about…"

"Don't give me all the credit," Woody broke in holding up his hand, not wanting to rehash what she reported to O'Brien. "Shepard concocted it and we simply reaped the benefits of their work; the thieves stealing from the robbers. Not a bad deal."

A smiling Billy slid over on the couch and slapped Woody on his jelly-like shoulder. "C'mon, you did more. Wasn't it your idea to have your dying old man sign the phony trust agreement right before he croaked, leaving you what turned out to be his hidden, but nonexistent nest egg?"

"Not me," Woody added, shaking his head. "Your sister thought that one up. That would create a plausible explanation of where we got the money, just in case the cops wondered why I quit. Or, if we couldn't bury it in the company. However, I do suspect the cops will have some more questions for me when they find out I resigned. But I've got a convincing reason."

"Then you both deserve a pat on the back."

"I don't want that," Woody added, shaking his head. "But, I

will take a job starting at a quarter mill, along with a piece of the action."

"Well, ah, you've got it!" Rhodes replied, in a thick Boston accent. "I had that down pat for that *eye-talian*. I figured that way he'd concentrate searching in that area."

"We planned every little detail ahead of time," Woody interjected. "But hey, there's another, important item that goes along with my new job."

"What's that? You want a car?"

"Nah. But we have to get together more often. Especially now that we're partners and colleagues."

"While I'm thinking of it, partner here's my new cell number. It's always on. And let's not forget another important item." Billy laughed loudly as he unbuttoned his shirt, exposing a tight-fitting white tee-shirt emblazoned in bold, black letters of the EAST BOSTON MARAUDERS. "The truth is that the three of us make a great team. And I don't mean softball. We played hardball like the fucking pros." Billy raised his glass, "To the East Boston/Parsippany Marauders."

CHAPTER FORTY-EIGHT

Erik was waiting patiently on the dark, rural road. Peering through a pair of cheap binoculars, he saw so many lights illuminated in the Montgomery household that he figured they must be stockholders in the local electric company. While waiting until certain Woody's daughter was tucked away, Erik pondered the depressing drive along Route 46. He was unfamiliar with Jersey, but was convinced that its architecture must have sprung from an act of sorcery. There were high tension towers with wires that seemingly reached to the clouds and acres upon acres of gray concrete that made up desolate towns with grimy motels and restaurants with windows so dirty you could probably scrape a meal off them. The fast-food outlets were the only things interrupting the depressing landscape, with garish fluorescent signs announcing their presence. The twenty-four hour donut shops probably comprised most of the nightlife in a State sandwiched between New York City and Philadelphia that even Benjamin Franklin had referred to as a keg tapped at both ends. But when compared to New York, Jersey had a lower State income tax, confirming that the tightfisted airline pilots cared more about their wallets than anything.

While waiting he was shivering, the prickly chill slowly climbing the vertebrae of his spine like walking up steps leading to a church, fear exacerbated because he didn't know the true persona he was dealing with. A common criminal? Sociopath? The anxiety was compounded by the penetrating dampness on a night when summer was taking its last gasp, a time when the northeast winds replaced the comforting southern breezes, bringing the first hint of cold weather. The autumn-like wind whining through the leaves caused the tree branches to rustle and sway, their branches clicking together, sounds that cooled his body even further. A number of times he wanted to start the car and flip on the heater but couldn't, lest someone discover his presence.

Montgomery's front door abruptly opened and a man much larger than Woody emerged. Erik's jaw muscles began twitching, followed by a warm feeling fueled by anger and forged into a steel-like rage that spread throughout his body. With head bowed, he silently exited the car.

Rhodes had to meet later that night with an architect at a posh upper east-side Manhattan condo he had just made a down-payment on, so he begged off more wine and bid *adieu*. Riding a high, he didn't pay attention to the tall blond guy who passed him. But Erik noted the build, rat-like features and birthmark. Although there was no beard, with slick money and bullshit written all over him, this had to be the scumbag. The guy got into a shiny black Mercedes with New York plates and drove off. Erik kept repeating the plate number aloud until he got back to his car and jotted it down.

The Montgomery houselights were being extinguished as Erik walked toward his destiny. The doorbell was answered by a smiling, heavyset woman, dressed in what appeared to be a white linen skirt with a large crucifix encircling her neck. Erik surmised she was Woody's wife.

"Billy, I thought you were leaving..."

So, Billy is the guy's name.

"Excuse me," as the smile vanished, "I thought you were someone else." The woman stood perfectly still until she finally asked, "May I help you?" She was nodding her head, like she ought to know the person standing on her doorstep, but couldn't quite place him.

"I wanna speak with Woody," Erik brusquely told her, quickly measuring her assets versus liabilities. The latter easily won out.

"May I say whose calling?"

"Erik Preis." He almost heard the blood rushing to her head. Would she puke? Faint? "And tell him it's urgent."

She stepped back and wiped her hands briskly on the side of her skirt for a long moment. Erik thought she would slam the door in his face, but finally whispered, "I'll see if he's in." Leaving him standing outside, she disappeared inside.

"Erik Preis!" a smiling, very married looking Montgomery bellowed as he offered his hand, which Erik ignored. The devils we anticipate are never quite as intimidating when we meet them face-to-face. "C'mon in," Woody finally half-heartedly uttered while motioning Erik inside, a deer in the headlights look on his face as he studied the floorboards.

Erik scrutinized the entranceway where the walls looked soft, perhaps weakened by so many lies? "I'll cut right to the chase, mister Airframe and Powerplant mechanic," he commanded in a loud voice. His heart was thudding as he held back the pent up anger that wanted to release itself with the fury of a summer thunderstorm. The woman was peering over Woody's shoulder with dark eyes darting back and forth between them. Her face was the color of paste, like the guy who just left. Pointing to her Erik said, "She knows?"

"That's Ingrid, my wife. What does she know? What are you talking about?"

"I won't play your fucking game all night, so I'll talk turkey. I know you took our money." He let the last sentence just hang in the air, begging for a reply. None came.

Woody reassumed his plastic veneer and replied in a voice full of self-righteous, but phony-sounding indignation. "What money? I don't know what the hell you're talking about."

"I also know that Billy, the prick who just left here and got into the shiny Benz was the one."

Woody's complexion turned whiter than Santa's beard as he began to reply, "But..."

"I want *our* money. Every last fucking dime." Although it was obvious that Woody wanted to say something, nothing came out. His skin tone changed to beet red and he took a wobbly step backwards. Did he have a gun? With response mechanisms revving in high gear and at the ready, Erik nodded in the direction of the street. "I got his plate number so it will only take some simple checking to unearth where Billy lives. But he fit my partner's description to a tee, right down to his ugly fucking face and birthmark."

"But..."

"By the way, just in case you never discovered my associate's true identity—"

Ingrid roughly pushed Woody aside and spat out, "We know. He's—"

With makeup thick as cake frosting that tried to mask a complexion riddled with pock marks, Erik pointed and commanded her, "Shut up!" From what he had just witnessed, Woody must have met this bimbo at an anti-testicle rally. These two people were the ones. Although trying to contain his fury, Erik discovered that a restrained response wasn't possible. There's a very fine line between justice and revenge, and his made for a difficult path to walk. He struggled to keep a balance—too far to one side of that line or in the other direction wouldn't work. He hissed, "Since you *think* you already know so fucking much, allow me to fill you in on a few more details that weren't on the voice recorder. My associate is a *paisan* who would love to even the score with *every* person responsible for his beating." He added with a haughty grin, "Once your buddy whacked him he developed a bad case of Italian Alzheimer's; when you forget everything but the grudges." He paused to allow his words to sink in. "Wanna hear more?" Only silence. "But I'm here to offer you a deal."

"Go ahead," Woody replied in a quavering voice with a mix of what Erik took to be either embarrassment or self-loathing.

"Wait a goddamn minute!" Ingrid shrieked in surround sound, throbbing arteries clearly visible in her puffy neck, her face actually looking like it might crack. "You don't have to cut any deals with this fucking prick. What's he gonna do? Go to the cops? Fuck him. If he does that he'll—"

"That wasn't what I had in mind," Erik hissed. "Maybe you read about those recent murders in Brooklyn Heights?" recalling some headlines in that morning's *NY Post*. "The cops don't know who committed them but I do. Wanna hear more?"

Woody looked like he would cry. His face was contorted. Was it rage or fear? He shouted, "Ingrid, for once just shut the fuck up!" Turning around, he rubbed his face with his hand, and offered in a subdued tone, "What's your offer?"

"Offer? Fuck you. This is *no* offer. It's a demand. I want it *all*, every last dollar. In exchange, I'll keep my mouth shut."

Pushing Woody aside, Ingrid screeched, "How the fuck do we know that?"

"I'm afraid you'll just have to take my word. The way I see it you have no choice."

Woody began, "I don't have immediate access to the cash. It will take me a while to get—"

"Not my problem," Erik interrupted, now in a businesslike tone. "Let me make it clear what will happen to you—all of you—if I don't get every last dime or if I meet with an accident." Standing on his tiptoes craning over Woody's shoulder, he added, "By the way, where's your daughter? Um, what was her name? Stephanie?"

"Fuck you, you little—" Ingrid hollered as she tried to get to Erik, but Woody grabbed her by the arm and squeezed it, the red marks his fingers left clearly visible when she roughly pulled it away.

"Take your bullshit act to Vegas, honey. I've arranged for all the info to be relayed to my associate." Now looking Ingrid directly in the eye, Erik added, "I included your names, your daughter's and this address. Wanna hear more?"

"But I can't come up with the cash right this minute. The money's not here," Woody begged.

Erik hoped he wouldn't have to wait, but was prepared. "You have until tomorrow morning to deliver it to me, here. If you fuck with me or take any, the letter goes out and you'll all be history, including Billy, 'cause another letter will go out early tomorrow with his plate number on it. Understand?"

Woody simply nodded his head.

"No excuses and no extension."

A somber Woody nodded again.

"Any questions?"

"What time will you be here?"

"Not important. But, if the money's not in my hands by sometime tomorrow morning, the info gets sent. Thinking about clearing out? Don't bother 'cause we'll track your asses down." Erik turned and left. He heard the door slam shut.

After Woody closed the door, Ingrid's facial red hot contours of anger began to melt, replaced by a cloudburst of fear. She immediately grabbed her cell off the table and called the number her brother had just given them. He was halfway back to his Manhattan apartment, content listening to the new Mercedes' hum of the tires on the blacktop. He answered on the second ring.

"It's Ingrid."

"I said we'd have to keep in touch more often, but I didn't mean…"

She cut him off. "There's been a serious complication. We just finished with a surprise visitor and his call wasn't a social one. It had to do with events in Boston a short time ago."

"Holy shit. Is he still there? Who?"

"He's gone. Just come back to the house! Now!"

"I'm on my way," Rhodes replied, making a tire-screeching U-turn on the roadway, oddly pleased at how well the Mercedes handled. A short time later he bounded up the steps and upon reaching the top Woody swung open the door. Both men plopped down on the couch.

"Who was it?" Rhodes pleaded breathing heavily, features so hard and pale they resembled a death mask. He was frightened out of his mind, afraid the reply would be Rosario.

"Erik Preis."

Rhodes let out a whoosh of air and asked, "What the hell did *he* want? What did he know?"

Their expressions conveyed his worst fear. "The whole

fucking thing. He even knew you were the one. He said he copied down your plate number and..."

"OK! OK! Enough, for Christ's sake!" Rhodes yelled, waving his hand in the air. "What the fuck does he want? His cut?"

"I wish. He wants it *all*, every last dime. If we don't give it to him by tomorrow morning Rosario will come after us, including you and Stephanie. What the hell can we do?" Woody begged, features contorted.

Ingrid shrilly broke in, "The little bastard's blackmailing us. The hunter doesn't fear the lion. Respect it? Yes. Fear it? No. When he comes to pick up the money we'll get rid of him. We can't—"

"Now *you* wait one fucking minute," Rhodes shouted, his eyes compressing to the point they resembled surgical incisions. "What the fuck are you talking about? The heist was one thing, but murder is *not* in my DNA."

"What the hell are we supposed to do? Just fucking hand over the money?" Ingrid hollered, the color of her face again matching the *Chateau Lefils* remaining in the decanter.

After only a short pause, a brooding Rhodes asked while shaking his head, "What other fuckin' option we got? I won't have any part of killing this prick 'cause we really don't know how many people he's already told. No doubt someone would find out, including his partner and maybe the cops."

"All right! You made your goddamned point," Woody shouted. "Can we get the money here by tomorrow morning?"

"I'll have to. It's in a safe place and like I said, it's even in the same bags. But that represents every last dime for the startup capital. I, we, can't open without it. And my apartment and car will have to go too." He hesitated only a moment, thinking aloud. "But the alternative's worse. Come to my place tonight and I'll have it there. Just make certain this motherfucker doesn't follow you. He might have my plate number, but he might not be certain who I am or where I live."

"Somehow he found out your first name."

"What? How the hell? You tell him anything?" Before Woody could reply he added, "I don't want his buddy to know *anything* about me. Who knows what that fucking lunatic might do?"

"I'll leave in about a half-an-hour."

"Make certain you're not followed." Rhodes reiterated. He turned to leave but hesitated and instead looked them both directly in the eye. "You guys better not be scamming *me*. If I find out you are..."

Woody's face matched Ingrid's as he pointed a fat finger at Rhodes. "Scamming *you*? Fuck you, asshole. We just finished dinner together and you offered me a job. Who the fuck you think you're dealing with? Some lowlife scumbag?" Calming down, he asked aloud, "What the hell am *I* going to do?"

"Maybe you can get your job back?"

"No fucking way. Especially after what that cunt Shepard said."

"What exactly *did* she say?"

"That's not important. All I know is they won't rehire me."

"I can't help you. I don't know what the hell *I'm* gonna do?"

"Remember, do *not* take any of the money," Woody reiterated. "He probably knows exactly how much and if you do..."

"Shit. I was going to hold back enough to tide me over and pay for my place 'til I can, hopefully flip it."

"You know, you make selfishness into an art form. Do *not* do that! We don't want that little guinea coming after us! It's bad enough that without a job I won't be able to make ends meet. If I know your sister, she'll probably force me to sell this joint and who knows what's next?"

    "I gotta go," Rhodes said.

CHAPTER FORTY-NINE

Erik returned to his dump motel a different person, a stick figure with a jumble of blond hair and lots of lost innocence. He grabbed a bite at a fast food joint down the block, but it just laid in his stomach. He watched TV for a while, but sleep wouldn't come. Fully dressed, with head wedged between two musty pillows he constantly tossed and turned. He had to escape this garbage heap, find his way to a pay phone and call Christina, disguising his voice in case the cops were listening in. He'd meet her at an out of the way place, tomorrow after he had the money. She was still out sick and the news he had to impart would certainly make her feel better. He'd passed a bank of phones at a gas station, so he drove there after getting quarters from the same slimy desk clerk. *Maybe I should boil the coins before using them?* He dialed her number and put in three quarters. Would that gorilla David answer? Instead, another male voice identifying himself as Officer Spinelli picked up. Erik thought it was a joke, but when the cop gave his badge number the anticipation turned to foreboding. Was Christina arrested? Were they interrogating her, now? Would he be next? He played dumb. "Sorry. I was trying to reach a friend at this number, Captain Christina Shepard."

"You a member of the immediate family?"

Erik recalled the night the cops questioned him. This was the same tone of voice. "I'm just a flying buddy who called to say hello. Everything all right?"

"I'm sorry, but Ms. Shepard passed away earlier today."

All Erik could blurt out was, "This some kind of sick joke?"

"Right now, all indications point to a major seizure-related head injury."

"What…?"

"I'm sorry. What did you say your name was? Perhaps you can shed some light…"

Erik slammed down the receiver. Christina dead? The news hit him like a blast of red-hot jet exhaust. He felt helpless, but since there was nothing more he could do, he returned to the motel. After saying a silent prayer, he was wide awake and also paranoid that Woody or his partner might attempt some shit. While pondering the faceless concrete wilderness surrounding his room, he continually glanced at the dial of the small clock permanently affixed to the scarred night table. Its luminescent numbers were seemingly glued in place. He traced the trails the cars' headlights left on the ceiling over and over, like bright rivers running through the crevices of a mountain range. Occasionally a car would stop. Would the flimsy door come crashing down? Was Christina *really* dead?

Per the norm, Juni and Angela Rosario began their routine before sunrise. It was a rough night, as his thoughts kept returning to what he'd heard on *Fox* News. A well-known woman pilot, Captain Christina Shepard had died from head wounds associated with a fall during an apparent grand mal seizure. As he sat at the kitchen table barely picking at his breakfast, Anita asked, "You OK?"

"I got so much shit on my mind..."

"About the bakery?"

"Lots of stuff." Although media interest in Christina's death would quickly abate, Juni knew this was a personal tragedy that would drag him down also. Pondering this he said, "Funds are so low that I don't know how the hell we're going to make it. Antonio must sense that something's wrong, because he's considering dropping out of school to work here. I don't want that."

"He and I spoke about it," Angela replied, "and he wants to help."

"But if he stays in school he can have a better life." A moment later Juni got up, went to Angela and put his arms around her. "My family deserves better. If I'd ratted out that prick at the bank none of this would've happened. Not a day goes by that I don't regret it."

"You did what you thought was right."

Juni softly kissed her, went into the spanking clean bakery, switched on the fluorescent sign and the world knew the Genoa Italian bakery was open for another day.

Like flying westbound into the strong jet stream, Erik felt the dawn would never reach its final destination. At first light, he breathed a sigh of relief. As daylight took possession of the outside world, the wind ceased blowing through a crack in the window molding and the low-hanging mist vanished, seemingly sucked up into the air. As the longed-for light finally burned through the yellowed curtains, Erik prayed this personal nightmare would end, soon. When he looked into the mirror, even though the eyes staring back were badly swollen, they could pass muster. He stepped outside into the still dank air, cautiously glanced around and saw nothing out of the ordinary. After throwing his belongings into the back seat, he hoped this would be the end of a crazy scheme hatched by Christina Shepard, seemingly a lifetime ago. He started the car and a nearby diner provided temporary solace, even though the rock-hard English muffin along with three cups of acid brew didn't help his stomach.

He circled Woody's place twice. Nothing appeared amiss. There were no other cars in sight including the Benz, so he pulled up directly in front. With nerves and muscles on full alert, he cautiously approached the front door and almost jumped out of his skin when it abruptly swung open. Woody was standing there, arms folded as if showing he had nothing to hide. Ingrid stood beside him along with four upright, large green duffels.

"There it is," Woody gruffly said.

"Open them," Erik demanded, somewhat surprised by the confidence in his voice.

Woody fumbled, but did as told.

"Turn them toward me. How much?"

"Every last dollar, approximately two point three million."

"It better all be there. Put the clips back on and hand 'em to me."

A sniveling Woody added, "You know that 'cause of you I'm going to lose everything. I already resigned from Shuttle Air and thanks to what fucking Shepard said, they won't take me back."

"That's great. I gain a seniority number. Plus, you're a shitty pilot anyway, so everyone will be safer."

The color drained from Woody's face and Ingrid began to utter something, but Erik's words shut her up. "It wasn't your money to start with."

There were lots of questions in her eyes as an obviously overwrought Ingrid finally snarled, "How do we know you won't tell your cohorts?"

"I'm afraid you don't. That's exactly the way I want it because you didn't only steal, you're also guilty of murder."

"Murder? You are a fucking head case!" Ingrid hollered. "That thug buddy of yours didn't die. Even you—"

"Christina Shepard is dead. Complete silence. "And the way I see it, you're as guilty as if you shot her."

"Dead? How? Was she murdered?" an ashen-faced Woody asked?

"Read about it in tomorrow's paper."

Neither Woody nor Ingrid uttered a word. Erik took a step back and stared from Woody to Ingrid. "I'm speaking for Christina when I say I hope you go to bed every night for the rest of your lives wondering who might be comin' for you." Erik watched his words sink in, hoping they would ultimately percolate down through their gray matter and remain with them as he clumsily picked up the bags. This seemed all *too* easy? While dragging the bags to his car, he felt like a cowboy in a John Wayne movie, with a rifle sighted on his back. But he fought off the impulse to glance over his shoulder. Once the bags were in the trunk, he looked back at the still-open doorway. It was as empty as a tomb.

As Erik drove away, Ingrid said, "He's got the money, but you think he'll tell his buddy?"

"I hope not."

"Yeah, but he said..."

"Goddamn it, Ingrid. I heard what he said. But he probably cut his own deal and left that guy out. He's as guilty as we are."

"I can only pray you're right. We should have removed a few hundred thousand for ourselves."

"Oh, really? And what happens if I'm wrong, he does split it and his partner doesn't get his full share? You heard what he said yesterday about Stephanie. Instead, you'd better be thinking about how the hell we're going to make ends meet. We're flat broke, on our asses, and—"

"On *our* asses? Fuck you. First, it was the Navy where they wouldn't let you fly 'cause of your boozing. It was just a matter of time until the same thing happened at the airline. Now, we'll add this to *your* list. I thought I'd married into the big time with you, but the bush leagues would be more appropriate. I called the real estate agency and they're putting our house on the market, tomorrow."

CHAPTER FIFTY

Once the victim's identity became known Daly and Morganthaler were immediately summoned to the Burger King. As Daly donned his gloves and glasses and gazed at the body, he recalled how incredibly beautiful Christina Shepard was in life. It bothered him tremendously to see her entire body covered with blood from a gaping head wound. The NYPD crime scene forensic technicians were just finishing up with their measuring, scraping and photographing and were ready to remove the body to the morgue. Morganthaler knew one, a nerdy-looking thin Medical Examiner with a pencil mustache and thick glasses who was dressed in a jacket that was about five sizes too large. "What's it look like?" he asked the ME.

"Pending the final autopsy findings, it appears she had a tonic-clonic seizure and struck, then snapped her head back hard on the railing," he said, pointing to the area where customers stood in line waiting to be served. "Preliminary findings point to a ruptured major external carotid artery to the brain and she bled to death, both internally and externally."

Daly just sighed, relieved that she didn't lose control of bodily functions as frequently happens. Morganthaler ordered her apartment roped off and the two cops drove there to search with the hope of finding some clues to the robbery. After ducking under the yellow tape, the first thing they noticed was a package in the mailbox. Opening it, they saw it contained a bottle of a prescription medication called Keppra that was sent by a mail order pharmacy based upon a prescription written by a Doctor Friedman. However, it was addressed to a Miss Megan Bauer in care of Christina Sheppard. Was it sent by mistake? That was doubtful. The only error was in the spelling of Christina's last name. They were puzzled because they'd been told the only other person who lived here was Bennedeto.

They gloved up and began at the rear of the cheerless house, working their way forward from the kitchen. The place smelled of dirty carpet and had more than a few areas of dust. More than living quarters, it better resembled somewhere to hole up from the real world. The dank bathroom, a nasty-looking place with oozing toothpaste on the counter, a cracked soap dish and strands of creepy-looking black mold throughout, was so small that both men couldn't fit in together. Daly entered and found a free sample bottle of Epecol with the name of the same Doctor Friedman on it. "Who and what do you suppose this is for?" he asked Morganthaler, holding the bottle up to the light. "And who the hell is Megan Bauer?"

"I don't have the slightest idea. Why don't you call the doctor?"

"Let me first check with our lab people." Daly phoned the FBI's New York lab, gave the guy who answered a brief background and read off the names and prescription numbers. A few moments later the technician called back and said both medications were primarily used as seizure prevention medications for people with epilepsy. Daly then called Doctor Friedman, gave his FBI shield number and explained why he was calling. "Is Christina Shepard a patient of yours?"

Friedman checked his computer records and relayed that he had no patient by that name.

After Daly gave him a physical description, the neurologist said he had another epilepsy patient who fit that description and who lived with a Miss Sheppard.

"I know you can't give me the name of this other patient, but did she pay for her visit with health insurance?"

"No. She paid cash. She claimed she had no insurance."

Daly was now starting to get the full picture. He sat down and phoned O'Brien. After discussing Shepard's death, asked, "Do you know if she had epilepsy?"

"She's been out sick for a while with a cold or something. But, epilepsy? No. She couldn't have. That permanently disqualifies a pilot from flying."

After thanking O'Brien, he hung up.

Continuing their search, they found a checkbook and bank statements in the kitchen hutch, along with several overdue Con Edison electric bills and letters threatening to shut off the power. Daly noticed her cell phone lying on the kitchen table. Scanning the numbers showed several made to area code 612, Minneapolis. That piqued his interest, so he called that number and after identifying himself and giving his badge number had a conversation with Mimi Johansen. After relaying what happened, she informed them Shepard was her adopted daughter's biological mother. This news came as a surprise and was followed by a lengthy discussion with Laurel, who filled him in on the history and Christina's epilepsy. She went on to tell him an anguished Christina had told her she feared that she could no longer afford to pay her college tuition due to her disease. This was not the sign of a person who had stolen over two million. Daly thanked her and hung up. "I just can't understand this," Daly said. "She needed money. But, although the motives are present, there's zero evidence pointing to any involvement." Morganthaler just nodded his head.

In the living room, Morganthaler pointed to the empty space on the wall where the large screen TV and stereo were located on their last visit. He mumbled to Daly, "I wonder where those went?"

"I don't know, but they're not anywhere in the house. It appears that lowlife Bennedeto also left because there is no male clothing in the drawers, or anywhere." They checked and discovered he had called in sick for work.

"Let's pay that dirtbag a visit." They drove to the address of the Brooklyn apartment he had previously provided. A dark-haired, scantily clad young girl answered their knock. After flashing their credentials, she reluctantly let them into the small apartment where the stale air smelled like dirty feet and unwashed bodies. They hollered out to Bennedeto and impatiently waited in the tiny hallway where the once beige-colored carpet looked like people had been wiping their mud-caked feet on it for years. Morganthaler took out his pad and asked the girl, "What's your name?"

"Mary. Mary O'Rourke, sir" she stammered.

He jotted it down. "How old are you?"

"I'm, uh, eighteen," she finally managed, not looking at him.

"You don't look eighteen."

"I am," she maintained, staring at her bare feet.

"Give me your address."

She complied and a moment later David finally emerged from the bedroom clad in boxers and put his arm around her waist.

"You guys just won't stop harassing me. Whaddaya want now?"

Daly spoke. "You know anything about what happened to

Ms. Shepard?" Morganthaler tapped Daly on the shoulder and pointed to two items off in a corner of the apartment while David had his back turned.

"What happened? I haven't even spoken with that bitch. What kind of bullshit did she feed you?"

"She's dead."

"Dead! What the hell happened?"

"We thought perhaps you could enlighten us?"

David put up both large hands as if to stop them. "Now wait one goddamned minute. We broke up a while back and—"

"Shut up and put your hands down," Morganthaler ordered, detecting a large chink in Bennedeto's phony armor. "When did you steal these? Were you lookin' to make a quick buck?" pointing to the stack of TV and stereo equipment.

"Those are mine," he shot back in the same tone of voice a man would use if he'd been caught by his wife with a naked hooker.

"Oh really? Perhaps then you can explain how Ms. Shepard had previously showed us credit card receipts in her name for those."

"I, I don't know—"

The young girl put her hand to her mouth. As he roughly spun David around and placed handcuffs on him, a sneering Morganthaler took out a small card and brusquely read David his Miranda rights. "At this time you're being arrested on suspicion of aggravated burglary of one giant screen television and a Bose surround sound stereo." Pointing to the young lady he added, "You are also suspected of engaging in sex with a minor. You may remain silent and are entitled to an attorney. Anything you say can and will be used against you."

David began to protest, but realized it was fruitless. Quickly deciding on a new approach he tried sucking up by informing the cops that Christina had recently been diagnosed with epilepsy. "If anyone found out it meant the end of her career." David wouldn't mention the strange shipments out of fear he might somehow be implicated in whatever happened, or the baggage heists, meaning additional, big troubles.

"We already know that."

"How did you..? Can I at least get dressed?" he begged, sounding like he might break down and cry. Morganthaler removed the cuffs and guarded him closely while his request was honored. Once dressed in jeans and tee the cuffs went back on, even tighter. They drove both he and the young lady to the nearest NYPD precinct where David was booked and held, pending a bail hearing. Mary O'Rourke was released into her parents' custody after they confirmed that she had run away and was fifteen years old. At David's court arraignment later that morning the magistrate set bail at one hundred thousand dollars on each of the two counts. His court-appointed attorney stated that he couldn't come up with that amount so he was remanded to Riker's Island. To the cops, no bail money meant he also probably had no involvement in the heist.

Leaving the courtroom, Morganthaler smiled for the first time in a long while. "At least that reprobate is off the streets."

A cheery Daly suggested, "Let's give him one more for the road." He called David's boss, informed him of the pending charges and that he was being held at Riker's. The supervisor stated he would immediately be placed on unpaid leave pending the outcome. If convicted on any count or if he accepted a plea bargain, he would be terminated.

That part was easy, but the distinct whodunit smell remained, gnawing away at both cops. "What about Preis?" Morganthaler ruminated as they headed to their car.

"What about him?"

"The T and L sheets keep pointing to the flight. It's the perfect connection, except so far it isn't. But, I just can't dismiss it completely. I wanna leave him on the suspect list even though the taps haven't turned up anything and although from what we know it would have been virtually impossible for him to carry it out alone. If he somehow arranged the heist without the other pilots' knowledge maybe he'll show his hand now? I'd also like to double-check his recent cell calls and keep monitoring all his financial transactions until someone upstairs tells us otherwise. I'll track him down and get his cell." Morganthaler added. "Not having a solid lead is making this investigation rather frustrating."

"I agree. It's like we're running in a blind alley marathon. Go ahead with Preis," an apathetic Daly informed him.

As the initial shock of Christina's death gave way to guilt, it ripped at Juni's gut like a searing blade. Recalling she had a young son living somewhere in Florida, although funds were extremely short he would get the kid's address and somehow send some money. Although he'd returned to East Boston and attended a number of softball games, it turned out there wasn't even a team called the Marauders. He also tried contacting Joey Martino, but his calls went unanswered. There wasn't even a recording on the other end. Juni thought maybe Martino skipped town with their dough since the trail ended so abruptly. However, he quickly learned Joey had died from a massive coronary, leaving his old lady penniless. Who the hell had their money?

CHAPTER FIFTY-ONE

The money in the trunk was like a dog constantly yipping at his heels and Erik was totally paranoid, driving a circuitous route, constantly checking his rearview mirror and quickly changing lanes to determine if he was being followed. He saw nothing. His part of this game had been played out and thus far he had won, but with far less grace than he would have liked. These emotions competed with even more depressing thoughts of Christina. While driving past Jersey City on Route 3 he spotted a deserted road off to the left and quickly pulled onto it, sped past a dilapidated wooden wharf protruding into the filthy waters of some unnamed tributary and jammed on the brakes. There was no company here except for the hulks of derelict cars bleeding rust, unpainted vacant buildings and light brown swamp weeds swaying in unison with the wind. The sewer seemingly drained here, with the soil tainted like the money. His gas tank might be full, but his adrenaline tank read empty, so he got out and opened the trunk. While inspecting his cargo, he pondered tossing the bags into the filthy water. Would his icicles of misery also ebb away? That answer was, no. Instead, he needed to plumb the past to bring the future into clearer focus, meaning coming clean with Carol. They would then decide how to spend it.

He slammed the trunk closed and sped back onto the highway.

As he fought the narrow lanes of the Goethals Bridge, the weather changed. The windshield wipers brushed away the intermittent rain and New Jersey with its belching smokestacks. Back in New York he *almost* felt whole again, but was still burdened by the wave of sorrow passing through him like a powerful X-ray. They would no doubt bury Christina in her home town in Florida. Bury; such a final word for someone who was so young and full of life. He pictured the line of mourners at her graveside, no doubt led by her son. Attempting to soften these thoughts he purchased a single red rose from a roadside vendor and detoured under what felt like a cold and friendless sky to her place. As he rolled to a halt, the billowing curtains of the now-lifeless shell she had called home waved in the air, seemingly beckoning him to enter. But the sense of death in attendance ruled that out. He ducked under the yellow tape and inserting the rose into the screen, he could almost feel her torment invading every inch behind it. Time passes quickly and Erik made up his mind to atone for what he had already wasted. Almost silent thoughts rolled off his lips and tears from his eyes as a closing goodbye. There was no room in his conscience for Christina's death. It was already crowded enough. How long would it be before a For Rent sign went up and a new saga began?

He forced himself to become all business and drove a circuitous route to his apartment, again checking for a tail. After checking for a police stakeout and seeing none, he dragged the duffels into the clammy basement. He opened a small door, pushed the cobwebs away with his hands and locked the bags in the dark recesses of this unlighted and unventilated closet like the guilty secret they were. No one wanting to breathe fresh air would even go near it. He next phoned Carol, asking in what he hoped sounded like good spirits. "How about we have dinner tonight?" No reply.

"At *Chez Nous*?"

"Can we afford it? The owner will probably charge us this time and that money could be better spent."

"We'll worry about that later. There's something more important...oh never mind. Be ready at seven." After hanging up he called and reserved a table for eight o'clock. Erik showered and dressed in a white shirt, black striped tie and charcoal-colored sports jacket and drove to Carol's. She was captivating in her short, size six green satin dress, replete with a white scarf and mesh stockings. As he pulled her close and they kissed, her clean hair that still smelled of shampoo tickled his nose.

Although Erik looked more handsome than ever, with eyes that resembled green ice, she sensed a foreboding. "You all right?"

"I guess?"

"Something's bothering you."

He didn't answer, just shrugging his shoulders because he was trying to hide the inner feelings of guilt. He didn't want to think of her with regret on sleepless nights, all alone. But he did want the life together, with her, he never had. He'd come clean and beg for understanding.

Except for the radio they drove in silence, which heightened the tension. Forty-five minutes later they were seated in the same enchanting setting with the glitter of crystal on stark white cloth. Despite the ambiance Erik found himself awash in black feelings. Even the *maître d'* in his black tux more resembled a priest conducting a funeral when he recommended the rack of lamb and *pommes frites*. The circuits from Erik's brain to his taste buds were so out of whack that the man could have been recommending a burger and fries to go with the inexpensive bottle of Merlot he ordered. Once it was poured he viewed Carol through the red mist while holding the wineglass in front of his face without a hint of a smile.

He had only sins to confess. How would she react? What roadmap would his life now follow? Could he crawl from the abyss he'd created?

"You look like something is wrenching at your gut. What's wrong?" she demanded. "And don't tell me it's nothing."

The time had arrived. His heart thrashed around inside his chest like it was trying to escape his body. The words were inside him, and like a noisy jet, had to be heard. He inhaled deeply. "Remember that missing money I told you about?" No response. His throat burned like someone had poured gasoline down it and struck a match. This wasn't easy. It entailed inviting someone else into a private place where the past could *not* be used as building blocks of the future. "Well, I *was* involved in the theft of it." The words came out barely audible. *Why was he telling her this? She was hurting. He could tell.* "It wasn't only me," he immediately added, "Captain Shepard and another guy..."

Carol still didn't grasp the full implications of what was spoken, other than the obvious. "*That* woman," she hissed through tightly clenched teeth, "the one who had her arm around you."

He held up his hand. "She's dead."

"Dead? Murdered?" She almost choked on her napkin.

"No. She had a seizure and died."

She had grasped the all too obvious. Forcing her repertoire of questions into temporary storage, darkness crept into the edges of her vision as the implications of what was spoken hit home. The softness in her eyes melted away, replaced by a wounded look. "Tell me the rest."

"First, you have to believe that I wasn't involved with her. You're the only person I've ever loved. I believe you only run into someone who's a perfect fit once. Then, you do *whatever* it takes to hold on. Now you own a part of my soul. There's no way to describe how I felt when you and your family welcomed me, especially after all the time I spent trying to get away from mine. Everything positive surfaced. You're the light that led me out of a bleak tunnel." He considered telling her why his father dealt with him the way he did but again, decided against it. The one secret he was about to reveal was deep enough.

"Why'd you get involved?"

"I didn't ask to." Awkward silence bobbed on the surface. He could tell she was hurting, so he took her hand in his. But it felt like she had just removed it from the freezer and she pulled away. "Taking the money was her idea. I swear. I was terrified of being caught and losing you, but was in a no-win situation."

"Jesus, Erik. Just explain", anger pushing away her fear.

"The money issue was paramount. Until your Dad came through I was gonna lose my job. Then, I fucked up during that emergency in Boston and she noticed. It wasn't serious, but could've been. And she could've made my life hell, said if the chief pilot knew he might fire me. I'm brand new. If that happened, I'd owe even more money to Shuttle Air. Either way, I was stripped down, nerves exposed and afraid of falling into a bottomless pit." His moss-green eyes filled with pain. "I *had to* hold onto my job. Then, she brought in this guy Juni..."

"Who?"

"She needed another person for this thing to work and she met this guy, Juni Rosario through her boyfriend. He's his uncle. Juni needed money to keep his family-run bakery afloat. She believed he'd bring the know-how that we lacked. In short, he removed money that was aboard our plane, in the cargo hold. Our only part was to create a minor mechanical diversion for a couple of minutes on a foggy Boston taxiway with a contrived problem. That gave him enough time to remove the cash."

"Why did she do it? Greed?"

"Maybe. She told me about paying lots in alimony and child support. But apparently she also had epilepsy. If the FAA finds out about that, you can't fly. She probably needed money 'cause of that."

"Why didn't you report this to your boss? Or the cops?"

"I considered that, but decided not to. First, I'd still owe the money. That wasn't going away, meaning my job was on the line. Of course, she'd have denied it all. Who do you think they'd believe? If they wanted to set up a sting, I didn't know if I could play out my role knowing the cops were watching. I'm a pilot not an actor. Also, her boyfriend is this big guy, David who looks like he takes steroids, a baggage handler at the airline and he might've come after me." He stopped, sipped some water and continued. "Also, the idea of being labeled a turncoat didn't sit well. The other pilots would shun me when word got out, so I didn't know if I could continue at Shuttle Air." He stopped to gauge her reaction, expecting to see tears brimming up. But she seemed as composed as a seasoned captain conducting an instrument approach. "Her plan *almost* worked. The first part did. Juni got the money, over two million, but then someone hit him over the head and took it."

"Two million?" she whispered, raising her eyebrows. "Hit him? Took it?"

"That was his story and I also had doubts." Erik paused and sipped more water to moisten his throat, which now felt as though he had been eating volcanic dust at thirty-three thousand feet. "But I knew it was true when I saw his injuries. I kept mulling it all over and over but couldn't figure out what happened."

"You mentioned this guy Juni and Shepard," she interrupted, trying to put the pieces together. "Anyone else involved? What about the copilot?"

"We agreed that we didn't need him. It would be only the

three of us. But the copilot, Woody Montgomery turned out to be the one. An accomplice of his hit Juni, in the process laying all the suspicion at our feet. Montgomery's a former Air Force maintenance officer who oversaw repairs on lots of Boeing-built jets. He probably became suspicious why Shepard and I were speaking in the cockpit. So, he got a hold of the voice recorder that had our entire discussion on it."

"How do you know this?"

Erik filled her in on all the details.

"What about the money?" she asked still wearing outward sorrow.

"I went to Montgomery's house and saw the guy who hit Juni. After he left, I rang the bell, told Montgomery and his wife, who was also in on it that I knew what happened and demanded the cash. I made up a story, told them if they didn't cough it up Juni would come after their family. They delivered it this morning. Right now the money's locked up in a musty closet in my apartment basement." He waited a moment. "I'm sorry I lied," he pleaded with heart still pounding, "and kept this from you. But I didn't know how to tell you or how you'd react." His stomach clenched. "Prior to meeting you I never came close to knowing the true meaning of the words love or trust. I figured strutting around in my uniform and flying a big jet would fill the terrible void known as my life, deliver all the needed happiness. But that myth died and for the very first time *you* released an undefined inner peace. Prior to that I was just passing time, living in all the hell my parents created. It was like I was waiting for you to spring me from my prison on Violet Lane, which should have been more appropriately named Violent Lane. But now it's *our* turn to live, together. All I ask is that you *try* to understand my position." Sensing they were at the crucial point where their relationship would go from darkness to hope or the other direction, for emphasis he made a fist and placed it in her hand. This time she didn't pull away.

"Then tell me, what *exactly* do you want from me?" Although still appearing as delicate as a newly-blossomed flower he sensed in her an invisible aura of inner strength more akin to a power lifter with total confidence. She appeared cool. But Erik wasn't. His palms were like sponges and he rubbed each alternately on the knees of his trousers in a futile attempt to dry them, all the while keeping one hand in hers. When she looked at him, splinters of hope began to bloom. He saw a donut where others saw a hole.

She stared into the eyes she had come to love. "Look, you might not realize it, but we're at a crucial juncture between the rapidly closing jaws of your past and the still open door of what I believed was *our* promising future. Your secrecy's creating a knife of conflicting emotions that's slicing at me. Love is like exercising, the more you work at it the larger it becomes, meaning continually working on the trust and honesty drills." She knew he carried a lot of pain inside and whispered, "Maybe I can understand why you did this? But, the time for *trying* to understand is like your captain friend, gone and never to return." He began to speak, but before he could utter a word she held up her hand. "The pilot had his say. Now it's time for the flight attendant to come out of the galley and take the helm, so be quiet. I'm *very* unhappy that you kept this from me. But I'm also in love with you, rough edges and all, meaning we share *everything*." Her expression seemed softened as a flicker of mirth appeared across her flawless face. "This is no one-way relationship. You were also an answer to my prayers when you literally flew into my life. There's something special about you that caused everything to change when I committed myself to what *we* could become. That's the awesome power of love and it includes honesty and loyalty, which aren't part of today's plastic world. I want us to grow so we can live the chapters of our new lives together, one by one. I *need* your presence, your voice, your love— you." She shook her head. "To be honest, you've changed from my shining knight into a more human one with slightly-tarnished armor. But you're still my hero 'cause I know how much you wanted to be successful and worked your ass off to achieve your castle in the sky." She hesitated. "But that's enough on this. Nothing positive can come from rehashing it any more. Enough Erik flagellation. We've *got* to move on because the past is like a club. If you keep hitting yourself with it you'll do permanent brain damage. We can't keep looking back hoping that somehow the past will change." The lines in her face disappeared, as though just injected with Botox. "But, we're still dealing with a colossal unknown."

He breathed an audible sigh of relief knowing that she had the heart of a golden retriever. But their roles were reversed and she was now the strong-minded one. "Define colossal unknown."

"Look, I'm no self-beatified Saint Carol. I would love to have that dough. But do we want it? Money, or the lack of it, is pretty much the root of all evil. Keep it and instead of paradise, you'll be creating a hell."

"While driving from Montgomery's place I wound up on a deserted Jersey pier and considered dumping it into the water. But then I thought about Shepard and what it might have meant for her. Some day we could be in a similar situation." Carol was slowly shaking her head side to side, but Erik continued. "The airlines have become a boom and bust business. I don't know what'll happen to Shuttle Air. I want enough to—"

"What's this guy Juni like?"

"Like I said, Shepard dated this dirtbag baggage handler and she met Juni through him. He's a relative of David's, and—"

"You told me that. Is he a suspect?"

"No. No way. The cops couldn't even know he exists." He paused to take a sip of water from the etched glass. "Christina mentioned he became involved 'cause he's in dire straits, borrowed to the hilt for his bakery and is no doubt teetering on the edge of financial ruin..."

"No," she uttered, pouting. "What kind of a person is he?"

"He's no Mother Theresa, but a family guy with a couple of kids. He also mentioned struggling hard with whether or not to even get involved, said he had reservations but ultimately decided to do it for his family."

She took a deep breath and sighed, "It was probably luck that this guy hit him and took the money, 'cause otherwise it would almost certainly be a cinch for the cops to track *you* down. There are a million ways in today's computer age." She hesitated only a moment. "Give the money to him."

Her reasoning didn't taste right. "What?"

"Give it to him. Every last goddamned cent! Dad bailed you out and I don't want *any*. You wanna be looking over your shoulder for the rest of your life? I don't and won't." She whispered blackly. "The cops are out there, waiting. Watching." She paused, letting her words sink in, not wanting to take this to the next level, her or the money.

"That's imposs—"

"Bullshit! Grow up!" the retort came as sharp as a knife, her milky pallor taking on a reddish tint, her eyes glowing like there was a light inside each. "They're somewhere in the shadows. Maybe even here. Now. I can guar-an-damn-tee you they won't rest. And you won't have a clue 'til it's too late. You'll see the minute you start flashing some. They probably have your phone tapped. And mine too."

It became apparent that he was at the place she *really* lived, so he gave up trying to be his own defense attorney. *Grow up?* Thoughts of those words made him realize that in reality he'd actually never believed he'd be caught. For the very first time he wondered how long would his sentence be? Five years? Jail. He'd be prime meat for the psycho animals that did nothing but lift weights and had no gender preference. One of them would no doubt want him for his bitch. Just like his involvement in the robbery, he really had no choice now. Erik didn't want the helium to escape from their romance balloon. He couldn't let that happen. After a period of silence that felt like weeks, he nodded in agreement with the young lady who sounded more like a mature woman as her words settled into his mind and like seeds began sprouting their first buds.

Exhausted, she told him, "I need your touch." She got up as he slid back his chair and sat sideways on his lap. The cushioned chair creaked and groaned under the strain of their combined weight. Other diners sent smiles at the striking young couple, obviously in love. Clutching her tightly, he now knew that destiny also clutched them firmly in its grip. As if also sensing this, she put her arm around his neck and gently kissed him, her sweet breath covering his face. "Now we'll be safe."

But still, give away over two million bucks?

CHAPTER FIFTY-TWO

After his final flight Erik checked his six, went to a pay phone and called the Genoa bakery. Juni answered.

"Juni. It's Erik Preis."

"Why the hell you callin' me? I told you…"

Erik was now the captain. "Just shut up and listen."

"If this is about Christina, it's been all over the news."

"That's not the reason—," Erik began, but Juni interrupted.

"I wonder how her kid is doin'. You have his address? I wanna send some money. I don't have much, but—"

Erik cut him off. "Did you get my letter?"

"What letter?"

"Never mind. We have to meet. Tonight."

"I don't want to be seen anywhere near you. The cops are probably all over you like stink on shit."

"Believe me, this is worth the risk."

Silence. Did Erik have a lead? "All right," Juni sighed. "Let's meet at that same Brooklyn restaurant after dark, around nine," loudly adding, "but make absolutely certain you're not followed."

"Don't go inside. Wait in the lot. If I get there before you I'll do the same. If I don't show it's 'cause the cops were watching."

"But, why—" Juni began, but there was a click and the line went dead.

Erik drove to his apartment, picked up a FedEx package delivered earlier that day and threw it into the car. He wouldn't—couldn't—open it; not yet. After spotting nothing suspicious, he waited 'til dark, went to the closet and put the now foul-smelling bags into the trunk of his car. After again driving an overly circuitous route and making certain there was no tail, he finally pulled into the lot across from Pepi's. The magic hour hadn't arrived, so he just sat there, listening to an Eagles CD, trying to cut through the tension that flowed from his body like waves in the ocean. The night was clear with the moon lending a sense of warmth, its radiance in the cool air bringing on fading summer memories. Looking westward, the New York City lights reflected off the high cirrus clouds making them appear like a carpet of lights. After again eyeing the package lying on the seat next to him, he ripped it open. Truth in a FedEx box. Its contents only served to reawaken horrible memories, a world of oppression where legitimacy was never considered.

For the next five or so minutes Erik's fingers tapped the overnight envelope in time with the music until Juni's old clunker rattled into the lot and got his attention. It pulled alongside and Juni looked drained, with circles under his eyes so deep they could have been etched with a knife. Wearing a dark tee shirt and black lightweight jacket, with both hands in the pockets of his baggy jeans he walked slower than grandma without her cane. But, no doubt his scoping job was as good as a deer's before entering a field to feed at dusk. He finally ambled over to Erik, whose heart was rapping. He was at the cusp. After shaking hands, Erik asked, "How's the head?" adding, "and the bakery?"

"The head's comin' along, aside from an occasional bad

headache. The bakery? Well, that's another story," he replied taking a deep breath and exhaling with a loud whoosh. "How'd you make out?" Juni still kept a wary eye for anything amiss. "Sorry I couldn't help, but I'm on my ass."

"I got the money from my girlfriend's father."

"You held on to the job?"

"Yeah. But it came right down to the wire."

"At least one of us made out."

"Make that both of us. I have something for you." He sauntered to the rear of the car with a silent Juni in tow and popped the trunk.

"Holy shit! Where—how—did you get it?"

"I found out who it was and got 'em."

Juni's mood was immediately uplifted. He opened one bag, stuck his hand in and rubbed the old bills between his fingers, fleetingly seeing Hamilton, Jackson, Grant, and even Franklin. They were more like cloth than money. There must be millions of stories behind each. He finally asked, "And?" Hesitation. "Who was it? I'll deal with him."

It was Erik's turn to hesitate. Should he say any more? "It wasn't just a him, but rather them. And, they're probably already taken care of."

"Whaddya mean?"

Feeling an undercurrent of adrenalin, Erik related the entire story, adding, "And the best part was Woody already resigned from the airline, figuring he was set for life. No way will they take that prick back. He'll lose everything. Don't go near him, 'cause we got ours and he got his. The same thing probably applies to his ugly comrade whose first name is Billy." Erik hesitated. "I got the plate number of his Benz, which is probably for sale as we speak." He handed Juni the slip of paper with the number on it.

"Did you count it?" Juni asked, seemingly brushing aside Erik's last remarks. But a momentary, churning rage surged through his face as he put the paper in his pocket.

"It's probably a bit over two million," Erik answered.

"Over a million apiece. No, make that seven-hundred thousand. I'll get Christina's share to her son. Somehow. Some day. Is that OK with you?" Juni sighed, torn between sadness over Christina's death and renewed hope for his future.

Shaking his head, Erik said. "I don't want *any*. The fire burning in my belly was to find out who had it. The money's all yours. Do whatever you want."

"But, but, we were partners."

Erik shook his head. "You said not to tell anyone, but I had a lengthy discussion with my girlfriend. Excuse me, but she's my fiancée now. I proposed last night and she accepted. I told her everything and she strongly urged that I give it all to you. *We* don't want any. I only got involved to pay off my loan and that's behind me. We're planning a long and happy life together and don't want this shit hanging over our heads."

Juni just stood there speechless, his nimble mind navigating the uncharted waters Erik's actions had awakened. Hope is the dream of every person, but this would enable him to reach fulfillment. He put his arm around Erik and while hugging him, sobbed, "Thanks," tears involuntarily streaming down his cheeks and onto his jacket. Not even trying to wipe them away, he added, "I will *never* forget what you've done for me and my family. I'll also figure out a way to get Christina's share to her kid. It will take time, but I'll do it. Maybe a college scholarship for starters?"

"She would have wanted that. Just be *very* careful."

"It's the least I can do. And please, if there's ever anything you need, I'm always there. *Never* forget that."

Erik nodded his head and helped transfer the bags to Juni's trunk. As Erik drove off he looked up at the moonlit sky, at the clouds floating like distant weightless balloons with many thoughts filtering through his brain, all competing at once for his attention. But now, only one person remained front and center, Joe. He was determined to take this memory flight to its final destination. Was he ready to disembark? Information can be like an endless circle, taking power from someone and handing it to another. He could still recall standing in his room as a boy, ear to the wall, tears streaming down his cheeks hearing Joe's accusations and wondering if he was really his father. He fought his entire life to keep these feelings tucked away. Should he now return to the place he once called home and inform both parents that Joe really is his father? Countering this were the vile memories, honed over the years with jagged edges of repressed anger. All for nothing. He hesitated. No, it was done. Over. His mother and father were lost. Joe couldn't hurt him anymore because what was formerly unknown was no longer. The past is what you make of it. What his parents had done to themselves was bad. But what they had done to him was worse. When his mother cheated, she also cheated him out of his childhood. Even though those demons were in the past, right now he didn't have an inkling of what the word forgiveness meant. Maybe some day, but not now. His closing chapter would be to put Joe and Ursula out of his life. Between Carol's love and enabling Juni to return from the land of the dead, he'd go a step further and pull off a personal Lazarus.

He sped off, hopefully to a fairly certain future. Despite what he'd done for Juni, the reality remained that he still wasn't one of New York's finest citizens in line to receive an award. With this fact in mind, he reached over and retrieved the small black briefcase from the passenger side floor, rested it on the seat next to him and opened the latches with two loud clicks. Although trying to smile his mouth wouldn't cooperate as he glanced at eight thousand bucks. *Not bad for a night's work. After all, I have to pay for Carol's ring.*

THE END

ACKNOWLEDGEMENTS

I've worked for almost my entire adult life as an airline pilot, with the idea for this book surfacing when I told my beautiful and awesome wife of many years, Lorraine, that I had witnessed money being loaded into the cargo compartment of my 727 jet. The very first words out of her mouth were, "Maybe we can take some of it?" I truly love her for her spontaneous and innocent outbursts (among other traits). But that was when the brainchild for this book was hatched. For that I will always be grateful, along with her enduring patience and silent indulgence while I spent untold hours in my office perfecting and rewriting the manuscript. The same love is extended to our amazing children, Lorrainie, Christy and Matthew, who have made me very proud of what they have become. I have the best family a man could ask for, and they will always be loved and appreciated. That same love is extended to my grandchildren, some of whom, like Olivia and Sara, already show a genuine propensity for the creativity needed for writing.

Many thanks are also extended to former NYPD organized crime plainclothes detective Nicky Castellano, who since I didn't take my wife's original advice and find out for myself, provided me with the necessary "insider" info on police investigative techniques, tactics, and procedures.

I also extend my sincere gratitude to Stephen Penner from Ring of Fire Publishing for giving a first-time author that needed big break. The feelings that go with being told for the first time, "We want your book" are indescribable and will never be forgotten

ABOUT THE AUTHOR

I became enamored with flying at a young age, and my career spanned almost forty years, starting with securing a commercial pilot license, instrument rating and flight instructor certificates. At age twenty, I flew as a flight instructor and charter pilot and secured my multi-engine rating. I was then employed as a captain for a commuter airline. I finished out my vocation after approximately thirty-six years of piloting five different jets for two major airlines on both domestic and international routes. I now devote my time to my family, writing and fishing.

—*George Jehn*

RING OF FIRE PUBLISHING

www.ringoffirebooks.com

16973018R00188

Made in the USA
Charleston, SC
20 January 2013